I0746845

LADY SPY

SERVING MAGIC
BOOK FOUR

TONI CABELL

Copyright © 2022 by Endwood Press LLC

All rights reserved.

The characters and events in this book are fictitious. Any similarity to real persons, living or dead, is coincidental and not intended by the author.

No part of this book may be reproduced in any form or by any electronic or mechanical means, including information storage and retrieval systems, without written permission from the author, except for the use of brief quotations in a book review.

Book by Toni Cabell

Cover Design by Mayflower Studio

Published by Endwood Press LLC

 Formatted with Vellum

CHAPTER I

Mara pulled the cobalt blue door closed and inserted a large silver key, covered with runes, into the lock. She turned the key to the right, listening as the bolt clicked into place. Pressing her palm against the front door of Katrine's Klockworks, Mara waited. The door vibrated beneath her touch, thrumming with protection wards cast by her fay boss. Mara's fingers tingled as the powerful magic settled around the automata toyshop.

Pulling on her leather gloves, Mara turned and walked briskly down High Street. The spring evening was chilly, a fine mist coating everything. Mara had worked well past closing; her rumbling stomach reminded her of the lateness of the hour. The other shop owners had closed their establishments hours earlier. Even the constables had ceased their evening foot patrols.

Mara noticed the shadows shifting ahead, and her senses went on high alert. She reached into the pocket of her midnight blue cloak and withdrew a pair of brass knuckles, which she slipped over the fingers of her right glove. The only trouble Mara typically encountered on her walks home was the inebriated, flirtatious male variety, which she discouraged with a sassy mouth or if necessary, a right cross to the jaw.

She continued walking, and whatever lurked in the shadows seemed to melt into the dressmaker's shop several doorways down. Mara crossed the street, the heels of her tall leather boots clacking on the damp cobblestones. She glanced into the plate glass windows of the shops that had reopened since the war. Many others were still boarded up, their owners missing or deceased. Flickering light from the gas lamps lining the road reflected off the darkened windowpanes, revealing nothing other than Mara herself, bundled into her cloak, scuttling along the empty sidewalk. Even so, something felt off, not quite right.

As she peered into the next row of shop windows, she noticed movement behind her. A large, oddly shaped shadow seemed to be following her. Maybe someone had learned of her undercover work for the Valerran government and was out for revenge. Mara swallowed hard, her pulse quickening with her pace, each stride bringing her one step closer to home.

She heard slow, shuffling steps behind her, as if someone were dragging himself along the sidewalk in his stockinged feet. Mara bent down, reached inside the shanks of her tall boots, and withdrew a dagger from each one. She rose from her crouch and spun around, her daggers glinting in the light cast from the gas lamps. Mara shouted, "State your business or be off. I'm in no mood for coddling drunkards, and I've nothing to rob!"

The lumbering shadow sneezed. "No hurt me. Need help."

Mara lowered her daggers, frowning. "Farleigh? Is that you?"

The grihm, a half-human, half-wolf crossbreed, took another step closer so Mara could see his mangled features in the flickering light. Crossbreeding was illegal, but that hadn't stopped Glenbarra's Fallow sorcerers from doing it anyway, using crossbreeds to create terror wherever they went. Most grihms were about the size of an average man, but Farleigh had been six-and-a-half feet tall before the Glenbarrans had captured and crossbred him with an over-sized wolf.

Grihms had a bushy tail and four wolfish legs, with a pair of furry human hands for paws up front. While their forehead and eyes looked like a man's, their snout and muzzle were one-hundred percent wolf. Despite their ferocious appearance, not all grihms served their Glenbarran overlords. Farleigh and his friends had been instrumental in helping the Valerran resistance turn the tide of the war. Mara trusted him.

Most grihms lost the power of speech, but a few, like Farleigh, could make themselves understood. Nodding his shaggy head, the grihm yipped, "Aye, Farleigh. Friend." He added, "Need help."

Mara re-sheathed her daggers inside her boots and glanced up at the enormous grihm. "Why do you need my help? I thought you moved to the grihm preserve outside the city."

"Can't stay. Bad men."

"Bad men at the preserve?"

Farleigh nodded. "Aye. Very bad."

Mara sighed. She'd put in a long day at Katrine's Klockworks since her boss was gone this week taking care of urgent fay business. Mara had been looking forward to a simple meal of toasted cheese, followed by a long soak in the claw-foot tub she shared with the three other residents on her floor. It was her turn to go last, which meant she could bathe longer; all in all, not a bad compromise.

"Have you eaten?"

Farleigh shook his head vigorously. "Farleigh hungry."

Mara rolled her eyes. The super-sized grihm wouldn't be satisfied with the simple fare in her apartment. He needed a good meal with a lot of protein. "Come on," she grumbled. "Let's see what Remy's cooking."

Farleigh's muzzle twitched. "Remy. Good friend."

Mara arched a blonde eyebrow. "A better friend than me?"

Farleigh looked up at the darkened sky, thinking. Shrugging, he grunted, "Better cook."

Mara burst out laughing. "True enough. Remy is the best cook I know."

Mara led Farleigh down High Street several more blocks, trying to keep him in the shadows as much as possible. They turned right at Market Street, passing the various food vendors and guildhalls, all closed for the night, until they reached Queen's Way, a small residential side street that ran perpendicular to Market Street. Mara couldn't imagine why the city's founders had named her street after the queen—whichever queen was reigning at the time— since the palace was twenty blocks away on the other side of downtown Bellaryss, the capital of Valerra.

Mara guided the nervous grihm to Remy's apartment building, which was adjacent to hers. Well-to-do families had once lived in the large, elegant townhomes, but with so much of Bellaryss's commercial and residential districts destroyed during the war, builders had hastily rehabbed abandoned homes into multi-family dwellings. The exteriors were attractive enough, constructed from golden sandstone, with arched doors and windows and weathered gray trim. However, the interiors consisted of narrow, dim corridors, shared bathrooms, and cramped flats. She and Remy were renting their tiny studio apartments for the same reason as everyone else—housing was scarce, and the rent was cheap for an in-town location.

Mara pulled open the door to Remy's building and stepped into the foyer, forgetting for a moment that a gigantic grihm was lumbering behind her. A woman with a toddler in tow took one look at Farleigh and shrieked. She grabbed her little girl and ran in the opposite direction.

Farleigh hung his head. "Sorry."

"Don't be. It's not your fault. Although I'd rather get inside Remy's flat before we run into anyone else. Far less explaining to do." What Mara didn't add was that she thought the frightened woman might send for help. Mara didn't want to have to explain to a constable why Farleigh was wandering around downtown Bellaryss with her, especially since she had no idea herself why Farleigh had run away from the grihm preserve.

Mara rapped on Remy's door. The door cracked open, and the scent of Remy's homemade stew from one of his mother's cherished recipes made her mouth water. Mara smelled freshly baked bread and brewed coffee too. Remy pulled the door all the way open, his hazel eyes widening at the sight of Farleigh towering behind Mara.

Tall, husky, with wavy brown hair and a love of good food and long naps, Remy had often played the part of the class clown in school. But that was before the war, before they'd both lost friends and family. Despite the fact he was her ex-boyfriend, Mara knew Remy wouldn't turn her away. He'd help her and Farleigh.

"Come inside, quickly." Remy stepped back to let them pass and then looked down the corridor in either direction before closing and locking the door. Although everyone had become more security-conscious since the war, Mara noticed that Remy's left eye twitched, signifying he was nervous. Something was unsettling him, and she didn't think it had anything to do with the grihm in their midst.

Remy had furnished his apartment practically overnight, by scrounging from junk shops and castaways. Bunk beds that tilted precariously occupied the side of the room opposite the tiny kitchen, along with a scuffed-up wardrobe missing its door, and a single, stuffed chair for reading. In the center of the room sat a wobbly, oblong table and four mismatched chairs. A squat, pedestal gas lamp stood between the kitchen and the door, casting as many shadows as light around the apartment.

Mara ushered Farleigh into the apartment ahead of her. "Why are you being so paranoid? I know it's a bit strange walking around with a grihm, but—" The sight of two gorgeous blue-haired men sitting at Remy's table drove the words right out of Mara's head. Remy had lit several candles, casting a soft orange glow on their upturned faces.

She recognized Efram, one of their fay friends who'd helped the resistance overthrow their Glenbarran occupiers. The other man appeared to be related, with his luminous gray eyes, brown complexion, and curly blue hair. The vivid blue hair was the only outward clue that both men were fays—well, that and their matching silvery, stretchy tunics, trousers, and capes. And their amazing good looks. Mara had yet to meet a fay man or woman who wasn't easy on the eyes.

Mara was certain she'd never met the other man, since she would surely remember him. He wore his hair longer than Efram, his wavy blue locks grazing the shoulders of his silver cape. The planes of his face were more angular than

Efram's, his chin more chiseled. When he rose from the table and gave a graceful bow, Mara noted his broad shoulders and the muscles straining across the stretchy fabric of his tunic. He raised his head, his eyes locking onto Mara's, and the corners of his perfect bow-shaped mouth tipped up in greeting.

Efram walked over to Mara, bowed, and then took her hands in his. "It's good to see you again." Turning to Farleigh, he bowed a second time. "And you as well. I've heard how much you helped the resistance here in Valerra, and I'm glad to be able to finally thank you."

Farleigh seemed suddenly shy and dropped his head to his chest. *Poor Farleigh*, thought Mara, *he's probably been feared, insulted, and reviled since being turned into a grihm.* Mara decided to rescue the large wolf-man. Nodding at the other fay, she asked, "Would you please introduce us?"

Efram grinned. "Of course. Mage Mara, Grihm Farleigh —this is my younger brother, Arnestarious the Fourteenth."

"But everyone calls me Arnesto." Efram's brother smiled. "Eframallium the Thirteenth is my elder by fifty-eight months." Mara arched an eyebrow, trying to calculate Arnesto's age, which she tagged around eighteen, the same as her.

Remy whistled. "Arnestarious the Fourteenth? Eframallium the Thirteenth? I'm glad you don't mind using nicknames."

"Not only don't we mind—we prefer them!" said Efram.

"That is most certainly true," agreed Arnesto. "Although Auntie still prefers to use our more formal names." Arnesto's stilted speaking style, so unlike his older brother, surprised Mara. Arnesto sounded as if he'd learned the Valerran language from a textbook, with an ancient instructor as his speech coach. She hoped the auntie he mentioned hadn't been his tutor.

Farleigh sniffed the air and whimpered. Mara recalled the poor grihm was famished. Bowing, Mara said, "It's very nice to meet you, Arnesto." Turning to Remy, she added, "Farleigh is quite hungry. Perhaps once he's eaten, he can tell us why he needs help. And I'd like to hear more about the Fay Nation, and what's been happening these past few months."

"Aye, coming right up." Remy served up two more bowls of meat and vegetable stew. He placed Farleigh's bowl on the floor, where the grihm could lap it up, while the two fays made room at the table for Mara. Their conversation centered on the weather—the arrival of spring accompanied by melting snow, sudden downpours, leaking roofs, swollen rivers, and puddles everywhere.

Arnesto chewed his spoonful of stew thoughtfully, as if the weather were a topic of utmost importance to him. "Chilled spring is a challenging season. The temperatures are still too cold and the weather too unpredictable. One moment you may have high winds and thunderstorms, and if you simply turn down a different path, you may come upon weak sunshine, or if you are truly lucky, an occasional crocus or hyacinth bud. Give me gentle spring, or any of the summer and autumn seasons. My favorite is auburn summer."

Mara had never found the weather to be a particularly engaging topic. Perhaps it was a fay thing, all this interest in the weather. "What is auburn summer?"

Arnesto's sandy brown eyebrows rose nearly to his hairline. "Why, it is that special time of the year, after Midsummer and before Autumn Solstice, when the days grow shorter, the air is tinged golden, and the late summer flowers—the hydrangeas, camellias, and asters—are in bloom. There is both sweetness and sadness to that season, would you not agree?"

Mara didn't know what to make of Arnesto, except that she could watch him describing the weather all evening. Arnesto's gray eyes lit up as he spoke, and he waved his hands expressively, as if he could conjure auburn summer right in Remy's flat. Since he was a fay, perhaps he could. Efram shook his head at his brother. "What did I tell you about waxing poetic about the weather?"

Arnesto drew his brows together. "You did mention that most people find weather to be somewhat boring, which I cannot fathom. Oh, and I think you said something about the seasons, and how we like to describe them in seven categories, but everywhere else, there are only four seasons. I honestly do not understand that last bit. Clearly, there are seven seasons."

Efram rolled his eyes. "You're hopeless. How are you going to become a scout if you can't learn to blend in a bit more?"

Arnesto ran a hand through his shoulder-length blue hair. "You are right, of course. I shall need plenty of practice and to immerse myself in Valerran culture. But that is why we are here, is it not? For me to learn how to interact with your human friends."

Efram groaned. "Please, don't ever say that again."

"What, precisely, shall I not say again?"

"Don't say 'human friends.' You make them—or us—sound like alien creatures. In fact, don't use the word 'human' at all. Excise it from your vocabulary. And watch your speech patterns. You sound too much like Auntie Yelenarra."

Mara figured that ancient Auntie Yelenarra had been

Arnesto's tutor. She still couldn't understand why Arnesto's speech and mannerisms were so very different from his brother's. It was almost as if the younger fay had been raised in a pod somewhere and spoon-fed tidbits of Valerran language and culture.

Arnesto sighed. "Very well. I will no longer speak of humans."

"And?"

"And I will do my best to speak less and listen more." Arnesto leaned back and gave his brother a smile so stunning that Mara was glad she was sitting down. She was not a swoony sort of girl, but Arnesto bordered on bedazzling. Was it a fay thing or an Arnesto thing? She'd never noticed it with her fay boss, Katrine, or with Efram or Wreyn, her fay friend they'd lost during the war. Mara frowned as she recalled what happened to Wreyn. No one should be murdered and then raised from the dead by an evil necromancer to do his bidding.

Arnesto glanced over at Mara. "You seem saddened all of a sudden. I cannot imagine it has anything to do with our discussion of the weather."

Mara took a deep breath and sniffed. "I was thinking about another fay scout who became a good friend over the past year."

"Wreyn," Efram whispered huskily, deep grooves creasing his smooth brow. Clearing his throat, he added, "The best scout I've ever known."

Arnesto stared at his brother. "I have always thought of you as the best scout there is."

Efram gazed into his wineglass. He took a long swallow before setting his glass on the table. "Thank you for saying so, but Wreyn was the very best. She could blend into any environment, and she seemed to know just who to target as a willing informant. Her loss was a heavy blow, and not just because of our friendship."

Arnesto reached over and gripped Efram's shoulder. "I will not let you down, brother, I promise."

Efram didn't look up, but nodded. "I know," he said softly. "You'll be brilliant if you put into practice everything you've learned."

Arnesto leaned back, his expression serious. "Perhaps it is time we shared the reason for our visit."

"Aye." Efram took a deep breath and then turned to Remy and Mara, his eyes clouded, his mouth set in a straight line. "We're here about King Roi."

"What about that Glenbarran war criminal?" Remy crossed his arms across his chest. King Roi had master-minded the invasion of Valerra, the rise of necromancy, and the spread of dark sorcery across the continent. Of course, the crazy king had a lot of help from a Fallow master mage named Mordahn, but Mara's friend Linden had finally dispatched Mordahn permanently to the realms of the dead. The last anyone had seen of King Roi, he was retreating with the remnants of his battered army, running away as fast as his horse could take him. When Valerran troops had caught up with his defeated army, the Glenbarran king was gone, escaped to no one knew where.

"King Roi is back," announced Arnesto. "Stirring his sorcerous cauldron of Fallow intent once more."

EFRAM WINCED, SHAKING HIS HEAD AT HIS YOUNGER BROTHER, "Sorcerous cauldron of Fallow intent? Really?"

"Too much?" asked Arnesto.

"Completely over the top," grunted Efram. "No one speaks like that anymore."

"Auntie Yelenarra does."

"Auntie Yelenarra is eighty years old! Besides, she's not being trained as a spy."

Arnesto started to object, "True, but—"

Mara interrupted before the blue-haired brothers spent any more time bickering about their fay aunt. "If King Roi has been spotted near Valerra, then let's inform the authorities so they can arrest him for his war crimes."

"Well, that's part of the problem," admitted Efram. "We've lost the fay scouts who've reported seeing Roi. After their initial reports, they returned to the king's last known location to track his activities and..."

"And unfortunately, they have not been seen since." Arnesto completed his brother's sentence. "But fear not, I have come to take their place. I shall infiltrate the king's filthy nest of vipers and carry on, without fear or trembling."

Efram groaned and held up his hand, palm outward. "Just don't say anything else, at least not until I finish explaining." Arnesto canted his head but remained silent. Efram turned to Remy and Mara. "Arnesto will be an amazing scout, once he learns how to blend in. That's actually why we've come to you. Katrine wants the two of you to help Arnesto acclimate to Valerran culture—teach him how to be 'human' as he likes to say. Otherwise, I'm afraid my brother's career as a fay scout will be very short-lived."

Remy nodded. "I'm happy to help, but I'm not sure what I can do."

"For starters, Arnesto needs a place to live."

"No problem." Remy turned to Arnesto. "You can stay with me. I know it's not much, but..."

Arnesto placed his hand over his heart. "Your kind offer touches me deeply. I shall endeavor to be as unobtrusive as possible. Where can I find my suite of rooms? Through that oaken door perhaps?" Arnesto pointed to the only door in Remy's flat—the exit.

Remy opened his mouth, closed it, and then tried again. "I realize you may be accustomed to something larger, but this is home for now." Remy pointed to the bunk beds leaning against the wall. "You can have the top bunk."

Arnesto raised one perfect eyebrow and lowered the other. "Smashing. I look forward to sleeping so close to the ceiling."

Mara turned to Efram. "He's not going to last five minutes."

Efram coughed and avoided making eye contact, which told Mara she wasn't going to like what came next. Efram spread his hands wide, palms outward. "Well, that's where you come in."

"Me? How so?" Mara folded her arms and glared at Efram. Not that she wouldn't mind spending time with the remarkably good-looking Arnesto, but she had a shop to run, clockwork toys to repair, and her undercover work for the provisional government. She simply didn't have the time to teach Arnesto how to be a good spy. Despite what Efram said about his brother's talents, she feared it would be a full-time job, and a fatal one, if she didn't train him properly.

Efram gave Mara an apologetic look. "You've been asking for backup for weeks. Arnesto is your backup."

Mara's voice was an octave higher than usual. "But I asked for a well-trained backup, not someone who speaks like a popinjay and is so ridiculously handsome he'll never be mistaken for a Glenbarran delinquent. Arnesto will wind up getting us both killed inside a week!"

Arnesto turned the full force of his smile on Mara, and she felt her resistance to the hare-brained idea cracking just a little. "Do you really believe I am ridiculously handsome? Humans are so intriguing."

"Well, I don't think you're ridiculously handsome," grumbled Remy, sounding like a jealous ex-boyfriend.

Arnesto ignored his new flat mate, lost in thought. "Although I do not know what a popinjay is, I believe that part was not meant as a compliment."

Mara threw her hands up in the air. "None of it was meant as a compliment or as an insult. The fact remains you have a long way to go to become adept at undercover work in Valerra. No offense."

"None taken." Arnesto inclined his head at Mara. "You

are in agreement with my brother and with Katrine. However, as you shall soon discover, I am a quick study."

Mara tucked a chunk of wheat-colored hair behind her ear and frowned. If her fay boss wanted her to take on Arnesto, then she'd have to find a way to make it work. *Since I'm going to be stuck with the awkward yet gorgeous Arnesto anyway, I'm going to make him earn his training.* "Very well. If you're going to be my backup, you may as well work alongside me at the toyshop. Katrine told me I could hire a shop's assistant. There's no better way to learn how to blend in than to wait on customers all day long. Besides, we run some of our undercover operations from that shop, so it's as good a place as any to teach you the art of blending in."

"I look forward to waiting for your customers, although I wonder if there might be something more I could be doing whilst I am waiting, that is?"

Mara gritted her teeth. "I said *waiting on* customers, not *waiting for* customers. Waiting on customers means helping them find what they are looking for at the toyshop."

"Ah. You are using an idiom to describe the activity of aiding customers to find a suitable purchase at Katrine's Klockworks. I see I have much to learn about the finer aspects of your language."

"And the art of blending in," added Efram.

Without her help, the stunning Arnesto wouldn't last even one day on his own. Mara was going to teach him to be a proper spy, or literally die trying. "Speaking of blending in, will you be using a glamour to change your appearance?" The fay's bright blue locks were a dead give-away, not to mention his sparkly silver get-up. Although Efram knew quite well how to makeover his appearance while in Valerra, she doubted Arnesto had gotten the hang of it yet.

Arnesto rose from the table and stood near the bunk beds in the crowded flat. Farleigh was dozing on the floor next to his empty bowl of stew, having polished off three helpings. Mara glanced at the bedraggled grihm. She still had no idea what had spooked Farleigh so much that he ran away from the preserve, but she was determined to find out and help him if she could. She owed Farleigh that much at least.

Arnesto cleared his throat, and with a wave of his right hand, changed his appearance. Instead of blue hair, his longish locks were sandy brown like his eyebrows. He'd traded his sparkly silver garb for a green cape with a paler green satin lining, layered over a brown-and-green striped tunic and brown leggings. A dark green felt fedora, with a wide brim and a long burgundy feather tucked into the leather hatband, was perched at an angle on his head. His tall leather boots were the same shade of burgundy as the feather, and he pulled on a pair of matching burgundy gloves. He looked as if he were preparing to audition for the role of a wood nymph with a traveling troupe of actors.

Arnesto adjusted the brim of his fedora. "I have been studying Auntie Yelenarra's books on Valerran culture. Although there were few illustrations, I came across some excellent descriptions of the dress code."

Mara found her voice first. Efram and Remy seemed to have been stunned into silence. "How old are the books in your aunt's library?"

"Oh, they are quite old. I do not believe my aunt has acquired any new editions for perhaps the past forty years or so. Why?"

"It's just that, well, um…" Mara paused, trying to figure

out how to tell Arnesto he couldn't possibly walk around Bellaryss dressed like that. Either he'd be laughed at or mugged, possibly both.

Efram waved his hand at Arnesto's clothing. "You look as if you walked off the pages of one of Auntie's storybooks. Wait a minute!" Efram narrowed his eyes. "I seem to recall an illustration in *Collected Valerran Folktales*, the one about the wood nymph who robs from the rich and gives to the poor. You look just like him!"

Arnesto bowed. "Well done, brother. You have an excellent visual memory." He tapped the brim of his hat. "I am quite partial to the fedora. I believe it lends me an air of credibility."

Efram muttered something under his breath about kid brothers. Mara said, kindly but firmly, "Efram is right. You do look as if you stepped right out of a storybook. We're going to need to make some adjustments."

"You are the expert. Tell me what I need to change."

Mara rose from the table and swiped a newspaper from the floor next to the stuffed chair. She circled Arnesto twice and then paused directly in front of him. Mara began making wardrobe suggestions, using the illustrations in the newspaper to get her point across. With each flick of his wrist, Arnesto implemented Mara's suggestions, his clothing undergoing one change after another. Finally, Mara nodded and turned to Efram and Remy. "What do you think?"

Arnesto wore a dark brown wool jacket that accentuated his broad shoulders and nipped in at his waist, with a beige cravat folded neatly at his neck. Mara paired the jacket with brown and beige houndstooth slacks, their creases as sharp as if they'd been freshly ironed. Mara convinced Arnesto to skip the flashy fedora he preferred and choose a tasteful brown trilby instead.

"A remarkable transformation!" said Efram. "He looks ready for work at Katrine's Klockworks."

"But what about his undercover assignments? He'll need to dress the part of a down-at-the-heels Glenbarran too," pointed out Remy.

Mara pursed her lips and turned back to Arnesto. "Can you lose the jacket and the cravat, replace the linen shirt with a baggy, torn sweater, and add a few patches to your pants? Oh, and scuff up your boots. They're too shiny." With several minor magical adjustments to Arnesto's wardrobe, he transformed from a well-dressed shop's assistant or junior clerk to a man who might be panhandling for loose change or picking a pocket. Mara added one final touch. "Switch out your trilby for a knit cap and pull it down low over your forehead."

"That's brilliant!" Efram applauded, and even Remy clapped once. Mara thought she might need to have a private chat with Remy. She wanted to remind him they were no longer dating, so there was no reason Remy should feel threatened by Arnesto. *No reason at all*, thought Mara, since the fay was simply in need of a good field coach—period. Besides, absolutely nothing could interfere with their working relationship, including any passing attractions they might feel. Mara sighed. Perhaps she ought to avoid the topic entirely with Remy.

"Will he be able to maintain the glamour the whole time he's undercover? What happens if someone detects he's using magic to alter his appearance?" asked Remy.

"That's a fair point," Efram turned to Arnesto. "You'll need to go to the haberdasher's shop. There's one located on the same block as Katrine's Klockworks. Tell the owner you want six sets of clothing similar to the first set you were wearing. We can easily scrounge up some worn-looking garments for your undercover work. But a well-tailored suit takes much more effort and skill."

"Do you have any money to spend at the haberdasher? That shop is quite pricey," said Remy.

Arnesto had transformed back into the brown jacket and houndstooth slacks. Mara thought he might be a tad vain, or perhaps he simply hadn't had a chance to wear anything other than stretchy silver tunics and capes. The fay reached into the inside pocket of his wool jacket and withdrew a wad of bills—the equivalent of a year's salary for any shop's assistant. Remy's mouth dropped open. "Is this not enough?" asked Arnesto. He dug into a side pocket and pulled out a drawstring bag that clinked. "I brought some gold too. I was not confident that I had enough of your paper money."

"That's more than enough," said Mara. "Lesson number one in how to blend into Valerran culture: Don't display large amounts of cash, either paper money or gold coins. You will draw unnecessary attention to yourself. Other men will think you are showing off or foolish, and either way, they will attempt to relieve you of your money. Oh, and you're going to need a wallet to store the bills. We'll shop for one tomorrow. As for the bag of gold, keep it here in Remy's flat. You don't want to be walking around with gold coins clinking in your pocket."

Arnesto gave Mara a dazzling smile. "Thank you for taking me on as your apprentice. I look forward to receiving many more invaluable lessons and tips whilst working alongside you." He pointed down at Farleigh, who was whimpering in his sleep. "Do you think we ought to wake him? He sounds frightened."

Mara glanced at Remy, who shrugged. "Why are you looking at me? I've only gone undercover as a grihm. I have no idea what it's really like, and I hope to never find out!"

Arnesto leaned forward, the awe on his face apparent, staring at Remy as if he'd actually stepped out of a storybook. "You worked undercover as a grihm? But how? Now that's a story I must hear first-hand."

"There isn't all that much to tell. We needed someone to wear a grihm costume in order to get into the Valerran Museum, which was heavily guarded at the time by Glenbarrans, grihms, and some creepy undead necromancers, including Mordahn himself." Remy patted his stomach. "Since I filled out the costume without any need for padding, I was volunteered."

"Remy played the part to perfection—no one doubted he was a grihm," said Mara.

"I think Farleigh realized pretty quickly that I was not actually a crossbreed." They all turned to look at Farleigh, sleeping quietly now. Remy added, "I have a feeling we're not going to learn anything tonight from him. We may as well let Farleigh sleep through the night."

"But he can't walk around downtown Bellaryss in broad daylight. Who knows how many people he'll scare before he's either arrested or attacked," objected Mara.

"When Arnesto leaves in the morning, he can take Farleigh with him on his traveling mists," said Efram. "Farleigh will be safe in Katrine's basement until we figure out why he's here."

"Excellent plan, brother!" Arnesto turned to Mara. "What time shall I arrive at Katrine's Klockworks? I believe the shop opens at nine-thirty?"

"We have toys to repair before the shop opens tomorrow. Let's meet there at seven-thirty."

Arnesto's bright smile drooped somewhat. "You wish to begin at seven-thirty in the morning? I had no idea Valerrans begin their workday so early!"

Mara put her hands on her hips. "Is that a problem?"

Efram burst out laughing and slapped his younger brother on the back. "You'll get used to waking up with the birds." He explained to Mara and Remy, "Fays are not early risers, as a rule. Even our young ones rarely go to bed before midnight. It took me a month to make the adjustment."

"On that note," said Mara, rising from the table, "it's getting late, and we do have an early start tomorrow. Arnesto, I'll see you and Farleigh in the morning."

"I should be leaving as well," Efram stood up. "I'll walk out with you." As they left Remy's flat, Efram assumed his own glamour. Instead of his sparkly silver clothes, he wore a workman's battered gray jacket over dark corduroys. He pulled a knit cap down low over his light brown hair.

Outside Mara's building, which was a duplicate of Remy's right down to the weathered gray trim, Efram said, "I hope you don't hate me when I tell you it was my idea for Arnesto to train with you."

"Of course I don't hate you. But why me?" Mara and Efram stood beneath a sputtering gas lamp that cast flickering shadows all around them. The cobblestones were wet; it must have rained while they were inside Remy's flat. The air felt heavy with moisture, and the cloying dampness clung to Mara's hair. She shivered. *What had Arnesto called this season? I think it's chilled spring—a remarkably apt description.*

Efram removed his cap and ran a hand through his short, curly hair. "It's impossible to train one's own brother in the finer points of spying. I'll wind up throttling him, and Arnesto can't help himself. He was raised...differently."

"I can understand not wanting to train your sibling, but I think there's something you're not telling me." Mara made a mental note to find out what Efram meant about Arnesto being raised differently. She had no idea how fays were raised to begin with. She'd always assumed they lived with their parents and went to school just like Valerran children.

Efram peered down the street as if seeking answers in the gloom and mist. His voice dropped a decibel. "I don't want to make the same mistakes I made training Wreyn. Look how she ended up."

"Wait a minute. Are you telling me you were Wreyn's field coach?"

Efram's shoulders sagged. "Aye. Wreyn trained with me. As I told Arnesto, in many ways, her talents exceeded mine. But I obviously botched something critical for her to have been captured in the end."

Mara recognized all the signs of a broken heart in her fay friend. "You were in love with Wreyn, weren't you?" Efram nodded, casting his eyes downward. Mara shook her head. "And now you're beating yourself up because Wreyn was killed during the war and you survived. You must know, deep down, that it had nothing to do with Wreyn's training. She was a superb scout, but we're in a dangerous business. Even the best of us makes mistakes."

Efram pulled the cap back onto his head. "You don't."

"Don't be ridiculous. Of course I make mistakes. You should see the clockwork toys I've ruined trying to repair them."

Efram shook his head. "I'm talking about in the field. You are hyper-focused when you're on a mission. Whether it's gathering intelligence or fighting hand-to-hand, you are the best I've ever seen. That's why I wanted you to train Arnesto."

"But Linden is every bit as good as I am—even better when it comes to her magic."

"Linden is also the Faymon Liege and lives in Faynwood. Her attentions of necessity are directed elsewhere. And while she is a remarkable leader, Linden is not a spy. That is not her gift. But it is yours."

Mara snorted. "So there *is* something I'm better at than Linden, eh?" Mara and Linden had a complicated relationship. In fact, Mara hadn't liked Linden very much during their school years. She used to believe, wrongly so, that Linden was an arrogant stick-in-the-mud. When they'd been thrown together during the war, they had no choice but to cooperate in order to survive. Along the way, Mara discovered that Linden was shy, not stuck up, and eventually they became friends by choice, not by accident.

"Stop doing that," said Efram.

"Doing what?"

"Comparing yourself to others—and putting yourself down. Accept the fact you were part of an elite team that overthrew King Roi, his army, and his necromancers. And since then, your undercover work for Vas and Katrine has been nothing short of remarkable. How many Glenbarran operatives have you snagged and sent to jail in the past three months? Seven? Eight?"

"Nine, counting the two last week." Mara squared her shoulders. Her undercover work was not nearly as glamorous as she'd expected when she first signed on. Sometimes Vas assigned her to stake out certain locations. Mara spent more than her fair share shivering in the underground tunnels, playing the part of a disaffected shop worker looking to join one of the anti-government cells, which were led by Fallow mages or ex-Glenbarran soldiers still loyal to King Roi. Other times, Katrine assigned her targets to follow or to engage in conversation—small talk mostly. Mara's favorite assignment was working under-cover as a bar maid at the Cracked Cauldron, a local pub owned by a former resistance fighter. Mara enjoyed the easy-going camaraderie and free food. Plus, it was a lot warmer than working in the tunnels. Half of Mara's arrests had been the result of tips she'd picked up while pouring ale.

Efram's words had struck a chord inside Mara. Perhaps she did spend too much time comparing herself to others. She had some thinking to do, but it was well past her bedtime, and after her speech to Arnesto about starting at seven-thirty, she had to make sure she arrived on time. "Thank you for trusting me enough to train your brother. I'll do my best."

"I know you will, and Arnesto truly has some remark-able skills. Once you see him in action, you'll understand why he's destined to be a great fay scout—if he doesn't get himself killed first."

CHAPTER 3

Mara leaned over the worktable, biting her bottom lip in concentration as she repaired the broken wing of a clockwork mockingbird. The inner workings of the mechanical wing—tiny gears, shafts, and springs—were spread around the table in front of her. She cleaned, oiled, and replaced each part inside the wing's open casing. When she'd accounted for every item, she laid the top of the wing over the casing, aligned the edges, and snapped it closed. Mara rubbed her fingers over the sculpted feathering of the tin wing, wondering how Katrine had learned her craft. As a fay, she would have had no exposure to automata growing up, since too much magic interfered with anything mechanical. And fays were inherently magical beings. She'd never gotten around to asking her boss, and Katrine had never said.

Mara glanced at the brass wall clock ticking above her head—eight thirty-five. Arnesto wasn't off to a rousing start. Then again, he had a gigantic grihm to corral and translocate via his traveling mists. Ten minutes later, after Mara had managed to fix the leg of a small clockwork poodle, she heard Arnesto and Farleigh arrive before she saw them. The clatter of a dozen metallic toys tumbling over onto the shop floor alerted her.

Mara rose from her stool inside the long, narrow office, separated from the customer-ready front of the toyshop by a damask curtain. It was in the office at the rear of the shop that toys were repaired, supplies ordered, bills paid, tea and snacks procured, and where undercover operations were often planned in hushed whispers after hours.

Mara unbuttoned the white smock that protected her clothing from an errant splash of machine oil or a tiny metallic fragment and hung it on one of the hooks next to the worktable. She adjusted her long-sleeved, lilac silk blouse with the pointed collar, tucking it into the waistband of her wool challis skirt. The skirt's swirl of purple, lilac, and violet paisley grazed her ankles. Her saddle brown leather boots peeked out beneath her full skirt, and Mara decided she liked the juxtaposition of the colorful purple shades with the saddle brown.

"I apologize for my tardiness." Arnesto pulled aside the curtain separating the shop floor from the inner office and nearly collided with Mara. They each took two steps back, Arnesto bumping into Farleigh behind him, and Mara backing into the stool. "It shall not happen again." Mara noticed Arnesto had chosen to glamour himself into the outfit she'd helped him create the evening before. *Good,* she thought, *despite the fact he's over an hour late, at least he's listening to me.*

"My fault," moaned Farleigh. "All my fault."

"What's all your fault?" asked Mara.

Farleigh waved one large fur-covered hand in the air. "Late because of me. And Jerdahn...oh, Jerdahn!" The grihm howled, a loud mournful wail that set Mara's teeth on edge.

There was something about howling wolves—or grihms—that she found deeply disturbing.

"Tell us about Jerdahn. What's happened?" said Mara. Jerdahn and Farleigh had been crossbred at the same time and had escaped from their Glenbarran guards together. Jerdahn was the more cheerful of the two grihms, as well as the clumsier. She wondered if he'd been injured somehow. But that still wouldn't explain why Farleigh felt the need to run away from the grihm preserve and seek outside help.

"Told him worry not. Said new healer wouldn't hurt. Now, oh now," Farleigh howled again, so loudly this time Arnesto winced and covered his ears.

Mara shouted above the keening grihm, "Farleigh, get a grip on yourself. You're a trained Royal Marine! Act like one!" She realized it might be ridiculous to call the large wolf-man a marine, but Farleigh had attended the Royal Marine Academy. He'd been a corporal before he was captured and crossbred.

Farleigh clamped his mouth shut, drowning out the rest of his yowls. He hiccupped a few times and sniffled. "Aye. Trying. Harder in this form." He glanced down at his furry wolf body, his muzzle crumpling at the sight.

Mara could see he was on the verge of another bout of tears and interjected, "What about Jerdahn? You mentioned something last night about bad men. Has someone harmed Jerdahn?"

Farleigh whimpered and slowly told his story. Mara was accustomed to the grihm's garbled speech and could follow along. Arnesto drew his sandy brown eyebrows together as he listened. Mara thought Arnesto might be casting a spell to translate Farleigh's words as he spoke.

"New healer came to preserve. Let the others go." Farleigh shrugged his massive shoulders. "One healer's like another. Then Yeller, a loud fellow, got sick. Carried him to infirmary. New healer said he had to stay few days. Yeller came back different. Quieter.

"I figured Yeller still unwell and would be loud again. But Jerdahn said no. Said healer did something bad to Yeller. Jerdahn watched. When grihms went to infirmary, Jerdahn said they came back different."

Mara asked, "Did you think the grihms seemed different after leaving the infirmary?"

Farleigh shook his head. "I paid no attention. Grihms afraid of anyone with syringe. Then week ago, Jerdahn cut his paw. Bad cut, very deep. He begged me not take him to healer. But I did. Thought healer make him better. Two days later, Jerdahn returned to kennel. Said nothing, just curled up on blanket. Next morning, I poked him, and he bared his teeth. Scared me, so I dropped to my belly. Flattened my ears, showed him I meant no harm.

"He shuddered and said his head hurt. Then he groaned. His eyes rolled back. I thought he dead and I howled. Another grihm checked on him. My best friend was breathing but passed out from pain. Then I found it."

Mara frowned. "What did you find?"

"Small cut, right here." Farleigh pointed behind his head to a spot where his spine met his skull. He howled once before continuing. "Bad man put something in Jerdahn's head. And in other grihms too. When Jerdahn woke up, he remembered nothing. Not even why he went to infirmary.

"Then night before last, more bad happened. Jerdahn and other hurt grihms jumped up and ran out of kennel, howling. They disappeared, somewhere deep in woods of preserve. When they came back, Jerdahn's muzzle bloody. Same with others.

"When I asked what happened, where blood from, Jerdahn snapped his jaws. I scared he might attack. Then he whimpered and said his head hurt. He crawled onto blanket and slept. I waited until almost sunrise and left kennel. Ran to edge of preserve and followed fence. Found good spot for burrowing underneath. Hid during day and ran during night. Had to find my friends from resistance. Had to find you." Farleigh raised his head, his brown eyes bloodshot, and he looked directly at Mara.

As Farleigh spoke, a knot had been slowly forming in the pit of Mara's stomach. She nodded, swallowing down the bile rising in her throat. This had all the hallmarks of a Glenbarran scheme, a new twist on King Roi's horrific abuses. But this time, instead of using Fallow magic to control the grihms, were the Glenbarrans inserting mechanical devices into their heads? "You did the right thing, Farleigh. I don't know what's going on at the preserve, but I'm determined to find out. I'll get a message to Vas, and we'll help Jerdahn and the other grihms."

Arnesto placed his hand on the grihm's shoulder. "Grihm Farleigh, I give you my word. This mystery shall be solved forthwith. Wrongs shall be righted, and the nefarious perpetrators brought to justice!"

Farleigh furrowed his brow and hiccupped. "Don't understand. Think you want to help. Thanks."

Mara glanced at her worktable. She still had several more clockwork toys to be repaired for customers, but she also had to get word to Vas about the problem at the grihm preserve, and she had to start training Arnesto. Mara decided it would be simplest for Arnesto to deliver a message to Vas on her behalf. She leaned over her worktable and drew a slip of parchment toward her. Pulling a bottle of indigo ink from the shelf above her table, Mara dipped a clean quill into the ink and scribbled out a note for Vas.

> *Farleigh is at the shop.*
> *Trouble at the preserve.*
> *Meet Arnesto, my new trainee.*
> *~M*

Mara waited for the ink to dry and then folded over the parchment. After she addressed the note to *Colonel Martel Revas, Provisional President of Valerra*, she heated a few drops of blue wax and used her signet ring to seal the note. The gold ring had been a gift from her father when she turned sixteen—a sword slicing through the downward stroke of the letter *M*. Her stepmother had thought the ring inappropriate for a young lady, but Mara loved it just the same. Before her father had remarried, when it was just the two of them, he used to call Mara his little warrior princess. She'd been in more scrapes in the schoolyard than any boy her age, generally to protect her father's honor with her fists.

Mara's father, Benes Pensk, had failed in his first commission as a young marine officer during the last border war. Benes had ordered his unit to retreat when they should have charged, and the general in charge had demoted him on the spot. Lieutenant Pensk lost both his officer rank and his reputation on one fateful afternoon. Mara's father later admitted he'd been scared, terrified of losing all his men and women. He'd elected to pull back. His failure may have been less noticeable had not another young marine officer, Ric Arlyss, taken over command and led the marines to a decisive victory that day. It took Mara a long time to get over her resentment of that other officer and his daughter, Linden, who eventually became Mara's friend.

Mara handed the note to Arnesto and gave him directions to the provisional government's headquarters, located inside an abandoned savings and loan building on Market Street. The beautiful old parliament building had been demolished during the war. She asked Arnesto to repeat the directions back to her, which he did flawlessly. "It's important for you to ensure that Vas, and only Vas, receives my message. Then please come back here immediately. The store will be open soon and I could use the help."

"You may rely on my speed and discretion. I shall return momentarily." Arnesto gave a small bow as his fay traveling mists encircled his legs.

"But wait, you can just walk there—" Mara frowned. She'd have to remind Arnesto to avoid using his fay traveling mists during the daytime, particularly to translocate several blocks to the savings and loan building. If he were going to learn to blend in, he'd have to travel like everyone else, by foot, by horse, or by steam-powered locomobile.

Mara turned back to a forlorn-looking Farleigh. She had some shelving to be moved in the shop. Perhaps a little bit of useful work would be good for his spirits. "Come on, Farleigh. I could use some help before the shop opens." Farleigh grunted in agreement.

Katrine's Klockworks catered to anyone—child or adult —who enjoyed a touch of whimsy in their toys. Wind-up cats with glittering green eyes, mechanical dogs in a variety of breeds from small poodles to mastiffs, dancing ballerinas, and toy soldiers lined the shelves of the shop, alongside miniature cows, horses, birds, locomobiles, and even a few griffins. Farleigh patiently moved a new shelving unit to several different locations in the shop before Mara nodded. "That's perfect, thanks. And now you may as well make yourself comfortable in the basement while we wait for Arnesto to return with Vas's response."

Mara had no sooner unlocked the door to the shop and flipped the sign in the window to *Open*, when she heard a racket in the basement, followed by shouting. She hastily re-locked the door, turned the sign over to *Closed*, and ran behind the counter. She parted the curtain separating the public toyshop from the office and worktable and stepped inside.

Mara scurried through the cluttered office to the rear alley entrance of the store, which was stacked floor to ceiling with boxes and crates full of tiny gears, shafts, and cranks. Mara's boss also kept a trunkful of knapsacks inside the rear entrance. Each knapsack contained a basic healer's kit, food rations, and a canteen of water—useful supplies that were close at hand for Mara and the other undercover operatives in their network.

Vas's voice carried upstairs from the basement. "Queen's Crown! How dare you snatch me from my office! Who *are* you, anyway?"

"You have my sincerest and utmost apologies, Provisional President. I conveyed you here on Mage Mara's orders."

"Mara ordered you to kidnap me? I think not, whoever you are."

Mara rolled her eyes as she flung open the door to the basement and dashed down the stairs. Vas rounded on her, his dark eyes flashing. "What's this all about?"

Farleigh yowled, "My fault, all my fault!"

Vas hadn't noticed Farleigh, who'd been curled up near the back of the basement behind a row of supplies. "Farleigh? Were you kidnapped by this crazy fay too?"

"I beg your pardon, sir. While I may have misinterpreted my orders and brought you here against your will, I can assure you I am most definitely of sound mind," said Arnesto with a toss of his head, the burgundy feather in his green fedora bouncing in indignation. Mara groaned inwardly. Not only had Arnesto kidnapped Vas, but her fay trainee had changed into his wood nymph garb again.

Vas crossed his arms and drew himself up. "Enough! I want answers—and I want them from Mara." He turned to Mara, his dark eyebrows pointed downward in an unhappy scowl.

Of medium height and build, Vas was most comfortable wearing baggy sweaters and rumpled corduroys. Instead, he was dressed in a navy jacket, gray cravat neatly topping his white linen shirt, and dark gray slacks, which meant he'd been preparing for an important meeting with the other leaders of the provisional government. Vas's face and hands bore the scars of someone accustomed to hard fighting. His piercing brown eyes missed nothing and likewise gave nothing away. He wore his blue-highlighted brown hair—the blue streaks inherited from his Faymon parents —cropped short.

Faymons hailed from up north in Faynwood, where her friend Linden was now the Liege. According to Faymon legends, the blue streaks were due to their mixed heritage. Faymons were mostly human, but they had traces of pure fay in their ancestry. This sometimes led to wariness and even resentment among their Valerran neighbors, who were far less magical and one-hundred-percent human.

In Valerra, only Serving Families such as Mara's possessed magical abilities, which had been acquired many centuries earlier. Three Faymon seers, driven by prophetic visions, had traveled southward to teach a select group of

Valerrans the rudiments of Serving magic. That rare gift of magic had been carefully nurtured through successive generations of Valerra's Serving Families.

Across the border in Faynwood, however, Serving magic thrived everywhere. From kitchen maids to clan chiefs to young girls and boys, everyone could cast spells. So much Serving magic swirled about the place that Faymons didn't use modern technology, like telegraphic transmitters or gas lighting or steam-powered locomobiles. All that magic interfered with the operation of mechanicals. Mara had missed the conveniences of technology during the brief period she lived in Faynwood. However, she'd quickly learned to become more reliant on her own Serving magic, which had improved dramatically among the Faymons.

Mara gave a quick recap of Farleigh's story, with the grihm adding a chorus of grunts and whimpers throughout her retelling. Vas's face darkened when she reached the part about all of the grihms running out of the kennel at the same time and returning with blood on their muzzles. "And so I asked Arnesto to deliver my message to you personally, given the urgency."

"Was kidnapping me to catch my attention the actual message, or did you have something more mundane in mind, such as a handwritten note?"

"A note, of course." Mara tilted her head at Arnesto, who stared at his burgundy boots, studiously avoiding eye contact. "Arnesto, where is the note I asked you to deliver to Vas?"

Arnesto reached into the pocket of his green cloak and withdrew the sealed piece of parchment. With a deep bow, he handed it to Vas. "Your message, sir."

"We're going to have a chat about following directions

after we discuss Farleigh's situation with Vas," said Mara, her voice steely. She wondered whether she ought to send Arnesto back home now, before he got himself into any real trouble. She could simply let Katrine know Arnesto wasn't ready yet to assimilate into Valerran society. He needed a break-in period—maybe with Efram or another of their fay acquaintances—who could help corral Arnesto's overenthusiasm, which was perhaps more dangerous than apathy in a spy.

Vas broke the seal and quickly scanned the note. Since Mara had already filled him in on Farleigh's sad situation, the only other news was that Arnesto was her trainee. Vas glanced at her, doubt etched in the deep lines of his face. "How can this wood nymph, who kidnapped me in front of half a dozen witnesses, possibly be your new trainee?"

"Arnesto is Efram's younger brother and has been...ah... in training for undercover work. Katrine has sent Arnesto to me for his field coaching. And presumably, to help me here at the shop."

"You've got to be kidding." Vas waved his hand at Arnesto, who continued staring at his boots. "He won't last five minutes in the field. And I'll not have you putting your life on the line, training someone without the first notion of what's at stake." Vas folded his arms and addressed Arnesto, who looked as forlorn as Farleigh. "Young man, look at me."

Arnesto raised his head and looked directly at Vas, his gray eyes shining. Mara almost felt sorry for him. Vas asked, "What were your precise orders from Mara?"

Arnesto cleared his throat, and looking a bit surer of himself, repeated back Mara's directions. "I needed to ensure that you, and only you"—here Arnesto bowed again to Vas—"received her message. I also needed to return here forthwith. The store shall be opening momentarily, and Mara will need my help."

"Where's the part about using your fancy fay mists to translocate me against my will?" asked Vas.

Arnesto removed his ridiculous wood nymph hat. He twisted the felt brim in his perfectly manicured hands and hung his head. "I may have gotten somewhat carried away with my first assignment. After all, you are the famous resistance leader and Provisional President of Valerra. I wanted to make a lasting impression."

The corners of Vas's mouth quivered in amusement. "You certainly made a lasting impression, son, although I'd recommend against kidnapping in the future. It could back-fire on you or even get you killed."

"Aye, sir!" Arnesto's head snapped up, a hopeful note in his voice. "Does that mean I can stay?"

"That's up to Mara. After all, she is now your field coach."

Arnesto poured on the full force of his fay charm. He seemed to grow in stature and presence, becoming, if anything, even more bedazzling. Arnesto turned his lumi-nous gray puppy-dog eyes on Mara, who felt herself becoming uncomfortably warm. "I only wish to serve as honorably as my brother. I know I have much to learn, and who better to teach me than you?"

Mara knew when she was being manipulated; on the other hand, her fay boss had sent Arnesto to her for coach-ing. She wondered why Arnesto was so determined to become an undercover operative, and why Katrine and Efram seemed to think he had the skills to succeed. So far, she'd seen nothing to persuade her that he would become adept at spy craft.

Mara decided she would give him another chance, as

many as needed, until either he improved or completely washed out. Or until he got them both killed.

Mara put her hands on her hips, deciding to take a firm approach with Arnesto. He was frankly too darn good-looking to allow him any leeway. She'd have to be as tough with him as she was with…well, with everyone else. "Fine. I'll do my best to train you, but you must listen carefully and follow my lead. And never, ever wear that ridiculous wood nymph outfit again!"

Arnesto bowed gracefully, and when he straightened, his appearance had transformed. He was wearing the clothes he'd arrived in that morning. "Thank you, Mage Mara, you will not regret this."

"Just Mara is fine."

"Just Mara it is, then."

Vas nodded. "Now that's settled, let's get down to the most pressing matter at hand. Farleigh's disturbing story of the goings-on at the preserve."

Farleigh had been sitting on his haunches. Now he raised his head and howled. "Bad men at the preserve."

Mara said, "This sounds like some sort of a Glenbarran scheme, one of King Roi's tricks."

Vas shook his head. "I wish it were that simple."

"Huh?" Mara couldn't imagine why Vas thought a Glenbarran plot would be simpler than what was really going on at the grihm preserve. "What do you mean?"

Vas sighed. "We've been keeping tabs on King Roi, or attempting to anyway. He's been spotted in the southern provinces, near the barrens. Every time we close in on him, he manages to escape, but not before he takes out the scouts and marines who are tracking him. However, there have been no reports of the king inside Bellaryss or anywhere near the grihm preserve. It seems that whatever is happening at the preserve is an altogether different problem. I will, of course, contact Harlan Lewyn about this situation."

"The same Harlan Lewyn who retreated to his horse farm during the siege of Bellaryss, while many officers and mages, including his own nephew, lost their lives defending our capital?" Mara would never forget how easily Harlan Lewyn, one of the wealthiest merchants and landowners in Bellaryss, simply abandoned his post at the city walls and went home.

Vas pursed his lips, which meant Mara would be in for a lecture. "At some point, you're going to have to forgive Harlan Lewyn. He has made many amends since then, and besides, his company is managing the grihm preserve."

"I thought the preserve was run by the provisional government."

"It's sponsored by our government, but we have limited resources and no training in caring for grihms. Lewyn's company has been doing a fine job running the grihm preserve—far better than we could have managed otherwise."

"Until now, that is."

"Let's get all the facts, but if what Farleigh has seen is affecting a large number of grihms, then I will hold Lewyn personally responsible. Unfortunately, we're facing an even larger problem at the moment."

"What do you mean?" Mara wasn't sure she wanted to hear Vas's answer.

The president's face darkened. "Someone inside Bellaryss, someone not connected with King Roi, is trying to foment a rebellion."

CHAPTER 4

Mara took a step back, unable to believe her ears. Someone they trusted, someone who'd fought alongside them to overthrow Glenbarra, was now undermining them. It made no sense. "But why? To what end?"

"There are those who oppose the monarchy. They have no desire to return Valerra to its former glory. Instead, they intend to create so much chaos and uncertainty that it would be unsafe for Queen Ayn to return from the colonies and resume her royal duties."

Mara crossed her arms, angry that anyone who might have once been a friend would oppose the crown. "I know things have been rocky since the end of the war. What's happening that has you more concerned than usual?" Mara knew Vas well enough to know he was a perpetual worrier.

Farleigh whimpered softly. Vas patted the large grihm's shoulder. "There's a growing movement among the various guilds to decommission the use of magic. Some guild leaders claim it was the clash of two magical systems— Serving magic versus Fallow sorcery—that nearly destroyed Valerra."

"But that is illogical thinking, if I may be so bold," said Arnesto. "Serving magic saved Valerra from the dark forces of Fallow sorcery. Do these anti-magic proponents not understand?"

Vas raised his shoulders in a half-shrug. "Perhaps not. Or perhaps it's simply a ruse to gain the upper hand at this delicate time in our nation's rebuilding. After all, King Roi, Mordahn, and their thugs nearly wiped out the Serving Families of Valerra." Most Serving Families, realizing the Glenbarrans aimed to destroy them and their magic, split up at the start of the war. A lucky few evacuated with the queen, while others attempted the dangerous trek to the colonies on their own. The rest remained in Valerra to fight against the relentless tide of Glenbarrans invading their homeland.

Mara had elected to stay behind and fight, despite her father's entreaties. He'd packed up his two younger daughters and his second wife and purchased passage for them on a merchant vessel. Unfortunately, Valerrans such as Mara's family fled Bellaryss in late autumn, when storms came up without warning on the Pale Sea, creating huge waves that swamped everything in their path. Mara had no idea whether any of her family had survived the arduous trip.

"The resistance relied heavily on the fays to break down Mordahn's Fallow spells at Wellan Pass. I do not believe you could have overthrown Glenbarra without our magical assistance," said Arnesto.

"Aye," agreed Vas. "And our friends from Faynwood used veils of drabness to slip into Bellaryss, right under King Roi's nose. 'Tis true, without the aid of Serving magic, we would still be occupied—which is why this anti-magic movement is so disturbing."

Arnesto began pacing around the cramped basement, dodging shelves filled with broken or partially assembled clockwork toys, as well as glass jars containing tiny screws, gears, shafts, and springs. He muttered to himself in the buzzing language of the fays, waving his hands in the air. Mara narrowed her eyes, surprised to see her new trainee so unsettled. "What is it, Arnesto?"

Arnesto spun around suddenly, wearing his sparkly silver cloak, tunic, and trousers. He ran one slender hand through his vivid blue waves, his gray eyes troubled. "I need to visit Auntie Yelenarra's library to examine her collection of old scrolls. There is something about the anti-magic movement and rising opposition to the monarchy that feels familiar to me. I need to do some research." He hesitated before adding, "That is, with your permission, Coach Mara." Arnesto gave a deep bow.

"It's just Mara, and if you think there may be a clue in an old scrap of fay prophecy, by all means go."

Foggy tendrils twined around Arnesto's legs. "I am seeking one of the oldest manuscripts in existence, written by the most revered...." The traveling mists enveloped Arnesto, and he was gone.

Mara shrugged. "I guess we'll learn more once he returns."

"In the meantime," said Vas. "I want to move Farleigh to a location where he will be safer and far more comfortable than this basement."

Farleigh raised his shaggy head and yipped. "And help Jerdahn."

"Aye, I promise I'll get to the bottom of what's going on at the preserve. I'll help Jerdahn and the other grihms." Vas walked to the stairs and said over his shoulder, "I'm going back to headquarters so I can pick up my locomobile. Wait here for me. We're going to visit one of my oldest friends. He owns a large orchard north of the city. You'll have plenty of space to roam."

Farleigh tilted his head to one side. "Apples?"

Vas smiled, "Aye, he grows apples, plums, and pears."

Mara followed Vas up the stairs. "I'd better get the shop open before Katrine's customers start complaining."

Vas returned to pick up Farleigh about an hour later. He used a veil of drabness to hide the grihm and snuck him out the rear entrance of the shop into a waiting locomobile. Mara knew Farleigh would be looked after by Vas. She was less certain they would be able to help Jerdahn and the other grihms, if they'd been surgically altered. She just hoped they could prevent any more grihms from coming to harm—or from harming others in their altered state.

Mara had a steady stream of customers throughout the morning. Before she'd started working at Katrine's Klockworks, she had no appreciation for the number of people with an interest in clockwork toys. Shortly after noon, Mara locked up the shop and posted a sign on the door, hand-lettered by Katrine: *Enjoying a Leisurely Lunch—We will Reopen Before We Close.*

The first time Mara saw the sign, her first day on the job, she thought Katrine was joking. But when Katrine had flipped over the sign on the door, she'd told Mara to follow the instructions. Shrugging, Mara had taken a long lunch, close to an hour, and when she returned, the shop was still closed. Katrine didn't reopen the shop for another hour, and Mara quickly learned that a fay's sense of time was more elastic than a Valerran's. Katrine refused to be bound by a timepiece. She explained to Mara that fays simply could not fathom how Valerrans built their lives around the hands of a clock.

Mara reminded herself of that fact when Arnesto still hadn't returned to the shop by mid-afternoon. She found herself wondering whether something had happened to her fay trainee. *Hang on, what am I doing? I've known Arnesto for less than a day, and I'm already worrying about his whereabouts? I need to get a grip—he may be charming, challenging, and gorgeous—but he's also frustrating, ridiculous, and unreliable. And I'm his field coach. I need to maintain my distance. Otherwise, Arnesto's antics will definitely get us both killed!*

Mara was counting the day's cash receipts when Arnesto materialized behind her, wearing his silvery fay garb. "I must apologize for losing track of time."

Mara jumped, losing her place; she'd have to start over and recount the receipts. She spun around, torn between relief Arnesto hadn't gotten himself in trouble and frustration he had no inkling how much time had passed.

"I realize fays and Valerrans have a different sense of time. However, you and I are going to need to work on your reliability." Mara noticed a troubled, almost haunted look in Arnesto's eyes, something she'd not seen there before. She softened her tone. "What have you discovered?"

Arnesto ran a hand through his long blue hair. His eyes shifted to the cash receipts Mara held in her hand. "Since I interrupted your important work, please allow me to finish the count for you."

"Are you sure?"

"Quite sure. You may trust me to count your paper money and coinage with speed and accuracy. According to Auntie Yelenarra, my fast-math skills are second to none."

Mara wasn't sure what he meant by fast-math skills, but she reminded herself that Katrine trusted Arnesto. She placed the bills and coins in the fay's outstretched hand. He moved so quickly that all Mara could see was a blurring motion, one second Arnesto's hands, the next second bills flipping through the air, followed by coins.

"Two-thousand, three-hundred and twenty-two denare." Arnesto announced, handing the money back to Mara with a small bow. Mara knew from experience it sounded about right. *Can Arnesto really count that quickly? If so, what other hidden talents—other than his fay-born magic—does he have up his silvery sleeves?*

She arched her eyebrows. "Thank you...that was very fast indeed."

"And accurate," added Arnesto, with a twinkle in his eyes that quickly faded. Something was really bothering her new trainee. Mara placed the bills and coins in a depository bag, which she carried into the small office behind the counter and locked in the bottom drawer of the worktable.

Arnesto followed her into the office and sat on a stool with a sigh. Mara pulled the other stool out from under the worktable and sat down across from him. "Do you want to tell me about it?"

Arnesto nodded and took a deep breath. "I believe you've visited the realms of the dead before?"

"Aye." Mara's scalp prickled. Not only had she visited the realms of the dead, but she'd almost been trapped there. Mara and her friends had pursued King Roi's most powerful necromancer, Mordahn, all the way into the lowest of the realms, where they battled the dark sorcerer and his protectors until Linden managed to dispatch Mordahn for the last time. He was gone for good, but what Mara saw in that other world still gave her nightmares. She'd seen where darkness and evil eventually lead—to a swirling, swiftly flowing river that sweeps its occupants into a lake of fire.

Arnesto said, "My mother was a reaper, but a special

kind known as a reaper-extractor. She extracted the undead from our world and returned them to the realms of the dead, where they belong."

"You mean like Katrine?"

"Aye. I am related to Katrine, a very distant cousin, through my mother's side of the family."

"You mentioned your mother *was* a reaper—past tense. Did something happen to her?"

Arnesto nodded. "During her last reaping, something went horribly wrong. My mother managed to escape from the realms of the dead, but an undead creature followed her back to Havynweal, back to our family's home." Arnesto rubbed a hand over his face, struggling to compose himself. Mara felt a stab of sympathy for him, but she resisted the urge to pamper her new trainee. Arnesto wouldn't be coddled once he was in the field—quite the opposite, in fact.

"My mother cast every protection ward and defensive spell she could conjure to shield us, but she was too weakened from her battle in the lower realms to sustain the spells. When the beast broke through Mother's wards and crashed through our front door, its dark, misshapen spirit seeped into every corner of the house, crept inside my head, and crowded out every happy thought I ever possessed. I cannot say what I found more frightening—its appearance or its presence."

"What did it look like?"

Arnesto drew his sandy brows together. "Dark bristles, each as thick as my finger, covered the creature's body, which seemed to be a cross between a panther and a lizard. When the creature opened its mouth, I saw row upon row of jagged, pointy teeth. That hideous thing killed my mother and my pet griffin with several powerful swipes from his razor-sharp claws."

"Oh, Arnesto, how horrible for you. I'm sorry you had to see that. How did you escape?" Mara's heart constricted in her chest, her sympathy swelling at the thought of a younger version of Arnesto, witnessing the deaths of his mother and his pet.

Arnesto stared at a spot above Mara's head, his eyes somewhat unfocused, as if he were once again facing down the undead creature. "The monster turned his fiery orbs on me. I ran through the house screaming, out the back door, and into the kitchen gardens before he caught up with me. The beast threw me onto the ground and slashed at me with his front claws. He shredded my tunic and scored my chest, and then he paused, panting heavily. His breath smelled of rot and decay.

"The monster leaned over and sank his long fangs into my neck and shoulders. I cried and thought, 'this is it...at least I will be with Mother.' But instead of joining my mother, the creature howled as if *I* had injured *him*. He flung me so hard I hit my head on a red oak tree in the center of our garden. When I came to, I was lying on a healer's cot. I later learned that most of my family was out tracking the beast. Efram wasn't old enough to be tracking, so Father sent him away to study with the monks on Sanrellyss Island. I was only five, too young to be sent to Sanrellyss Island with Efram. So Father turned me over to Auntie Yelenarra, my mother's elder sister, for protection."

"For protection from the beast?"

"No. My father eventually tracked him down, with the help of Auntie Yelenarra and the rest of Mother's family."

"Are they all reapers?"

"Aye."

"So if your family tracked the creature down, why did your father believe you still needed protection? Who was after you if not the beast?"

Arnesto squirmed and avoided meeting Mara's eyes. The stool was darned uncomfortable; Mara's back was killing her, but she didn't think that was why Arnesto wouldn't look at her. "The others," he said.

"What others?"

"The dark fays from the outer demesnes."

CHAPTER 5

"The dark fays from the outer demesnes? I've never heard of them. Who are they?" Mara wondered whether Arnesto's imagination was running ahead of him. The story of the monster following his mother out of the realms of the dead was entirely believable, and given her experience, altogether likely. However, none of her fay friends had ever mentioned dark fays from the outer demesnes. Perhaps Arnesto was weaving a tall tale to explain why he'd been gone so long.

"It's not so much who they are, but what they are."

When Arnesto didn't continue, Mara said, "Alright. You've roused my curiosity. What are they?"

"The descendants of fays who have been banished from Havynweal over the centuries for misuse of magic."

Mara had only known one person who'd misused his magic—Stryker Soto, her friend Linden's ex-fiancé. Mara had had an enormous crush on Royal Marine Corporal Stryker Soto before the war, but he'd pursued Linden instead. Later, when Stryker had turned into an envious, overbearing boyfriend, Mara realized she'd dodged a bad situation. And when, in a fit of jealous rage, he'd misused his magic and nearly injured a lot of innocent people, she'd felt sorry for Linden and what she'd had to endure. Bad boyfriends were bad news—period. The Faynwood Council expelled Stryker Soto, sending him to work out his sentence on a Faymon ship in the Pale Sea.

"Here in Valerra, and up north in Faynwood, misuse of magic is a serious crime. But I had no idea fays also misused their magic."

The corners of Arnesto's mouth twitched up. "Although humans veer into Fallow sorcery and necromancy, you believe we fays are immune to the pull of the dark ways?"

Mara's face turned pink, which she hoped Arnesto couldn't see in the light of the single gas lamp she'd left on in the office. She realized she had a lot to learn about fays. Nodding, Mara said, "Aye. My understanding of fays is based on what I've learned from Katrine, Efram, and others. And also from the fay tall tales my father used to read to me."

Arnesto hopped off his stool and bent from the waist in a deep bow. When he straightened, he'd changed back into his brown jacket and houndstooth slacks. "I would be deeply honored if you would permit me the privilege of instructing you in fay ways. However, I am famished, and I trust you are as well. Might I escort you to a pub some-where for a simple meal?"

Mara resisted the urge to consider this a date, which would be inappropriate. After all, she was Arnesto's field coach. Mara was sure that somewhere in the Valerran Handbook of Covert Operatives, which she'd never read because Vas was still writing it, there was some sort of an injunction against dating your fellow spies. And if there wasn't, there should be. Arnesto was way too distracting in the abstract, without becoming emotionally entangled with him as well.

Mara stood up and smoothed down her skirt. She reached for her midnight blue cloak, dangling on one of the coat hooks. Arnesto was beside her in an instant, helping her slip first her left arm, and then her right, into her cloak. She noticed his scent for the first time, of loamy earth mixed with tangy citrus. Mara took her time buttoning up. "Thank you. Dinner sounds like a great idea. We'll consider this your 'welcome' celebration and I'll treat you."

Arnesto brought his hand to his chest and nodded. "If that is your custom in Valerra, then I am happy to oblige."

Arnesto followed Mara through the shop, ensuring every gas-lit wall sconce was turned down. Mara locked up and placing her hand on the doorframe, waited until she could feel Katrine's various protection wards and charms thrumming with power. She led Arnesto several blocks west to Bellwether Street and the Cracked Cauldron.

Arnesto pulled open the thick wooden door of the pub and ushered Mara inside. The low murmur of many different conversations, punctuated with occasional laughter, swelled around them. Mara figured the Cracked Cauldron's original owner must have been a carpenter, with its scarred, wide plank floors, polished mahogany and brass bar along the back wall, and dark wood booths lining the other three walls. To the right of the bar was the requisite dartboard, where a boisterous group of young men were engaged in relieving each other of their day's wages. Idyllic prints of pre-war Valerra dotted the pub's dark green walls —mostly rural scenes from the rolling farmland, valleys, and quaint villages to the west of the city. Mara scanned the room and spotted an available booth along the wall nearest the door. She and Arnesto slid into a pair of well-worn benches across from one another.

After they had eaten their fill of meatloaf, stewed root vegetables, and fresh bread, the owner of the establishment stopped by their table. A petite, dark woman in her late thirties, her brunette hair pulled back in a bun, placed two steaming mugs of pub coffee in front of them. Although each pub varied the recipe somewhat, the rich black coffee contained a hint of cinnamon, a dash of cocoa, and a shot of strong spirits, with a dollop of whipped cream floating on top. "Compliments of the house."

Mara smiled at the woman. "Thank you, Gemala. I'll pop over tomorrow for a quick chat."

Gemala handed their empty platters to a young boy of about twelve, one of her nephews, and then she wiped down their table. "You must introduce me to your companion."

Mara made the introductions, adding, "Arnesto will be working with me at the toyshop, and aiding me with Katrine's many other projects." Mara intentionally emphasized *other projects*.

"I predict Katrine's toyshop will gain new foot traffic, once word spreads about the handsome young shop's assistant she's hired." Gemala grinned, her brown eyes twinkling.

Arnesto smiled. "Thank you, madam. I am touched by your kind words and your gift of pub coffee, which I look forward to imbibing."

Gemala chuckled. "Aren't you a cheeky lad?" She winked at Mara and moved on to a nearby table to take their order. Gemala reminded Mara of a sleek black cat that slipped into and out of tight spots quickly; when you looked around for her, she was already gone, on to her next destination.

Arnesto nodded at Gemala. "A friend of yours?"

"Aye, and one of our work colleagues." Mara had met Gemala, or Gem as she'd been introduced, during an undercover operation in the final months of the occupation. It had been Mara's first experience working alongside Vas and his resistance fighters, and she'd loved everything about the covert operation—the danger, the adrenaline surge, the belief that what she was doing really mattered—until they'd lost a valued team member. Although she hadn't known Burr personally, Vas and the others had been devastated at the time.

Arnesto arched his right eyebrow. "Are there many such work colleagues in Bellaryss?"

Mara shook her head. "Actually, very few whom I trust completely. Gemala is on my short list." She paused and took a sip from the steaming mug. Glancing up at Arnesto, Mara said, "Tell me about the dark fays and why they were after a five-year-old boy."

Arnesto focused on his mug of pub coffee and sighed. "Father believed they wanted to kill me, but Auntie Yelenarra thought they were more clever than that and wanted to experiment on me."

Mara grimaced at the idea of subjecting a child to experiments. What could have made the dark fays—whoever they were—so interested in a small boy? "But why? What is so unique about you?"

Arnesto waggled the fingers of his right hand slightly, and whispered, "Drape us in a veil of gauze, hide us from inquiring eyes." A gauzy veil immediately snapped into place. Mara could invoke a veil of drabness too, although it would take her multiple repetitions of the incantation to conjure the veil. Wreyn, her fay friend, would repeat the incantation three times before the veil materialized. Mara was beginning to grasp that Arnesto's magic was far from ordinary, even for a fay.

With the veil of drabness firmly in place, they were effectively hidden in plain view from everyone else in the pub. If other diners happened to glance over, their eyes would skim past the gauzy grayness without realizing anyone was present inside. In addition, the sounds of their voices were also muffled so no one could eavesdrop.

Arnesto untied his beige cravat, and Mara's eyes widened. *What does Arnesto think he is doing? This behavior is entirely inappropriate.* Arnesto must have been aware of what she was thinking, because he gave her a mischievous wink. His face grew serious again, as he undid the top three buttons of his white linen shirt. Mara realized he wanted to answer her question about why he needed protection from the dark fays—and the most proper way to partially undress before a single young woman was to do so in a public place. It would still be considered scandalous, if anyone observed them, but Arnesto had solved that problem by casting the veil of drabness over their booth.

Arnesto grasped the edges of his shirt, which he abruptly tugged open to reveal white scars crisscrossing his chiseled brown chest, as if a sharp rake had been dragged across the flesh, first in one direction, then another. Mara shook her head, horrified at the damage wrought by the undead creature. She wanted to offer a word of comfort, something to break the silence, but Arnesto tilted his head and pushed aside his sandy brown hair. The skin between his left ear and the top of his shoulder was punctuated with deep, vicious-looking scars—as if a monster had sunk its fangs into his neck.

Mara inhaled sharply, her throat tightening at the sight of Arnesto's scars. She struggled to come to grips with the fear and trauma he must have suffered as a young child. He'd witnessed a brutal attack on his mother and his pet griffin, before the monster had turned on him. And yet, Arnesto had managed to survive and even thrive. Did he have invisible scars from the attack as well, ones he kept well hidden?

Arnesto dropped his hair, hiding the bite marks once more, and he buttoned up his linen shirt. Mara asked, "How did you escape with your life?"

The fay ran his fingers across the silk of his cravat and retied it, though somewhat crookedly. He sipped his pub coffee and then placed the mug carefully on the tabletop before replying. "Well, that is the question, is it not? How did a five-year-old untrained fay boy not only escape, but manage to kill an undead creature from the lower realms?"

"Wait a minute—you killed it? I don't understand."

"My father, Auntie Yelenarra, and the rest of the family tracked the monster for three days, following the path of destruction it wrought. Fortunately, the creature did not kill anyone else, but it tore a path through auburn summer, damaging trees and meadowlands, and attacking a herd of unicorns, before collapsing beside a stream and drinking itself to its second death."

"But you were nowhere near the creature when it died. How could you have killed it?"

Arnesto pointed to the area below his left ear, hidden beneath his hair. "That monster started to drink from me, and apparently, my blood was toxic. My father believed the creature was driven by an unquenchable thirst. Apparently, so did the dark fays when they learned of it."

"Why would they have cared?"

"Can you imagine the power one could wield inside the realms of the dead, if you possessed the ability to send something undead to its permanent home in the lake of fire? Using the threat of extinction, you could gather to yourself the very worst of the undead and build an army that defies imagination."

Mara had never heard of dark fays. They sounded worse than Mordahn, who was the darkest sorcerer she'd ever battled, a Fallow mage bent on destroying Serving magic and all who practiced it. She believed that once Mordahn had been dispatched to the lake of fire, their undead problems were over. Maybe she'd been uncharacteristically optimistic, which would be a first for her. Her friends always teased her about her gloomy outlook. What they didn't realize was that Mara chose to be a tankard-half-empty pessimist because she couldn't bear to be disappointed at every turn. If she always expected the worst, then once in a while she could be pleasantly surprised when something actually turned out right. Looks like she'd been wildly optimistic about their undead problems.

Mara stirred her lukewarm pub coffee, sifting through Arnesto's story. Efram had said something about Arnesto's childhood being different. The pieces were starting to fall into place. "And so you were raised by your aunt, who protected you from the dark fays?"

"Aye. But my auntie did more than protect me. She taught me how to defend myself and how to fight back."

Mara tried to imagine an elderly fay woman teaching Arnesto how to fight. Based on Arnesto's stilted speech patterns, courtesy of Auntie Yelenarra, she held out little hope he'd been taught to fight using ordinary weapons. "What were your aunt's weapons of choice?" *Please don't say knitting needles and frying pans.*

Arnesto smiled. "I suspect you might be concerned my auntie taught me how to use weapons close to hand—a boiling cauldron of water, a fireplace poker, or a piece of broken pottery—and you would be right. However, Auntie Yelenarra possesses extraordinary skills with many weapons you would recognize, and a few you might not."

Mara thought perhaps she'd underestimated Arnesto's fay aunt. "What weapons have you mastered?"

Arnesto drew back his shoulders and said, with more than a hint of pride in his voice, "I know my defensive wards and offensive spells inside and out. In fact, I am a twelfth-level fay wizard."

Mara nearly choked on her drink. "I didn't know fays assessed themselves on levels of magic."

"Of course. It is quite similar to how Valerrans advance through your magic levels."

Valerrans generally recognized three levels, apprentice, mage, and master mage. When Mara had lived in Faynwood, she'd attended the famous Faymon magic trials. Faymons evaluated their students at each stage between apprentice and master, breaking down the mage category into sub-levels: novice, junior, and senior mage.

Mara wondered what it meant to be a twelfth-level fay wizard. "How many levels of magic are there in Havynweal?"

"Twelve."

"Twelve?"

Arnesto gave her a wry grin. "I perceive you are surprised that I have achieved mastery of my magic—both Serving magic and elemental magic—although there is very little cause for commanding the elements most days."

Mara rubbed the back of her neck. An image of Arnesto, his blue hair blowing as he commanded a mighty wind, popped into her head. Since she was not a girl prone to visions, Mara dismissed it. "What sort of physical weaponry have you mastered?"

"The staff, the flint, and the plunger."

Mara's face fell. *This is worse than I thought. None of these weapons will be of much use to an undercover operative in Bellaryss.* "Anything else?"

"Darts."

"Darts?"

Arnesto nodded. "Auntie Yelenarra set up a dartboard in the woods behind our home. I have become quite skilled at hitting the center of the target. My aunt believed dart throwing would be a useful skill to acquire, since it is a popular pastime in Valerran pubs. She thought I could throw darts with the locals and pick up useful tidbits of information along the way."

Mara would have liked to have a word with the ancient, and by all accounts, formidable Auntie Yelenarra. Her assumptions about Valerran culture could get her nephew killed. On the other hand, Mara had to agree that dart throwing might be a good way to develop relationships with potential informants. However, knowledge of more conventional weapons would be even better. "Have you received training in sword fighting or knife throwing?"

"Naturally. I am adept at both, and a fair hand with a bow and arrow."

"Why didn't you say so? Here I was thinking we'd need to find you a fencing coach immediately."

"You asked me what weapons I had mastered. While I am accomplished with the sword and dagger, I do not consider myself a master."

"Alright, that's helpful. I will book us some time with my fencing coach and see how we can help you improve."

Arnesto smiled, his teeth practically sparkling in all their pearly whiteness. "Thank you for taking me on as your trainee. I recognize I have much to learn, and I believe you will help me to achieve my heart's desire."

Mara's eyebrows rose. Should she ask? Did she really want to know? Her curiosity got the better of her. "And what is your heart's desire, if I may be so bold?" *Gah! Now I'm starting to sound like Arnesto.*

Arnesto placed his hand over his heart and intoned, "To serve honorably, use my magic wisely, and prevent the dark fays from destroying Valerra."

CHAPTER 6

"Wait...what?" Mara massaged her temples. She was beginning to get a migraine, and she laid all the blame on Arnesto. He was confounding, confusing, and perhaps a bit crazy, too. What had she gotten herself into, agreeing to take on this odd, awkward, amazingly good-looking fay as her trainee?

"The dark fays intend to infiltrate Valerra. This is why Katrine asked me to come to Bellaryss, and why Efram wants you to train me. We cannot permit the dark fays any foothold inside your homeland. The Glenbarrans and their Fallow sorcery are bad enough; the dark fays from the outer demesnes are worse. Much, much worse."

Mara felt like she had a lot to unpack in that statement, but she was too exhausted and headachy to draw Arnesto deeper into conversation. The dark fays from the outer demesnes would have to wait until she had a good night's sleep, and she could question Arnesto more closely.

Mara asked Arnesto to lower the veil of drabness so Gemala could find their table. When Gemala made her way over to the two of them, she waved away the bills that Mara pulled out of her reticule. "Your meal is all taken care of."

"Who?"

Gemala grinned. "A certain handsome young shop's assistant." Two men started to argue loudly near the billiard table, located opposite the dartboard on the other side of the ornately carved mahogany bar. Gemala headed toward the bickering men and called out over her shoulder, "Have a good evening!"

Mara looked at Arnesto and waited for an explanation. He gave her a sheepish smile. "When you visited the ladies' lounge earlier, I took the liberty of paying for our meals. For all our meals, actually."

"All our meals? How much money did you give to Gemala?"

"I believe she said, 'Son, you and Mara can eat as many meals as you would like here, for as long as you like, or at least until you are as old as I am."

Mara shook her head. "You paid for our meals for the next twenty odd years? How much did you give Gemala?"

Arnesto lifted his shoulders. "I did not count out the gold."

Mara frowned. "Are you telling me you gave Gemala your entire bag of gold?" When Arnesto nodded, she said, "But you didn't have the gold with you earlier. How did you manage to retrieve it from Remy's apartment and hand it over to Gemala while I was in the ladies' lounge? I wasn't gone all that long."

Arnesto stared at the wall behind Mara's head and avoided eye contact. Mara realized this meant her fay trainee was trying to weasel out of telling her the truth. Since fays couldn't tell a lie directly, they had mastered the art of avoidance, misdirection, and partial truths. "It has been rather a long day," said Arnesto. "Do you think we could start walking in the direction of our flats?"

Mara folded her arms across her chest. "Aye, once you answer my question."

"Fine." Arnesto waved his hand in the air. "I might have cast a tiny spell to freeze everyone inside the pub for sixty seconds, just long enough for me to travel by mist over to Remy's flat, pick up the bag of gold, and then return."

Mara didn't know what bothered her more, that Arnesto had frozen everyone inside the pub, or that he didn't seem to realize he'd broken a couple of cardinal rules. "What if something had happened here in the pub while you were gone? Or, what if someone saw you using your magic? You would have blown your cover on your first day."

"I was gone so quickly that no harm could have come to anyone in the pub. And I can guarantee no one saw me."

"Can you also guarantee that some Fallow sorcerer inside Bellaryss didn't pick up on your magical signature and realize an unknown fay was using Serving magic in the area?"

Arnesto's mouth turned down at the corners. "Ah. I see the problem now."

"Well?"

"I had not considered that possibility. I am sorry."

Arnesto looked so contrite Mara's attitude softened somewhat. Besides, he'd paid for all their meals for the next two decades. How long could she really stay mad at him? On the other hand, Arnesto had to be more careful, especially with all his talk about dark fays.

Mara said, "I must ask you to remember, every waking moment, that you are no longer in Havynweal. You and I must watch every step. Any misstep could harm our cause and perhaps get ourselves injured, or worse."

"Of course. I never make the same mistake twice. It shall not happen again."

Mara smiled. "I know you meant well, and I am grateful for the free meals for the next twenty years."

"You should do that more often."

"Do what?"

Arnesto waved his fingers in front of his face. "Your smile lights up your entire visage. You are quite lovely all the time, but when you smile, well then—"

Mara cleared her throat to interrupt Arnesto before he said anything more about her looks. She didn't want to even consider that *he* might find *her* attractive. She was not crossing that line with her fay trainee. "Would you look at the time? It's later than I thought. Shall we leave?" Mara started to rise from her booth, but Arnesto reached out his hand and whispered, "I believe Gemala may need some assistance."

Arnesto nodded at the two loud, brawling men, whom Gemala was attempting to separate. The tall, skinny man pushed Gemala out of the way as his companion, a thickset fellow in a threadbare coat and patched trousers, lifted a small tube to his mouth and blew through it. The tall man grabbed his throat and tumbled backward, knocking over one of the servers carrying a platter of food. Several women screamed as the stout man ran through the crowded room toward the door. Mara stood up and hissed, "Follow that man, but don't engage him. Find out where he's heading. I'll stay here and see if I can help the injured man."

Arnesto sprinted from the booth, his long legs blurring with the speed of his movement. Mara found herself wondering again about Arnesto and his many hidden talents—one of which seemed to be speed—whether counting the day's receipts or chasing after a criminal. She found herself asking more questions about the fays during the past day than she'd asked in the past year. Was Arnesto unique, or perhaps simply unusual, where fays were concerned?

Mara knelt beside the fallen man as Gemala checked his pulse and shook her head. "He's gone."

"But how? What could have killed him so quickly?" whispered Mara.

Gemala pointed to a spot of blood on the side of the man's neck. "Looks like something sharp pricked him. A needle perhaps?"

Mara gently turned the man's head to the side and found the culprit—a tiny metal splinter lay on the floor beneath him. Mara bent to examine it further and leaned back on her heels. "He was poisoned," she said, her mind whirring with the possibilities. Who was this gaunt stranger lying in Gemala's pub, and why had he been killed? The only clue was his chef whites, peeking out from beneath his plain wool coat. Mara pointed at the miniscule glint of metal. "Looks like a very small dart, nearly impossible to see unless you're a few inches from the ground."

Gemala handed Mara a cloth napkin. "Here, wrap that dart up and make sure you don't touch it. Whatever killed him was extremely potent."

Mara carefully rolled the dart up inside the napkin and tucked it in her reticule. Something about this whole scene didn't sit right with her, beyond the fact a man had been murdered in plain view of thirty or so people inside the Cracked Cauldron. She had not encountered poisoned darts before—knives, swords, daggers, arrows, and axes, mostly, and the occasional pistol—but guns, like clockwork toys, failed around too much magic. *This is no ordinary crime. Poisoned darts are an assassin's weapon.*

Mara rose from the floor with a sigh. She wished she hadn't sent her inexperienced trainee after an assassin who killed with poisoned darts. The door to the pub opened, sending a blast of rain-swept air into the room. Mara hoped to see Arnesto returning from his chase. Instead, two constables arrived, their wool cloaks damp, their black umbrellas dripping water on the scarred wooden floor. Mara berated herself for having left her umbrella back at the shop; the rain had stopped when she and Arnesto had left for the pub.

Gemala hurried over to greet the new arrivals, a fortyish baldheaded man with blue eyes and an impressive handlebar moustache, and a slightly younger woman with glossy black hair pulled into a low bun, fair complexion, and gold-rimmed spectacles.

The woman strode across the floor, the heels of her boots clacking against the floorboards. The man followed in her wake, pulling out a small leather-bound notebook and a pencil from the inside pocket of his cloak. "I am Chief Inspector Talias, and this is Inspector Foxx," said the woman, her loud voice carrying across the room. "Please do not leave the pub until Inspector Foxx and I have taken down your statements." A general murmur, along with some groans, arose from the crowded room.

One woman called out, "But I have my young ones with me, and it's getting late, past their bedtime."

Chief Inspector Talias waved her hand. "We'll move this along as quickly as possible. Meanwhile, I'm sure Gemala will be happy to keep you well supplied with something to fortify your nerves." Gemala took the hint and offered a round of free drinks to her patrons, including warm mugs of cider for the children.

Mara hadn't moved away from the man's body when

the constables entered the Cracked Cauldron. It seemed disrespectful somehow to leave him lying alone on the scuffed floor. The chief inspector's spectacles, which glinted from the gas lighting inside the pub, settled on Mara. "Do you know this man?" When Mara replied no, Talias frowned. "Then why are you standing over him? What is your interest in this dead man?"

"I wanted to see if I could do anything to help him."

"Are you a healer?" Talias drew closer to Mara and the body.

Mara shook her head. "No, but I have battlefield experience. I've stitched up more than my share of wounds."

Behind the chief inspector's spectacles, a pair of almond-shaped brown eyes flashed darkly. "So, you are not a trained healer, but you felt called upon to examine him. Did you move the position of his body in any way?"

Mara sensed that Talias would not be pleased with her answer. "I moved his head to peer more closely at his neck."

The furrow between the chief inspector's brows deepened. Shaking her head, Talias knelt beside the man's body. Foxx hovered nearby, ready to take notes. Talias pointed at the pinprick of dried blood on the man's neck and called out her observations to Foxx. "Small wound, right side of neck, paralysis of face and limbs, bluish cast to skin, white foam on his lips." Rising, she added, "This man was poisoned, but how? If that's the entry wound, where's the weapon?"

"I found this on the floor and wrapped it up to prevent anyone from touching it." Mara reached into her reticule and withdrew the cloth napkin, which she handed to Talias.

Chief Inspector Talias carefully opened the napkin and showed the tiny dart to Inspector Foxx, before turning back to Mara, her face hardening. Mara resisted the urge to squirm. "You should not have touched anything, neither the man's head nor the dart that delivered the poison. Should you ever encounter criminal activity again, wait for the proper authorities. You are neither a trained healer nor a trained constable. In fact, you are barely out of school and have no business interfering in matters you know nothing about."

Mara felt herself growing warm in direct proportion to her rising temper. She took a deep breath, and then another. She would not rise to the bait tossed her way by Talias. This was no ordinary crime scene, no straightforward scuffle between two inebriated men that ended tragically. Mara knew it, and so did the chief inspector. No one carries around poisoned darts unless he intends to swiftly and permanently dispatch someone to the realms of the dead.

"Aye, Inspector."

"That's Chief Inspector."

It took all of Mara's willpower to refrain from an eye roll. "Aye, Chief Inspector, ma'am."

The Chief Inspector nodded curtly. "Return to your table. Do not leave until Inspector Foxx and I take your official statement." Talias turned to Inspector Foxx. "Let's see about getting some volunteers to move the body into another room until the coroner arrives to examine him." Foxx found several ready volunteers from among the patrons, and together they carried the dead man into the rear room of the pub, generally reserved for Vas and his staff when they ate there. Vas required an extra measure of privacy and security these days.

Chief Inspector Talias started on the side of the pub closest to the murder and moved methodically across to the other side of the room, stopping at each table to interview witnesses. Meanwhile Inspector Foxx scribbled in his leather notebook and occasionally interjected with a question of his own. They released each table as they went. Mara noticed they skirted around her table, forcing her to wait until every other witness had been questioned.

Mara kept checking the timepiece in her reticule, worrying about Arnesto. When two hours had passed with no sign of her fay trainee, Mara wondered where to start looking for him. She had no idea how to contact Efram and ask for his help. She could try to reach Katrine, although she preferred not to bother her fay boss just yet. She didn't want Katrine to know she'd sent Arnesto into a dangerous situation without backup.

Mara was not a girl accustomed to sitting around and waiting. She drummed her fingers on the wooden tabletop, until the chief inspector sent her a withering stare. She rose from her booth and took two steps toward the ladies' lounge, hoping to stretch her legs, but Foxx waved her back to the table. "We'll be with you shortly. Please remain seated in the meantime."

Mara massaged her temples, her stress over Arnesto's tardiness giving her a mighty headache. She glanced over at Gemala wiping down tables. Foxx was nowhere in sight. Perhaps the inspector had gone in search of another notebook; the man had scribbled enough notes to fill an entire volume. Talias finally reached Mara, but only after she'd cleared every other table in the pub. The chief inspector slid into the bench opposite Mara and noted the half-empty mugs on the table.

After jotting down Mara's name, place of work, and home address, the chief inspector asked, "Where's your companion, Miss Pensk?"

Mara played with the blue-and-white checked napkin in front of her. She knew the constables would want to interview Arnesto, if and when he showed up. Arnesto would tell the truth, probably with panache and drama, but he would answer all of Talias's questions. Yet Mara couldn't reveal that she and Arnesto had their own interests in this case or that they worked undercover for the provisional government. "He chased after the culprit—the murderer—although we didn't realize the other man had died."

The chief inspector scowled. "What is your companion's name?

"Arnesto."

The chief inspector leaned closer. "Arnesto? What about a surname?"

Mara shook her head, realizing how little she really knew about Arnesto. The woman grunted. "And where is Arnesto now?"

"I don't know. He never returned to the pub."

The chief inspector slapped the table with her hand. Mara jumped, her nerves frayed with worry. "The last thing I need is another dead body. Why couldn't you leave the investigating and the chasing to the experts? Everyone thinks they're a constable these days."

Arnesto couldn't be dead, could he? Mara took a deep breath and rubbed her forehead. She had to wrap up this interview and start searching for Arnesto. Her new trainee had trusted her, and she'd let him down. *I'm a terrible field coach—the absolute worst. I should give up now before anyone else gets hurt because of my stupidity.*

The chief inspector softened her tone. "Let us hope Arnesto has enough common sense not to confront the murderer."

Mara bit her bottom lip but didn't reply. Arnesto might

be the most magically gifted fay in his family, but his common sense was in short supply. Talias watched Mara closely before exiting the booth. "When your friend turns up, please send him to the station for questioning. You're free to go."

Mara slid out of her seat and stood up, grateful to stretch her legs. She slipped her arms into her cloak, grabbed her reticule from the table, and called out good-night to Gemala. Mara dashed out the door of the pub and then hesitated. Thankfully the rain had stopped, but the cobblestones were slick. Where to go first? Mara didn't want to search the seedier streets of Bellaryss by herself this late in the evening. She started to jog toward Remy's flat. He might be her ex, but he was still her closest friend in Valerra. He would help her find Arnesto.

Mara sprinted up the steps to Remy's flat, unbuttoning her cloak as she went. By the time she reached the third floor, she was huffing slightly. The humidity from the spring rains seemed to have followed her into the building. Mara wiped her damp forehead the back of her sleeve. She peeled off her cloak and looped it over her left arm before pounding on Remy's door.

Mara detected voices and faint laughter inside. She wondered whether one of Remy's friends from the Bakers Guild had stopped by. Arnesto's safety was more impor-tant, so Remy's friend would have to understand. Remy cracked open his door. "What's wrong? You look like you ran the whole way here." Mara realized she must look a mess. Her ponytail had come half undone as she jogged, and she'd pulled out the ribbon, her long blonde hair tumbling down around her shoulders like a tangled web.

"It's Arnesto. He's missing!"

Remy started to shake his head, "No, he's—"

"Your full puff pastry rivals my auntie's for flakiness and flavor," called out someone from inside the apartment —someone who sounded an awful lot like Arnesto. "I must present Auntie Yelenarra with your recipe on my next visit home."

Mara shoved her cloak and reticule at Remy and then barreled into the small studio apartment. Her chest heaved as she took in several gulps of air. Her emotions warred within her. One instant she felt relief Arnesto was safe and the next she wanted to scream at him. She yelled, "Why didn't you come back to the pub?"

Arnesto's large gray eyes grew round. He started to answer, but Mara stalked over to him waving her hands. "Do you have any idea how worried I've been? I had no idea where you were or how to contact you! I thought you'd been murdered!"

"Murdered? But why would you possibly think that?" sputtered Arnesto.

"Why were you so worried about him?" grumbled Remy, sounding slightly jealous. "He's a fay and can take care of himself."

Mara rounded on Remy. "Really? How can you possibly say that after what happened to Wreyn?"

Remy frowned. "But that was down to Mordahn and he's gone for good. Nothing else undead is roaming the streets of the city."

Arnesto folded his hands in front of him. "Mara is right. Being a fay is no guarantee of safety. Far from it, in fact." He squared his jaw and peered into Mara's eyes. She felt the oddest sensation, the smallest fluttering inside her chest, which had nothing to do with Arnesto's gorgeousness, or his nearness, or even his fayness. She felt the stirrings of a *connectedness*, deep within her inner core, as if she and Arnesto had an invisible string linking them together.

"Maragold Gracelyn Raeburn Pensk," he said, enunciating each syllable of her name.

Mara stumbled backward, her heel catching on a loose floorboard. Unable to break her fall, she flailed her arms, waiting for the painful thwack when her skull struck the wooden floor.

CHAPTER 7

As Mara fell back, she sensed movement beneath her and found herself landing in Arnesto's arms. He scooped her up before she crashed into the floor and cradled her against his chest. "I am terribly sorry. I had not realized..." Arnesto stared down at Mara, his brow creased. Mara had never been this close to Arnesto. She smelled loam and citrus, wondering at the unusual pairing, which seemed fitting somehow.

Mara peered up at the smooth planes of Arnesto's face, her heart beating out a disjointed rhythm. She needed to get herself under control and fast. She cleared her throat. "I think you can put me down now. I can't very well carry on a conversation like this."

Arnesto carried Mara over to the single stuffed chair in Remy's flat. He gently deposited her and stepped back.

Mara brought her hand up to her head. She probed beneath her tangled locks and didn't find any lumps. "What just happened?"

"Arnesto said your name, you stumbled, and Arnesto

caught you somehow," said Remy. "I've never seen anyone move so fast."

"That's not what I meant. Something happened to me when Arnesto said my name—my full name." Mara glanced up at Arnesto, who stood before her, his hands clasped in front of him. She waved at the old ladder-back chairs around Remy's kitchen table. "Do you mind sitting down? I feel disoriented enough without constantly looking up."

Arnesto pulled out a chair and sat down. Remy glanced from Mara to Arnesto and back to Mara, the silence in the tiny apartment lengthening. Remy sighed. "I think I'll brew us a pot of tea. I can see this is going to take a while."

Mara narrowed her eyes at Arnesto. "I never told you my full name. How did you—"

"Katrine told me."

"Why would Katrine tell you my name?"

"She said I would need it. But I did not think that would happen."

"I still don't understand what happened."

Arnesto crossed his long legs. "You have heard that names have power?"

"Aye, but I've never experienced anything like that before."

"That was my fault," said Arnesto sheepishly. "I spoke each syllable of your name too energetically. I wanted to get your attention, but I fear I went overboard. I shall be more careful in the future."

Mara leaned her head against the cushioned seatback, trying to sift through the meaning behind Arnesto's words. If he could speak her full name out loud and get her attention—and he certainly proved he could do that—could she do the same? If she knew Arnesto's full, complete fay name, wouldn't she be able to call out to him when she needed to reach him? Mara asked, "Does it work the same way, if I called out your full name?"

Arnesto nodded. "Aye. In fact, I have been remiss. I should have provided you with my full name at the first opportunity. I could have prevented the misunderstanding this evening, which led to your anxiety about my whereabouts. That is my fault. I am sorry." Arnesto hesitated. "I feel as if I have done nothing but make mistakes and apologize for them since arriving in Valerra. I did not expect to be failing so spectacularly as your trainee or to be feeling so bereft about it."

Remy handed Mara and Arnesto each a mug of tea. He clapped a hand on Arnesto's shoulder. "Buck up, old chap. We all fail when we learn something new. Don't be so hard on yourself."

Mara took a fortifying sip of the black tea, which Remy had sweetened with honey. "Remy is right. We all make mistakes when we are learning—and even after we are experienced—we are only human, after all."

Arnesto sighed. "And therein lies my deep sense of failure. I am not human but fay."

"I hope you're not suggesting that fays don't make mistakes, because I know that's not true," said Mara.

Arnesto shook his head. "Not at all. But it is a well-known fact that humans make more mistakes than fays."

Mara and Remy looked at one another and burst out laughing. Mara said, still chuckling, "Look, I can't begin to tell you who makes more mistakes or who fails more spectacularly, because I don't know. But I can tell you the fays I've known make plenty of mistakes, even Chief Pryl." Pryl, Chief of the Fay Nation, had been a close ally during the war with Glenbarra. Pryl was currently taking a holiday from all official fay business—his first ever—while Katrine, his half-sister, subbed for him at the fay council meetings. Since fay council meetings could last days, even weeks, Katrine was stuck in Havynweal for the time being.

Remy nodded. "My mum used to say, 'Remy, my boy, you're like your father. You're going to make more than your fair share of blunders as you journey through life. Remember this: take your failures square on the chin, but don't write them on your heart. Learn from them, but don't let them crush you.' That's good advice for anyone, whether he's human or fay."

Arnesto clasped his hands around one knee. "Your mother's advice does have the ring of truth to it. I suppose an occasional miscalculation or misstep is only natural whilst one is learning."

Mara felt as if they'd wandered way off topic. She still had no idea what had occurred after Arnesto dashed out of the pub. "Now that we've established the fact no one is perfect, not even a fay, please tell me about tonight. Where did the murderer go?"

"Why do you persist in calling him a murderer?"

"Because he killed the other man with a poisoned dart. The tall man died almost instantly."

"Assassinated then?" asked Remy.

"Aye, looks that way, although the inspectors assigned to the case seem to want to treat this like a bar fight gone bad."

Arnesto jumped from his chair, spilling his tea on the floor. He waved his hand, muttering a spell under his breath, and the puddle of tea disappeared. "That man was assassinated? With fast-acting poison? This makes no sense."

"Why not?" asked Remy

Arnesto ran his hand through his wavy blue hair. Mara

noticed he always reverted to his natural hair color when no one else was around. "I tracked that man back to the corner of Market Street and Bellwether."

"But that's the location of the old savings and loan building used by the provisional government," said Mara.

"Aye. "

"Are you sure?"

"Positive. I watched the man enter the building. Then I ran back to the Cracked Cauldron, but a constable had been posted outside. He would not allow anyone back into the building. He took my name and told me to go home. Apparently, I shall need to present myself to the Royal Constabulary Headquarters in the morning. He mentioned something about making a formal declaration."

Mara sipped from her mug. "They want to take your statement, which is your eyewitness account of what happened at the pub. I will coach you on what to say."

"Shall I not simply tell the truth?"

"Aye, but there are certain truths you will need to avoid sharing, such as the fact you're a fay, and that you're training with me as an undercover operative, and that I asked you to track that man after he ran from the pub."

"Ah, I see. But you do realize that fays cannot lie. If I am asked a direct question, then..."

"Then you will provide an indirect reply," said Mara. "I'm not asking you to tell an untruth, but to avoid telling the entire truth. Like earlier this evening, when you tried to avoid telling me about giving Gemala the bag of gold."

"Wait a minute," interrupted Remy. "You gave that entire bag of gold to Gemala? What were you thinking? Do you realize what kind of a flat you could have rented with that much cash?"

Arnesto gestured toward Remy's half-empty cup. "Here,

allow me to top up your tea." Remy handed his mug to Arnesto, a puzzled expression on his face. Arnesto set both their mugs down on Remy's wobbly table. "I do apologize in advance for this."

"Huh?" said Remy.

Arnesto pointed a finger at Remy and incanted, "For seven full minutes, you shall be frozen in this space, after which you shall forget this spell ever took place."

"What are you doing?" Mara started to rise from the chair, but her legs still felt rubbery from her earlier backward tumble. She dropped down into her seat, wondering what had gotten into Arnesto and worrying because she couldn't see Remy actually breathing.

"I used a freeze and forget spell on Remy. We have six minutes and forty-seven seconds before it wears off."

Mara had never heard of a freeze and forget spell. That must have been what Arnesto had used at the pub earlier in the evening. Had he ever used it on her?

As if reading her thoughts, Arnesto said, "There are two things for you to know: I would never use that spell on you, since you are my coach and mentor. And Remy is just fine. When the spell wears off, he will not remember a thing."

"Why did you cast the spell on Remy in the first place? Was it because of the gold?"

"Not the gold per se, but because there are things I do not wish to discuss in front of Remy. It would be unwise for him to know the extent of my magical abilities for example, or my full fay name."

"Are you concerned that Remy can't be trusted? He's completely loyal to our cause."

"I do not question Remy's loyalty, but rather, his tendency to speak too much to anyone who will listen."

Mara sighed. "You've got me there. Remy has never

been able to keep a secret. That's why Vas and Katrine have not recruited him as an operative. They've told him it's because they need him to serve as an informant, working inside the Bakers Guild, which is partially true. But it's mainly because of his inability to keep his own counsel." Mara paused and decided she may as well get it over with. "I suppose he told you we used to date, and that I broke it off earlier this year?"

"Aye, Remy has mentioned that to me more than once. Apparently, he has had a crush on you since the fifth grade, which by my calculation would have been since he was ten years old. He has even described in detail the gold ball gown that you wore to your Teenth—your seventeenth birthday celebration."

Mara groaned. "Alright, I don't need to hear any more evidence about Remy's tendency to over share. I'll be more careful on the subject of your magic around him. What about your name? I like the idea of being able to contact you when I need to, but if your name fell into the wrong hands, couldn't that place you in danger?"

"Are you thinking of the dark fays?"

"Aye."

Arnesto smiled. "It is true the dark fays do not know my full fay name. However, I trust you to keep my name safe. I shall tell it to you now."

Arnesto stepped around Remy's chair and leaned over Mara. As he whispered into her ear, the stirring of his breath made her skin tingle. She took a deep breath and forced herself to focus. "My full fay name is Arnestarious Aziel Windstorm Lucato the Fourteenth. When you say my name aloud, I will come to you." At the sound of Arnesto's name, Mara felt that odd sensation of connectedness again, and the faintest trembling in her chest.

Arnesto dropped down into the ladder-back chair, his mouth pursed. "How very strange."

"Did you feel it too?"

Arnesto flapped his hand between them. "When I said your name earlier, I knew I had put too much energy into each syllable. Not only did you stumble, but I felt a pull as well. But this time, I merely whispered my name into your ear, and I sensed a peculiar flickering inside, as if butterflies were beating their wings against my rib cage."

"What does that mean?"

Arnesto gave a half-shrug. "I'm not entirely sure."

Mara's eyes widened. "You used a contraction in a sentence for the very first time. We'll make a Valerran out of you yet!"

"A contraction? Oh, you mean when I combined the pronoun *I* with the verb *am* and formed *I'm*. It does flow more easily off the tongue, doesn't it?" Arnesto grinned to indicate he was fully aware he'd used another contraction.

Mara laughed. "Aye. Actually, it's important to learn how to adjust your speech patterns to fit the undercover role you are assuming." She grew more serious. "What name should we use for you—what name did you provide to the constable outside the pub this evening?"

"I told him my name was Arnesto Luca."

Mara repeated the name aloud. She decided it sounded just right to her, neither too exotic nor too common. "It's a good name for you, one that's easy to recall and pronounce. Let's go over your story for the constables tomorrow."

Mara pretended to be an investigator and asked Arnesto the same questions she'd been asked. She coached Arnesto on his answers, reminding him not to volunteer more information than was required. Arnesto improved as they rehearsed together, but Mara thought he could use additional practice before he faced the chief inspector in the morning.

Remy grunted in his sleep. "I think he'll be waking up soon," said Mara.

"Aye, in another minute or so. We can spend that minute practicing, or we can talk about the strange set of coincidences we have uncovered."

"You mean the fact a man was assassinated in our presence, which is odd enough, and the assassin seems to be connected to the government?"

"Plus, we learned of an anti-magic movement from Vas, which may or may not be connected with what is happening to Farleigh's friends at the grihm preserve."

"And I learned there are dark fays who may be targeting Valerra."

"The dark fays are definitely targeting Valerra," said Arnesto.

"But why?" Mara found it hard to believe these other fays, whom she'd never heard of or encountered, planned to attack Valerra.

"For the same reasons the Glenbarrans attacked Valerra. Your country is rich in natural resources, with good farmlands, plenty of fresh water, and far better technological advantages than its neighbors. Valerran mages are also loyal to Serving magic, which the dark fays despise. Finally, Valerra has a long border with Faynwood, making it a secure location from which to launch an assault."

"So you're saying that Faynwood is the ultimate target?

"Anyone who opposes Fallow sorcery, injustice, and cruelty is their target. The dark fays hate Faynwood because of its close ties to Havynweal and the Fay Nation that banished them."

Mara didn't understand how fay magic worked. Havynweal was somehow tethered to Faynwood, so attacking the Faymons' homeland, where her friend Linden now lived, was akin to attacking the fays as well. "That does seem like a lot of coincidences."

"Too many for this fay to find any comfort." Arnesto noticed Mara stifling a yawn and rose from his chair. He gave her a hand up and bundled her into her cloak. "You look exhausted. Let me help you next door to your building."

Mara nodded and picked her reticule off the table. She was too exhausted to argue and still felt wobbly from the full-name-sharing experience with Arnesto. As tendrils of fog curled around her legs, Mara heard Remy mumble about his tea growing cold. She started to object to traveling by fay mists, but in the next instant she found herself standing on the second floor of her apartment building in front of her door.

"Goodnight, Mara. I shall see you in the morning," whispered Arnesto from within the soft cocoon of his traveling vapors. The mists winked out and he was gone.

Mara fumbled with the door key, her hands trembling with fatigue, and stumbled inside her flat. Tossing her cloak onto the coat rack just inside the door, she headed straight to bed, fully clothed. Mara kicked off her boots, slipped under the covers, and closed her eyes. She heard someone softly singing a fay lullaby on the other side of her wall. She thought it was probably the young mother in the flat next door serenading her small son. Mara's father used to sing the same lullaby to her when she was a child and afraid of the dark.

"Come now softly, lead me nigh
Where dreams come true, and hopes runs high.
Sprinkle your fay dust, stay by my side,
Keep me from harm all through the night."

Mara yawned, smiling at the familiar lyrics, and nestled deeper into her pillow. But the melodious voice grew harsh and raspy, and a chill swept down her spine as the lyrics changed. She was certain the young mother next door was no longer singing this version of the lullaby.

"Maragold Gracelyn Raeburn Penske, beware
When nightmares come true, and fears run high,
Wild magic takes hold as we stalk by your side,
Menace unleashed all through the night."

Mara struggled against the wave of sleep overtaking her. She desperately tried to open her eyes, wanting to search for the source of the voice. The lullaby's magic was too strong, however, and Mara drifted off to sleep—but not before she shrank under her covers, afraid of the dark once again.

CHAPTER 8

M

Mara slept until the morning sun streamed through the two tall, arched windows of her flat. Despite its diminutive size, she'd fallen in love with the classic architecture of her flat, especially its arched windows and doorways. The apartment building, converted from a private residence, reminded her of pre-war Bellaryss, before the Glenbarrans had invaded her homeland. More than half of the city's buildings, constructed with Valerra's famous golden marble and yellow sandstone, now lay in ruin and rubble.

Mara had a few delicious moments of forgetfulness as she came awake. She thought she was waking in her father's elegant three-story townhome, her younger sisters sleeping down the hall. Mara tried to recall whether she'd finished her homework. Then reality came crashing in on her and she remembered the horrors of the war with Glenbarra and the loss of her family and so many friends. Mara clutched her sheet closer, her grief still raw, her chest aching.

She swiped her moist eyes and swung her legs over the side of the bed, surprised to find she'd slept in her clothes.

Her skirt and blouse were wrinkled beyond recognition and would need a trip to the laundress. Mara shook her head. Arnesto's stories about undead monsters and dark fays from the outer demesnes were taking a toll on her wardrobe and her peace of mind.

She couldn't quite remember what had bothered her so much the night before, just as she was falling asleep. Mara felt as if something important sat just beyond her reach, swept away along with the rain and clouds.

The bright morning sun formed patches of light on her scraped oak floorboards. Mara's timepiece was in her reticule, but she didn't need to check the time to know she would be late for work. She wished she could glamour herself into a new outfit and conjure up some fay traveling mists for a quick morning commute.

Mara forced herself to stand and hastily made up her bed. She'd have to use old-fashioned willpower to push herself through her morning rituals and speed walk to the shop. Even so, she'd be a good hour late opening it up. While Katrine's customers didn't object to the quirky hours kept by the owner herself, they expected Katrine's assistant to be more reliable. Mara didn't feel as if she'd been particularly reliable during the past few days. But then again, she had a new trainee who was throwing her off schedule, or off kilter, more like.

Arnesto was more than he seemed at first glance—and she didn't mean his lean, muscled build or heart-throb-handsome face—but his eccentric upbringing, lightning-fast speed, and fay magic that rivaled even Katrine's. How many twelfth-level wizards were walking around Havynweal anyway? The Valerrans could have used their help during the war, and they could still use their help, especially with poison-toting assassins, a growing anti-magic movement, and whatever was going on at the grihm preserve—plus the new threat from the dark fays that worried Katrine and Arnesto.

Mara knelt on the floor and dragged out a long, flat trunk from beneath her bed. She retrieved the key from her reticule and unlocked the trunk, flipping back the lid. She removed a dark blue leather scabbard from inside and rose to her feet. Dozens of multi-faceted sapphires covered the golden hilt peeking out from the scabbard, the jewels winking cheerfully in the morning sun.

In one fluid motion, Mara gripped the hilt with her right hand and withdrew the sword. Ancient fay hiero-glyphs danced along the blade, which blazed bright blue. Mara placed her left hand on her hip and parried the empty air in front of her, satisfied that her sword had not lost any of its fay-spelled magic. If she had to face these dark fays at some point, she'd want her ensorcelled sword at her side.

She and Remy were the only ones left inside Valerra who still possessed the remarkable fay swords, which they'd discovered inside the Valerran Museum during the siege of Bellaryss. At the time, Mara had believed that she'd chosen her sword, but she later learned the weapons did the choosing—her sword did not light up blue for anyone else—and the same was true for Remy's blade, which blazed bright red when he gripped its hilt. Mara returned her sword to its scabbard and placed it carefully inside the velvet-lined trunk, a gift from Katrine. She re-locked the trunk and slid it back under her bed. It was past time to focus on the toyshop and her tasks at hand.

Mara opened the door to her flat, saw that the shared bathroom was currently vacant, and made a mad dash for it. She felt better after she washed off the grime from the previous day and changed her clothes. Mara selected a soft gray-and-burgundy jersey skirt that reached to her ankles and a pale gray, long-sleeved blouse with little pearl buttons. Examining her brown leather boots for scuff-marks, she set them aside and pulled her tall black leather boots toward her.

Mara knew it was the height of luxury in post-war Bellaryss to own two pairs of tall boots, but she had indulged herself and had no regrets, especially on mornings when she was running late and hadn't the forethought to polish her other pair the night before. She stepped into her boots, fastened the dozen buttons on each leg, and then she slipped her thin, narrow blades, each sharp enough to slice through a piece of parchment midair, into the holsters stitched inside the shanks. After a quick survey of her flat to ensure she hadn't forgotten anything, she drew on her midnight blue cloak, grabbed her reticule, and locked her door. If she speed walked, maybe she'd only be forty-five minutes late opening the shop.

When Katrine had offered Mara a steady job as her assistant at the toyshop after the war, Mara looked forward to returning to some semblance of normalcy, despite the rundown conditions inside the city. She soon discovered that she enjoyed learning the mechanics of automata and had become nearly as adept as her boss at repairing the clockwork toys. Only a few weeks into her new job, Vas had approached Mara with the idea of working for Valerra's new provisional government as an undercover operative.

Mara had jumped at the chance to do something that could give her a true sense of purpose again, after the highs and lows of the previous year. When she and her friends had fought against Mordahn, King Roi, and their army—comprised of Glenbarran conscripts, as well as Fallow mages, necromancers, and their undead minions—Mara had felt as if she'd found her calling. After the war, she'd started wondering what to do next with her life, especially since her closest friend, Linden, had settled into a new relationship and important role inside Faynwood. Mara couldn't help feeling left out. She'd decided to make a go of it in Valerra, where she'd been born and raised, rather than resettle in Faynwood.

She'd started dating Remy, hoping their long-standing friendship might bloom into romance. But that never happened. While Mara cared for Remy, she quickly realized she could never love him *that way*. Remy wasn't surprised when she broke up with him. If anything, he might have been the tiniest bit relieved. Mara held high expectations of everyone—her friends, her ex-boyfriend, and most of all—herself.

When Mara reached the corner of High Street and Prospect Avenue, she nearly collided with an old woman peering through the plate glass window of Katrine's Klockworks. The woman wore a long, purple cape that flapped around her legs in the stiff spring breeze, her striped blue and pink silk stockings at odds with her burnt orange scarf. She held onto her brown felt trilby with one hand to prevent it from blowing off her gray curls in the wind. Mara withdrew the large, ornate shop key from her reticule and apologized for the lateness of the hour.

The old woman waved away Mara's excuses. "It matters not, lass, as I have only just traversed the mists myself. However, I could use a strong cup of tea with a hint of bergamot. I find I do not translocate as expeditiously as in my youth. I seem to have gotten quite turned around—I visited all seven seasons before arriving here on your doorstep."

Could this be Arnesto's Auntie Yelenarra using a glamour to disguise herself? Mara nodded. "Aye, ma'am. Let's get you inside and out of this wind." Mara inserted the key in the lock and placed her left hand on the doorframe. She turned the key and waited for the protection wards to stop thrumming and disengage before opening the door. "Please come in. I'll just turn up the gas lighting in the shop, and then I'll heat up some water for our tea."

"Go ahead and take care of your business. I shall glance about this odd selection of automata."

Mara turned up the gas-lit wall sconces set into the side and rear walls of the shop. Then she slipped behind the counter and through the damask curtain to the office, where Katrine had installed a small kitchenette in the back. Mara tossed her cloak onto the coat hook near her worktable and then scurried to the kitchenette. Using the hand pump above the narrow sink, Mara filled a battered teakettle with water. She scooped an extra scuttle full of coal into the cast iron stove next to the sink and then struck a match to light the coal. Placing the kettle on top of the stove, Mara turned around to find the old woman had wandered into the office and sat down on a stool.

The woman removed her brown trilby and patted down her flyaway hair, which turned a vivid shade of blue before Mara's eyes. She dropped her glamour entirely, her clothes transforming from an eccentric elder to a stately fay—her stretchy silver cape neatly layered over a long, sparkly empire-waist dress, the silken fabric woven into tiny swirls of silver, ivory, and gold. On the fay woman's feet were a dainty pair of silver ankle boots that Mara immediately envied. She idly wondered whether a Valerran shoemaker could craft her a pair.

While she waited for the water to boil, Mara grabbed an apple from the shelf above the sink, cored and sliced it, and then arranged the pieces on a platter she offered the fay elder. The woman thanked her and took a few bites, chewing slowly. "Ah yes, the tree-borne fruit of Valerra. It is every bit as sweet as I recall, although it has been many years since I last took a bite. What is this called again? Is it a pear or perhaps a pomegranate?"

"That is an apple, ma'am." *If this woman tutored Arnesto,* thought Mara, *then I needed to give him more credit for how quickly he's adapting to Valerran culture.* Mara bowed from the waist. "I am Mara Pensk, Katrine's assistant. Are you by any chance related to Arnesto?"

The fay woman's face broke into a wide grin. "Aye, Arnestarious is my youngest nephew. I am called Yelenarra." Pointing at the teakettle, she added, "I believe that is near boiling."

Mara retreated to the kitchenette and pulled down the porcelain teapot from the shelf. She measured out the loose tea and poured in the hot water. While she waited for the tea to brew, Yelenarra said, "I thought I would drop in whilst Arnestarious was otherwise occupied with the constables. Terrible business at the pub last night. First the grihms and now this. I must say I expected the Bazeerka to be subtler, although they must have inside help from a few traitorous humans, no doubt."

Mara concentrated on pouring out the tea into two mismatched teacups. How did Yelenarra know about the assassination last night and about the grihms? Did Arnesto visit his aunt after delivering Mara to her apartment the previous evening? Mara handed a cup to Yelenarra, who thanked her and took a sip. "Delicious. I have always said the Valerrans know how to brew a good cuppa."

"Who are the Bazeerka?" Mara had a pretty good idea, but she wanted to hear it from the fay woman herself.

"The dark fays from the outer demesnes, descendants

of Bazeerkalim, who was banished from Havynweal more than a millennia ago. I was under the impression that my nephew had explained about them."

"Arnesto told me about the dark fays, but he didn't call them Bazeerka." Mara took a bite of apple and chewed slowly. "What I don't understand is why I've never heard of the dark fays until now."

Yelenarra laughed, a pleasant tinkling sort of sound that reminded Mara of Mage Mother Pawllah. An ancient and powerful fay woman who'd since passed on, Pawllah had offered Mara and her friends much-needed refuge on Sanrellyss Island after the fall of Valerra. Perhaps Yelenarra had spent time there in her youth. "The Bazeerka are very, very good at hiding—and they have been content with making mischief in Havynweal rather than here in Valerra for the past hundred years or so."

"What's changed?"

"Why you and your friends, of course."

"Me and my friends? How so?"

"You defeated Mordahn, the worst necromancer in generations, and you are routing Fallow sorcery from Valerra. You are upsetting the magical balance of power, or at least, that is how the dark fays would think about it."

"But that was months ago, and really, my friend Linden, the Liege of Faynwood, battled Mordahn in the realms of the dead. The rest of us, myself included, played supporting roles."

Yelenarra waved her hand. "The young Liege could never have defeated Mordahn without assistance from you, Katrinareus, and the others. Eframallium has told me of your courage and your skill with the sword and dagger. No, lass, let us be frank with each other. There is something more to you than meets the eye, as pleasant as that may be."

Mara frowned, confused by what Yelenarra was saying, or perhaps not saying. "I'm sorry, but I'm not following."

Placing her teacup on the saucer tucked into the small square of the worktable that Mara had cleared away, Yelenarra tilted her head. "Think back to your trip into the realms of the dead."

"I'd really rather not."

"Katrinareus has told me how you helped her wrestle the last of Mordahn's undead protectors into the boat. She said she was thoroughly exhausted and could not have overcome the last protector without you by her side. I would like very much to hear that story from your perspective."

Mara placed her teacup on the worktable, next to Yelenarra's. She whispered, "I'd prefer not to speak of it. I still get nightmares. Even last night, I dreamt something that frightened me, although I couldn't recall it this morning."

Yelenarra nodded. "Aye, lass. That is the influence of the darker powers attempting to break free. But speaking of it will lessen their influence over time, I promise."

Mara sniffed. "But this is not a good place or time to tell that story. A customer may come in at any moment, and I may be indisposed." What Mara couldn't bring herself to say was that she might break down into sobs. She abhorred whiney, weak girls and never, ever wanted anyone to see her as anything other than strong and in command of herself or her situation. That was one of the main reasons she'd become friends with Linden, who didn't fall apart at the first sign of trouble. If anything, Linden dashed headlong right toward it, an admirable quality in Mara's book.

The fay woman waved her hand. "You shall not be having any customers whilst I am visiting."

Mara quirked an eyebrow. "Oh?"

Yelenarra nodded. "I cast a forgotten spell over the shop. Katrine's customers will walk on by for the time being."

Mara sighed. "Very well. But please don't forget to lift the spell when you leave, or Katrine will not be pleased with the day's receipts."

Yelenarra winked. "Aye, lass. Now, tell me your tale."

CHAPTER 9

Mara closed her eyes for a moment, forcing herself to recall the gloomiest, saddest, creepiest place she'd ever visited—the lowest level within the realms of the dead. She shivered and Yelenarra reached over to place a steadying hand on top of hers. "Deep breaths, lass. I promise your nightmares shall lessen over time. However, this is still very fresh for you. Was it four months ago now?"

Mara opened her eyes. "Aye, this would have been last fall, late in the season." Why was she finding it so difficult to tell this story? Mara blew out a puff of air and rubbed her arms. She could do this. "It's the place itself that gives me the nightmares—or more accurately—it's what happens when the music stops that still scares me."

"The music? I am not following."

"Didn't Katrine tell you about the singing spirits?"

When Yelenarra shook her head, Mara said, "It's difficult to grasp the strangeness of the place without understanding about the singing and the silence afterward. There's a rhythm to the lowest realm, sort of a natural cycle, and music is part of it."

Yelenarra waved her hand. "As a reaper, I have traveled throughout the realms of the dead, except for the lowest realm. Few reapers travel there—only Arnestarious's mother and Katrinareus have made that journey in recent memory—and now you. Tell me about this cycle and the music."

"The cycle always started the same way. A group of wispy, translucent figures gathered on the far shore, along the river separating the good spirits from the unsavory ones. During the singing phase, the spirits of the newly departed—those who led decent, honorable lives—glided across the river effortlessly and were welcomed on the far shore. I felt certain my mother, who died when I was very young, stood somewhere on that far shore, and I thought about crossing over myself just to see her again. I even wondered whether the rest of my family had arrived there as well."

Mara paused, a lump forming in her throat. She felt such a longing for her family and had no idea whether they had survived their grueling trip to the colonies or died along the way. Mara's father had paid for five berths on a merchant ship when it became clear the city's defenses were failing, and Bellaryss would fall to the Glenbarrans and grihms. But Mara had refused to leave with her father, sisters, and stepmother.

She had vowed to never abandon her duty to her homeland; what she'd left unspoken was that she intended to clear the family name. She would be courageous where her father had failed. In the eighteen months since the start of the war, Mara had come to understand the horrors of the battlefield. She'd faced more than her share of sword-wielding grihms and Glenbarrans, as well as necromancers and their undead army. Along the way, she'd learned how easily one's courage could fail. She'd come to understand her father, and his decision to retreat in the face of overwhelming odds. She only wished she could see her father again to tell him she now comprehended the incomprehensible. She'd long since forgiven him.

Yelenarra waited until Mara's brow cleared before she said, "Please continue, lass. What happened when the spirits ceased their melodious singing?"

Mara took a sip of tea. She hated to even think about what happened next. Mara returned her cup to the saucer on the worktable, but mentally, she was standing in the lowest realm of the dead. "As the music faded away, another group of spirits arrived at the opposite shore. They immediately began fighting over the few boats lining the shore. Let's just say that none of the unsavory ghosts made it to the opposite shore—they either drowned in the churning water or were swept away by the strong current. It was horrible to watch." Mara paused, rubbing her arms to bring back the circulation. She felt cold all over, as if she carried with her the gloom inside the realms of the dead.

"Tell me about your fight with Mordahn's protectors," coaxed Yelenarra.

Mara rose from her stool opposite Yelenarra, finding it easier to tell this part of her story standing up. "Since Katrine has already told you what happened, I'll not repeat all of it again. You asked me about capturing that last protector. As you know, Mordahn had raised four undead necromancers, who remained by his side at all times. They wore long black robes, with red runes at their cuffs and hems. They smelled of rot and corruption, their eyes fiery orange sockets, and their mouths were mostly teeth, as the flesh had worn away." Mara shivered but forced herself to continue. She paced around the small office, moving her hands as she spoke.

"We had to capture the protectors one at a time, drag them into a boat, row out to the deepest part of the churning river, and toss them overboard. They fought us all the way, screaming curses at us as the current drew them into its depths.

"Katrine and I were down to battling the last protector. The protector's hands closed around her throat. I could see Katrine was exhausted by then and struggling. I swung my blade and lopped off the protector's right arm." Mara paused in her pacing, the image still crystal clear in her mind. "That undead thing's arm continued to wriggle on the ground, groping its way toward me. I picked up the flopping arm and flung it into the river, where it sank beneath the brackish water. The creature turned on me with a mighty howl. When the protector lunged, I whipped my blade out and caught the necromancer in the face as its fiery eyes blazed at me.

"The thing tore my blade from my hands and gripped me by the hair. It opened its jaws to bite me, but I jammed my elbow into its lower jaw. By then, Katrine had recovered sufficiently to toss her ensorcelled rope around the protector's torso and tighten the lasso. I retrieved my sword and together we tugged the creature into the last boat. While Katrine held him down in the boat, I rowed us out to the center of the river. Together, we shoved him overboard as he screeched at us. I used my last remaining strength to row us back to the beach. And well, you know the rest of the story. Not all of us escaped, and I vowed to never, ever, leave someone behind again."

"You helped to defeat four undead necromancers and

saved Katrinareus in the end. I would say you fully discharged your duty."

Mara dropped back down to the stool, suddenly drained. "I suppose you're right. Even so, I hope I'm never faced with that sort of decision again."

"And if you are, I trust you shall do what is right. Sometimes we must sacrifice the one to save the many."

Mara canted her head to the side. It occurred to her that Yelenarra was speaking from her own experience. Mara imagined the elder fay as a young woman, battling against the Fallow sorcerers and dark fays in her day.

Yelenarra reached inside her cape and withdrew a lace-bordered linen handkerchief, which she handed to Mara. Mara blotted her moist cheeks, unaware she'd been crying. When she offered to return the handkerchief, Yelenarra closed her hand around Mara's. "Keep it, lass. I have searched long and hard for the likes of you, among the Valerrans and the Faymons. Katrinareus was right about you."

"What was Katrine right about?" asked Mara, her throat scratchy. She picked up her cup and took a sip of the cold tea. With a grimace, Mara returned the teacup to the worktable. She'd have to brew a fresh pot later.

"You will be the perfect partner for my dear nephew."

Mara's eyes bulged and she sputtered, "But I hardly know Arnesto, and I don't believe in such arrangements."

Yelenarra frowned. "What are you saying? You do not wish to work with Arnestarious to defeat the dark fays?"

"You said something about being his partner."

"Aye, it is critically important to never, ever, attempt to face the dark fays alone. That seldom goes well."

The meaning behind Yelenarra's words slowly dawned on Mara. "Have you been seeking a colleague for Arnesto—

someone he can train alongside and work with to fight the dark fays?"

"Aye, that is what I have been trying to say." Yelenarra drew her pale silver brows together. "Ah, I believe I might have confounded you with my use of the term *partner*." Yelenarra giggled. "When it comes to the coupling activities of young people, I shall certainly not interfere...but to clarify, I have been searching for a suitable comrade-in-arms for Arnestarious."

Mara's face reddened. She'd leapt to conclusions about Yelenarra's intentions for her nephew. On the other hand, Arnesto was beyond attractive, and working closely together was bound to get complicated.

Yelenarra rose from the stool. "Thank you, lass, for a lovely cup of tea and a rousing good story. Arnestarious shall be arriving shortly, and it is time that I return home." Yelenarra paused and drew herself up to her full height, which was about half a foot shorter than Mara. Bowing, she intoned the Serving magic pledge. "Mage Mara, may your magic serve in peace and lead through service. This is the true path."

Mara bowed. "Thank you, Lady Yelenarra. It has been an honor to meet you. May your magic serve in peace and lead through service." The traveling mists twined around Yelenarra's legs. As the fay vanished in a cloud of vapor, Mara called out the remainder of the pledge, "This is the true path!"

Mara used the hand pump above the sink to wash the mismatched porcelain teacups and saucers, her mind sifting through the visit with Arnesto's formidable aunt. She mulled over Yelenarra's words, not quite sure what to make of them: *You will be the perfect partner for my dear nephew...I have been searching for a suitable comrade-in-arms for Arnestarious.* Mara shook her head. Arnesto's aunt was as confounding as her fay trainee—and just as impossible to understand.

The bell above the shop door tinkled, and Mara hurried through the office to the front of the shop expecting to find a customer. Instead, a young boy with a smear of jelly on his face, wearing a rumpled gray sweater and dark pants two inches too short, held a crumpled piece of parchment in his fist. He thrust out his other hand, palm open, waiting for a tip before releasing the note. Mara glanced at the boy holding the smudged note with a sinking feeling in her stomach. Arnesto should have arrived at the shop by now, following his interview with the chief inspector. Even worse, the only people she knew who relied on street urchins to deliver messages were inmates at the jail.

"Oh, just a moment." Mara retrieved her reticule and withdrew a coin, which she pressed into the boy's outstretched palm.

"Thank ye, mum," said the boy, thrusting the note in her hand and turning to leave.

"Wait, don't you need a reply?"

"Nay, mum. Yer needing to show up to post yer mister's bond." The boy pocketed the coin and dashed out the door.

Mara glanced at the spidery handwriting on the note, her sinking feeling turning into a leaden pit in her stomach.

CHAPTER 10

Mara had no doubt Arnesto penned the note, which he addressed to *M. P. at Katrine's Klockworks*. "It appears I shall be unavoidably detained. Inspector F. has declared my answers unsatisfactory. I fear I must ask for whatever aid you can provide. Most sincerely, A."

Mara posted the *Be Back Soon* sign on the shop door and locked up. Since she had no idea how long this would take, Mara decided to turn off all the gas lamps in the shop before she left. She swooped through the office to pick up her cloak and reticule and then slipped out of the shop's rear alley entrance, locking the back door behind her.

Mara briefly considered asking Vas to intervene but realized she needed more information. She had to know what questions Arnesto's interview might have raised before deciding who could best help. Mara half-jogged to the Royal Constabulary. Along the way, she skirted around an overturned flower cart, hothouse lilies and roses scattered across the road, and nearly collided with a large constable chasing a short man in the opposite direction.

She arrived in short temper at the drab, sad-looking yellow brick building and stopped in her tracks.

Walking down the concrete steps of the building was her fay trainee, impeccably dressed in a charcoal gray blazer and navy slacks, with a gray fedora angled low over one eye. Arnesto was chuckling alongside his companion, none other than the chief inspector herself! Talias spotted Mara first and actually smiled at her.

"Ah, Miss Pensk, I'm afraid you have been called away from your shop unnecessarily. We've cleared up Mr. Luca's paperwork."

The chief inspector shook Arnesto's hand. "It's been a pleasure, Mr. Luca." She nodded pleasantly at Mara as she passed by and then climbed into the passenger seat of an idling locomobile, driven by Inspector Foxx. The insignia of the Royal Constabulary, a white lily surrounded by three gold stars, was emblazoned on the side panel of the sleek black vehicle. Mara often wondered who'd designed the symbol for the metropolitan police force, which she liked despite the fact it made no sense as a symbol for law enforcement.

Arnesto descended the steps and gave a small wave to the departing locomobile. "I shall explain everything when we are out of earshot of this building."

Mara arched an eyebrow. "I'm overcome with curiosity, given the note that was delivered to me not twenty minutes ago."

Arnesto took Mara by the elbow and guided her across the street. He waited until they'd crossed two more streets before he said, in a voice so low Mara had to lean closer to hear him, "She is a fay."

"What? I don't believe it," hissed Mara.

"At one time, she was Chief Pryl's top fay scout inside Valerra."

"What happened?"

"She met someone who convinced her to stay here in Valerra, rather than return home to Havynweal at the end of her tour of duty. A gentleman by the name of Exeter Talias."

Mara stopped walking and stared at Arnesto. Exeter Talias had led Valerra as its Prime Minister for nearly a decade until his untimely death six years earlier. Mara's father had greatly admired Talias, and Mara had written school papers about the illustrious leader. Unfortunately, Prime Minister Talias had died under mysterious circumstances. His widow claimed he'd been assassinated, but nothing ever came of the investigation. Mara shook her head, the implications of what he'd told her just sinking in. "Wait a minute. Are you saying Exeter Talias was the chief inspector's husband?"

"Aye. After his death, she joined the constables and rose rapidly through the ranks to her current position."

"What can it mean?" Mara wondered aloud. They stood across the street from the shop and waited for a locomobile and two horse-drawn carriages to clatter past on the cobblestones before crossing.

Arnesto quirked his eyebrows but didn't say anything until Mara had unlocked the shop door and they were safely inside. "You mean the fact the chief inspector is a fay, or the former PM may have been assassinated, or the dark fays are becoming more active here in Valerra?"

Mara lit a gas lamp and paused, waving her hand. "All of the above. And let's not forget about whatever is happening at the grihm preserve, and whether they're related. I don't know where to even begin. Does the chief inspector believe the dark fays might have had something to do with her husband's death six years earlier?"

"She didn't say, but she implied there has been a growing Fallow presence inside Valerra for some time now. With the Glenbarran invasion eighteen months ago, Fallow sorcery has become more prevalent. However, Fallow mages have been plotting inside Valerra for years, decades actually. And wherever Fallowness exists, the dark fays are sure to be involved."

One of Katrine's regular customers interrupted any further discussions. The elderly woman pulled open the shop door, her hat askew, and clutched her reticule to her sizable bosom. "Finally! I declare I must have walked up and down High Street four times before I found the shop. I must make an appointment with my healer. Something's very wrong with my eyesight!"

Mara glanced at the old woman guiltily. "Oh dear, perhaps you simply became turned around this morning. Please do take a seat, Mrs. Montague, and one of us will brew you a cup of tea."

"I shall whip you up some tea forthwith." Arnesto stepped forward and introduced himself as the new shop's assistant.

Mrs. Montague smiled gratefully at Arnesto, obviously charmed by the tall, good-looking young man waiting on her. "Oh, I almost forgot. I've brought a little something for our tea." Mrs. Montague handed Arnesto a small wicker basket, covered with a linen napkin on top. "I know how much Miss Pensk enjoys my chocolate scones." Arnesto thanked her, bowed from his shoulders, and then retreated behind the counter to the office and kitchenette.

The elderly lady sat in one of the two stuffed chairs Katrine had strategically placed in front of a tall looking glass along one side of the shop, which provided an unimpeded view of all the clockwork toys on display, as well as a means for observing the street outside through the large plate glass window. It was an ideal perch for an older lady or gentleman seeking to make a purchase as well as to keep an eye on the comings and goings on High Street.

"Perhaps you're right," sniffed Mrs. Montague. "I've not been sleeping well lately. I've been hearing things as I drift off."

Mara's scalp prickled with anxiety. What could be disturbing the sleep of a kind old woman like Mrs. Montague? "Oh?" said Mara, hoping to prompt a response.

The elderly customer nodded, her wispy gray strands visible beneath the pillbox hat she'd pinned on top of her head. "Aye, Miss Pensk. I swear I hear a low voice rasping in my ear, telling me I must bake more scones and biscuits for my friends. Isn't that just plain silly?"

Mara sat back, relieved that Mrs. Montague's rasping voice seemed harmless. Perhaps Mrs. Montague needed to see her healer after all; she might be mixing the wrong herbs into her bedtime tea. They chatted amiably until another customer came through the door, and Mara left to wait on the middle-aged man looking for a clockwork bird for his wife.

Mara and Arnesto wound up skipping lunch entirely, having barely enough time to split the last apple above the shelf in the kitchenette, as a steady stream of customers visited the shop, some to make purchases, others to drop off a toy to be repaired. Many of the customers complained they'd stopped by earlier in the morning, but the shop was either closed, or they'd managed to walk on past it. At half-past five, Mara said, "Let's post the *Closed* sign at the front door and lock up. We've more than made up for the fact we were closed most of the morning. I've been run off my feet, and I'm positively famished!"

While Arnesto performed his fast–math on the day's receipts, which exceeded the day before, proof Mara had been run off her feet, Mara turned off the lamps and tidied the shop. She locked the receipts in the bottom drawer of the worktable and straightened up, her stomach rumbling. She opened her reticule to withdraw the large, ornate shop key, and her eyes settled on Yelenarra's handkerchief. Mara had forgotten to tell Arnesto about the visit from his aunt.

Arnesto had followed her into the office and was standing close behind her, waiting. Mara withdrew the lace-bordered square of linen. Before she could say anything, Arnesto's eyes clouded, his face taking on a steely quality Mara had not seen before. "When did my aunt visit you? And why did you not tell me?"

Arnesto sounded hurt, as if she'd slighted him some-how. Mara quickly explained about the timing of his aunt's visit, assuring him she would have told him immediately, if so much else hadn't happened in the meantime. Somewhat mollified, he said, "But I still do not understand why she came to speak with you and not me. It is most unusual for my aunt to travel outside of Havynweal."

Mara cleared her throat. "Your aunt asked me some very personal questions. Someone else might have considered them downright impertinent, but I recognized she was really trying to protect you. Apparently, she wanted to see for herself whether I was up to snuff as your coach."

Arnesto stared down at his impeccably pressed navy slacks, the crease as sharp as ever. Was it a fay thing, this ability to look fresh as a field of asters at the end of a long, tiring day? After all, Arnesto had been locked up for a period of time that very morning. "I am sorry about that. Auntie

Yelenarra is quite protective and frankly, a bit nosy too. But she means well, and she is the closest thing to a mother that I have."

Mara slipped into her cloak. "We had an... interesting visit. Your aunt has given me a lot of food for thought. Speaking of food, since you've purchased all of our meals for the next two decades, how about we actually partake of something more than half an apple?"

The corners of Arnesto's mouth twitched up. His face broke into a brilliant, heart-stomping sort of a smile that made Mara feel weak in the knees, which she decided to attribute to hunger. "It shall be my pleasure to accompany you to the Cracked Cauldron."

Mara beat back any internal fluttering that her fay trainee induced and gave him a curt, businesslike nod. "Very well. First, we'll eat, and then we'll find Vas. We need to provide him with an update." Arnesto followed her outside and waited as she locked up.

"You wish to visit the provisional president this evening?"

"Aye. Vas hardly ever sleeps. Besides, he conducts at least half of his undercover work in the evenings. We need to tell him what we've learned so far."

"You mean about the dark fays?"

Mara nodded. "And about you tailing the assassin back to the old savings and loan building. Normally, I would have called upon Vas early this morning, but well, it's been a day."

"Aye, Mara Pensk, it certainly has. I am beginning to see why Efram and Katrine were so insistent that I train with you."

A small line formed between Mara's brows. "And why is that?"

"Because you do not sit and wait for something to happen—you rush straight into the dragon's lair."

"Some might say that only fools rush in."

Arnesto's eyes twinkled. "Or brave lady spies determined to save the world, one mission at a time."

Mara chuckled, but she knew, deep down, that was exactly what she planned to do. She'd not give into Glenbarran thugs, or Fallow sorcerers, or these infamous dark fays. No one was going to be taking Valerra by surprise again—not on her watch.

CHAPTER II

ARNESTO PAID THE DRIVER OF THEIR HANSOM CAB AND OFFERED HIS hand to Mara as she climbed out of the coach. He watched as the man clicked his horse's reins and drove away. "I do not understand why you wish to expend paper money, when I could simply translocate us here on my traveling mists."

"Unless we encounter an emergency, we'll be using non-magical conveyances to move us from one point to the next. Even the most accomplished Valerran mages travel by horse, locomobile, or their own two legs. Think of this as part of your training in our culture." Mara led the way up the driveway toward a three-story brick home, located on a quaint side street in Bellaryss's southernmost district.

This section of the city had escaped the worst of the fighting and looting during the war. Mara could almost imagine she was walking down a pre-war gravel drive, when her biggest worry was what to wear the next day. Instead, she had to deal with dark fays, an assassination by an unknown assailant, a quirky new spy trainee, and a clockwork toyshop to run with an absent boss. Plus, there was Farleigh, who weighed on her mind precisely because she hadn't had any time to think clearly about the grihm and the strange happenings at the preserve.

Mara rapped the brass knocker on Vas's dark green front door and waited for someone to answer. Vas did not employ a butler, housekeeper, or any other servant; instead he surrounded himself with a few trusted friends who performed multiple duties in his household. Vas's friends had been members of the resistance during the war and formed part of his spy network now. No one entered the president's inner circle without being fully vetted, either on the battlefield or in a darkened alley, where hand-to-hand combat was the norm.

They waited a full five minutes, and Mara wrapped the knocker again. "Are you certain the president is home and receiving guests?" asked Arnesto.

Mara shrugged. "We started at the savings and loan building, and the attendant at the front desk told us Vas had left for the evening. We stopped by his three favorite pubs, including the Cracked Cauldron, on the way here. If Vas isn't home, then I'm out of ideas."

Arnesto leaned against the door and listened, and then he pulled back, straightening his cravat. Mara heard someone unlocking the double bolts on the other side. The front door creaked open. "Ah, Miss Pensk," said Qwidd, "I do apologize for keeping you waiting. And who is your companion?"

The eldest member of Vas's team, a lean man in his late fifties with iron gray hair and a heavily lined face, squinted into the gloom. Arnesto swept his fedora off his head and bowed. Qwidd wore the white padded jacket, thick gloves, and cropped white pants of a fencing coach, which was one of his other functions on Vas's staff. Qwidd kept Vas and everyone else on the team, including Mara, on their toes with his sword and dagger skills.

Mara made the introductions, and Qwidd stepped back to allow them to enter. She nodded at Qwidd's padded jacket. "Who's here tonight?"

"The usual—Nahn, Sami, and of course Vas. Any news on when Katrine will be back?" asked Qwidd, trying not to sound hopeful. It was obvious to everyone except Katrine herself that Qwidd had a massive crush on her. So far, he hadn't worked up the courage to do anything about it, other than buy more clockwork toys at her shop. Mara figured by the time a man had reached Qwidd's age, he would have learned how to let a woman know his feelings, but Qwidd couldn't seem to get past 'hello' when Katrine was in the room.

"She's going to be tied up for a while, unfortunately, but she promised to pop in occasionally. I'll let her know you were asking about her," said Mara.

"Oh, no need. I was just curious," Qwidd shrugged, a pink flush spreading across his craggy face. He clamped one large, gloved hand on Arnesto's shoulder. "Come along, lad. Let's see what you're made of."

Arnesto's eyebrows rose almost to his hairline. "Sir, I am made of flesh and blood and magic, like any other mage. I do not understand how you intend to verify my constitution."

Qwidd canted his head to one side, his bushy brows drawn together. Then he threw back his head in a hearty laugh. "Oh, I can see we're going to get along famously. What a sense of humor! Come with me, and I'll get you fitted out."

Arnesto smiled uncertainly and followed the giant of a man. Mara fell in beside Arnesto and explained they would be joining Vas's regular fencing sessions, which occurred every evening the president was at his residence. "The only way to actually speak with Vas after hours is during fencing practice, or afterward, but he expects you to show up early enough to participate. Vas is a big believer in physical conditioning for his team."

"So in order to share our intelligence with the provisional president of Valerra, first we must fence with him?"

"Aye," Mara nodded. "Or with someone else who's gathered here tonight. Consider it a minimum requirement."

"I see. Well, I suppose it is preferable to facing a swarm of goblins or attending a fay council meeting."

"How could you give those two vastly different experiences equal weighting?"

"They are equally unpleasant," said Arnesto.

Qwidd held open the door to Vas's basement. They could hear the sounds of blades swishing and making contact below them.

Mara descended the stairs behind Arnesto. "Poor Katrine. She must be very grouchy by now, since she's presiding over the fay council in her brother's absence." She paused at the bottom step to ask. "Do you really have goblins in Havynweal?"

"Of course. They are magical creatures, after all. But they are a belligerent, untrustworthy bunch. Give me a bevy of trolls any day—to calm a troll, all you need to do is offer him food, preferably a full puff pastry."

Mara made a mental note to learn as much as possible about Havynweal. The more she heard about the land of the fays, the more she wanted to see it with her own two eyes. She wondered whether Arnesto could take her for a visit one day.

She followed Qwidd and Arnesto into the dimly lit basement, which Vas had set up for training his team. The walls were padded with thick quilts in a variety of patterns, giving Mara the sense she'd stepped into a street bazaar. The concrete floor had been overlaid with several layers of threadbare carpets. Three mismatched armoires lined the padded wall to the right of the stairs. One armoire held the fencing and boxing gear, including facemasks that were used only for new recruits. Once Vas determined a trainee's skill level, the masks came off. He wanted the training to be as realistic as possible. A second large wardrobe held a variety of outfits, uniforms, and costumes useful for all manner of undercover work.

The third and largest armoire contained their practice weaponry: swords, sabers, daggers, bows, arrows, and pistols. As far as Mara was concerned pistols were next to useless, since they were mechanical devices and all things mechanical malfunctioned around too much magic. Mara left archery and pistols to the ex-marines. Her preferred weapon was anything with a blade, and more recently, a length of rope. Katrine had been teaching Mara how to lasso in the alley behind the shop. As it turned out, lassoing was a useful skill in the realms of the dead; Mara intended to become as proficient as Katrine in case she found herself in the lower realms again.

A couple of plain wooden benches occupied the wall to the left of the steps, as well as a pair of fabric-covered folding screens, which served as makeshift changing rooms. Two narrow slits in the concrete served as the only windows on the back wall, along with a second exit from the basement, a thick wooden door that connected to one of the many tunnels beneath Bellaryss. Vas, Katrine, and the rest of the covert operatives made regular use of the tunnel system—and so did the Glenbarran thugs and Fallow sorcerers determined to bring down the new government.

Nahn and Sami were fencing with longswords in the center of the oblong room, with Vas acting as coach and referee. Qwidd, Mara, and Arnesto watched in silence, not wanting to interrupt the fencers. Nahn seemed to have the upper hand, and when she jabbed the tip of her blade into the padding in the center of Sami's chest, Vas declared her the winner.

Nahn, the only other woman in the room, was as tall as Mara, with long dark hair she pulled into a ponytail and a jagged scar slicing across her right cheekbone, courtesy of a run-in with a Glenbarran sword. Mara liked the former marine captain, who'd served with Vas since graduating from the Royal Marine Academy. Nahn was as no-nonsense as Mara herself, a quality that Mara appreciated in the other woman.

When Mara was still in school, before the Glenbarran invasion, her friends used to think she was hardhearted. What they didn't understand was that Mara had layers of defenses, which she'd been acquiring since the age of six. A pug-nosed boy had followed her around the schoolyard during recess one day, calling her father a coward for ordering his unit to retreat. Mara had used her fists to pommel the boy until he cried and tripped over his own feet, splitting his lip. Her father had paid the headmaster a hefty bribe to allow Mara to remain at the school. That fist-fight was the first of many for Mara. Each name-calling incident, each sarcastic remark about her father, had forced Mara to reinforce her invisible armor a bit more.

Sami rounded out Vas's household staff. A former master sergeant, Sami had served for two decades in the marines, battling Glenbarrans, grihms, sorcerers, and the undead. A short, barrel-chested man, Sami wore his thick blue-streaked black hair in a single braid down his back. His complexion was a few shades darker than Arnesto's, and his round face was as unlined as a teenager's.

Qwidd cleared his throat and announced their arrival. "Mara is here, along with her new recruit, Arnesto."

Vas spun around, a smile creasing his lined face. Vas was a decade younger than Qwidd, but Mara thought he seemed older of late, more burdened than when he'd been a resistance leader during the war. Mara respected Vas and trusted him enough to spy for him, but she still found him to be an enigma. She couldn't understand why he agreed to be the provisional president since he hated politics, but good candidates for the job had been in short supply.

Vas greeted Mara and then turned his attention to Arnesto, who bent from the waist to acknowledge the president. Vas said to his team gathered around them, "Here is the lad who kidnapped me from my office in order to deliver a message."

The others chuckled and Arnesto dipped his head in embarrassment. He mumbled his apologies and fidgeted. Mara felt a stab of sympathy for her fay trainee and tried to give him some cover. "Well, it *was* an emergency of sorts, and Arnesto *did* deliver my message with lightning speed."

Arnesto raised his head, his luminous gray eyes locked onto hers. He smiled and Mara's heart gave the tiniest of flip-flops, which her inner voice squelched with a stern lecture about staying focused.

Vas pointed to the armoires. "Suit up in fencing gear and grab a couple of swords. Oh, and Arnesto, wear a mask. Katrine would never forgive me if I send her cousin home with cuts on his face."

Arnesto nodded wordlessly and followed Mara. They selected padded white jackets, cropped pants, and thick gloves from the equipment armoire, and a pair of swords from the weapons armoire. Mara slipped behind a folding screen to change out of her skirt and blouse and into her gear. She heard Arnesto changing behind the other folding screen and found herself looking forward to seeing his sword fighting skills on display.

When Mara and Arnesto emerged from behind the dressing area, Vas and Nahn were standing in the center of the room, ready to spar. Qwidd pointed to Arnesto, "Lad, you'll spar with Vas while Mara spars with Nahn. After four minutes, you and Mara will switch places and then spar for another four minutes. Sami, you'll call time in two-minute increments. When the eight minutes are up, I'll pronounce the winning team: either Vas and Nahn, or Mara and Arnesto. Questions?"

Mara flexed her legs at the knees and raised her sword in front of her chest, the tip of the blade pointing to her left shoulder, the hilt near her right hip. Her muscles tensed as the adrenaline surged through her veins. Mara felt as if she came alive when she sparred, her every nerve on fire. She sensed Arnesto steeling himself next to her and hoped he could last at least a minute against Vas.

Qwidd stepped out of the fighting circle. "On guard! Begin!"

Nahn and Mara danced around each other, well aware of their sparring partner's strengths and foibles. Nahn charged Mara's left side, swinging her sword in a powerful arc that Mara blocked as she sidestepped to her right. Their blades clashed, ringing out with each fresh riposte and parry. They lunged, blocked, and counter-attacked in a series of swift, taut moves.

One minute passed, and then another, as Sami called out the first two-minute segment. Next to her, Mara heard Vas and Arnesto's blades whipping through the air and clanging when they made contact, Arnesto meeting every one of Vas's thrusts with a block and counter-attack. *Good for Arnesto, he's keeping up.*

Sami shouted, "Four minutes!"

Qwidd called out, "Blades down! Mara and Arnesto, switch now!" Mara caught her breath as she passed Arnesto, who seemed preternaturally calm, as if he spent each evening in Havynweal fencing with his aunt. Perhaps he did.

Qwidd yelled for them to begin once again, Arnesto sparring with Nahn this time, and Mara with Vas. Mara spotted Nahn charging Arnesto out of her peripheral vision, and Arnesto pivoting gracefully. She had no more time to think about her fay trainee. Vas whipped his blade in front of her face and then swung his sword underhand, intent on jabbing its tip into the side of her padded jacket. Mara knew Vas favored this offensive move, and Qwidd had taught her how to defend and counter the attack.

Mara brought her sword down with both arms, instead of swinging upward, as Vas expected. She batted Vas's blade out of the way and pivoted to his unprotected side, swiping her sword against him as she slipped past. She managed to make contact with Vas's padded jacket before he jumped out of reach; Mara had scored serious points in this bout. Vas rarely found himself on the receiving end of a blade.

By the time Sami called out the two-minute warning, all four fencers were panting. Mara longed to sit on a bench, remove her boots, and wiggle her toes. Instead, she poured on every ounce of energy she possessed, determined to win this bout for herself and Arnesto.

"Time's up, swords down!" hollered Sami. Mara was relieved to lower her sword and catch her breath. She noticed Arnesto's brow was damp and he was huffing slightly. It looked like her fay trainee was as competitive as she was, which she took as a good sign. Mara reached out and shook Vas's hand, and then Nahn's. Vas clapped Arnesto on the shoulder and said, "You can have my back any day, A."

"I second that," agreed Nahn, who turned to the fencing master. "Alright, Qwidd, who won this friendly little bout?"

"It was close, very close." Qwidd grinned at Mara. She realized in that moment she and her new trainee had accomplished the impossible. They'd actually won against two of the most formidable swordfighters in the country. She wanted to jump up and down but restrained herself. "However," said Qwidd, "I'm calling this for Mara and Arnesto. Congratulations to you both!"

"Well done," said Vas. He accepted a towel from Sami and mopped his brow. "Now tell me about the murder last night."

CHAPTER 12

Mara tucked a loose lock of wheat-colored hair behind her ear. "So you've heard about that?"

"Aye. Gemala stopped by my office this morning. But she said you had a better view of what went down, and apparently Arnesto chased after the assailant. I figured that's why you came tonight, to tell me what you know."

Mara nodded and wandered over to one of the benches propped against the basement wall. She pulled off her boots, wiggling her toes inside her socks. Arnesto sat down at an adjacent bench, placing his palms on his thighs. Mara thought he seemed tense again, not nervous as before, but mentally preparing himself to tell them his part of the story —the part about the potential dark fay tie-in, which she suspected most fays preferred not to discuss with anyone outside of Havynweal.

Mara told Vas everything she could recall about the murder and then asked Arnesto to describe his pursuit of the man after he ran from the pub. Arnesto provided a detailed description of the murderer, as well as how he weaved in and out of streets and alleys before arriving at the corner of Market and Bellwether. "I observed him entering the old savings and loan building, and then I left to report back to Mara."

Vas's eyes narrowed at the mention of the savings and loan building, where he worked everyday alongside the rest of Valerra's provisional authorities. "Are you certain it was the same man? After all, he led you on a merry chase and it was a dark, stormy night. You could have confused him with someone else."

Arnesto held his ground. "The man I followed to provisional government headquarters was the same man who ran from the pub. Of this, I am certain."

Vas drew his brows together and started to pace around the worn carpets in his basement. Mara wondered how much Vas's pacing had contributed to their shabby state. He addressed the others in the room: Sami, sitting cross-legged on the bench closest to the stairs, Qwidd, tidying up the gear in one of the armoires, and Nahn, lounging on the other side of Arnesto. "What do you make of it? Any thoughts who the murderer might be? And why he'd be running into the building that late at night?"

Qwidd, who was a master at multi-tasking, pulled his head out of the armoire. "How did the assailant enter the building?"

"What do you mean?" asked Arnesto.

Qwidd waved a facemask in the air. "Did the man use a key? Did someone open the door for him from the inside? Did he magic himself into the building?"

Arnesto ran a hand through his hair and sighed. "I was concerned about being spotted, so I kept my distance. I cannot be certain, but I do not believe he used a key. He entered the building very rapidly—he did not pause to unlock the door."

"So either someone was waiting for him and let him in immediately, or he translocated inside," said Nahn.

Arnesto nodded slowly. "Aye, it would seem so. If the latter happened, then he would most certainly be fay."

"What do your senses tell you? Was he fay-born or human?" asked Sami.

Arnesto shrugged. "I got no impression of him being fay or being anything else either. In fact, I could not pick up any emotional readings from him, either before or after he killed the other man."

Fays were well known for their ability to read emotions, which gave them great advantages when they were negotiating. Mara reflected that was probably why the fay council meetings took so long—every fay was reading every other fay and trying to jockey for position. She felt sorry for her boss all over again, stuck in Havynweal with the fay council. Katrine hated the politics of governance, whether human or fay.

"So we have someone who can mask his emotions well enough a fay can't read them, who kills with a tiny poisoned dart, and who melts into the savings and loan building." Vas waved his hands, frustrated. "I don't know what this all adds up to, but I don't like it one bit."

Mara said, "This may be completely unrelated, but it seemed to me Chief Inspector Talias was treating the murder at the pub like a routine bar fight gone bad, even though the evidence pointed to an assassination. Could she be conducting a different kind of investigation?"

"Such as?" Vas folded his arms.

"Looking for clues about different connections altogether? Either tied to her husband's unexplained death years earlier or tied to the fays somehow. Or both," said Mara. "After all, Chief Inspector Talias is a fay." Vas didn't seem surprised about Talias, so perhaps he'd known about her true identity all along. She turned to Arnesto. "This is a good time for you to explain about the dark fays from the outer demesnes."

"Huh?" said Qwidd. "What dark fays?"

"Where are these outer demesnes located?" asked Nahn, who had a passion for cartography. She collected and drew maps of pretty much everything, which Mara thought was an eccentric, although oftentimes useful, hobby.

"The Bazeerka," whispered Sami, and everyone stared at him. Sami shrugged. "My grandmother was a storyteller. I've heard tales of Bazeerkalim's descendants, the dark fays."

Vas turned back to Arnesto. "Alright, tell us about these Bazeerka. Who or what are they, and why should we care?" Arnesto provided Vas and the others with the same dark fay history lesson he'd given to Mara, except that he left out his personal story.

Mara didn't want to push him into sharing more than he was comfortable with, but she really believed Vas needed to hear about Arnesto's unfortunate connection to the dark fays. Before Mara could prod Arnesto about his past encounter, Sami spoke up. "My gran always said the Bazeerka were after one thing, and that's the end of Serving magic."

"But how can these Bazeerka possibly succeed if they're outcasts from Havynweal? Are they truly that powerful?" asked Vas.

Mara glanced at Arnesto, and a look passed between them. He rose from the bench next to Mara. Sweeping aside his wavy, shoulder-length hair, Arnesto pointed to the jagged bite marks on his neck. "When I was a young boy, an undead creature, whom my father believed was under a

Bazeerka spell, killed my mother and tried to kill me." He let his hair fall back into place and added, "It is unwise to underestimate the dark fays." Everyone peppered Arnesto with questions. He patiently answered them, the horror of his childhood experience becoming evident as he spoke.

Even tough, fearless Nahn looked chastened when he was finished. "I think we need to find a way to monitor their activities on their own home turf. How can we find the outer demesnes?"

Arnesto compressed his lips and shook his head. "One of most challenging things about the dark fays is pinning them down to a single location. While they have been relegated to the outer demesnes, they can travel anywhere but Havynweal itself. And the outer demesnes are inhospitable to humans; even dark fays cannot rest comfortably there for long. I believe that may be one of the reasons why they are always so ready to leave and bother some other place."

"Why can't they find rest in the outer demesnes?" asked Qwidd.

"Because of the heat."

"Is it located in a desert?" Nahn tilted her head, as if she could already see the edges of the outer demesnes. Mara figured she was preparing to construct a map of the inhospitable region the dark fays called home.

"You're not far off. The outer demesnes are anchored between the barrens south of Valerra, and the lake of fire within the lowest realm of the dead."

A hush descended inside Vas's basement, as everyone took in the reality of the Bazeerka's exile. Mara grimaced. She couldn't imagine a worse place to be forced to live, stuck between certain death in the lake of fire and the forbidding climate of the barrens. They must be very evil fays to have been sentenced to such a region for all time.

Sami spoke into the silence. "So the Bazeerka live with the constant reminder of their eternal punishment—unless they behave—which of course they cannot or will not do."

"Which is it, I wonder?" said Qwidd, who tended to toward philosophizing. "That they can't behave, or they won't behave?"

"It is most certainly the latter!" Arnesto's sandy brown eyebrows drew together in a deep frown. "The Bazeerka have the same free will as the rest of us. They choose Fallow sorcery over Serving magic—every time. They choose to abuse others to gain the upper hand—every time. There has yet to be a recorded instance of a dark fay doing something good!"

Qwidd gave a half-shrug. "I'm merely suggesting that the very nature of their exile might encourage them toward darker pursuits. I mean no offense, but I'd like to understand their motivations."

Arnesto's shoulders sagged. "I do apologize for my outburst, Master Qwidd. As you can imagine, this is a highly emotional subject for me."

Arnesto returned to the bench next to Mara, and leaning his head against the quilted wall behind him, closed his eyes. Mara noticed how his long eyelashes fringed his cheekbones, pale lace on sculpted brown skin. She yearned to place her palms on the sides of his face and soothe him, to lend some comfort to the small boy who'd witnessed such horrors, and to the impossibly handsome man he'd become. Instead, she blinked rapidly and berated herself for her not-so-idle thoughts.

Vas cleared his throat. "What did the Bazeerka do that got them permanently banned from Havynweal?"

Sami glanced at Arnesto, whose eyes were still closed. "I

can relate what my gran told me, and perhaps Arnesto can correct any errors."

Arnesto pinched the bridge of his nose and opened his eyes. "Aye, please do. I would like to hear the story that has been shared outside of Havynweal. It may be instructive for us to compare notes."

Sami rose from his cross-legged position near the stairs and stretched his legs. He began to pace, a habit Mara assumed he'd picked up from Vas. "What I'm about to share occurred over a millennia ago, after centuries of civil war and internal strife had nearly destroyed the fay race. A struggle arose between the last two fay clans still able to raise a sword or cast a spell. The rest had fled with their families to Faynwood to wait out the longest war. It was these fay ancestors who gave me, Vas, and other Faymons the blue streaks in our hair, and an extra measure of magic in our spells."

Sami glanced at Arnesto. "Am I on the right track so far?" Arnesto gave Sami a thumbs-up, a Valerran custom Mara didn't think her fay trainee had acquired yet. Sami nodded. "Good, because now we get to the heart of the matter. What happened between those two clans, and why was one banned forever from their homeland?"

Sami waited a few beats before picking up the threads of the story. "Imagine a field of frozen white ice and snow, and two fay clans arrayed for battle in darkest winter, where all the fighting inside Havynweal occurred. They would have been dressed in thick furs to prevent frostbite, their swordfighters lined up on the plain in orderly rows, and their archers in the tallest evergreens. Every able-bodied man, woman, and child, some as young as seven, stood on that field, awaiting the start of the final battle for control of Havynweal and by extension, the human realms as well, inside Faynwood and beyond.

"You see, this battle would determine not only who led the fays, but how outsiders, including the human populace, would be treated or mistreated. Chief Archipryllius the First—that would be Chief Pryl's forefather—took his calling as seriously as any fay chief before or since. He and Chief Bazeerkalim were half-brothers, and unfortunately, Archipryllius had no delusions about his sibling's proclivities. As a boy, Bazeerkalim had thought nothing of tearing the wings off butterflies, or stealing the horns from unicorns as they slept. Bazeerkalim was a wicked fay, through and through.

"However, even Chief Archipryllius hadn't expected his brother to pore over the ancient, forbidden scrolls in his quest for power. Bazeerkalim stumbled upon the darkest of all sorceries—what we know as Fallow magic—and uncovered the necromantic spells. He called upon the undead to aid his clan in their battle. Even worse, he invited the undead to make their home in Havynweal, should they claim victory in the final battle. The unsavory undead, those spirits deemed unfit to cross the river and spend eternity on the other side with their departed loved ones, were highly motivated to win at all costs. After all, what had they to lose? They were already dead and damned."

"How bad was it?" whispered Mara, entirely engrossed in the tale. Sami had clearly inherited his grandmother's storytelling gift.

"Take your worst nightmare, multiply it by a thousand-fold, and you can begin to grasp the horrors. The undead slaughtered most of Archipryllius's clan, tearing the limbs off some, flaying the flesh off others, and ignoring the cries for mercy. Every spell incanted by Archipryllius's clan rebounded back on them, Bazeerkalim's Fallow spells succeeding where Serving magic failed. Archipryllius had no choice but to surrender, and so he did."

"But Bazeerkalim saved the worst for his brother. First, he strung Archipryllius upside down on a frozen tree. Then, he selected a whip made from five leather straps banded together. The outer edges of each strap were tipped with sharp metal barbs. Bazeerkalim used that cruel instrument to flog his brother over and over, until Archipryllius wept to be set free. Bazeerkalim cut his brother down and left him to freeze to death on the bloodstained snow beneath him. Fortunately, Bazeerkalim underestimated Archipryllius's magic; after all, he was a twelfth-level wizard of Serving magic, whereas Bazeerkalim had not progressed beyond the seventh level.

"With his dying breath, Archipryllius called upon the power of every Serving mage, across every realm and continent and race. His dying magic, which is the most powerful magic of all, banished Bazeerkalim and his descendants to the outer demesnes, where they rightfully belong. His spell also cast the undead into the lake of fire, cleansing Havynweal of their malice."

Sami stopped speaking. No one seemed willing to break the silence until Arnesto said, "You spoke the tale well and truly. I will add only this: the dark fays have not learned their lesson. Bazeerkalim's descendants are as intent as ever on overthrowing Serving magic, and Valerra sits squarely in their sights. The Bazeerka intend to complete the destruction wrought by the Glenbarrans. They will stop at nothing—and destroy everything you hold dear—until either they win or we defeat them."

CHAPTER 13

Someone was pounding on Vas's front door, rapping the brass knocker over and over. Qwidd closed the armoire and took the steps two at a time to answer the summons. Nahn glanced at Vas. "Expecting anyone else tonight?"

Vas furrowed his brow. "Nay. But neither am I surprised. Too much is unsettled at the moment."

Qwidd descended the stairs with a telegram in his hand, which he gave to Vas. "The messenger is waiting in the foyer for your reply."

Vas tore open the sealed envelope and read the message. The lines about his mouth tightened, and the creases on his forehead deepened. He handed the telegram to Qwidd. "Read it aloud, please."

Qwidd complied, his rich baritone rising in surprise. "UPRISING AT GRIHM PRESERVE STOP MANY CASUALTIES STOP THREE GRIHMS ESCAPED STOP REMAINING GRIHMS DESTROYED STOP."

Mara brought her hand to her mouth to keep from crying out loud. One of the escaped grihms must be Farleigh, but who were the other two? She hoped Jerdahn had managed to escape, although she had no reason to think that was true. She wondered why the authorities hadn't thought to report Farleigh's escape until now; perhaps a single missing grihm was inconsequential compared to an uprising, casualties, and the destruction of the remaining crossbreeds. Mara shook her head, thinking of the grihms, all of them crossbred by Fallow mages against their will. "I knew many of those grihms. They would not have led a rebellion unless they'd been compelled. I've let Farleigh down, and now his friends are dead. I feel awful about this."

Vas replied gruffly. "If anyone should feel awful, it's me. I'm the provisional president, and it was under my authority the grihms were placed in that preserve. Farleigh warned us, but I allowed other priorities to get in the way. I'd planned to travel to the preserve yesterday to conduct a surprise inspection, but I had to reschedule. I planned to travel again today but was forced to cancel a second time. I vowed to place lives above politics, but this time, I failed miserably."

"How many people knew of your upcoming trip to inspect the preserve?" asked Arnesto.

Vas spun around. "A handful. Why do you ask?

Arnesto shrugged. "I wonder whether something other than routine politicking interfered with your travel plans?"

"Arnesto may be on to something." Mara rose from the bench. "What if the destruction of the grihms had been planned all along, but with Farleigh's escape and your pending investigation, the timetable was moved up? And your schedule intentionally disrupted?"

"But that would mean someone close to Vas was involved," said Nahn.

"And perhaps a handful is an understatement. I had to

rearrange my schedule, including a ribbon cutting ceremony for the new Children's Hospital, a meeting with the Merchant's Guild, and several other engagements. I may have mentioned something about a short trip out of town to visit the preserve." Vas sighed. "So let's assume my trip to the preserve was intentionally disrupted. Given that Arnesto tracked an assassin back to government headquarters, it's a fair assumption."

Sami asked, "Does anyone know why the man in the pub was killed? Or who he even was?"

"He was dressed in chef's whites," said Vas. "But the victim had no identifying papers on him. No one matching his description has been reported missing either. The chief inspector doesn't know who he was or why he was targeted for assassination." *Vas and Talias have been discussing the assassination,* thought Mara, *so Talias knows this was more than a brawl gone bad.*

"Sir," said Qwidd, now acting the part of Vas's unofficial butler instead of his fencing master. "The messenger is still waiting upstairs. What is your reply?"

"My reply is simple: WHAT IN QUEENS CROWN HAPPENED STOP."

"That's it?"

"Aye," Vas squared his jaw. "Let's see what their investigation comes up with. Meanwhile, we'll investigate who might have been behind the sudden scheduling conflicts that caused me to postpone my trip."

Qwidd gave a slight bow and sprinted up the stairs. They heard the door open, close, and then someone banging the brass knocker again. Mara assumed the messenger had left his gloves behind, but then she heard the urgent murmur of a familiar voice. Her ex-boyfriend rarely strayed outside after midnight, since he had to rise at three o'clock for his job as a baker's apprentice. Qwidd descended the steps, Remy hot on his heels.

The worry lines on Remy's forehead eased when he saw Mara and Arnesto. He was winded from running and waved his hand at them as he gulped some air. "I thought you were both dead."

"What? Why would you think that?" Mara didn't know whether to be annoyed Remy was checking up on her or concerned something major must have happened to rouse him from his flat after midnight.

"It's the shop," Remy huffed. "Katrine's Klockworks. It's badly damaged, some sort of a gas explosion."

"That can't be! All the gas was turned off when I left the shop." Mara's stomach turned to a fistful of lead. She couldn't imagine High Street without its quirky toyshop.

"How did you find out?" asked Arnesto.

Remy turned toward him. "When you didn't show up by midnight, I went over to Mara's flat to see whether everything was alright." Mara refrained from rolling her eyes at her overprotective ex. He'd been checking up on her again. "When Mara didn't answer, I decided to take a walk. I wandered around a bit and wound up at High and Prospect. The fire brigade was already there, tossing buckets of water on what remained of the shop. The fire chief told me the flames were still too hot for them to enter the building. He didn't know if anyone had been inside at the time of the explosion."

Mara shook her head. "How bad is it?" *Will Katrine blame me for the shop fire? Will she decide to rebuild? What will I do in the meantime? I no longer have a job!*

"At least half the shop is completely gone, nothing but charred bricks and misshapen bits of metal." Remy bit his lower lip, which Mara noticed was trembling. "I can't explain it, but I felt something dark and twisted surrounding the shop. I flagged down a hansom cab. The driver was heading home, but he gave me a lift as far as his own neighborhood, and I ran the rest of the way here. I know you often come here for fencing practice, and I hoped that was the case tonight. I figured Vas would know what to do, if... well, if you and Arnesto had been caught in the fire." Remy hung his head.

Arnesto went over to his flat mate and gripped his shoulder. "Thank you for your concern. This is a grave piece of news indeed."

Mara joined Remy and Arnesto, clustered in the center of the basement. "We're safe, Remy, but I'm in shock over the shop."

Remy drew Mara into a quick bear hug and then stepped back. "Aye. It's a shocking sight to behold."

Vas said, "I'll ensure there's a thorough investigation into the cause of the fire. In the meantime, perhaps we—" Vas paused at the sound of loud pounding at the front door. He glanced at Qwidd, who sighed and sprinted back up the stairs. Mara heard the murmur of voices again, and footsteps as Qwidd headed down the stairs alone. A look passed between Qwidd and Vas. The provisional president followed the fencing master back up to the first-floor foyer.

Mara strained her ears, overcome with curiosity at this latest arrival. She heard Vas say, "Penray!" but the rest of his words descended into a buzz of urgent whispers. Mara glanced at Nahn and Sami. "Who's Penray?"

"Chief Inspector Penray Talias," hissed Nahn.

"The chief inspector and Vas." Sami shrugged. "They are friends."

The way Sami emphasized *friends* made it clear that Vas and Talias had a personal relationship, which Mara found surprising. She'd never seen Vas with a woman; in fact, she'd never seen him in any social engagement that was not connected to his role as provisional president. The Vas she knew worked all the time. Even his evening fencing sessions revolved around the work they did, either officially or unofficially, for the government. Whatever social life he'd once had was long gone. All Mara knew was that Vas had lost his wife and daughter years earlier, before the war.

Mara returned to her bench, torn between extreme fatigue and the promise of a feather mattress, and her unbridled curiosity to know what brought Talias to Vas's door so late in the evening. Arnesto sat next to her, sharing his bench with Remy. She didn't think Talias came to report on the shop fire. Although a heavy loss to Katrine, the fire would not normally engage a chief inspector's attention. There must be something else that drew Talias out this late and kept her whispering upstairs with Vas.

The steps leading down to the basement creaked with footfalls. Qwidd came alone, his face ashen. "Vas requests that we report upstairs immediately. Chief Inspector Talias brings disturbing news."

Qwidd led them upstairs to the front parlor, a room so unlike Vas that his late wife or perhaps his mother must have decorated it. Pale pink and blue florals competed for attention everywhere, from the paper hangings on the walls, to the patterned carpet on the oak floorboards, to the floor-length drapes and chintz-covered furnishings. Two large sofas faced each other, bookended by a pair of wing-backed chairs on one end, and an enormous stone fireplace on the other. The grate inside the stone hearth was devoid of wood and flame despite the chilly spring temperatures. Everything about the room seemed faded, unused, a reminder of its female inhabitants long since gone.

Vas lit several wax candles on the low table in front of the sofas. He and Talias sat in the wing-backed chairs. Vas pointed to the sofas, where Mara took a seat between Remy and Arnesto, and Nahn plunked herself down next to Qwidd. Sami sat cross-legged on the carpet, his back to the cold fireplace.

Strands of loose hair peeked out from Talias's normally neat bun, and she'd missed one of the buttons on her blouse. She frowned at Remy. "Martel, who is your guest?"

Vas cleared his throat and introduced Remy to the chief inspector, adding, "Mr. Zel looks over-tired to me."

Talias nodded. "Aye, I believe he might benefit from a good nap."

Remy objected. "Oh, don't bother about me. I'm fine."

"Mr. Luca, would you mind?" Talias arched an eyebrow at Arnesto. "We shall await your return."

Arnesto rose from the sofa and bowed from his shoulders. "Aye, Chief Inspector, Mr. President." Fay traveling mists snaked around Remy's legs and torso.

Mara heard Remy call out, "But I want to stay!" before he and Arnesto vanished in a cloud of vapors. Mara slid closer to Vas and Talias, making more room on the sofa for Arnesto when he returned. She assumed Remy would be placed under a sleeping spell, one that would magically fade at three o'clock when he needed to rise for work. She just hoped all of the spells he'd been subjected to lately weren't addling his brain.

Mara thought the polite thing to do would be to make small talk while they waited for Arnesto; however, she'd never been much for needless conversation. That had been the purview of her stepmother, a decent woman who'd accepted and even loved her husband's unhappy young daughter. Mara found herself missing her stepmother more than she'd expected, and at the oddest times, such as now, seated in a silent parlor awaiting more bad news. Her stepmother would have known how to ease some of the tension in that room.

Mara picked at a loose thread on her fencing jacket and stared down at her stockinged feet. She'd dashed up the stairs behind Qwidd, anxious not to miss the news, and hadn't thought to slip her feet back into boots. Her stepmother would have been mortified at Mara's lack of proper attire, and her father would have merely chuckled.

Barely a minute passed, although it seemed much longer. Arnesto emerged from a puff of mist and lowered himself onto the sofa. Mara detected fatigue in her fay trainee, which she found somehow reassuring. He wasn't some super-fay-wizard who needed no rest, but a young man of flesh and blood and magic, much like the rest of them, although more so in the magic department.

"All is well?" asked Vas. When Arnesto nodded, Vas turned to the chief inspector. "Penray, would you be so kind as to repeat your news for my team's benefit? I'd prefer they hear this firsthand from you."

Although Mara had earned Vas's trust fighting alongside the resistance during the war, and later working as an undercover operative, this was the first time he'd considered her a member of his inner circle. She leaned forward, anxious to hear the chief inspector's news and determined to not let Vas or the others down.

Talias nodded. "The fire at Katrine's shop was not an isolated incident. Explosions have rocked the docks, damaged part of the Valerran Museum—" Everyone gasped. The museum housed the largest collection of ancient fay and Valerran artifacts anywhere in the world, a veritable treasure trove of old scrolls, artwork, tapestries, weaponry, and knowledge. "And destroyed the old savings and loan building. Vas's office is nothing but a smoking hole in the ground."

"What about our records, all our work, tracking and documenting the Glenbarran underworld operating inside Bellaryss?" asked Sami.

"Gone, I'm afraid. Even worse, there's been a prison break at the constabulary, with several of my officers slain." Talias's shoulders drooped. "It's been a difficult and sad night for the fire brigade and for my constables. I shall be leaving shortly to visit with the families of the slain officers."

"But first, we must decide how to approach this attack, which threatens to undermine everything we've fought so hard for." Vas's mouth thinned. "This level of violence has not been seen since the siege of Bellaryss. We had no inkling a coordinated attack of this magnitude was about to occur. Our intelligence was sorely lacking."

Mara bit her bottom lip, her head spinning with all the bad news. However, one thing truly did not make sense to her. "I can understand targeting the docks, the constabulary, and the government offices, as well as the museum, which is symbolic of our culture and the ascendancy of Serving magic. I can even understand instigating an uprising at the grihm preserve to create instability. But what does Katrine's toyshop have to do with any of this?"

"Her role as a former resistance leader is well known. Perhaps it was payback for that?" Qwidd crossed one leg over the other and clasped his hands around his knee.

Mara shook her head. "There are many other resistance fighters in the city who've returned to their pre-war activities, without interference or consequences. Why Katrine? And why now?"

Nahn stretched her long legs out in front of her. "Katrine is Chief Pryl's sister and one of the most powerful fays in Havynweal. Perhaps her shop was simply a convenient target for a disgruntled fay?"

"Not likely," said Arnesto. "Fays will bicker and barter for days on end, but every fay agrees to abide by the Great Havyn Accords, established half a millennia ago. Physical violence against another fay, except during a declared war, is outlawed, punishable by banishment."

Talias canted her head to one side, deep in thought. She frowned. "But maybe Nahn isn't so far off the mark."

Sami glanced at the chief inspector. "I'm not following."

Talias ticked off the points on her hand, one finger at a time. "Katrine's Klockworks was owned and operated by a fay. Chief Pryl purchased the old savings and loan building after the war, and he was renting it to the provisional government for next to nothing as a personal favor to the Valerran people. The Royal Constabulary, led by yet another fay, was attacked and my officers slain."

"What about the docks?" Qwidd asked. "I'm not aware of any fays working at the docks."

"That's not entirely true," replied Vas. "The Valerran Brotherhood of Dockworkers is comprised mostly of Valerrans, a handful of Faymons, and two fays. It just so happens the current leader of the brotherhood is a fay by the name of Bruhmwel."

"Bruhmwel's a fay?" Nahn's eyebrows rose.

"Aye," said Talias quietly. "That's not well known. Neither, for that matter, is Katrine's fay heritage, nor mine. Chief Pryl is the only one of us known to be a fay."

"Chief Pryl is also revered by the Valerran people for the assistance he provided during the war with Glenbarra," said Arnesto.

Vas scrubbed his face with his palm. "These are far too many coincidences for my liking. Someone is targeting fays inside Bellaryss."

Talias shrugged. "Or sending fays a message."

"What about the dead man at the Crooked Cauldron?" asked Mara. "What's his connection to all of this—if there is one?"

The chief inspector sighed. "In the midst of everything else, I neglected to mention we discovered the dead man was a pastry chef by the name of Jakob Kornish. He'd recently moved to Bellaryss to work for Chef Desna. However, we have no lead on the murderer. Arnesto tracked him back to the savings and loan building, where the trail went cold. I don't believe that's a mere coincidence, given tonight's events."

Vas closed his eyes and rubbed his temples, which Mara knew meant he was deep in thought. He grunted suddenly, and his eyes flew open. "Queen's Crown! He was a pastry chef?"

Talias stared at Vas, her dark eyes widening. "A gentleman from the Bakers Guild dropped off a large basket of pastries at the constabulary this afternoon."

"And someone—I'm not sure whether it was a man or woman—delivered three boxes of pastries today to the savings and loan building." Vas squared his jaw. "I think it's high time we keep a sharper eye on the Bakers Guild. Mara and Arnesto, accompany your friend to his place of work tomorrow, and ask for an introduction to the owner. Chef Desna happens to own the largest bakery in Valerra, and he's also president of the Bakers Guild. Apply to him for baking apprenticeships."

Mara sat up straighter, grateful to be given an assignment, but wondering how she could pull this off. "Remy told me there are no openings for new apprentices at any of the bakeries."

"I believe you will discover there are several openings when you apply in the morning," Talias said severely. Mara nodded but didn't probe. She'd prefer not to know Talias's plan for ensuring a couple of inexperienced apprentices would be welcomed into the Bakers Guild. Would she find the suddenly unemployed bakers some other means of occupation? Or cast a sleeping spell on two of the laziest, ensuring they missed work?

Vas rose and offered his hand to Mara and Arnesto, a signal for them to be on their way. Mara was more than ready to head back to her flat. "Thank you for taking on this assignment. I have no idea what you may uncover, but I feel certain there must be some connection between the guild and the events of today. I know you'll need to rise in a few hours, so please be on your way."

"Aye, sir." Mara stood up and wiggled her toes in the patterned carpet. "How should we get word to Katrine about the shop? She will want to be involved in the investigation and the cleanup."

"I'll contact Katrine in the morning and fill her in," said Vas. Mara nodded, the implications sinking in. If Vas could contact her fay boss that readily, then he must know Katrine's full fay name, which made sense; they had led the resistance inside Valerra during the war. Still, it rankled Mara that the provisional president could reach Katrine whenever he wanted, but Mara had to wait for her boss to contact her.

Arnesto stood next to Mara and canted his head. "Under the circumstances, may we travel by mists this evening?"

"Aye, I'm ready to go home by any means available. But

let's change first." They said goodnight to Vas, Talias, and the others, and returned to the basement.

Mara slipped into the dressing area behind the folding screens where she'd left her clothes. She dressed quickly and rejoined Arnesto, wearing his navy blazer and gray slacks, and looking as fresh as if he'd just completed his morning ablutions. Mara's hair was pulled back in a messy ponytail, and her blouse had fallen to the floor, so it was badly wrinkled. Arnesto's vaporous tendrils wrapped themselves around her legs, and she thought once again of her small flat and cozy bed. Although this evening, she'd be fortunate if she'd get two hours of sleep before she'd need to waken.

"But before we head to our flats..."

"You wish to see the shop?" asked Arnesto.

Mara bit her bottom lip. "I need to see it for myself."

Arnesto cast a veil of drabness over them as they landed across the street from the toyshop, but he needn't have bothered. The fire brigade had moved on to other locations and the street was deserted. Mara could understand why Remy would have panicked when he arrived at the corner of High Street and Prospect Avenue. No one would have survived the blast that reduced Katrine's Klockworks to ashes and ruin. Smoke still wafted up from the smoldering rubble, burning her eyes and nose. Bells clanged from the chapels and private residences in the downtown area, a call for additional hands to fight the fires. Black smoke and bright orange flames lit up the skyline. A sob escaped from Mara's lips, her memories of the war still too fresh.

Arnesto put his arm around her shoulders. It felt so natural Mara didn't shoo him away. She coughed, the smoke stinging her throat.

"Shall we head back to the flats?" he asked gently.

"Aye, I've seen enough."

In a blink, they were standing in her flat with the gas lamps turned on, courtesy of Arnesto's magic. While fay mists continued swirling around Arnesto, the vapors dispersed from Mara sufficiently so she could step clear. Arnesto waved silently as the mists whisked him away. Mara was grateful Arnesto hadn't tried to engage her in any further conversation. He must have realized how exhausted she was, and how deeply she mourned the losses that night, especially Jerdahn and the grihms, and Katrine's Klockworks.

Her fay trainee had read her emotions accurately. Arnesto's abilities—his sensitivity, his speed, and his skill with a sword—were rising in her estimation. If she could coach him to speak more like an average Valerran, he would make an excellent spy.

Mara hung up her cloak and draped her blouse and skirt over the back of a chair. She pulled on a nightgown, kicked off her boots, and tumbled onto her feather mattress. She was certain she'd not fall asleep, with all the bad news and crazy stories about dark fays muddling up her brain, but sleep came swiftly and mercifully.

As Mara drifted off, she thought she heard a raspy voice whispering her name, followed by cries for mercy, barely more than an echo, from somewhere beyond the city's boundaries, deep inside the territory known as the outer demesnes.

CHAPTER 14

"Tell me again why you want to come to work with me?" Remy rubbed the sleep out of his eyes as Mara and Arnesto hurried along beside him. They were due to arrive at the Best Bellaryss Bakeshop, better known as the Triple B, by three forty-five. They were running late because every time Remy asked a question, he stopped walking.

For a fay unable to tell a lie, Arnesto managed to skirt around the truth quite neatly. "With Katrine's Klockworks damaged by fire, Mara and I are seeking employment. We heard that Chef Desna at the Triple B is in need of two apprentices who can begin work immediately. This seems to be an ideal solution all around."

"But what I don't understand is how you heard about the openings at the bakery. We were fully staffed yesterday."

Mara rolled her eyes, but Arnesto patted Remy's back. "Very true. However, I do have a fay's sixth sense about these things. Plus, I know how highly regarded you are among the other bakers. Your recommendation will surely go a long way with Chef Desna."

"Ah," Remy puffed out his chest, "I see. Well, I'll do whatever I can to help you land these apprenticeships. Try not to be too disappointed if you're not selected though, since they are highly sought after and there's usually a waiting list for admittance."

"Thank you, Remy. I shall appreciate all you can do to help make our case with your employer." Arnesto smiled at his flat mate.

Meanwhile, Mara kept her hands balled up in fists, thrust deep in her pockets, to keep herself from nibbling on her knuckles. She was a bundle of nerves. What would they do if Talias hadn't been able to free up two apprenticeships for them? What were they even looking for anyway? She found it hard to believe that Chef Desna was an enemy of the monarchy and plotting against the government; the palace had been his number one customer before the war.

The three of them arrived out of breath and five minutes late at the Triple B. Remy led them around to the rear of the bakery and pounded on the back door. One of the bakers, a thickset man wearing a muslin apron splotched with flour, opened the door. A wave of warm, yeasty air wafted into the alley. Mara wondered whether they were permitted to eat any of the baked goods. A berry muffin and cup of coffee would do nicely for the breakfast she'd skipped that morning.

The baker grunted at Remy. "Good thing you showed up, lad. Two others sent notice they're quittin'. One needs to care for her ailing mum, and the other inherited a farm in the western province. Can you believe that?" The man finally noticed Mara and Arnesto. "And who 'r you?"

"These are my friends, who are looking for work. Is Chef Desna around?"

"Aye, but best brace yerselves. Chef's in a right foul mood."

The baker waved them into the largest kitchen Mara had ever seen, occupying more than half the building. Coal-fired brick ovens lined the walls on either side of the room, tended by a pair of young boys with sooty faces and coals-cuttles in their hands. Four long wooden tables filled the center of the kitchen, with a couple of bakers stooped over each table, some hand mixing flour, sugar, suet, and water in large bowls, others kneading the dough into various shapes—some rounded or braided, others folded or molded—and then placing them on metal trays, ready for the ovens. The far wall contained a long counter punctuated by a pair of deep sinks with hand pumps for washing bowls, pans, plates, and utensils.

The kitchen was noisy, even noisier than Katrine's Klockworks the week before Winter Solstice, when the shop was packed with holiday customers. One man wearing a tall white baker's toque and dressed in a blue striped shirt and dark slacks, his snowy white apron protecting his clothes, shouted to be heard above the rest. Remy guided Mara and Arnesto toward the man, who turned ice-blue eyes on the newcomers. "Mr. Zel, you're late! If it happens again, I'll dock your pay."

Chef Desna was a middle-aged man with a shaved head, even features, and a no-nonsense air. He jutted his jaw at Mara and Arnesto. "Who permitted you entry to my kitchen? The bakery doesn't open until six o'clock. Come back during business hours."

"Sir, these are friends of mine, applying to be your apprentices."

Desna cast Remy a chilly look. "You know the rules, Mr.

Zel. There's a waiting list to join the guild. Escort your friends to the door and get to your station without delay!"

Arnesto flapped his wrist and hissed, "For forty-five seconds you shall be frozen in this space, after which you shall forget this spell ever took place." All noise in the kitchen ceased, and everyone—the young stokers, the bakers, Desna, and Remy—were motionless.

"What are you thinking? The bread and cakes may burn!" huffed Mara.

"They'll be fine for the reminder of the spell, which is thirty-three seconds. Our only hope is for me to persuade Desna that he's already hired us."

"Can a fay really do that?" Mara was incredulous, and more than a little disturbed by the idea of using mental persuasion.

"A twelfth-level fay wizard can do it, but on two conditions: the mage who incants the spell receives no personal gain, and another person of equal or higher status agrees."

"But how can I agree? I'm not a fay wizard."

"No, but you are my field coach. Fourteen seconds."

"I don't like it, but I can't see any alternative." Mara expelled a puff of air in frustration. "Go ahead. Let's hope this works."

Arnesto gave her a business-like nod. "Of course it will work." He murmured an incantation in the fay language, which sounded like a lot of buzzing to Mara's ears. When the spell unwound, everyone returned to their tasks at hand, although the bakers found to their surprise that their breads and cakes had browned faster than expected.

Chef Desna frowned at them, and Mara figured he'd toss them out of his kitchen any moment. Instead, he sent Mara to the front of the shop and put Arnesto to work in the kitchen. Mara found a white apron with the Triple B emblazoned in green lettering on the front and tried to make herself helpful to the other apprentices setting up for the morning rush.

Arnesto carried a tray of small cakes, delicately frosted in pastels and topped with tiny rosettes, through the swinging kitchen doors and into the bakery's storefront. "Have you found anything yet?" whispered Mara.

Arnesto lowered his sandy brown eyebrows. "In between carting and washing these trays, timing each batch in the ovens, ensuring the stokers stay on top of their tasks, and jumping whenever and wherever I am needed, I have not had a moment to contemplate finding something."

Mara took a step back. Arnesto was downright cranky. This was a first, and she wasn't sure whether it was due to lack of rest or lack of progress. "Alright, keep your eyes open."

Arnesto returned to the kitchen through the swinging doors, and Mara scurried to aid the other apprentices behind the counter as a steady stream of customers entered the Triple B. By late afternoon, Mara struggled to keep from yawning in front of both staff and customers. She wondered yet again what possible purpose she and Arnesto could serve in the bakery. On the other hand, she reasoned, they did need to work somewhere, and since Katrine's Klockworks was out of commission for the time being, the bakery was a sound alternative. And given its foot traffic, she ought to be able to pick up some useful intelligence.

"Time to close up," said one of the apprentices working alongside Mara, a sturdy young woman named Bea.

"But it's only five o'clock. I thought the bakery closed at six?"

"Except when we have guild meetings, like tonight. We close early so we can attend the meeting."

"Does everyone attend?"

Bea flipped the sign over to *Closed* in the shop window and bolted the front door. "Aye. It's mandatory for apprentices. Not sure why; it's mostly just a lot of boring business stuff and the usual shouting."

"Shouting?"

Bea drew her dark brows together and leaned forward. "You think Chef Desna is the only one who yells in the kitchen? They all shout and holler to be heard over each other. I go home each month with a pounding headache."

Mara sighed. "I see. Something to endure but not enjoy."

"Aye, but they do feed us. You'll get a decent meal out of it anyways."

Mara hung up her apron next to Bea's and followed her through the swinging doors to the kitchen where the apprentices, Arnesto among them, were wiping down the long tables. Apparently, most of the bakers and Desna had already left for the guild meeting. The same baker who'd admitted them that morning shouted instructions to the apprentices, a large key ring in his hand. When the head baker was satisfied with the kitchen's cleanliness, he sent everyone into the alley and locked up. Mara fell into step beside Arnesto, following behind Bea, Remy, and another apprentice, a young man with a thick mop of curly black hair.

"Chef was crankier than usual, don't you think?" said Bea.

Remy shrugged. "Perhaps, but he's always tense on days we have guild meetings." The young man with the curly mop of hair agreed.

"I apologize for my surliness earlier." Arnesto spoke quietly, so only Mara could hear him.

Mara glanced up at him and noticed the dark smudges under his eyes. "Don't worry about it. I'm surprised the lack of rest is getting to you though. I didn't think fays needed as much sleep as everyone else."

Arnesto shook his head. "Where do these ideas about fays originate, I wonder?"

"Storybooks, mostly. Until I met Chief Pryl during the war, I hadn't even thought fays were real. And storybook characters are pretty indestructible as a general rule."

Arnesto snorted. "Well, to set the record straight, I do need sleep. More than that, I am not an early riser. I have newfound respect for Remy's profession."

"Aye, me too, especially since Remy loves to sleep; he used to nap all the time in school." Mara pursed her lips, wondering whether they'd actually learned anything that day. "I just wish I could come up with an angle or a lead. I don't know what we're looking for, beyond the oddity of baked goods being delivered to some of the buildings before they exploded, and one dead baker killed by a poisoned dart."

"Perhaps we might discern something tonight at the guild meeting."

Mara nodded. "Let's split up and circulate."

Bea was right about two things: the excellent meal served to the guild members—broiled whitefish, roasted root vegetables, and a remarkable array of sponge cakes, courtesy of Triple B—and the volume of yelling involved during a guild meeting. Mara rubbed her temples to ward off a headache. Arnesto had attached himself to a group of boisterous bakers from one of Desna's competitors. He sat across the guildhall, a large boxy room that smelled not unpleasantly of tobacco and ale. Gas wall sconces sputtered, casting as much shadow as light on the wood paneled walls and doors.

Mara hoped Arnesto was having better luck gathering useful information. So far, half a dozen women, whose ages ranged from a stoker in her early teens to a head baker well past retirement, had questioned her about Arnesto. It took every shred of Mara's dwindling patience for her not to roll her eyes or tell them his fay charm was attracting them. But that wasn't entirely accurate. Arnesto was charm itself, regardless of his fayness. Right now, he was chuckling along with the other young bakers in his group. At least he was blending in, which was more than she was managing.

Mara joined Bea, speaking in hushed whispers with several apprentices from another shop. They stopped whispering when she joined them. "I'm sorry, I didn't mean to interrupt."

Bea waved her hand. "She's alright, a new apprentice at Triple B."

One of the apprentices, a boy of about sixteen with thick black eyebrows, nodded. "We're talking about the fire at government headquarters."

"And at the constabulary and museum," added his companion, a slender girl with large brown eyes.

The boy nodded. "We think it's the Glenbarrans."

Bea whispered, "Well, that's what you think. I'm fairly certain it's even worse."

"Worse than the Glenbarrans?" The boy's brows pointed downward, like a blackbird diving for its dinner.

Bea crossed her arms. "Much worse. It's the dark fays."

"Don't be ridiculous," the girl's eyes widened. "There's no such thing as fays, dark or otherwise."

"Why do you think it's the dark fays?" asked Mara. The

boy and girl shook their heads and wandered off in search of more sponge cake.

Bea leaned over. "Because I've been hearing voices when I fall asleep at night, and my mum always said that was a sure sign of a dark fay infiltration."

Mara whispered, "Was your mum a fay?"

Bea waved her hand. "Nay, but she hailed from Faynwood, a refugee from their civil war."

Mara glanced at Bea's too-black hair. Bea patted the top of her head. "I color over the blue highlights."

"But why? There are plenty of other Faymons living in Valerra these days, including the provisional president."

"I'd rather be blonde, like you, or brunette or ginger, anything but a girl with blue streaks in her hair."

"You've been teased about it?"

Bea snorted. "More than teased. I've been pushed and shoved and bullied. It was my mum's idea to hide the blue, leastwise while I was in school. Then afterward, I just kept doing it."

A pang of regret jabbed Mara. Had she ever considered how Linden felt, growing up with vivid blue streaks running through her dark hair? Before the war and before they'd become friends, Mara had been jealous of Linden, convinced her life was perfect, with her famous war hero father, her prime minister uncle, and her grandmother Nari, the highest-ranking master mage in Valerra. Mara hadn't thought about the bullying Linden must have received because of her heritage. Mara wished she could turn back the clock and apologize for her surly younger self. She couldn't do that, but maybe she could help Bea.

"I think the blue streaks are lovely, actually."

"You do?"

"Aye. I quite adore the vivid blue hair of the fays too."

Bea gripped her arm. "You are a believer, like my mum, aren't you?"

"You mean that fays exist?"

Bea nodded, and Mara dropped her voice. It wouldn't do to draw attention to themselves or their conversation about fays, dark or otherwise. "Of course they exist. The old fay tales are more truth than fantasy. And the fay lullabies actually do work, you know." Mara had once relied on the sleep magic in an old fay lullaby to incapacitate some nasty prison guards. Besides, if she'd had any doubts, they'd been long since dispelled by all the fays in her life. These days, she counted more friends among fays and Faymons than Valerrans, an unexpected outcome of the war with Glenbarra. The ongoing conflict between Serving magic and Fallow sorcery went largely unnoticed by the non-magical population of Valerra, except when buildings collapsed or caught fire, and the rivers turned red from Fallow spells. Even then, Valerrans just blamed the Glenbarrans.

Bea's voice grew wistful. "You sound just like her, you know."

Mara assumed that Bea, like everyone else living in Bellaryss, had lost most of her family to the Glenbarrans and their Fallow sorcerers, who'd managed to overwhelm even the strongest defensive wards that had once protected their city. "I wouldn't mind a few blue streaks myself. Except I'd never use dye to cover my natural hair color."

"You wouldn't?"

Mara shook her head. "It's a plain fact that it damages the hair follicles. Might even lead to premature hair loss."

Bea smoothed her dyed hair. "I'll think on it."

Mara needed to bring the conversation back around to the dark fays. She didn't want any eavesdroppers and whispered into Bea's ear. "I've heard their voices too."

Bea's eyes widened. "The dark fays?"

Mara glanced around and then murmured, "I've heard them just as I'm falling asleep."

Bea gave a shudder. "But why are only some of us able to hear them?"

"I don't know. Maybe because we believe they exist?"

A loud clanging interrupted them; apparently the Bakers Guild employed a large copper bell to bring the guild to order. Straight-backed chairs scraped against the floorboards, and Bea beckoned Mara to follow her to where the other apprentices were seated in the back of the guildhall. They sat down under the watchful eye of a couple of elder bakers, arms folded across their chests, waiting for any of the apprentices to get out of line.

One of the bakers, the guild's secretary, read aloud the minutes of the previous guild meeting. Mara's head started to droop, but Bea pinched her awake before any of the supervisory bakers noticed. Following the reading of the minutes and some tedious debate about the fund for pensioners, Chef Desna said, "And now we come to the new business. First, let us recall Jakob Kornish, a new baker to our local chapter and to the Triple B, having transferred here recently from the western province. As you know, Baker Kornish was killed in a bar fight earlier this week."

Everyone bowed their heads in a moment of silence, unified in their display of respect for someone they hardly knew. Mara suspected that show of unity wouldn't last long. Desna added, "The constables have encouraged anyone with information to please come forward. Your anonymity will be protected." Mara thought the last part was a bit unusual. Chief Inspector Talias must believe that an offer of anonymity would encourage someone to speak out who might not otherwise.

Chef Desna leaned forward on the table where he and the other officers of the guild were seated. "The next topic is the recent fires in the downtown area and their impact on our bakeries and customers."

A woman hollered from the center of the hall, "We need a recall vote! Our city is in a shambles and the government's not doing enough."

"At least your bakery wasn't damaged by the fires yesterday! It'll be weeks before I can reopen," yelled a man with a goatee, sitting near the front of the room.

Bea whispered, "That's Chef Osman. His bakery was next to the Valerran Museum and suffered smoke damage. He's ordered his apprentices to clean and repaint the bakery while he takes a short holiday. He'll be open inside a week. He's always complaining about something."

Chef Osman turned and shouted at the audience, ensuring his voice carried across the guildhall. "Queen's Crown, how much more of this can we take? We're at the mercy of anyone with magic—they think nothing of starting fires and leaving the rest of us to fend for ourselves. It's not right!"

Another man, seated in the first row of the hall, rose from his chair. His square build and bushy sideburns seemed familiar. He walked up to Chef Desna and whispered a few words. The chef nodded. When the man turned around to face the crowd, Mara narrowed her eyes, recognizing him instantly: Harlan Lewyn, leader of the Merchants Guild and owner of the company who'd ruined the grihm preserve.

Harlan Lewyn raised his hands and began to clap. Others took up the clapping, and soon the entire hall resonated with the sound. Lewyn lowered his hands and boomed in a loud voice, "My fellow workers and loyal

Valerrans, I have come on behalf of the Merchants Guild for two reasons: First, to express our condolences at the loss of Baker Kornish due to a senseless act of violence, which has been on the rise since Martel Revas assumed leadership of the provisional government. Second, to ask for your support in corralling the flagrant use of magic within our borders."

A woman hollered from the back of the hall, "Aye. It's the mages that's the problem!"

Several bakers began debating with the woman, but Lewyn raised his hands and they quieted down. "I'm not suggesting that mages have *started* these fires." There were a few grunts and grumbles from the audience, and he waited for them to settle down. Harlan Lewyn knew how to work a crowd. "What I *am* suggesting is that we need to *control* the use of magic in our land, to ensure it doesn't get out of hand again. None of us wants another war."

Chef Osman shouted, "He's right. We should outlaw magic!" An argument broke out in the guildhall with bakers hollering over each other to be heard. Harlan Lewyn gave Chef Desna an apologetic shrug and took his seat. Meanwhile the argument he'd instigated took on a life of its own.

Mara curled her hands into fists, her temper flaring at the ignorance on display in the guildhall. *Outlaw magic? After Serving mages sacrificed themselves during the Siege of Bellaryss? After the Faymon clans marched down from Faynwood under a veil of drabness and launched a surprise attack on the Glenbarrans? After the fays lost countless women and men retaking Wellan Pass, which ultimately led to King Roi's defeat?*

Bea noticed Mara's balled up fists. "Don't get angry. You'll just give yourself away."

Mara huffed. "Give myself away? What's that supposed to mean?"

"You're a mage, right? None of the chefs will openly hire a baker's apprentice with magic skills."

Mara bit her bottom lip. "How can you tell I'm a mage?"

Bea snorted. "You believe in fays, you hear voices, and you like the blue-streaked hair of the Faymons." Bea glanced over her shoulder and then leaned closer. "Look, I'm not just apprenticed to Chef Desna. I'm apprenticed to a Serving mage as well. Your secret is safe with me."

Mara's brow wrinkled. She never considered that she might have to hide the fact she was a Serving mage. *Crow's feet, this is Valerra, where Serving families were once highly respected, even revered. This makes no sense. Even Harlan Lewyn once claimed to be a Serving mage, although he's refuting it now.* "Why would no one hire a baker's apprentice who could handle magic?"

"The chefs are worried that an apprentice with magic skills could simply conjure a perfect cake. Most of them don't really understand how magic works. Conjuring a cake that looks beautiful and tastes as good as it looks would require master-level abilities, which no apprentice would have anyway. But no one wants magical competition in the Bakers Guild, so the use of magic at any of the bakeries is prohibited."

Mara relaxed somewhat; she could see their point. The chefs wanted a level field for their bakeries, with no one having an unfair advantage. It didn't mean they supported the anti-magic laws that Lewyn was proposing. Mara glanced at Bea and wondered what it would be like to serve two apprenticeships at the same time. "How can you possibly find the time and energy to be apprenticed to both a chef and a mage?"

Bea shrugged. "I want to learn my spells well enough to become a full-fledged mage someday. In the meantime, I need to pay for my room and board. So I bake during the day, and most evenings, I spend studying my spells and practicing with my mage tutor. Maybe now you can understand the other reason why I don't want to reveal my Faymon heritage. While Chef Desna is more open minded than most, he might feel it necessary to withdraw my apprenticeship."

Chef Desna struggled to be heard above the din of shouting bakers. He soon gave up and clanged the copper bell again. The guildhall gradually settled into an uneasy silence. Bakers with magic in their bloodlines were likely disturbed by the anti-magic talk that evening. Desna sent Osman a chilly glare. "Any more outbursts like that, and I'll personally remove you from this hall." Osman shrugged but didn't respond. Anyone looking at the two men would lay odds on Desna, since he was taller and broader than Osman.

Desna's ice-blue eyes surveyed the guild members, lingering on several of the louder men and women. "As for the rest of you, let's remember that we are neither politicians nor magicians. We are bakers. We ensure Valerrans have fresh bread for their tables and treats to lift their spirits. This guild has never taken—and never will take, at least while I'm here—an anti-magic stand." Desna gave a quick bow to Harlan Lewyn, acknowledging their difference of opinion. Lewyn nodded his head amicably.

"Our one rule, which is a good one and fair to all bakers, whether magically gifted or not, is that we do not use magic in our kitchens. If you don't like our guild's policies, I suggest you leave now."

Desna sipped from a glass of water and waited; his blue eyes narrowed. No one left the room. "Alright then. I will thank you to keep your political opinions to yourselves and remember we are here to discuss guild business. Period."

An older woman raised her hand. Desna acknowledged her. "What is it, Chef Rosita?"

Rosita stood. "I suggest that a small group of us bring forward a petition to the provisional authorities, requesting more constables be added to foot patrols, and that we fund an extra fire wagon for the downtown area." A number of others voiced their agreement, and Desna took a vote. The resolution passed.

The meeting lasted another thirty minutes, as more mundane topics were addressed or tabled for the next meeting. Harlan Lewyn slipped away from the guildhall unnoticed. Mara respected how deftly Chef Desna managed the noisy group of bakers. While he'd made a point of stating he was a baker and not a politician, he handled the opinionated crowd and got them moving mostly in the same direction, a feat Mara hadn't thought possible at the start of the meeting.

They filed out of the hall and fell into step behind Chef Desna and Chef Rosita, who leaned heavily on a cane as she walked. Arnesto joined Mara, while Remy came alongside Bea, the four of them walking abreast. It occurred to Mara they were four mages, or more accurately, one fay wizard, two mages, and one mage apprentice. She glanced about, curious as to how many other bakers and apprentices were intentionally hiding their magical abilities due to the current climate. She found herself becoming annoyed all over again, but she reminded herself this was an undercover assignment from Vas and not a permanent position.

Desna helped Chef Rosita climb into a hansom cab, handed up her cane, and waved goodbye. Desna waited until the cab pulled away, and then he started to cross the cobbled road. A sleek black locomobile accelerated down the street, heading straight for the chef. "Look out!" cried Mara.

Desna spun around and saw the locomobile barreling toward him, but his reactions were too slow to avoid the speeding vehicle. Arnesto sprinted into the street and grabbed the chef, dragging him out of the path of the loco-mobile. Everything happened so quickly that all Mara could see was a blur of motion, but she thought she heard Arnesto cry out as the locomobile whizzed past.

Desna and Arnesto tumbled onto the cobbled sidewalk in a tangle of arms and legs.

CHAPTER 15

"ARE YOU HURT?" REMY REACHED DESNA AND ARNESTO FIRST.

The chef took a shaky breath. "I don't think so, thanks to my newest apprentice who's sprawled beneath me." Desna took Remy's outstretched hand and grunting, rose slowly to his feet, careful not to step on Arnesto.

While Remy and Bea fussed over Desna, Mara knelt beside Arnesto, who'd pushed himself up on one elbow. "Did you break anything?"

Arnesto winced but shook his head. "My bones still seem to be knit together. I do believe I shall be quite bruised in the morning, however." Mara helped Arnesto to stand, but he wobbled and clutched his side. She put his free arm around her shoulder and instructed him to lean on her.

Chef Desna reached out his hand to Arnesto, who shook it awkwardly, draped as he was over Mara. "Thank you, Mr. Luca. I am in your debt. I don't believe I would have walked away from that accident."

Arnesto dipped his head in acknowledgment. "I am grateful that we both escaped from that speeding vehicle without serious injury. But sir, this did not feel like an accident to me."

Desna's eyebrows rose, but he didn't reply. A small group of bakers, who'd observed the near miss from across the street, hurried over to them. "Do you need to see a healer, Chef?"

"That driver should be reported!"

Desna assured the knot of bakers that he was fine, just a bit shaken. One of the bakers flagged down a hansom cab for the chef and helped Desna climb inside. Desna leaned out before the driver pulled away. "Mr. Luca, I will not expect to see you in the morning. You will be sore and will need a good lie-in. I will not expect you either, Miss Pensk, as I imagine you will be overseeing Mr. Luca's care. If there is need for a healer to be consulted, please send the bill to me."

Desna pounded on the roof of his cab to signal the driver he was ready to depart. The driver flicked the reins and his chestnut mare drew away from the curb. The group of bakers disbursed until just Remy, Bea, Arnesto, and Mara remained.

Remy noticed Arnesto was still leaning on Mara and frowned. Before he could object, Mara said, "Remy, why don't you walk Bea home? I don't think any of us should be walking alone at the moment. I'll help Arnesto get back to the apartment."

Bea didn't think she needed an escort, but Remy shook his head. "Mara is right. These are strange times, and I'd feel better knowing you were safely home."

Bea tilted her head and gave a shy smile. "Alright then."

As soon as Remy and Bea rounded the corner, Mara said, "I want to get you home as quickly as possible. Maybe you should cast a veil of drabness and use your mists to translocate us."

"But I thought you objected to using my fay mists for travel?"

"I do, except in special circumstances, such as when you save someone's life and get yourself banged up in the process."

The corners of Arnesto's mouth quirked up. "Duly noted." Arnesto murmured the incantation for a veil of drabness. "Drape us in a veil of gauze, hide us from inquiring eyes." He needed to repeat the spell several times, which told Mara he was more severely injured than he was letting on. Mara repeated the words of the spell with him to reinforce the magic.

The gauzy veil draped over them, although Mara thought the edges looked ragged, as if the spell were as wobbly as Arnesto. She wrapped her arms around him more tightly, concerned he might crumble on the cobbled sidewalk. Wispy tendrils wound around their legs and snaked up their waists.

Mara felt Arnesto's weight shift in mid-transfer. He pitched to the side, and she struggled to keep him upright. Mara felt nothing beneath her feet but air; they were suspended within the traveling mists, surrounded by a cloud of vapors. Arnesto's head lolled to the side. They dropped suddenly, falling far too quickly to whatever lay below. Mara didn't want to think about where they might land or the pain of impact when they did.

"Arnesto," she screamed, "wake up! You need to get us home!"

"Home," mumbled Arnesto.

They touched down on something soft, much softer than the wooden floorboards in either apartment. Mara peered through the mists, but she couldn't see anything in the dark. Arnesto slumped forward. Mara caught him under both arms and laid him down where they'd landed, which turned out to be a grassy expanse of lawn. The yards fronting the row of apartment buildings where she and Remy lived were mostly scrub grass and weeds, so she didn't think they'd arrived near either flat.

A globe of cool white light flared ten feet away, blinding Mara as she knelt beside Arnesto. "Hello," she called out, hoping whoever held the lamp was friendly. "We need a healer right away. My friend has been injured."

The white light jostled about and a reedy voice called out, "My nephew is hurt? What caused his injuries?"

Well that clarifies things. We're in Havynweal! I've always wanted to visit the fay lands, but not like this.

"Arnesto ran in front of a speeding locomobile to save a man's life."

Yelenarra hurried over and knelt beside Arnesto, across from Mara. The fay woman placed a palm-sized crystal egg, which glowed from within like a moonbeam trapped in glass, on the ground next to her. Her empire-waist gown and matching cape were the same sparkly silver that Efram and Arnesto usually wore, rather than the gold, silver, and ivory swirly fabric she'd worn earlier, when she'd called on Mara at the toyshop.

Yelenarra's hands gently probed Arnesto's arms, legs, and torso. Arnesto cried out when she reached his right side. "He cracked a few ribs, which will heal, but I fear internal bleeding. Please stay with him whilst I retrieve the healer."

Yelenarra vanished in a puff of mist, taking her light globe with her and plunging them into darkness once again. Arnesto wheezed, "Auntie Yelenarra?"

"Aye, she left to find the healer. You brought us home—to your home in Havynweal. How do you feel?"

Arnesto coughed a few times, gasping with each breath. "It hurts to breathe."

"Your aunt said you cracked some ribs. Here, let's try this. It might help." Mara scuttled behind Arnesto and propped his head up on her lap. "Is that any better?"

"Aye." He coughed again. His chest heaved a few times as he caught his breath. "You called me your friend just now. Did you mean it?"

Mara paused, because she wanted to answer Arnesto honestly. She'd been so consumed with worry, she hadn't really thought about what she was saying to Yelenarra. The words had tumbled from her lips. But it was true; she did think of Arnesto as her friend and perhaps something more. Mara reminded herself, yet again, that she was Arnesto's field coach and anything more than friendship wouldn't be possible. She already felt emotionally entangled with her fay trainee, despite her best efforts.

The one thing she could offer Arnesto was her friendship, and she'd gladly receive his in return. "Of course I am your friend. I hope you're mine as well."

Arnesto took a wheezy breath and sputtered, "I, Arnestarious Aziel Windstorm Lucato the Fourteenth"—he reared his head up from her lap, coughing into his fist before leaning back against Mara and gasping—"accept your friendship, Maragold Gracelyn Raeburn Pensk, and I pledge the same to you."

Mara placed her hand on his shoulder. "Hush now. The healer will be here soon." The ground shuddered beneath her, and she tingled all over, as if tiny needles were pricking her face and arms and legs. If she hadn't been sitting on the well-sodded lawn with Arnesto's head in her lap, she would have toppled over, just as she'd fallen in Remy's apartment the first time Arnesto had used her full name.

Arnesto whispered, "I shall endeavor to live up to your expectations."

"Thank you. I shall endeavor to do the same. Now you must rest." *Gah! What's wrong with me? I sound just like Arnesto, all formal and proper.* Mara used her hands to brace herself against the ground as her head continued to spin. The piece of whitefish she'd eaten at the guildhall threatened to rise up like a clockwork bird in her stomach.

A small part of her innermost self felt strangely—and strongly—connected with Arnesto, who'd finally quieted down, although his breathing was shallow. Something profound had just passed between them, but Mara had no clue what it was. Perhaps Katrine could shed some light on fay customs about friendship, if Mara could ever find her fay boss inside Havynweal. Mara was sure she'd need a fay escort. She didn't think ordinary humans were permitted to wander about the fay lands on their own.

A cool white moonbeam appeared through a haze of vapor, followed by a second beam, this one a warm yellow light. Mara draped her arm protectively across Arnesto's chest and he gripped her hand, entwining their fingers.

Yelenarra and a second figure, draped from head to toe in heavy veils, emerged from the mists. Holding the yellow globe of light aloft in its hand, the veiled healer leapt to Arnesto's side, moving more like a large cat than a human or fay. Mara sensed the healer probing her mind telepathically, and she immediately incanted under her breath, "Block heart and mind from probing spells, all remains hidden till I choose to reveal." Mara might not be a twelfth-level fay wizard or a Valerran master mage, but she knew her Serving magic spells, and she resented anyone poking around inside her skull.

The healer reared back at Mara's resistance. She addressed Yelenarra, pronouncing each *S* with extra emphasis, making her sound almost catlike. "Let us move Arnestarious to some place more comfortable than this human's lap."

"Now, now, Zornamayne. Katrinareus has asked this young woman to aid my nephew as he learns Valerran ways."

"What a ridiculous waste of time for a twelfth-level fay wizard," sniffed Zornamayne. Mara decided the healer was a rude, prejudiced female fay of indeterminate age and fairly high rank, given Yelenarra's deference. "Let us transfer him inside where I may examine him properly, and let us dispatch this girl to the human realm forthwith."

Arnesto gripped Mara's hand harder and wheezed. "No! My friend stays."

The lighting was far too dim to catch Yelenarra's facial expression, but Mara noticed that she tilted her head and gave the barest of nods. The healer sighed dramatically. "Very well, Arnestarious. If you have chosen her, then she may stay."

The two fays incanted in their buzzing language. Mara's lap suddenly lightened as Arnesto levitated two feet above her. Since he refused to loosen his grip on her hand, Mara managed to awkwardly roll to her knees and then stand. She thought she detected a little snicker from the veiled healer. Mara couldn't stand the woman, but if she could stop Arnesto's internal bleeding, she'd hug the nasty crone.

As Yelenarra and Zornamayne murmured, Arnesto rose to Mara's hip and glided toward a tall, arched doorway, stretching twelve or so feet above their heads. The curve of the arch was covered in gold and silver runes that flared up as they passed beneath. Mara kept pace with Arnesto, his hand still wrapped around hers. Thick carpets muffled the sound of their footsteps; all Mara could hear was the quiet buzzing of the women's incantations and Arnesto's wheezing. Mara compressed her lips, concerned with how labored his breathing had become.

Arnesto's hand went limp in hers. "Hurry, he's passed out again!" urged Mara.

Zornamayne held her yellow globe above Arnesto's face and leaned over. She swiped at his lips with one very furry, paw-like hand. "He is definitely bleeding from within. Quick, there is no time to lose." They passed through cavernous rooms, some generously furnished with curving sofas, low tables, and tapestry-covered walls, while others were devoid of all accouterments, with nothing but plain walls, bare floorboards, and tall glazed windows.

They climbed four stories of winding stairs and entered an enormous round bedchamber with a large mahogany bed on the left side of the room, its bed curtains drawn apart. The two fays gently guided Arnesto onto crisp linen sheets. Yelenarra waved her hand, lighting every candle in the chamber at once—inside the wall sconces, on top of two tall dressers, in the candelabra on the brass stand behind the sofa, and on the night stands on either side of the bed.

Mara stepped away and stood near one of the tall, narrow windows inside the round chamber. She waited while the healer examined Arnesto, the woman grunting as she probed his chest and side. Arnesto writhed in pain but didn't waken. Zornamayne removed her veils, and Mara pressed her lips together to keep from gasping out loud. The healer was a hybrid, part large feline, part female fay.

Unlike the misshapen forms that grihms had been forced into during crossbreeding, Zornamayne was breathtaking, with lovely green eyes, a small, pert nose, and delicate whiskers above her pink mouth. She had pointy cat's ears on top of her head, and her fur was champagne colored with touches of black on her front and back paws, her tail, and the tips of her ears.

The healer turned toward Mara. "Tell me exactly what you saw, frame by frame, leaving no details out. This will help me visualize the extent of the injury."

Mara struggled not to stare at the feline-fay healer, who was strange, beautiful, and frightening all at the same time. As she took a deep breath and recounted the accident, Zornamayne peppered her with questions about the angle of the locomobile, the position of Arnesto's body as he fell, and when she first noticed he'd been seriously injured. When Mara finished, Zornamayne turned back to her patient. The healer murmured in buzzes and hisses, and a flask appeared in her paw-like hand. As Yelenarra lifted Arnesto's head from the pillow, Zornamayne poured the potion down his throat. Arnesto choked on the liquid, batting away Zornamayne's hand, but the healer was determined he drink every drop. Arnesto eventually stopped thrashing and fell into a drugged sleep. As Yelenarra laid his head back on the pillow, Mara tiptoed to the bed for a closer look.

Zornamayne waved her hands above Arnesto's injured side and the layers of his skin parted, revealing sinew, muscle, ribs, lung, stomach, and spleen. Mara bit down on her knuckles to keep from crying out. The healer reached into Arnesto's side, muttering incantations as she ran her fingers over the cracked ribs, which knitted themselves back together as Mara watched. She touched the tear in his lung, which closed, and then she reached behind his stomach to gently massage his spleen.

Zornamayne's incantations changed tone and tempo. Rather than hissing and buzzing, she hummed her healing spells while running her furry hands over Arnesto's injuries. His muscles, sinews, and skin repaired themselves before their eyes. Zornamayne's humming changed to whispers. She waved both her hands in the air in a final healing ritual and then stepped back, her shoulders slumped in exhaustion. Yelenarra pushed a small chair beneath the healer, who collapsed into it. "I have done all I can. And now we wait."

Mara stared at the healer. "You mean Arnesto might not improve? That your fay magic may not be enough to save him?" Mara's voice sounded high-pitched and whiney. Anger coursed through her, at the driver who'd intentionally targeted Desna and struck Arnesto, and at this strange cat-woman, who had the worst bedside manner she'd ever encountered.

Zornamayne's head snapped up, and she hissed at Mara. "You can not be so stupid as you sound, not if Arnesto has befriended you. Fays die, just like humans. The fay army suffered heavy losses helping Valerra defeat the Glenbarrans at Wellan Pass, as you must know."

Yelenarra joined Mara on the other side of the bed. She patted Mara between the shoulder blades, a surprisingly motherly gesture, and Mara's eyes stung with unshed tears. The three women: one human, one fay, and one feline-fay hybrid, watched their patient closely for any signs of improvement. Mara's legs grew weary with the waiting, which Yelenarra must have sensed, because Mara found a small cushioned chair behind her legs and dropped down into it. Yelenarra pulled another chair from somewhere in the chamber and sat beside her with a heavy sigh. Mara felt a stab of sympathy for the old woman, who'd raised Arnesto as her son.

Mara stared at Arnesto until her eyes burned, hoping to see whatever sign they were looking for. She was the first to notice the color beginning to creep into his lips again, turning from sickly pale to their normal pinkish color. "Look, I think his color is improving."

Zornamayne rose from her seat to examine Arnesto, pulling down his eyelids, and peering into his mouth. She withdrew a narrow, foot-long silver tube from her robe. Setting one end of the tube against his injured side, Zornamayne placed her ear over the other end and listened. Mara held her breath as she waited.

The healer drew back and smiled, instantly transforming her feline face from scary to serene. "Arnestarious is out of immediate danger, but he needs complete bed rest until the next moonset, and then he may return to normal activities. If he becomes feverish, rub a cloth soaked in witch hazel over his skin. Whilst he is on bed rest, feed Arnestarious a cup of bone broth mixed with a tablespoon of ground angelica root, a pinch of aniseed, and a dash of turmeric."

Mara let out a ragged breath, the anxious knots in her stomach lessening somewhat at the good news. Yelenarra leaned over and kissed Arnesto's forehead. "Thank you, Zornamayne. You always know what to do."

Zornamayne, her veils firmly in place, said, "You may always call upon me. My clan owes you more than we can ever repay." The healer turned to Mara. "I expect our paths shall cross again, since you are Arnestarious's friend."

Mara bowed low to express her gratitude. "Thank you for saving Arnesto's life. He was under my supervision in

Valerra, and I failed him as his coach and friend. I am in your debt, madam healer."

Vaporous tendrils twined around the veiled hybrid, swishing about like the tails of half a dozen alley cats. Zornamayne canted her head to the side. "Aye, I suppose you are. Very well, I shall be sure to collect the debt, friend of Arnestarious." The healer nodded as she vanished into the mists.

CHAPTER 16

Arnesto's hands twitched on the sheets, and he mumbled something unintelligible. Yelenarra gave Mara an apologetic look. "I must prepare the bone broth. Would you stay with Arnestarious until I return?"

"Of course." Mara pulled the small, cushioned seat up closer to the mahogany bed. "I'll be right here, keeping watch over him."

Yelenarra's face softened. "Katrinareus was right about you. My nephew has chosen wisely, but then he has always been a perceptive lad. I sometimes wonder whether the attack that killed his dear mother caused him to dig deeper inside himself and to develop inner reserves of strength and wisdom. He is certainly the youngest fay wizard to achieve twelfth-level mastery."

Yelenarra snapped her fingers and disappeared in a small puff of vapor. Mara assumed Yelenarra didn't have to travel far, probably to her stillroom to grind the herbs and then to her kitchen to make up the broth. However, the distances could be deceiving, since the manor felt more like a museum than a home.

Arnesto stirred occasionally. Each time, Mara reached across the bed to take his hand, which immediately calmed him. While Mara knew the basics of healing, gained on the battlefield, she would be the first to acknowledge she was no healer. She pondered why the touch of her hand soothed Arnesto. Did it have something to do with the fact he thought of her as his field coach and therefore an authority of sorts? Or was it because they had declared their friendship, which seemed to take on special significance inside Havynweal?

Arnesto started mumbling again and seemed more agitated. "Hush now, you need to rest," she whispered, slipping her hand inside Arnesto's. He sighed and settled down again. Mara stifled a yawn and tried to calculate how many hours she'd been awake. She'd been managing on a couple of hours of sleep for the past few nights, and she hadn't stopped once since arriving at the bakery at three forty-five the previous morning. Mara figured she'd had maybe six hours of sleep in the past seventy-two hours, and it was starting to take a toll.

Her eyelids grew heavy. She tried blinking herself awake. Yawning again, she thought she might lay her head on the coverlet briefly. Arnesto was still gripping her hand, and she couldn't lean back against the chair without disturbing him. She closed her eyes and drifted into a fitful sleep, dreaming in odd little snippets of Arnesto: pulling pack his hair to show her the scars left by the undead creature; dueling in Vas's basement with a mastery she'd been surprised to see; falling as he was struck by the speeding locomobile. And then came the image she'd seen before, Arnesto's fay-blue hair blowing and his arms raised in the air, commanding the elements in a mighty windstorm.

Mara woke to the low murmur of voices somewhere

nearby, perhaps in the hall outside the bedchamber. She raised her head from the coverlet and grimaced at her stiff neck. Arnesto was resting quietly and had finally released her hand from his grip. She brought her freed hand up to rub the back of her neck and leaned against the chair. She had no idea how long she'd been asleep, but she could see blue sky beyond the narrow windows of the round chamber and she heard birdsong.

Mara glanced down at her crumpled blouse, missing two buttons, and at her grass-stained, torn skirt, and wrinkled her nose. She was a sore sight, but there was nothing to be done about it. She had no change of clothes at hand and had more important things to worry about than her wardrobe. She had liked the blue jersey skirt, though, which was ruined. At this rate she'd have to purchase an entirely new wardrobe, although without a steady paycheck that would be impossible. No matter, she had to help Vas and Katrine figure out who was behind the fires, and she had to keep Arnesto safe.

Mara drew her brows together. Where had that last part come from? Why did she think she had to keep Arnesto safe? She thought about her dreams, shaking her head about the last image of Arnesto raising his arms in the midst of a storm. She was forgetting something—something important about him that she'd realized as she slept.

She looked at Arnesto, running her dream images, all of which were fading rapidly from memory, through her head. If she could just recall that one critical connection she'd realized while she slept, then she could tell Yelenarra and Katrine. And of course, Arnesto, once he was recovered. Together, they could figure out what it meant.

"I thought I heard you stirring," whispered Yelenarra, who'd entered the room silently and tapped Mara on the shoulder. "Come, lass, follow me. I trust you could benefit from a spot of breakfast, a lie-down on a real bed, and then perhaps a bath and change of clothes."

Mara couldn't decide what she wanted most: to stretch out on a bed, take a bath, or change her clothes. However, she knew she ought to have something to eat first. She'd been too busy snooping around at the guildhall the previous night to eat much of her dinner. Mara followed Yelenarra out of the bedchamber and down the winding stairs. "I thought I heard voices earlier, when I first woke up."

Yelenarra nodded. "Aye. Katrinareus has come and gone."

Mara sighed, unable to keep the disappointment from her voice. "I'd hoped to be able to speak with Katrine while I was visiting. There's so much to catch her up on."

"She peeked in to check on Arnesto and say hello to you, but she could not stay. The fay council occupies most of her time, now that the chief has taken his holiday."

"Is it worse than usual?"

"Aye. Katrinareus cannot get them to agree on how to handle the latest threats from the dark fays. And if she is gone too long, the council will take a vote without her, and then half the council will believe the other half has snookered them. They will wind up bickering for another week or two and accomplish nothing." Mara had heard stories about the fay council from Chief Pryl, Katrine's half-brother. The fay chief had traveled back and forth to Havynweal all the time for one vote or another, which always left him grouchy afterward.

"Why not just disband the fay council, if it's so ineffective?"

Yelenarra arched one eyebrow and lowered the other,

which Mara felt certain Arnesto had learned from his aunt. "Nay, that would be much, much worse. Legends and fay tales have been written about Havynweal before the last remnant of fays laid down their weapons, ending the five-hundred-year civil war that nearly wiped out our race. We are far better off with councilors who fight with words and votes than with swords and arrows. Far less bloodshed."

"I suppose it's not much different from what Vas has to deal with right now with the provisional governors. They argue constantly, about nearly everything."

They reached the bottom stair and Mara had her first real glimpse of Arnesto's home. Early sunlight streamed through the floor-to-ceiling windows of the largest parlor Mara had ever seen. Curved sofas in bold splashes of color dotted the room, which was punctuated by tall potted plants, dark teakwood and marble low tables, a pianoforte in the far corner, and silver candelabras sitting on end tables or standing behind sofas, positioned for an evening of entertainment or quiet reading.

One massive triptych painting occupied the longest wall opposite where they stood. Mara glanced at the triptych and took a step closer, surprised to see the legend of Sollara, the young fay girl whose magic defeated an evil giant and created the Swords of Five, depicted on the wall. Yelenarra nodded at the last illustration, showing the swords upheld in battle by Sollara's five brothers, the original owners of the ensorcelled weapons. "Which one do you own?"

Mara skirted around a blue-and-gold sofa and several end tables so she could stand in the center of the room. She pointed at the sword with the blue hieroglyphs flashing brilliantly and almost felt her sword calling to her, from under the bed in her flat.

The details in the painting were remarkable. But who was the artist? And how old was the painting? Based on what Mara and Katrine had pieced together about the five swords discovered at the Valerran Museum, some unknown fay had hidden them in the Weapons Room two hundred years earlier.

"I own the blue sword, or more accurately, the blue sword chose me, back in the Weapons Room at the museum. We'd tried to select our own weapons, but these swords have a mind of their own. I'm just surprised at the level of detail and accuracy here in this painting. Who is the artist?"

Yelenarra raised her palms to the ceiling. "That triptych is as old as this house, which has been in our family since the beginning."

"Since the beginning?" Mara followed Yelenarra out of the parlor and down a wide hallway. Plush rugs in rich jewel tones covered the dark wooden floor; vivid blues, deep reds and purples, and bright greens and golds formed swirling patterns that reminded Mara of constellations captured in silken thread. All the walls were whitewashed stucco, clean and spare.

"The beginning of our family tree. My ancestors claimed this mountain and constructed this home at the end of our long civil war. None other has ever lived within its walls." Mara didn't realize they were on a mountain. She wondered whether she could explore the area with Arnesto when he was feeling better. Valerra had lovely green hills, but none could ever qualify as a mountain.

"Eframallium! I did not hear you arrive." Yelenarra's face lit up as she greeted another of her nephews.

Efram bowed to his aunt and Mara. "I came as soon as I heard. How is Arnesto?" Efram's eyebrows rose almost to his hairline as he took in Mara's rumpled appearance. He was impeccably dressed in his stretchy silver garb, which never seemed to wrinkle, pill, or tear.

Mara hadn't even had a chance to comb her hair, which had come undone from its ponytail and now hung about her shoulders in a mass of blonde tangles. She stifled a sigh. Mara never left her flat without ensuring every hair was in place, her boots shined, and her outfits tasteful and well accessorized, right down to the handkerchief inside her reticule. But in the span of a week—ever since Arnesto had entered her life—she'd become an unfashionable wreck and utterly useless spy.

Yelenarra took Efram's arm, and they continued down the hallway past a library that beckoned to Mara with its shelves of books, a morning room decorated in shades of rose and teal, and a great hall that was devoid of most furnishings. Large enough to fit Mara's entire apartment building, the hall was composed of white walls, dark floors, a row of low tables pushed against one wall, and a scattering of colorful floor cushions stacked beneath the unadorned windows. Eight chandeliers hung from the center of the arched ceiling.

Yelenarra gave Efram a quick summary of Zornamayne's visit and Arnesto's condition. "I need to bring your brother his bone broth. Please take Maragold into the small dining room where I have laid out your breakfast. And then show her to the Amber Room."

Yelenarra turned to Mara. "I almost forgot, Katrinareus left this note for you." Yelenarra withdrew a folded piece of parchment from the pocket of her apron. She handed the note to Mara, who wished she could escape to a private spot to read it immediately. Instead, she thanked Yelenarra and tucked the piece of parchment inside her ruined reticule, which had been dangling from her left wrist during the accident and somehow she'd managed to retain—one more essential accessory from her dwindling wardrobe in need of replacement.

Efram guided Mara to a long, low teakwood table inside the "small" dining room, which could easily accommodate Katrine's entire shop within its four walls, plus the haberdashery and Desna's bakery. Cheerful silk rugs covered the room's dark floors and muffled their footsteps. The mansion was silent as a monument and far too quiet, reminding Mara once again of a museum, not a home. How had a young, troubled fay boy ever gotten to sleep at night, up in that turret bedroom all by himself?

Efram gestured at the gold-tasseled, red floor cushions near one end of the table, which had been set for two. He insisted on serving Mara, pouring her a mug of hot coffee with cream, and piling up her plate with scrambled eggs, strips of crispy bacon, a berry scone, and seasoned potatoes. She thought perhaps he was trying to feed her three meals for breakfast.

He sat opposite her and waited until she'd had a few forkfuls of egg, a strip of bacon, and a bite of her scone. "Tell me about the accident."

Mara took a long swallow from her mug and then set it down on the table. She repeated the same details she'd shared with Zornamayne. When she was finished, she added, "I'm so sorry. I should have protected your brother better, warned him about the dangers of speeding locomobiles."

Efram shook his head. "Please stop. This is not your fault. Arnesto is no fool. He took a calculated risk, saved a man's life, and was injured in the process. Thankfully,

Zornamayne is the most talented healer in Havynweal, and if she believes Arnesto is on the mend, then he is."

Mara nodded but didn't reply. Her emotions were as tangled as her hair at the moment, and she couldn't explain herself even if she tried. The only things anchoring her were the belief that Arnesto would heal and her instinct that something about the accident was all wrong. If only she could recall the clue from her dreams that had to do with Arnesto, then she could begin righting the wrong.

Efram pointed at the note from Katrine, which Mara had placed next to her plate. "Go ahead and read it. I promise not to pry for at least ten more minutes, or however long it will take me to finish my breakfast. Besides, I expect that Katrine will ask me to escort you to wherever she wants you to go inside Havynweal."

"How do you know she wants me to go anywhere?"

Efram gave Mara the same sardonic look Arnesto had mastered, his head tilted to the side and his arms folded across his chest. "This is Katrine we're talking about. She'll have something in mind for you to do while you're here."

Mara opened the note, drawing immediate comfort from Katrine's familiar scrawl:

Mara,

I'm thankful you and Arnesto were not injured in the shop fire, which was arson and not anything you did or didn't do. So stop feeling guilty about the fire and Arnesto's subsequent accident. I've informed Chef Desna of the extent of Arnesto's injuries and that you are required to nurse him back to health.

Something's afoot, but I can't say more at the moment.
Come see me this afternoon for tea. Efram knows
the way.
~K

Mara handed the note to Efram. He quickly read through the few lines and scowled. "Katrine can't say more or won't say more. Which is it, I wonder?"

"Maybe she'll tell us more in person."

"You may be right, given where we'll be meeting her later.

Mara tucked the note back into her reticule. "What's that supposed to mean?"

Efram snorted. "You'll see. In the meantime, get some rest. You look like you might fall over any minute. I'm sure Yelenarra will find you something suitable to wear while you're in Havynweal."

Mara waved a hand at her blouse and skirt, both beyond repair. "You mean this won't do?"

Efram grinned and then immediately sobered. "This isn't just about changing out of your stained clothes; it's about changing into a disguise. Where we're heading, we'll want to pass you off as a fay."

Mara touched her hair. "But how? Any fay is going to see right through whatever glamour Yelenarra might cast on me."

"My aunt is quite ingenious. Wait and see. But first"—Efram took a final bite of his second breakfast—"let me show you to the Amber Room."

"It sounds mysterious." Mara followed Efram out of the dining room. They turned down a series of corridors, all with the same white walls, dark wooden floors, and plush carpets. Mara became quite lost and didn't think she'd be able to find her way without an escort. While most of the doors were firmly closed, she peeked into any of the open rooms; one was filled with statuary, from beautiful nymphs and mermaids to ugly gargoyles and trolls; another was a greenhouse, with glazed windows on three sides and filled with an exotic variety of flowering plants and herbs. They walked past a square room with an enormous fireplace occupying one entire wall and a floor-to-ceiling map on the other. Various swords, spears, staffs, and bow sets hung on the remaining two walls. *Is that where Arnesto practiced his weaponry?* Mara wondered.

They started to climb winding stone steps similar to those leading to Arnesto's turret. "In case you're curious, the house boasts six such turrets. Five are private bedchambers and the sixth is an open tower, once used as a lookout, but now used for stargazing."

"How does your aunt manage with all these stairs? She's appears in excellent condition, but this is still a lot of climbing."

"My aunt travels by mists nearly everywhere these days. She only takes the stairs out of deference to you, as her guest."

"I see," said Mara, suddenly feeling insufficient for such a home and such remarkable magic on display everywhere. *Why would Arnesto want to leave all of this and become a fay scout in Valerra?*

Mara posed the question to Efram, who spread his hands wide, palms outward. "Arnesto is burdened by the past, by what he saw and survived when he was a boy. He believes it is his duty to prevent what happened to him from happening to anyone else."

"And he's convinced Bazeerkalim's descendants are targeting Valerra?"

"Aye. Katrine and my aunt agree. If Chief Pryl were here, he'd be in their camp as well. But the fay council..." Efram didn't finish his sentence.

"It's like the war with Glenbarra all over again."

"Nay, it's worse," grunted Efram. "The Bazeerka are fays, and as such, the fays in Havynweal have no excuse. The fay council knows what happens when evil is unopposed, but they are turning a blind eye, just the same."

Efram pushed open the heavy wooden door to the Amber Room and stepped aside. "I'm going to visit Arnesto now, and then I'll be back this afternoon, at three o'clock on your timepiece."

Mara frowned at Efram's awkward phrasing. "Why would it be three o'clock on my timepiece and not elsewhere? You've never set up an appointment that way before."

Efram grinned. "You've never set foot in Havynweal before. We don't use timepieces or clocks here." Mara reflected that probably explained a good deal about Arnesto's tardiness, although he had started improving. The mists twined around Efram's legs and waist. He waved goodbye before blinking out.

Mara entered the round bedchamber, as large and impressive as Arnesto's. But where his had been cool blues and dark greens, this room was, as its name suggested, decorated in shades of coral, peach, and amber. Like everywhere else in the home, the floors, doors, and trim were dark wood, and the walls whitewashed. Mara removed her boots before stepping onto the plush rug, a swirl of orange and yellow, with dashes of red. She wiggled her toes as her feet sank into the silken fibers.

A large bed occupied one side of the room, piled high with several feather mattresses. The ochre bed curtains were pulled back invitingly, and the coverlet turned down. On the opposite side of the room were a small sofa, a low table, and candelabra for reading at night. Eight tall, narrow windows gave a panoramic view of the world beyond Arnesto's home. In between two of the windows stood an enormous dresser-armoire combination, sizeable enough to fit Mara's entire wardrobe twice over.

She wandered over to the closest window, left open to air out the room, and gasped. Mara made a complete circuit around the chamber, peering out of each window before returning to the first one. Yelenarra hadn't exaggerated when she said the ancestral home had been built on a mountain. From Mara's vantage point, she saw low-hanging clouds floating by, a brilliant globe of yellow-pink sun shining through the windows behind her, an expanse of green lawn around the home itself, and then sharp crags and ragged peaks everywhere above and below them. Much farther down, in the valley below, she could see bright green grass and flashes of brilliant color in the meadows and gardens. She tried recalling Arnesto's favorite Havynweal season. Was it auburn summer? If so, it was a long way down to that lovely-looking valley. Mara wouldn't be exploring the grounds outside the home without an escort who knew the area well; otherwise, she might find herself falling into a crevice or tumbling off a ledge.

As compelling as the view was from Mara's turret bedchamber, she was so exhausted she could barely think. She'd hoped for a bath, or at the very least, a small washbasin and towel so she could wash off the grime from the previous day before lying down on the bed. She noticed a small crack in the round wall to the right of the sofa and drew closer. The crack was actually a seam, which ran up one side, across a span of about thirty inches, and then down the other side.

Mara placed her palm against the seam running along the right side and pushed. She heard several clicks, as if someone were unlocking a padlock, and the wall swung open to reveal a private bathroom suite. But when Mara approached the brass tub, which stood upon four sturdy-looking claw and ball feet, she couldn't find any faucets. The same was true with the delicate shell-shaped sink set in a marble shelf. Even the water closet had no levers or pulls for flushing. She threw up her hands, not sure how to go about requesting water. Did she have to descend the four flights of stone steps and search for Yelenarra?

She plunked herself down on the edge of the bathtub and heard the sound of warbling water nearby. She looked over her shoulder and jumped up, startled. Water was filling the bottom of the tub. When she hopped off, the water stopped. Shrugging, Mara sat back on the tub's rim and remained there until the tub had filled. She dipped a finger in the water, which was exactly right, neither too cool nor too hot. Mara searched the cupboard and found a towel and bar of soap, as well as a cotton robe hanging on a hook. She eagerly peeled off her clothes and stepped into the tub, enjoying a good soaking in the perfectly tempera-ture-controlled water. Even twenty minutes later, the bath-water was still comfortably warm.

Once again, Mara marveled at Arnesto's decision to leave all of this behind so he could live and work in Valerra at a variety of menial, and in some cases, dangerous tasks, in the off chance he might be able to do something about the dark fays. She hadn't appreciated him enough; she simply hadn't realized what he'd given up by deciding to leave Havynweal. That was true of her other fay friends as well—Wreyn, who'd died during the war, and Efram, who'd fought alongside his Valerran friends. Even Chief Inspector Talias had left this behind for the Valerran man she'd fallen in love with. And then there was Katrine, who'd chosen to live in Valerra as a young woman rather than return home to Havynweal. Katrine's decision had been more youthful rebellion than anything else, but even so, she'd given up a great deal when she'd moved to Bellaryss and kept her true identity a secret.

Mara climbed out of the tub, dried off with the towel, and wrapped herself inside the robe. She peeked inside the bathtub and watched as the water receded. She wondered whether the tub cleaned itself too. Now *that* would be very useful magic indeed.

Yawning, Mara opened the curved door of the bathroom suite and padded over to the bed. She climbed under the covers with a small sigh and fell immediately to sleep.

Mara woke some hours later, the back of her neck tingling. She felt uneasy, almost as if she were being watched. She opened one eye and noticed a shadow across her bed that hadn't been there when she'd turned in. Mara slowly reached under her pillow for the small dagger she always slept with. She remembered with a jolt she wasn't in Valerra any more—and her only weapons were still tucked inside her boots on the other side of the room.

CHAPTER 17

"My lady Maragold, please do not be alarmed," squawked a distinctly female, though somewhat birdlike voice.

Mara sat up and reared back against the bedpost, startled to find a miniature griffin standing on the bottom of the bed, cocking her head at Mara. The only griffin she'd ever met had belonged to her friend Linden. The griffin flicking its tail back and forth on her bed looked quite similar, even down to her coloring. She had the face of an eagle, framed by a shaggy red mane streaked with white, the compact body of a small lion, and a strong pair of wings. However, Mara had never heard Kal speak. A talking miniature griffin was an entirely new phenomenon, one that would take some getting used to.

Mara cleared her throat. "Greetings, Madam Griffin. I am at a disadvantage, since I do not know your name."

The griffin flapped her wings, which caused the bed curtains to flutter. "I am called Gloria. Although I am come for another purpose, I wonder whether you bear any news of my youngest son, Kal, Griffin Companion of the Lady Liege.

Mara wasn't sure of the protocol for greeting talking griffins, but she relied on her stepmother's etiquette training; when in doubt, go formal. "I am very pleased to meet you, Griffin Gloria. I am happy to report I saw your son, Griffin Kal, several months ago. He was in good health and accompanying Liege Linden back to Faynwood."

Gloria clicked her beak a few times and bobbed her head. "Thank you for confirming, Lady Maragold. A mother never ceases to worry about her offspring."

"Quite so," said Mara. "I believe you mentioned something about there being an altogether different reason for your visit?"

Gloria turned around and hopped from the bed to the rug. "Aye, but perhaps you might like to dress? I realize I have called upon you at a most inopportune time, given that you are still enrobed." Gloria padded over to the armoire and using her beak, pecked at the latch. The armoire swung open to reveal dresses—day dresses, evening dresses, ball gowns, even several riding habits—all in the current fashion, or what had been the fashion before the war. Mara wandered over and pulled out a pale rose dress with an empire waist and short cap sleeves. She held it up to herself.

"Oh, it shall surely fit, milady. It is magicked for your dimensions." Gloria tapped the adjacent dresser with her front paw. "You will find your undergarments in here. The next drawer down contains headpieces that will disguise your blonde hair color. And in the bottom drawer are shoes, dancing slippers, and ankle boots, all sized for you."

Mara swallowed, not sure whether she should be wearing any of the clothing. Perhaps they were intended for some other guest. Well, except for the headpieces, which seemed to have been designed for her. Gloria noticed her hesitation. "Lady Maragold, the last guest to stay in this suite was Arnestarious's dear mother. I can assure you, Lady Yelenarra has conjured these clothes for you. Please go ahead and dress. I shall wander over here to the open window to allow you some privacy."

Mara had nothing else to wear, other than the stained clothes she'd arrived in. She selected what she needed among the undergarments, and then found a pair of dusky rose ankle boots in the shoe drawer. Returning once again to the armoire, Mara sorted through the collection of hooded capes for outdoor use. The long burgundy cape would do just fine when she left to visit Katrine later with Efram.

Mara slipped into the bathroom suite to change. Searching the cupboard she found a hairbrush, a comb, and ribbons. After a dozen painful passes with the brush and some close work on a few remaining knots with the comb, Mara pulled her hair back into a low ponytail. She surveyed herself in the looking glass on the wall next to the cupboard. Gloria was right; the pale rose dress was a perfect fit.

Mara returned to the bedchamber. "I wonder whether there might be a reticule?" she said aloud.

Gloria turned around from the window. "Try the small drawer on the left." Sure enough, Mara found as many reticules tucked inside, as there were dresses in the armoire. She selected a burgundy that matched the cape.

Gloria bobbed her head. "I am sure you must feel better. It is always awkward to meet someone new when dressed in a bathrobe. Leastways, I would imagine that to be the case."

"Aye, thank you. This is much better," agreed Mara. "And now, please tell me why you are here."

Gloria clicked her beak a few times and wandered over to the sofa. She pawed at it. "You may want to have a seat, milady."

Mara was beginning to grow impatient with the griffin, who seemed to have something important to impart but was reluctant to get to the point. "Very well." She took a seat and peered into the griffin's amber eyes. "Why have you come today?"

The griffin curled her front legs beneath her and bowed forward. "I wish to offer myself as your companion, Lady Maragold, sworn friend of Laird Arnestarious the Fourteenth."

Mara wasn't sure what she'd expected, but this was surely not it. Gloria wanted to become her griffin? Or perhaps it was more of a mutual thing, where Gloria chose her, and Mara chose to accept or decline? But how could Mara refuse the companionship of a talking, magical, miniature pet griffin? On the other hand, how could she possibly care for Gloria in Valerra given the state of her finances?

Gloria noticed her confusion, and she dropped her head to her chest. "I see you are uncertain about whether you wish to accept my offer. I realize, of course, most griffins are decades younger when they choose to become companions, but my children are all grown with lives of their own. I am not a griffin to sit by the fire and speak of her glory days. Nay, my best days are ahead, serving milady and helping you fight the dark fays."

"My dear Gloria, I don't know what to say. I am flattered, and a bit flummoxed as well. I don't know how to care for a griffin—"

Gloria flapped her wings and squawked. "That is one advantage I have. I am quite capable of caring for myself, unlike Kal and my other younglings, who needed to learn to hunt and preen and fly. I can read and write too. Very few griffins boast those skills."

"That is quite impressive. Tell me, do you have much acquaintance with Bellaryss, where I live?"

Gloria bobbed her head. "I visited the Sunrise City several times in my youth. Quite a lovely sight to behold."

Mara clasped her hands together. "It was a lovely city before the war, but much of it is in rubble and ruin now. We are starting to rebuild, but then with the recent fires, I don't know how long it will be before we have a real city again. Do you really want to leave Havynweal for Valerra?"

Gloria hopped onto the sofa. "I wish to serve you, milady, and that means where you go, I shall follow. Your home shall be my home, and your friends shall be mine." Gloria rested her head on Mara's lap. Her sincerity touched Mara, warming some of the lonely places inside. *Here is a creature that wants to be with me, who chose me. How can I possibly turn this lovely griffin away? Besides, she seems as lonely as I am, or as I was, before Arnesto came along.*

Mara suddenly needed to see Arnesto, to check on him and ensure he was truly on the mend. And she needed to give the griffin her answer. Mara reached a tentative hand out to Gloria and rubbed between her wings. Gloria purred, nestling a bit closer. Mara laughed. "I think we will do just fine together, you and me."

Gloria clicked her beak excitedly. "Thank you, milady. I shall serve you with honor all my days. And now, I really think you ought to visit Arnestarious. I sense you are anxious to see him."

"Are you a mind reader, Gloria?"

Gloria clicked her beak and shook her head. "Not minds, but emotions. Griffins can read emotions even better than fays. Please go see him. I will find myself some lunch among the mice population down below. I shall return to accompany you on your visit to Katrinareus." Gloria hopped down and practically shooed Mara from the room.

Mara descended the winding stone staircase, confused by what had just transpired, but also excited. She now had a pet griffin, just like Linden. She wondered when they might see each other again. More than distance separated them, but circumstance and duty too. One day, when Bellaryss was safe again, Mara would take a trip to Faynwood with Gloria.

She reached the bottom of the stairs and retraced her path with Efram earlier, or what she could recall of it. Mara was fairly certain Arnesto's turret chamber was located on the opposite side of the house. She merely had to locate the large parlor with the triptych painting, and she could find her way from there. Easier said than done. Mara wandered about for a good twenty-five minutes before she found the parlor. She might have to ask Yelenarra to conjure a map for her if she were staying any longer.

Mara paused. Why did she possibly think she'd be staying in Havynweal longer? She had to return to the bakery soon, although she didn't want to leave Arnesto until he was feeling better. She hoped to spend some time exploring the fay lands, since she didn't think she'd ever have another chance. But Vas and Katrine were counting on her to uncover some sort of a clue at the Triple B or inside the Bakers Guild.

Mara was beginning to think the only clue she'd come across was what she'd already observed and what Vas already knew. There was a strong anti-magic movement among many Valerrans, and if the bakers were feeling that way, what about the other guilds? Further, what had some disgruntled anti-magic bakers to do with the fires the other night, the murdered baker at the pub, or the problems at the grihm preserve?

Mara was tired of all the half clues and theories. She yearned for action, not more talk, and she was ready—if only someone would point her in the right direction. She hoped Katrine would do just that when she saw her later in the day.

CHAPTER 18

THE DOOR TO ARNESTO'S CHAMBER STOOD OPEN. YELENARRA MUST have left to prepare more bone broth because Arnesto was alone in the room. Mara sat in the same chair she'd occupied earlier and observed him closely. He no longer thrashed about as he slept, which she took as an encouraging sign.

Arnesto stirred. His eyes still closed, he extended his hand across the bed toward her. Mara leaned over and took his hand. He entwined his fingers through hers and murmured. "You are still here."

"Aye," whispered Mara. "I won't leave until I see you are well on the road to recovery."

Arnesto's mouth twitched. "My aunt's horrible bone broth ought to do the trick nicely. The dregs alone would wake the undead."

Mara breathed a sigh of relief. If Arnesto could crack jokes, he must be on the mend. But why did she have this lingering feeling he was still in danger? Then Mara remembered her odd dreams about Arnesto during the middle of the night. She'd connected the dots while sleeping and promptly forgot them when she awoke. "The accident—it was no accident!"

"I believe I made a similar observation to Chef Desna."

"No, aye, you did, but that's not what I mean," Mara explained. "I don't believe Chef Desna was the intended target. You were."

Arnesto squeezed her hand. "I know, but please do not tell my aunt." His eyes fluttered open. "She will only worry and may do something rash."

"Very well. I won't say anything for now to Yelenarra, but I will tell Efram and Katrine. I need more eyes on you than just mine."

Arnesto's mouth twitched again and then he yawned. "Please come see me later, after you have spoken with Katrine." Then Arnesto did the most unexpected thing. He brought her hand up to his lips for a kiss.

Mara's heart thundered in her chest, all the while her head tried to understand what was happening. Her fay trainee should not be kissing her, period. And she should not be enjoying it, exclamation point. Arnesto fell back asleep, and Mara simply stared, still processing her feelings. His grip loosened on her fingers. She gently withdrew her hand and rose from the chair. Mara hurried to the door and then looked back to ensure Arnesto was still sleeping, still safe for the moment.

Yelenarra emerged from a puff of mist inside the chamber, carrying a fresh pot of broth in one hand and a large spoon in the other. The elder fay smiled at Mara. "You are looking much more rested, lass. Are you coming or going?"

"Just leaving. Arnesto woke briefly and then fell back to sleep."

"Did he say anything? Anything at all?" Yelenarra nearly spilled her pot of broth in her excitement.

Mara had promised not to say anything to Yelenarra about Arnesto being the intended target of the speeding locomobile. But she had to tell the woman something. "He complained about the bone broth."

Yelenarra's eyes crinkled in the corners. "It is working then. He only complains when he is starting to feel better."

Mara grinned. "Aye, your broth is definitely helping."

Yelenarra pointed at Mara's rose gown with her spoon. "Do you like it?"

"Very much. Thank you for your kindness."

The fay woman waved the spoon in the air. "It is my pleasure, Maragold. You are my nephew's friend, and as such you are now part of my family. Oh, I almost forgot—Eframallium is waiting for you in the library downstairs. Please fill me in after your visit with Katrinareus. Whilst you are gone, I shall remake a corner of your bedchamber for your Griffin Companion. I am so thrilled to have a griffin in residence again."

Yelenarra turned and headed toward the bed, intent on spooning the herbaceous broth down Arnesto's throat. Mara stared after the elderly fay, no longer surprised that everyone in Havynweal seemed to know what was going on at any given moment, before being told. But she wasn't sure what to make of Yelenarra's comments about having a griffin in residence. Mara wouldn't be staying *that* long. And she needed to ascertain the fay meaning behind being someone's friend. It seemed to take on special significance inside Havynweal. But perhaps the Valerrans had diminished the meaning of friendship over time and the fays had it right.

"How is Arnesto doing?" Efram had been reading a scroll on one of the study tables in the library. He placed two brass paperweights, one shaped like a griffin, the other a unicorn, on either side of the page to mark the spot where he'd left off.

"He woke up briefly, long enough to complain about your aunt's bone broth." *And to kiss my hand.* "I left my cape, and er, my griffin, upstairs in the Amber Room. I'll go retrieve them both now."

Efram jumped up from the desk chair where he'd been studying the scroll, knocking the chair to the floor. He bent down to right the chair. "Did you just say you had a griffin? When did this happen? And do I know the griffin?"

"This happened less than two hours ago. And the griffin's name is Gloria. She is Kal's mother."

Efram's jaw opened and closed, but no sound came out. He finally managed to sputter, "It's extremely rare for a griffin to attach itself to a human."

"You mean to a human who isn't destined to become the Liege of Faynwood, like Linden?"

"Aye, like Linden. But I'm curious...what did Gloria say when she offered to be your companion?"

Mara repeated what she could recall of the meandering conversation with the griffin. "And then Gloria curled her front paws beneath her, bowed to me, and said, 'I wish to offer myself as your companion, Lady Maragold, sworn friend of Laird Arnestarious the Fourteenth.'" Mara noticed Efram's eyes had popped open wider. "What? Why are you looking at me like that?"

Efram glanced back down at the scroll spread open on the table. "I'm not sure I know what you are talking about."

Mara drew her brows together. "I think you do know what I'm talking about, but you're avoiding it for some reason." Efram resumed studying his scroll, and Mara left to pick up her cape from her bedchamber. She knew Efram was right; it was unusual for a griffin to attach itself to an ordinary human. Mara still couldn't fathom why Gloria had picked her. She couldn't boast about any special qualifications, certainly none that would attract a griffin.

After coming home to an empty flat after work each night, finding Gloria waiting for her in the Amber Room gave Mara a cozy, homespun sort of a feeling. The griffin's presence soothed something inside Mara, smoothed over jagged places she hadn't realized were there. Mara spotted her tall leather boots shined to a gleam and canted her head. "Did you...?"

Gloria bobbed her head. "I thought perhaps you might want to wear your boots beneath your gown, since you can't very well hide your blades inside those little ankle boots."

Mara compressed her lips and thought about the implications. "But Arnesto has explained to me that fays no longer settle their differences with fisticuffs or blades."

The griffin hunched her shoulders forward. "And yet he carries the scars from an attack that killed his mother."

"An undead creature attacked him, not another fay."

"An undead creature under the control of a fay from the outer demesnes. Havynweal fays call the others the 'dark fays' or the 'Bazeerka' but they are all the same to me. They are dangerous fays and you must be careful, especially since Arnestarious is indisposed right now and unable to assist you."

Mara couldn't argue with Gloria's logic. She changed into her tall boots and slipped her thin blades into the holsters inside each shank. She transferred the contents of her ruined reticule into the new burgundy bag, including her brass knuckles and a small pocketknife, plus a fresh linen handkerchief from the dresser drawer.

Mara drew on the burgundy cape and headed to the

door, but Gloria called out, "Aren't you forgetting something?"

Mara turned back to find Gloria tapping the drawer containing the headpieces. "Aye, I'd completely forgotten about my hair."

Mara hurried back and opened the drawer. She surveyed the wimples, in a rainbow of colors to match the gowns, all of the same simple design—a sparkly gold or silver headband with a long scarf attached. She pulled out a pale rose chiffon and placed the gold headband over her head, adjusting it until the band fit squarely across her forehead. The wimple draped in graceful folds over her hair and shoulders.

"Yelenarra is a genius!"

Gloria cackled. "Careful not to say that in her presence or she will never allow you to forget it."

The two of them returned to the library together, Gloria padding alongside Mara as they descended the stairs and passed through wide, silent corridors. After introductions were made and Efram told Gloria how much he admired Kal, her son, the three of them left on Efram's traveling mists. They landed in a glade of dense maple and oak trees, their orange, red, and gold leaves beginning to turn metallic around the edges, indicating they would soon be ready to fall to the ground.

Mara pulled her cape more closely around her shoulders as a cool eddy of air swirled around them. "So we're somewhere in harvest fall then?"

"Aye, on the cusp of frosty fall, but not quite. Come along, you'll want to see this."

They stepped out of the copse of trees and onto a brick road. A country village lay a short distance away. Mara saw a number of fays milling about on the town green, where colorful tents had been set up. Efram stopped walking suddenly and smacked his forehead. "Oh, I almost forgot. If anyone addresses you, cross your forearms in front of you, your palms facing inward, and bow your head, like this—" Efram demonstrated.

"Why?"

Efram arched an eyebrow. "Unless you've learned to speak fay in the past few days, you won't have a clue what they are saying. Katrine and my aunt do not want it bandied about that we have a human in our midst. Old prejudices die hard, you know."

Mara scowled. It seemed everyone held to their own versions of what they believed to be true regardless of reality. Many Valerrans had anti-magic biases, which translated into distrust of Faymons and fays; Faymons struggled to believe anyone from Valerra could become a proper Serving mage given their weaker bloodlines; and in Havynweal fays simply didn't want humans around. She found it all so discouraging and told Efram.

He took her elbow and guided her toward the village. "When things get darkest, Valerrans, Faymons, and fays will band together, just like we did against the Glenbarrans and Mordahn."

Gloria agreed. "Eframallium is quite correct. In the meantime, please do not allow the pettiness of others to bring you down."

Mara took a deep breath of the fresh, crisp air and exhaled. "You're both right, of course. It's just such a huge waste of energy."

The sound of pipers striking up a lively tune on the town green cheered Mara somewhat. Efram sniffed. "I believe someone is selling iced cardamom buns, and I must have some with my tea. Come along, I can see Katrine over there haggling with her favorite bookseller."

"But I thought fays don't use money."

"We have no need of money since we rely on a bartering system to exchange magical favors. However, we do enjoy driving a good bargain."

Mara felt as if she'd entered a storybook version of a country village, with the large swath of green grass in the center surrounded on four sides by quaint gray stone buildings, most of them two or three stories. The buildings were a hodgepodge of shops and homes, with blue and red and green awnings over their glazed windows, and flowerpots filled with mums on every stoop. Striped tents ringed the green and were scattered haphazardly across the middle, with vendors selling everything from cauldrons to potions to books and cakes.

Mara's mood lightened considerably at the sight of her fay boss, her signature blue turban on top of her short curls. A small woman about sixty years young, with a strong chin and dark brown eyes that missed nothing, Katrine wore a purple flannel shirt and baggy red pants. That's when Mara noticed none of the fays on the green were dressed in their normal stretchy silver or gold fabrics. Instead, they wore flannel or cotton button-down shirts and baggy pants like Katrine, as well as dresses with high or low waists, and long or short sleeves, all in a variety of fabrics and colors. One young woman even wore a bright green ball gown with a long train, and her companion was dressed in black tails and top hat.

She turned to ask Efram about the odd-looking outfits on display and discovered he was no longer in his silver cape, tunic, and trousers. Instead, Efram wore a green cloak over a darker green cotton shirt and brown slacks. He leaned over to explain, "We like to dress the part of country villagers on market day in harvest fall. We will even haggle with paper money just for the fun of it."

"Ah, I see," said Mara, not sure what else to say. She glanced at Gloria, who gave a little shoulder roll as if to say she didn't get it either.

They approached the bookseller and Katrine, arguing in a series of buzzes and hisses. Everywhere around Mara the fays spoke and haggled, and she couldn't understand a single word. Then Gloria leaned against Mara's leg, and suddenly, every buzz and hiss instantly translated for her. Mara bent down to pat Gloria's mane and whisper, "Is this griffin magic?"

Gloria winked. "Aye, milady. I have gifted you a portion of my magic, which will activate anytime fays are speaking in your presence. You will be able to understand the fay language, and when you speak, they will understand what you are saying. Of course, it will be a good idea for you to learn fay language and customs, as time permits."

Mara hadn't given much thought to studying the fay language, but Gloria was right. If Arnesto, Efram, and Katrine could learn Valerran culture and language, she could do the same for them. Perhaps Arnesto could tutor her when he felt better. She thought of Arnesto, his dazzling smile and wavy blue hair grazing his broad shoulders, and her heart gave a little lurch. Mara frowned. She had to get her feelings under control, but Arnesto definitely made it harder, particularly when he entwined her fingers in his and brought her hand to his lips for a kiss, and when he looked at her with his luminous gray eyes, as trusting as a puppy.

"I won't pay a denare more, Bobolink. That's my final offer." Katrine put her hands on her hips.

Bobolink, a middle-aged fay with a round face and belly to match, slapped his hand on the table inside his booth. "You are a hard woman, Katrinareus. You're squeezing my margins to the point that it's hardly worth selling my books to you."

Katrine glared at Bobolink. "Save me your sob story. I know your margins as well as you do, and you'll be able to take a nice holiday from the proceeds of this sale."

The vendor sighed. "Very well. I can see your mind's made up and you've worn me down. Shall I deliver to the usual place?"

"Aye. Thank you, Bobo." The two fays shook hands and then Katrine turned to greet Mara and Gloria. Efram had wandered over to the baker selling her cardamom buns and the two were engaged in a friendly argument over the cost of a dozen. Mara noticed none of the vendors posted their prices, which explained all of the haggling.

"Oh, Katrine, it's so good to see you!" whispered Mara.

"Hush, lass, not here." Katrine leaned in. "I'm very glad to see you too." She straightened. "Come with me. I've reserved us a private room at the teahouse." Katrine tapped Efram on the shoulder as they passed and he followed them, carrying a brown baker's box with his precious cardamom buns inside.

Katrine led them into a shop decorated in neon pink and canary yellow, which offered twenty types of tea and a variety of pastries. Clusters of fays gathered around high-top tables to sip their tea and gossip, dressed in their afternoon finery, the ladies in ankle-length gowns and the gentlemen in gray and brown suits. Mara didn't see much difference between a fay teahouse and a Valerran one, other than the blue hair and buzzing syllables of the fays, and the fact that the fays used magic to refill their cups and plates.

Katrine waved to the woman behind the counter and continued down a hallway. She yanked opened a yellow door and pulled them inside, closing the door firmly behind her. The dark pink room contained a round table covered in a pink, green, and yellow floral tablecloth and four comfy chairs in pink chintz. Katrine mumbled an incantation as she withdrew a shaker of salt from one pants pocket and a vial of water from the other. Katrine walked around the room, sprinkling the salt and water around the entire perimeter and across the window sash.

There was a knock at the door, and Katrine quickly pocketed the items. "Come in!"

The woman from behind the counter entered the dark pink room. She carried a tray with a large pot of tea, four cups, saucers, and small plates, all in a pink and yellow rose pattern, plus assorted silverware and a platter of chocolate-ginger cookies. She arranged the tea things on the round table in the center of the room and stepped back. "Will there be anything else, Katrinareus?"

"No, thank you. We have all we need for the moment."

The woman closed the yellow door firmly behind her. Katrine withdrew the shaker of salt and vial of water from her pockets and proceeded to sprinkle both across the threshold of the door. She finished murmuring her incanta-tion and nodded. "That's it then, as secure as it's going to be for now. Please take a seat and allow me to pour the tea." Turning to Gloria she said, "It is good to see you again, my griffin friend."

"It is very good to see you as well, Lady Katrinareus." Gloria bobbed her head.

"Would you like a cookie?" asked Katrine, as Gloria hopped onto one of the chairs and circled three times before settling down.

Gloria shook her head. "No, thank you. I shall be quite content napping here whilst you have your tea."

Efram untied the white string around his box of iced cardamom buns and placed several on the platter next to the cookies. Mara tapped her foot impatiently as Katrine poured out the tea and selected a cookie from the platter. She wanted to jump up and down and shout at her boss: "*What are you doing? Your shop is gone and Arnesto is seriously injured and everyone is talking about the dark fays!*"

Katrine took a sip of tea and set the bone china cup down on its matching saucer. "You can stop tapping your foot, Mara. I know about the shop and about Arnesto and about the dark fays. I even know Arnesto was targeted by the driver of the locomobile, although I'd hoped we would have more time to prepare him—and you—before they found out."

Mara leaned forward. "Before who found out what?"

Katrine answered by asking a question of her own, which frustrated Mara almost as much as the fact her fay boss seemed unperturbed by all the disasters befalling them. "Who do you think was behind the fires and the attack on Arnesto?"

Mara had been giving that some thought and ticked off her top suspects on her fingers. "One possibility is the dark fays since by all accounts they are a rather nasty bunch. Although if they really were after us, I don't think they would set fires at night when no one was in the shops or buildings. They strike me as the type to injure and maim first, and ask questions afterward. On the other hand, there were casualties at the Royal Constabulary, but that still presents more questions than answers. For example, why would the dark fays bother releasing some Glenbarran thugs, since they consider humans beneath them?"

Mara paused and looked at Katrine, who said, "Don't stop now. You're on a roll."

Mara scratched beneath her wimple, grateful she didn't have to wear one all the time. "Another strong possibility is the hardcore anti-magickers. I don't believe they would hesitate to set some fires and even experiment on grihms. Every building that was set on fire or attacked had a fay connection. Some group with strong biases against fays could be sending a message, although neither theory explains the dead baker and the assassin who disappeared into the old savings and loan building."

Katrine put up her hand, palm outward. "Wait a minute. What's this about a dead baker and an assassin?"

Mara felt a small measure of satisfaction that her fay boss didn't know everything. She quickly relayed the short, sad tale of Baker Jakob Kornish, killed with a poisoned dart at the Cracked Cauldron.

"And Arnesto tracked the murderer back to government headquarters?"

Mara nodded. "Where the assassin disappeared into the building."

"Did Arnesto have any insights about the man who killed the baker? Was he human or fay?"

"That's the strange part. Arnesto couldn't pick up any emotional readings from the assassin, either before he killed Jakob Kornish or after. However, Arnesto saw no traveling mists when the man vanished into the building, leading him to conclude the murderer was human and someone was there to let him inside."

Katrine leaned back against her chair and nibbled on a cookie. "And what is your theory on a third possibility?"

"How do you know I have a third possibility?"

"Because you haven't mentioned the Glenbarrans yet."

Mara grunted. "Aye, it's true. King Roi could be involved, although Vas says he's keeping a low profile. But that doesn't mean he's not directing the Glenbarrans still loyal to him inside Bellaryss."

Katrine removed the turban from her head and ran a hand through her short blue curls. "So you believe we have three possible suspects who are setting fires and stirring unrest inside Bellaryss: the dark fays, who we know are active; the anti-magickers, who are on the rise; or King Roi, who still hasn't officially conceded defeat."

Efram stopped eating his cardamom treat long enough to say, "What about a fourth option—they're all working together."

CHAPTER 19

Mara stared at Efram. "You can't be serious."

"Why not?" he picked up another iced bun and waved it in the air. How many of those was he planning on consuming before dinner? "Bad actors often find their goals are aligned, until one of them believes they need to be in charge and gets rid of their competition."

"I think you've read too many fay tales."

Katrine rose from the chair and started pacing around the table. "Efram's theory has some merit. Let's not dismiss it out of hand."

Mara said, "I find it hard to believe anti-magickers like Harlan Lewyn would work with either dark fays or Glenbarran sorcerers. His followers are trying to outlaw magic."

"Is that really what they're trying to do?" asked Katrine. "I've known Harlan Lewyn for a long time. As a business owner in Valerra, I'm a member of the Merchants Guild. Lewyn is as trustworthy as a troll looking for its next meal. He would try any ploy to gain power."

"But that could backfire—"

A loud crash, followed by the tinkling sound of shattering dishes and teacups, interrupted Efram. Screams could be heard in the tearoom on the other side of the yellow door. Gloria raised her head from her chair and clicked her beak rapidly. "They have broken through!"

Katrine whispered, "Quickly now, Mara. Your sword, where is it?"

Mara's heart pounded and she swallowed hard. The last time she'd used her ensorcelled sword had been in the realms of the dead. "Under my bed, in the storage box you gave me."

"Let's hope the cloaking spell is still intact."

Mara didn't have time to ask why the spell would fail, or what would happen if it did, because there were more screams and then something thumped against the other side of the yellow door. Mara thought someone might have fallen against it. Katrine transformed instantly into her stretchy silver tunic and slacks, her sword in her right hand. She carried a coil of fay-spelled gold rope over each shoulder.

Katrine flung open the window and hissed to Gloria, "Get back to Yelenarra—make sure you're not followed— and tell her Mara is going to need her sword!" Gloria squawked. She leapt to the window, spread her wings, and flew off.

Mara jumped up from the pink chintz chair and bent down to retrieve her twin daggers from her boots. She joined Katrine, a sharp six-inch blade in each hand, and faced the door. She preferred to have her longsword in hand when attacked by something Katrine seemed to think came from the dark fays, or the realms of the dead, or both.

Efram dashed to the other side of Katrine, dressed now in his silvery fay garb and gripping his sword. Katrine grabbed one of her coils of gold rope and passed it to Mara. "You're going to need this too."

Mara took the coil, looping it over her neck. She draped the fay-spelled rope over her right shoulder and against her left hip. Her stomach twisted in knots as she recalled where she'd used the gold reaper's rope in the past. She had no desire to return to the realms of the dead.

The yellow door blew off its hinges. It took a moment for Mara to register that Katrine had magically blasted the door from the inside. "Let's go!" shouted her fay boss, charging through the opening. Mara followed behind, leaping over the man in black coattails she'd seen earlier on the green. He lay sprawled on the pink and white tiled floor, unconscious, his top hat gone.

The teahouse looked as if something had exploded inside. Overturned tables and broken china were scattered everywhere, with patrons lying on the tiled floor or slumped in their chairs, unmoving. In the center of the shop stood a huge, hulking monstrosity that reeked of death. Mara started to retch at the stench, until its beady eyes swiveled around to stare at her, giving her an instant chill.

Mara thought the thing was similar to the creature Arnesto had described, which had followed his mother out of the realms of the dead. Thick black bristles covered the beast's body, which seemed to be a cross between a panther and a lizard. One swipe from its long razor-sharp claws would slice open a man or woman. When the creature opened its mouth to screech, Mara spotted row upon row of jagged, pointy teeth.

She felt its twisted spirit seeping beneath her skin, displacing every happy thought with images of darkness and death. Her heart constricted in her chest, and she crossed her blades in front of her with a scream, "Oh no you don't!"

"Good thinking, lass!" yelled Katrine, who pulled Mara and Efram behind the counter. The woman who'd served them was curled in the corner, her arms over her head, passed out. The creature's explosive entrance must have knocked everyone in the tearoom unconscious. "Keep screaming at it. They are stupid and easily distracted."

"Aye, but how do we kill it?" hissed Efram

"We need to stab it through the eyes. Both eyes, at the same time."

Efram peeked over the countertop. The creature was roaring and shuffling from foot to foot. It picked up a platter of cakes and tossed them down its throat. "That beast is nine feet tall! How are we supposed to do that?"

"You're going to distract it while Mara and I lasso it to the ground."

Mara shook her head. "Huh? Will these ropes even hold a thing that size?"

"The ropes will hold up, but we might not, given its size and strength."

"How am I supposed to distract that monster?"

Mara watched as the creature snuffled about, picked up a tray of cookies, and scooped them into its mouth. "Look, it likes sweets. How many of your cardamom buns do you have left?"

Efram scowled. "Half a dozen. I don't mind sharing, but it frosts me to have to waste them on that undead monster."

Katrine glared at Efram, who sighed. He crept across the hall into the private room unnoticed, since the beast was busy going from table to table, eating whatever was left. The creature moved with surprising speed given its size.

Efram returned with his baker's box. "Ready?" he whispered. Katrine and Mara nodded.

Efram sheathed his sword and ran around the counter, the brown box under his arm. He waved one iced bun in the air. "Hullo there. I have in my hand the most delectable treat you will find in all of harvest fall. Iced cardamom buns. Would you care to try one?" Katrine and Mara sheathed their weapons and belly crawled to opposite sides of the tearoom, using the overturned tables for cover. Once in position, they readied their golden lassos.

The creature reared up on its hind legs and roared at Efram, who quickly tossed a bun into its rancid mouth. It chomped down on the bun and roared again. "Quite tasty, aren't they?" shouted Efram, as he pitched another bun into the monster's mouth.

"Dessert first!" screeched the beast. "Then I shall eat you!"

"Lovely," muttered Efram under his breath, as he threw another bun at the creature. "But you'll have to catch me first."

Mara unwound the coil of rope from around her shoulder and held the large loop in her right hand. She dashed from behind the overturned table, twirling her lasso and landing the loop of rope around the creature's shoulders. Katrine ran up and tossed her loop around one of the monster's front paws. They pulled at the same time, the creature screaming and swiping the air with his other paw. The beast managed to catch Efram in the leg with the edge of one sharp claw. Efram cried out and dived behind a chair near Mara for cover.

The monster yanked on the ropes, its strength more than a match for two women. Katrine lost her footing as he swung his trapped arm wildly, and she dangled in the air, holding tight to the end of her rope. Several blue heads popped up from behind overturned tables and toppled chairs, coming around after the creature's explosive entrance had rendered them unconscious. A few heads immediately popped back down, but two brave souls waved their arms wildly and hollered in an attempt to distract the beast.

The distraction worked, and Katrine was able to hook her legs around the beast's forearm and scramble up to his shoulder. The creature shook its head from side to side in an attempt to dislodge Katrine. Meanwhile, Mara yanked harder on the golden rope that still entrapped the beast's shoulders. She ran behind the beast and swinging on the rope, pulled herself up onto its back. She lost her footing as the monster shook itself to dislodge her. She tumbled to her knees, the creature's sharp bristles tearing through the fabric of her gown and cutting her legs. Mara hoisted herself up and continued to clamber up the beast's torso, gagging at the stench. She nearly fell again, when she realized the surface of its hide crawled with biting flies and spiders. Mara detested insects in general, and spiders in particular.

Mara reached the back of the monster's head and glanced at Katrine, bleeding from her nose, legs, and arms. "I'm not going to be able to climb up any farther, lass. This is up to you. But toss me your rope when you're on top of its head. I'll hold on long enough for you to finish this beast."

Mara's palms stung with blood and sweat, and her knees and legs smarted with cuts and scrapes. She gritted her teeth and climbed up to the top of the beast's malformed, bristly head. She straddled the creature's head between her thighs, wincing as the prickly bristles tore through her flesh.

Mara nodded at her fay boss and tossed down the end of her lasso, which Katrine wound around her back and then gripped in her hands. In one fluid motion, Mara withdrew her twin daggers and jabbed them hard into the red eyes of the monster. The beast roared and swung its head and shoulders so wildly that Mara and Katrine both fell off. They quickly scrambled away from the beast's sharp claws as it swiped blindly at the air and floor.

The beast swayed from side to side, its movements slowing. Mara wondered how long before it fell down. The creature dropped to its knees and shook its head, yellowish liquid streaming from each eye socket. "I am a servant of the one true king and ruler of the realms of the dead. Take heed and listen: King Bazra cometh now!"

The creature's voice changed, becoming raspier and if possible, more menacing, a hissy, shadowy sort of a sound that reminded Mara of a bad dream. "Fays of Havynweal, listen well. What happened today is a foretaste of what I have in store, unless you cease your senseless alliance with Valerra. Leave the humans to me, and I shall leave Havynweal alone. I give you two moonrises to decide your fate."

Why do fays have to make things so complicated? The next moonset for Arnesto's bed rest. Two moonrises until the end of the world.

The beast crashed face-first to the ground and withered on impact, shrinking down into a stinking pile of ash and bristles.

CHAPTER 20

Several pairs of hands lifted Mara from the floor and helped her to sit down in one of the righted chairs.

A middle-aged fay in a gold evening dress wailed, her two companions unmoving on the floor next to her. Mara feared they'd been crushed during the beast's explosive entrance. Fay men and women gradually came out from beneath their tables, their hats missing and clothing askew.

The young woman in the green ball gown sobbed, gulping for air. "How did that horrid creature get here? I have never been so frightened!"

The other fays in the tearoom swelled around Mara, the fear evident in their faces. An elderly man dressed in tweeds with elbow patches bowed toward Mara. "I shall never forget your bravery, milady." He glanced at the other fays and shouted to be heard above the wailing. "Let us thank— what is your name, lass?"

"Maragold Pensk."

The man in tweeds bowed a second time. "Thank you, Maragold Pensk. Your daggers surely saved us this day!"

The rest of the fays, other than the poor woman still weeping, bowed in unison and raised their voices in thanks.

"Indeed, but this level of violence is unacceptable. And who uses weapons in a tearoom?" inquired a woman with a double chin, dressed in a black bombazine gown. The woman addressed the room but stared at Mara. "After all, it is against the law to deploy such pointy objects in any of the seasons, except by proclamation from the council."

Mara glanced at Katrine, who was still sitting on the floor, catching her breath. The woman in black appeared to be waiting for an answer. Mara picked a large bristle out of her palm and winced, wondering how to respond truthfully without giving away she was human. "My griffin advised that daggers might come in handy today."

"Ah." The woman's double chin joggled as she nodded. "Griffins are wise. But still, it is most unusual."

"Would you rather have been eaten by that undead monster?" grumbled Efram from the floor. The man in black tails hobbled over to give him a hand up. Efram grimaced in pain and collapsed onto a chair.

"Of course not." The double chins wobbled indignantly.

"Then leave well enough alone."

Two women helped Katrine off the floor. She accepted a kitchen towel from the woman behind the counter, who was up and unharmed. Katrine wiped off her face and hands.

"Lady Katrinareus, will you advise the council to abandon its support for the human realms?" asked the young woman in the green ball gown, who was supported by the man in the black tails, his top hat back on his head. "I hope to never witness another monster attack inside Havynweal!"

"Nay, I'll not allow us to be bullied by the dark fays." Katrine tossed her head, her blue curls bouncing.

"But isn't that shortsighted?" asked the double chin.

"How so?" Katrine narrowed her eyes at the woman.

"What have the Valerrans ever done for the fays?"

Katrine put her hands on her hips. "Many of them died to preserve Serving magic in the human realm, and others fought to the very last man and woman to prevent the Valerran Museum from falling into Fallow hands."

"They failed in the end," pointed out the disagreeable woman in bombazine.

Efram spoke up. "For a short time, aye, but the museum, which houses the largest collection of magical artifacts anywhere outside of Havynweal, is safe once again, thanks to the Valerrans."

"Mara, step over here please. I'd like for you to remove your head covering," said Katrine.

Mara frowned, wondering whether Katrine had been knocked on her head. "Are you sure?"

Katrine gave her a curt nod. "Positive."

Mara hoped Katrine knew what she was doing. *Didn't Katrine and Yelenarra want to keep the fact of my presence under wraps?* She rose from her chair on shaky legs and moved closer to Katrine. She gripped the gold band across her forehead and yanked the wimple off her head. A chorus of gasps followed, along with denials of her obvious human heritage.

"Impossible! No human girl could fight off an undead creature and survive!" The man in tweeds shook his head.

Katrine waved her hand at Mara. "This human girl, without any thought to her own safety, defeated the beast and saved your lives today. Think twice before you say humans have never done anything for fays." Katrine stared down the woman with the double chin and glared around the teahouse. "We will be off now."

Katrine's traveling mists curled around her legs and crept along the floor to encircle Mara and Efram. Mara couldn't wait to see how Arnesto was feeling and tell him about the undead creature and Bazra's deadline. She glanced down at another ruined dress, shredded from her battle with the beast. Her hands, knees, and legs bled where the sharp bristles still stuck in her flesh.

When Katrine's mists cleared, they were standing inside a room with a stone fireplace large enough to fit Mara's bed inside. A cauldron sat on the hob, and several smaller pots sat on either side of the cauldron. The scent of fresh bread baking in the brick oven next to the fireplace reminded Mara she'd had very little to eat at the teahouse. Katrine guided Efram, who was limping badly, over to a long wooden table with a set of benches on either side. They both half collapsed onto the bench nearest the fire-place. Mara pointed to the gash in Efram's leg. "That's going to need to be cleaned and—"

"Don't say it!"

"I was just going to say your leg needs stitches."

Efram threw his hands in the air. "You went and said it."

"You mean stitches?"

"Aye." Efram shuddered. "I hate needles."

Yelenarra appeared in the kitchen and gave a little squeal when she spotted them. "Oh my stars! Please tell me the creature is looking worse than the lot of you!"

"Aye, Auntie, we bested him—although Mara gets the credit for the kill. I merely tossed sweet buns into his craw and got this for my troubles." Efram showed his aunt the gash in his leg.

She tut-tutted. "Up on the table, right now, Efra-mallium. There is no time to waste. I will need to clean that wound and stitch it right away."

"Aw, Auntie, no needles."

"I suppose I could call Zornamayne and ask her to knit your leg together. She does not use needles, but it shall hurt just the same."

Efram groaned. "Not Zornamayne! She's scary. Alright, go ahead and stitch me up."

Yelenarra disappeared for a moment and reappeared, carrying a black leather satchel containing a variety of healing implements, including tweezers, gauze, needles, and thread. While Yelenarra cleaned and stitched Efram's leg, Katrine told her about the undead creature and the visit from Bazra, with Efram and Mara adding a few details of their own. When she finished stitching Efram's leg, Yelenarra said, "Go on up to the Green Room and take a bath. I left a jar of salve on the dresser for your cuts."

"How did you know I'd need salve?"

Yelenarra raised her eyebrows. "When was the last time you visited without needing to be stitched or healed? I always put away extra salve when I know you are coming."

"Thank you, Auntie!" Efram grinned and vanished in a puff of vapors.

Yelenarra shook her head. "I do not know which of the boys I worry over more, Eframallium or Arnestarious. They are both prone to being in the wrong place at the wrong time."

Katrine said, "They are brave lads and will do their duty, which often leads to injury, as you well know."

"That is true, painfully so." Yelenarra patted the tabletop and Katrine climbed up. Yelenarra withdrew a pair of pliers from her healer's bag. Katrine's eyes bulged, but she compressed her lips firmly shut as Yelenarra proceeded to remove the sharp, stinging bristles from her arms and legs. When Yelenarra finished, she handed Katrine a jar of salve. "I know you shall be leaving for the council meeting, which has already been called to deal with this latest incident. Apply the salve three times daily, and do get some rest, Katrinareus."

Katrine took the jar and nodded. "Thank you." She glanced at Mara. "And thank you, lass, for your bravery. We'll send someone back to your flat to retrieve your sword. It's best to have it close at hand now that Bazra, the dark fay king, has made an appearance."

Mara had so many questions for Katrine, but the most important question centered on the only other ensorcelled sword in Valerra. "What about Remy and his sword? Could he be in danger even now?"

Katrine slapped her forehead with her hand. "I'd nearly forgotten about Remy. He's problematic to say the least."

"What do you mean?"

"Remy is a good loyal lad, but he can't keep his mouth shut. Once he sees Havynweal, he'll never stop talking about it."

"Can't you cast a forgotten spell on him?" Remy might drive her to distraction some days with his over-protectiveness, but Mara didn't want to see him left to his own devices against the dark fays.

"Aye, but I'd have to keep reinforcing it for the rest of his days or mine. Havynweal is unforgettable. Once he sees the fay lands, he won't be able to stop remembering, not without constant magical intervention."

"And this young man carries one of the Swords of Five?" asked Yelenarra.

"Aye," said Katrine. "He carries the red sword."

Mara added, "And he knows how to wield it."

Yelenarra's eyes lit up at the mention of the red sword. She muttered, more to herself than to the rest of them, "So that is where the red sword has been hiding. Very clever magic indeed." Mara had no idea what Yelenarra was talking about, or why she was suddenly so interested in Remy's sword. Yelenarra tapped a finger against her chin. "What if we bring the sword here and seek its new owner in Havynweal?"

Mara gasped. "But that could only happen if the current owner is deceased. I don't want any harm to come to Remy."

"Of course not. The plain truth is that Remy will be much safer in Chef Desna's kitchen than fighting the dark fays with his fay-spelled sword." Katrine glanced at Yelenarra. "What do you have in mind?"

"We shall cast an unremembered spell on Remy. He will forget he ever owned the sword. The magical connection between sword and owner will be broken." Yelenarra patted the tabletop, a signal it was Mara's turn to be examined by the fay woman.

"Would Remy forget how brave he'd once been, fighting against Mordahn and the Glenbarrans?" Mara clambered up and raised her shredded skirt above her knees. She grimaced as Yelenarra started pulling bristles from her legs with her pliers.

Yelenarra paused, pliers mid-air. "He would recall he had a role in defeating Mordahn, but he would be fuzzy on the details whenever he tried to remember using his sword."

"I'm glad Remy would still remember a lot of what happened since he's so proud of the role he played during the war." Mara gritted her teeth as Yelenarra pulled several bristles from her knees, which had been rubbed raw and were bleeding. "But if you brought the sword to Havynweal, wouldn't that mean we'd have to find a new owner for the sword?"

"Aye, but we shall not need to look far for the new owner."

Mara winced as Yelenarra plucked another bristle from her leg. "How can you be so certain? We found the weapons to be quite fickle when it came to selecting their owners."

"The new owner must be Arnestarious."

"Why Arnesto?"

Yelenarra extracted three more bristles before answering. "A twelfth-level fay wizard must wield one of the Swords of Five—the red sword to be precise—in order to defeat Bazeerkalim's descendants, the Bazeerka. Every seer says as much."

Mara groaned, half from the pain in her right knee as Yelenarra extracted a particularly long bristle, and half from the mention of prophecies, which had been the bane of her existence while she lived in Faynwood. Her friend Linden couldn't do anything without some seer predicting it would be so. The fays and Faymons relied heavily on prophecies and seers. "But aren't there other twelfth-level fays living in Havynweal?"

Yelenarra shook her head. "The only other twelfth-level wizard is a very old woman. She certified Arnesto after he passed his other levels. Her mind is still as sharp as the day she was born, but she is weakened by age."

Katrine stepped away from the two of them as her mists snaked up her legs. "I'll return before too long, as I haven't much hope the council will do the right thing in the face of Bazra's threat. In the meantime, we'll need to retrieve both swords from Valerra and bring them here for safekeeping.

Yelenarra, I'll count on you to figure out the right incantation to erase Remy's recollection of his sword."

"I shall take care of the spell shortly, as soon as I am finished here."

Katrine vanished along with her traveling mists. Mara stifled a small cry as Yelenarra extracted a bristle from her hand. "I do hate politics, whether human or fay."

"Aye, but yelling and name-calling are far preferable to maiming and killing."

"I can't argue with you there." Mara flinched as Yelenarra pulled a bristle from her wrist. "How is Arnesto?"

Yelenarra smiled. "Ornery, cranky, and asking about you every time I bring him his broth. Once you are cleaned up, please go visit him. Gloria is with him now, keeping him company."

Mara glanced down at the pale rose gown, now nothing but tatters. "I'm so sorry about this lovely gown. I hadn't expected to fight an undead creature inside a teahouse this afternoon."

Yelenarra threw back her head to laugh in her tinkling way, which caused Mara to chuckle. The idea of fighting an undead beast while having a cup of tea *was* ridiculous. Unfortunately, it also had been nearly deadly. Mara hoped to never encounter another bristly, smelly undead monster again.

Yelenarra laughed until she wheezed. "Ah, lass, I was due for a good laugh, which you made possible because you defeated that nasty beast. I wish I could have seen you climbing up the creature's back, wearing your rose gown and your tall leather boots with the twin blades tucked inside. That would have been a sight to behold."

Mara smiled at the visual image. "Aye. Well, come what may, I hope to avoid ruining any more gowns."

CHAPTER 21

MARA FELT BETTER AFTER A HOT BATH AND A GENEROUS application of Yelenarra's salve on all her cuts. She found a powder blue jersey dress with a square neck and three-quarter sleeves inside the wardrobe, which she didn't recall seeing earlier. No matter, the dress was comfortable and didn't require extra stiff undergarments, something she appreciated given the fact she ached all over.

Mara pulled closed the door to the Amber Room and wished, not for the first time, she could travel by fay mists to the other end of the massive house. She didn't relish climbing the four flights of stone steps up to Arnesto's chamber. *Stop your whining, Mara! You'll be stiff as a board in the morning if you don't move some more tonight.*

"Come in!" called out Arnesto when she knocked. It had taken her more than thirty minutes, ambling along at a snail's pace, to reach his turret bedchamber.

Mara pushed open the door and hesitated. Arnesto was propped up against several pillows in bed, chatting with Gloria, who'd climbed into a chair beside him. Although still technically on bed rest for another twelve hours or so,

Arnesto looked ready to jump to the floor and run a relay any moment. His wavy blue hair framed his handsome face, and his smile bedazzled as much as the first time they'd met. He wore a white linen shirt, open at the neck, which contrasted in the most attractive way with his brown skin.

Arnesto's gray eyes were no longer clouded with pain, but clear and bright. He frowned slightly. "Is anything the matter? You are walking rather stiffly. Are you injured?" He leaned forward, as if preparing to jump to the floor, but Mara rushed to his side, her leg muscles screaming with the effort.

"No, no, I'm fine, and you need to stay put. I don't want to have to tell Zornamayne you hopped out of bed because of me and wound up hurting yourself. I'm already in her debt as it is."

Gloria leapt from the chair and rubbed herself against Mara's legs. "Have a seat, milady. I am glad to see you are safe. I shall visit with you later, after I have had my dinner." She hopped to an open window, and flapping her wings, took off in search of her evening meal.

Arnesto stared intently at Mara, watching as she took her seat. She attempted to sit without wincing but wasn't successful. "You are unwell! What happened? Auntie has been noticeably distracted whenever I asked after you. And Gloria has been keeping me occupied with stories, some quite fanciful, in order to prevent me from seeking the truth about your whereabouts. Oh, hang on, what do you mean about being in Zornamayne's debt?" Arnesto crossed his arms, arching one eyebrow and lowering the other.

Mara found herself distracted by the way his biceps strained against the fabric of his shirt and took a deep breath to steady herself. She grew uncomfortably warm, although a late summer breeze blew through the open windows. Mara shifted in her chair, deciding she'd answer Arnesto's last question first. "After Zornamayne performed her healing ritual and saved your life, I thanked her and told her I was in her debt. After all, it was my duty as your field coach to keep you safe, and I failed. Zornamayne said she would collect the debt at some point."

Mara noticed the furrow between Arnesto's brows deepening. He looked like he was having a mighty internal struggle. Shaking his head, he reached for Mara's hand. She let him entwine their fingers, her heart flip-flopping as her mind scolded her for inappropriate conduct with her fay trainee. Once he was no longer bedridden, she'd have to set the record straight. "I fear you have been misled somewhat by my brother and me, and even by Katrine."

"Misled? About wanting me as your field coach?"

Arnesto squeezed her hand. "I wanted you to train me in Valerran culture and how to operate as a fay scout outside Havynweal. Efram and Katrine fully supported this, and still do."

"That's good, because otherwise, I'd have to question the whole notion that fays are unable to tell a lie." Mara smiled, but Arnesto compressed his lips in a thin, straight, unhappy line. *What is bothering Arnesto? This isn't like him at all.*

"What we didn't tell you was that Katrine had given me a special assignment. I was charged with keeping an eye on you and Remy."

Mara yanked her hand out of Arnesto's grip and jumped up from her chair, forgetting for a moment her sore muscles. She backed away. "*You* were spying on *me*? At my boss's request? I'd better leave right now, before I say something I'll regret." Mara turned and stalked toward the door, her legs aching with each step. A muscle throbbed in her temples, bringing on an immediate headache to match the pain in her chest. An overwhelming sense of betrayal washed over her, leaving a bitter taste in her mouth, of ashes mixed with bile.

"Wait, Mara—please!" called Arnesto. "My mission was not to spy on you, but to protect you and Remy from the Bazeerka!"

Mara's hand was on the door handle. She turned to face Arnesto, who'd swung his legs over the side of the bed, preparing to stand. She pointed her finger at him. "Don't you dare get out of that bed until moonset. I'll stay long enough to hear your explanation—which better be a good one—but only if you stay put. I'll not have you begin bleeding again because of me."

Arnesto grunted but cooperated, slipping his legs back under the covers. "I will provide an explanation, but only if you sit down over here next to me. I shall not shout across the room at you."

"I'm not sure you're in a position to make demands, but fine. I'm tired and sore because of these stupid Bazeerka, so I'll sit."

Arnesto waved a hand at her. "I was right all along. You are injured, and you say it is due to the dark fays? What happened?"

Mara pulled the chair farther back from the bed before she sat down. She'd not be holding hands with her fay trainee-turned-traitor. "I am not saying a word about what happened to me this afternoon, until you tell me why you were sent to spy on me."

Arnesto rolled his eyes, a distinctly Valerran habit he'd picked up from her. "I was not sent to spy on you. Katrine was certain the Bazeerka would target you and Remy because you own two of the legendary Swords of Five. The other swords are hidden away deep inside Faynwood, protected by physical guards and magical wards that would be nearly impossible for the dark fays to overcome. That makes your sword, and Remy's, much more attractive targets."

"So your real purpose was to keep our swords safe. It had nothing to do with protecting Remy and me." Mara bit her bottom lip to keep it from trembling.

Arnesto squinted at her, his eyes two narrow slits. "Stop twisting my words, Maragold." He spoke each word slowly and with emphasis. This was the first time Mara had seen Arnesto become angry. She sensed well-regulated power emanating from him, as if even in anger, Arnesto was in full command of himself. She decided he would be a formidable adversary, even without his twelfth-level magical abilities. "Efram told me of your exploits with the resistance and your skills as a field operative. I sought you out as my coach because I wish to be a fay scout like my brother. That is the truth. In addition, I came to Valerra to keep you and Remy safe from harm and prevent your ensorcelled swords from falling into the Bazeerka's hands, where they could manipulate the magic to their own devices."

"And Katrine was aware of this plan?"

"Aye. We planned this together."

"And Yelenarra?"

Arnesto leaned back against the pillows with a sigh. "My aunt is aware of the need to protect you and the swords from the dark fays."

"But?"

"She has her own motives, and they are somewhat different than Katrine's."

Mara was tired of fays and their secret motives, but she

was curious too. "Alright, I give up. Why else did Yelenarra want you to train with me?"

Arnesto locked his eyes on hers. She felt a small taste of his fay power in his gaze. Her untamed heart beat faster. "My aunt was seeking a partner for me, someone who had traveled to the realms of the dead and survived, someone who would help me face the Bazeerka and not flee at the first sign of danger." His voice dropped to a husky whisper, sending a small frisson of desire through her. She gave herself a mental shake-up and gripped the arms of the chair. "Someone I could call my friend."

Mara thought about her visit from Yelenarra. Arnesto's aunt had said much the same thing in her own circuitous way, except for the part about being friends. "Tell me, what does it mean to be a friend?"

"Is this a trick question?"

"Not at all. It's just that it seems to have special significance inside Havynweal."

Arnesto stared down at the coverlet on his bed and then out the closest window. His eyes flitted everywhere, except where she was sitting. He finally ran both hands through his blue hair. "Oh no."

"I don't like the sound of that. You'd better explain."

"But you offered me your friendship. I pledged mine in return. We even said that we hoped to live up to each other's expectations. I thought you understood..." Arnesto's face, so spirited a moment ago, looked forlorn.

Mara pulled the chair closer to the bed. "What is it?" she whispered. "What don't I understand?" He looked like a puppy that had just been kicked by its owner. If she could fix this, she would, despite her earlier anger at him.

Arnesto's mouth turned down. "It seems as if I have made a terrible mistake. I could blame my injured state, but that would not be truthful." He dropped his face in his hands. "Please leave. I need to be alone."

"My stars, what is wrong? Arnesto?" Mara reached out one hand tentatively and patted his shoulder.

Arnesto shrank away from her touch. "Be gone from me!" he shouted.

Mists enveloped Mara, as Arnesto and his bedchamber vanished from her sight. Her feet touched down on a cobbled walkway, but where had Arnesto sent her? It was after dusk, but there was still some natural light left in the sky overhead. She could just make out the shape of Yelenarra's mansion and its six turrets in the distance, but she wasn't quite sure how to traverse there. She supposed she could follow the walkway and hope it didn't wind up in a fay-inspired labyrinth or drop her down some crevice.

Mara had never seen Arnesto so upset and so unwilling to listen to her. She didn't know what disturbed her more, his anger or his sadness. Probably his sadness, since she'd felt her heart constrict when she saw him grappling with a revelation that she still didn't understand. It had something to do with their declaration of friendship inside Havynweal.

Mara remembered the odd prickling sensation that came over her after they'd pledged to live up to each other's expectations. Had that been a signal something significant had occurred? Probably, but she'd been such a dunderhead, she'd entirely missed the clue. "Oh, Mara, you've botched things badly," she said aloud, addressing the yew trees lining the path.

"This is definitely not your fault." Efram emerged from the shadows a few feet ahead of her, leaning on a walking stick. "Arnesto wanted to tell you his mission from the start, but Katrine and I were concerned you might simply refuse to take him on as your trainee if you knew."

Mara pointed to the walking stick. "How is your leg?"

Efram waited for her to come alongside him before answering. "It hurts, but I'll mend soon enough. How about you?"

Mara twisted her hands, forgetting about her cuts. She grimaced. "Confused and upset about Arnesto. First he was angry with me, and now he's just miserable and won't speak with me. What is so special about friendship here?"

Efram pointed with his walking stick to where the path diverged to the right. "'When you pledge your friendship, it's akin to promising you are exclusive to one another."

"Exclusive? You mean like dating exclusively?"

"Fays don't date, leastways, not the way Valerrans do. When we find a kindred spirit, we pledge our friendship— and in doing so, we pledge ourselves."

Mara rubbed the back of her neck, turning over Efram's words. She stopped walking and stared at him. "Are you trying to say, that is, do you mean to suggest—"

"You and Arnesto are betrothed."

CHAPTER 22

Mara sputtered. "But that's...but how...but why would he want to pledge himself to me?"

"Isn't it obvious?"

"Not at all."

"Oh come on, now. Don't tell me you haven't felt a spark between you two. It's been obvious to the rest of us since your first meeting. Even Remy noticed, and he wasn't too happy about it. He asked me to find Arnesto a different 'job' so he wouldn't spend so much time with you."

Mara's head was spinning so fast she felt dizzy. "Is there a bench around here somewhere? I need to sit."

Efram muttered an incantation and waved his hand. "One park bench, as you wish."

Mara plunked herself down on the dark green bench that materialized next to the path. She clutched her head. "What have I done? I've pledged myself to Arnesto without realizing it, and I think I just broke up with him without realizing it. All I do know is that I feel terrible, and not because my cuts are itching me right now, which they are."

Efram sat next to her on the bench, stretching out his leg. "You didn't break up with Arnesto. You can't, actually."

Mara dropped her hands into her lap. "Why can't I break up with him? Not that I want to, necessarily. I didn't even know we were betrothed."

"That's why Arnesto was so upset just now. He cast you out, quite literally, because he's realized that you're pledged—you're bound together—but you didn't realize what you were doing. It's his fault for not explaining beforehand."

"And it can't be undone, this pledging thing?"

"No."

"Because…"

"Because our word is our bond. This is what we mean when we say that a fay can't lie. We cannot break a pledge. He has pledged himself to you, and you have pledged yourself to him. Since you're not a fay, you could break your word, but you'd be reviled inside Havynweal as an oathbreaker."

"And I take it that's a really bad thing?"

"It's one of the things that can get you banished to the outer demesnes."

"What should I do?"

Efram used his walking stick to push himself upright. "My ridiculous brother needs to get over himself, and the two of you need to talk. You don't have to do anything, not now anyway. Fays are quite patient. The two of you might wind up marrying at some distant future date, or you may simply be friends in the Valerran sense of the word."

"Friends who can't date anyone else, ever, unless they want to be banished."

"Aye," Efram conceded. "Basically that's true."

"I need to do some thinking."

"Why don't I give you a lift to the Amber Room. I'll send

up a tray of food for you later. I told my aunt I'd make dinner tonight."

Mara felt suddenly drained, as if all of her strength had fled. She needed to curl up on the sofa and be by herself. "Thank you, I'll take you up on your offer of a lift and dinner later in my room. It's been a really long day—actually it's been a really, really long week."

"Aye, with more long days and weeks ahead." Efram nodded at Mara as the mists wound around her legs and snaked up her waist. She touched down on the plush carpet inside her bedchamber. She was so exhausted she didn't bother to light any of the candles in her room. Instead, she dropped onto the sofa, turned onto her side, and shut her eyes against the tears that threatened to spill over.

Mara didn't know how long she slept, but when she awoke, a full moon shone brightly through the window nearest the sofa. She heard a soft clicking nearby. "Gloria?"

"Aye, milady. I am here. Eframallium left you a tray outside your door, as I told him you were not to be disturbed."

Mara smiled at her somewhat officious griffin. "Thank you. I think I'd better light a few candles first."

Gloria tapped the sofa table with her front paw. "I found a few fire starters in the still room."

Mara picked up the jar of wooden matches and turned them over. Most of the flint had worn off their tips. They looked more like a castoff souvenir from some fay's visit to Valerra than an actual means of starting a fire. After all, fays didn't need matches to build fires or light candles. "Thanks, but I've got this." Mara opened her hands, palms facing up, and incanted a fire starter spell. "Turn wax and wick to flames so bright. Stop when burning true and right."

All the candles in the room lit up, casting a soft orange

glow inside the Amber Room. She opened the door and picked up the dinner tray left by Efram, which contained a mug of tepid tea, a small basket of crackers, a platter of cheese in a rainbow of colors from brown to pink to white, and a bowl of cut-up fruit, none of it recognizable. Mara tasted a morsel of the pink cheese, decided it was an amazing cross between raspberries and white cheddar, and polished off the rest of the pink cheese wedge in three bites. She sampled everything and proceeded to clean her plate, pausing periodically to answer Gloria's questions about the fight at the teahouse. Gloria interrupted her every so often with a squawk and a wing flap.

When Mara was finished, she set the tray aside and rubbed her eyes. Gloria watched her and cocked her head to the side. "You appear to have been crying. Tell me why. Griffins are excellent listeners."

Mara missed having Linden around to talk through their problems, especially when it came to their boyfriends or potential boyfriends. She hadn't had a real confidante since Linden returned to Faynwood and Mara remained behind in Valerra. She missed her friend, period, but she missed being able to bounce ideas off someone she trusted. It was a rare gift, one that she'd taken for granted. Even if Gloria couldn't offer any suitable advice, at least she could listen.

Mara slowly recounted her conversation with Arnesto, his anger and his hurt, and how he'd cast her from his room. She explained what she'd learned from Efram about friendship pledges, and Gloria clicked her beak. "Verily, verily, Eframallium is quite correct. You must not even consider becoming an oath-breaker. It is an unimaginable offense against all fays everywhere. Even fays who live among Valerrans would turn their backs on you."

Mara propped her elbows on her lap and rested her chin on her fists. "Even so, how can I keep my word? I didn't know what I was promising."

"Are you telling me you have no feelings for Arnestarious?"

"I'm not saying that at all. I do have feelings, but I don't want to be pressured to act upon them until I'm ready."

"Who says you have to act upon them? Did Arnestarious say anything to indicate you need to move with haste?"

Mara sighed. Her pet griffin asked really thought-provoking questions. "Not at all."

"So then what is the problem? If you like him and he likes you, and no one is in a hurry to publish the banns and hold the ceremony, why crack the cauldron?"

Gloria had a point. Mara supposed she could give it a try, although she doubted Arnesto would be willing to do the same. He'd literally kicked her out of his chambers and dumped her in the yard outside his home. That was not how you made friends or kept them. "I'll give it some thought, but quite frankly, Arnesto owes me an apology first."

Mara woke up in the morning to bright sunshine streaming through the windows. Gloria was gone, probably in search of breakfast. Her cuts and bruises were no longer itchy thanks to Yelenarra's salve. Mara rose and stretched, touching her hands to her toes to get some of the kinks out of her back. When she straightened, she noticed an envelope had been pushed beneath her door sometime during the night or the wee hours of the morning.

Mara picked up the note, her pulse racing at the spidery script. Arnesto had addressed it to "MGRP," using the initials of her full name. She tore open the note, her hands slightly trembling. Was he apologizing or kicking her out of his life?

Dearest Maragold,

Forgive me, please. At the risk of repeating myself, and sounding like a dunderhead (Efram's word for me), I shall write that again: Forgive me.

I am too often impulsive, occasionally ridiculous as my brother likes to remind me, and when it comes to you, entirely smitten. Aye, you read that correctly. To borrow from Valerran vernacular, I have fallen top hat over toes for you.

'How can that be,' you may ask, 'since our acquaintance is of such short duration?' True enough. However, I have been acquainted with your reputation for many months now, since I first heard about you from Efram and later from Katrine. I knew you were a human girl who owned one of the fay-spelled Swords of Five—quite remarkable, in and of itself—and that Katrine respected your courage and skills with a blade. Efram described your intense focus during a mission and your loyalty to Serving magic. I became fascinated with the thought of you, without ever having met you. I had to find a way to meet this remarkable girl. Could she really live up to her reputation?

Efram took me to the toyshop one afternoon when you were working there. Whilst Efram slipped into the back for a meeting with Katrine, I stayed up front. I watched as you patiently assisted an elderly customer searching for the perfect clockwork toy for her granddaughter. You will not recall seeing me, as I was disguised as an old man.

We only stayed a short while, but even in that quick visit, I found myself drawn to you. Later, when the opportunity came along to work beside you—and to ensure you were not in any danger from the Bazeerka—I leapt at the chance.

I am sorry for how I have handled, or mishandled actually, things between us. I never intended to place you in the awkward position of having to choose between being betrothed or becoming an oath-breaker. Please, do not consider the latter. Let us go on as before and perhaps, with repeat exposure to this besotted fay, you may develop reciprocal feelings for me. If not, we will traverse that moat when the time comes.

Yours forevermore, no strings attached,

Arnesto

P.S. Please do not leave me in suspense for too long. Tell me I am forgiven.

Mara read the note slowly, pausing periodically over a sentence, shocked at the depth of Arnesto's feelings. Her hands shook as she reread his words, her heart beating like the wings of a caged bird yearning for flight. Amazement and anxiety warred within her. At one moment she was thrilled *he* liked *her,* that the developing affection she felt for him hadn't been one-sided. Next, she worried he might not believe she could forgive him so easily or that he would doubt her feelings for him.

Mara raced through her morning ablutions, overcome with the need to find Arnesto. She'd tell him immediately he was forgiven. Only a girl with a heart of flint could read that letter and still hold a grudge. Mara began to hum in her strong contralto an old tune her father would sing when she was very young, when it was just the two of them. He would grip her small hand in his giant one and take her for a walk around the park near their home in Bellaryss. A few men and women, the kind-hearted ones, would stop and chat and even hand her a lollipop or piece of toffee. But most would turn and walk in the opposite direction, unwilling to address the coward who had retreated from battle, who'd turned his marines around and marched back across the muddy, gore-soaked field, withdrawing when he should have charged ahead.

Mara thought of her father, burdened by that one fateful mistake. He still found joy in simple pleasures, in singing to his daughter and taking her for pony rides and ice cream cones. And later, he re-married and welcomed two more daughters into his life. His was a different kind of courage, forged from failure. Something about Arnesto's letter prompted her to make a comparison between the two men, one traumatized by witnessing his mother's horrific death, and the other vilified for a single loss of nerve.

Mara opened the wardrobe door, intending to wear one of the lovely day gowns Yelenarra had created for her. Instead, she found three sets of stretchy tunics, leggings, and matching capes: a dark blue with silver sparkles, an aubergine with copper crescent moons, and a black set with gold stars. Mara drew her brows together in confusion. Why the change from pretty dresses to practical active wear, useful for fencing practice and lassoing, but not for visiting the man who'd written her a love letter?

Then Mara remembered. Bazra's warning had a date and time stamp. Tonight, at moonrise or thereabouts. Yelenarra wanted Mara to be well prepared, despite the fact the coming battle would be many hours away. Perhaps Yelenarra expected the Bazeerka to arrive sooner. Mara selected the black and gold tunic and leggings, adding a leather belt tricked out with pouches for her brass knuckles and pocketknife. She pulled on her tall black boots and slipped her twin daggers into the shanks. She looped her cape over her left arm and departed from the room, anxious to see Arnesto and have a heart-to-heart chat about the misunderstanding.

Mara hurried down the winding stone stairs from her turret bedchamber, her legs still a bit stiff from her battle with the undead creature the day before, but no longer painful. She skidded to a stop at the bottom landing in front of Efram. Sooty ash coated his silvery clothes and boots, his sides heaving as he caught his breath. His arms were wrapped around Mara's carrying case for her blue sword, which he held against his chest.

Yelenarra appeared in a puff of mist. "I thought I heard you arrive. But what has happened? Where is your brother?"

"The Bazeerka. They have Arnesto—and the red sword!"

CHAPTER 23

A knot formed in the pit of Mara's stomach. *The dark fays have Arnesto? What will they do to him? Kill him outright or torment him first?* Then she recalled him explaining that his blood had special properties. *Will they harvest his blood in order to rule the realms of the dead? I will never let that happen —not to any living soul and certainly not to Arnesto.*

Yelenarra had been carrying a cut-crystal vase filled with flowers from her garden: neon orange sunflowers, bright pink coneflowers, and lime green and navy mums. She staggered, dropping the vase. The flowers scattered across the carpet, reminding Mara of toy soldiers knocked to the floor when a child loses interest. Efram tossed Mara her carrying case and caught his aunt as her legs crumpled beneath her. "Oh, my poor boy. This is his worst nightmare come true!"

Efram's mists enveloped Yelenarra and Mara. In three blinks they were in the small dining room. Efram pulled out a floor cushion and gently deposited his aunt. He waved his hand, and a porcelain teapot in a butterfly pattern poured out three cups of black tea. Squares of cinnamon toast and cut-up fruit appeared on their plates. "I shall rescue my brother, Auntie. I will not let you down."

"Oh Eframallium, I will not lose you too." Yelenarra dropped her face in her hands, reminding Mara of the last time she saw Arnesto. *No, it will not end like this. We will not end like this.*

Mara leaned forward. "How was Arnesto captured?"

"I don't rightly know. I'd just left Remy's apartment with your sword when it happened."

Mara paled. "Is Remy...?"

Efram raised his hand. "He was taken along with Arnesto."

Yelenarra lowered her hands and raised her tear-stained face. "Tell us what happened, Eframallium, from the time you entered the young man's apartment."

Efram stared down at the table, his hands curled into fists on either side of his untouched breakfast. "We retrieved Mara's sword first and then went next door to Remy's apartment. Arnesto cast the unremembered spell on Remy, which took several minutes to complete. Meanwhile, I searched for Remy's carrying case, which shouldn't have been difficult given the size of his flat. I finally found it, wrapped in a smelly towel and stashed behind his dresser.

"I waited for Arnesto to bind the unremembered spell and handed him Remy's sword case. He told me to head back to Havynweal with Mara's sword and that he'd be right behind me. He wanted to test Remy's memory to be sure the incantation worked. I departed on my mists, but I felt a cold downdraft and a prickling down my spine. I immediately turned back, fearing the worst. A smoldering mist enveloped Remy's flat. Every surface was singed black, and a heavy cloud of smoke and ash filled the apartment, stinging my eyes and nose. I knew, even before my feet touched down on the floorboards, that Arnesto and the sword had been taken. I feared Remy would be injured or worse, but he was gone as well."

Yelenarra sighed heavily and waved her hand, a sparkly gold and silver cape now draping her ankle-length gown. "I must leave at once and inform Katrine and the council. I pray the council will take action, but I fear they will not. No matter, I shall travel to the outer demesnes and demand an audience with the dark fay king himself."

"No, Auntie, you mustn't. Then Bazra will have both of you! He could rule all the realms with that kind of power!"

"I don't understand," said Mara. "What sort of power?"

"My aunt's blood possesses similar qualities as Arnesto's. But instead of dispatching an undead creature to its permanent demise, Yelenarra's blood can raise the dead, without any necromantic incantation needed."

The ability to raise the undead seemed a heavy burden to carry. Mara couldn't imagine having such raw, unwelcome power. She gazed at Efram. "And what about you? Does your blood carry any unusual power as well?"

"Aye. But please know that what we are telling you has been told to no one outside our immediate family. It's far too risky." Efram ran a hand through his short blue hair. "My blood can quell the undead and bring them under my control."

Mara's jaw dropped. Between the three of them, they could raise the dead, control the undead, and send the undead to their eternal demise. She was thankful they were on her side, and convinced she had to prevent anyone else from Arnesto's family falling under Bazra's control. "We must take care that neither of you are captured by the Bazeerka. The consequences are unthinkable."

Yelenarra's shoulders sagged. "Even so, I have no choice. The Bazeerka have my dear nephew. I shall barter with Bazra—an even exchange—myself for Arnesto."

"No!" Mara pushed back from the table and bent down to the floor, where she'd deposited her carrying case. She murmured the opening spell and threw back the lid. She withdrew the sword, its jeweled hilt responding immediately to her touch. The ancient weapon came to life, its fay magic pulsing in vivid blue hieroglyphs up and down the blade. Mara stepped away from the table and raised the sword in her right hand. "We will rescue Arnesto and the others, and we will retrieve the red sword. The dark fays will *not* win this day."

The lines creasing Yelenarra's forehead softened. "Maragold, your courage is inspiring. However, this is a fight that shall test not only your bravery, but also your wits, your magic, and your heart. Bazra's authority within the outer demesnes is almost absolute. He will do everything in his power to break you and take your sword."

Mara sheathed her sword and looped the scabbard through her belt before retaking her seat. She would not allow Bazra's wicked Fallowness to crack her resolve. They needed a plan, and they needed help, as much as they could muster. "Katrine will help us, and I'm sure there are others willing to face Bazra."

Yelenarra compressed her lips. "Legends and stories to the contrary, most fays are not especially brave, leastwise, not anymore. It is only when our comfortable lives here in Havynweal are threatened with extinction that we will rise up and fight."

"But the fays helped us defeat the Glenbarrans during the war."

Efram said, "That was only because Chief Pryl finally

convinced the council that if we didn't stop King Roi's undead army in Valerra, he and Bazra might one day join forces. And that would be very bad news for Havynweal."

"I never knew that was the real reason the fays helped us."

"We don't discuss the dark fays with anyone outside the fay lands unless it's absolutely necessary," replied Efram.

Mara recalled Vas telling her about King Roi's latest sightings around the barrens. "Alright then, let's talk about the dark fays and the Glenbarrans colluding now. Wouldn't that argument work again?"

Yelenarra sat back down. "I am not following you, lass."

Mara turned to Efram. "How many fay scouts have gone missing recently?"

"We've lost three scouts in as many weeks. Each time, the scout reported on King Roi's activities, returned to track him further, and was not heard from again."

"Vas told us that King Roi has been roaming just beyond Valerra's southern border lately, near the barrens. Roi has a long history of dabbling in necromancy. What if he's been raising an undead army again?"

"That would be more bad news for Vas and the provisional government in Valerra. But what's the connection with Bazra?" asked Efram.

"The barrens. It makes no sense for King Roi to be messing around with his necromancers in the barrens. It's an inhospitable place, with blazing sun by day and frigid temperatures by night. The wind blows all the time, kicking up so much grime and dust that everything is covered in it. Even your food tastes gritty, and weeks after you've passed through, you're still washing the sandy soil from your hair."

"So you believe Bazra has struck a deal with the Glenbarran king? If the Glenbarran king is raising an undead army in the barrens, I can understand how Bazra might want access to that army." Yelenarra pursed her lips. "But what does the Glenbarran king get out of this?"

"Another chance at destroying Bellaryss. King Roi has never conceded defeat. And far too many of his ex-soldiers remained in our city after the war, hiding in underground tunnels and caves. Vas and his advisors believed it was because they had no good reason to return home, since much of Glenbarra had been decimated by the king's war. I think that was true for some of the Glenbarrans who didn't go home. However, it's become clear that others stayed behind to create trouble and commit crimes, perhaps waiting for an opportune time for their king to return."

"That is an interesting theory, one worth considering," said Yelenarra. "Perhaps with more time, we could bring evidence to the council that Bazra is colluding with the Glenbarran king. But our dear Arnesto is imprisoned by the Bazeerka as we speak, and Bazra's deadline approaches. We have no time for theories and debates. We must act."

Mara agreed. "Then we will take action. But we still need a plan that doesn't involve you negotiating with the dark fays for Arnesto's release. I don't see how that would ever go well. And we still need more than the three of us, if we are going to rescue Arnesto and Remy."

Efram squared his jaw. "Mara is right. We need to extend an *aidirasa*." He explained to Mara. "It's an ancient fay custom, rarely used, which is essentially a call to take up one's weapons and come to the aid of a neighbor. It's a call for help of a very specific kind. Anyone willing to fight alongside us will travel here to our mountain, set up their yurts, and sharpen their blades and arrows."

Yelenarra rubbed her forehead and closed her eyes for a

moment. "Alright. We shall send out an aidirasa. Then what?" Yelenarra opened her eyes, glancing first at Efram and then at Mara.

Yelenarra must be worn to a frazzle to be seeking advice from a human girl. Mara had many questions, but she asked the one question that would help her decide what to do next. "Can this aidirasa also include Valerrans willing to help us?"

Efram glanced at his aunt. "I don't see why not, so long as Auntie doesn't mind them camping on the grounds here."

Yelenarra raised her shoulders in a half shrug. "All who are willing to help us free Arnesto and Remy—and prevent Bazra from unleashing his Bazeerka on Valerra or Havynweal—shall be welcome here. My one stipulation is that you must be able to vouch for them."

"Of course," said Mara, already tallying the names in her head. "I'll need Efram's help traveling to Valerra and bringing them back here."

"Very well. Meanwhile, I shall find Katrine and tell her what has happened. And then I will issue the aidirasa. Please take care and hurry back. We have much to do and Bazra's deadline approaches."

"We'll be careful," Mara called out as the mists snaked up her torso. She snatched a square of cinnamon toast from her plate, before she and Efram vanished on his vapors.

Mara felt spongy grass beneath her boots and waited for the mist to clear away. She had no idea where Efram had brought them. Unable to see any familiar landmarks, she stepped around a thick, tall hedgerow and stopped in her tracks. "Why the Bellaryss Cemetery?"

"My gran's grave is over here, my dear." Efram spoke a little too loudly and steered her by the elbow toward an aboveground crypt near the western entrance of the grave-yard. Efram leaned into her ear to whisper, "Can't trust anyone these days, including that mourner behind us. He's heading in our direction."

Mara nodded and bent down to clear away some weeds from the side of the crypt, which she hoped marked the grave of a woman old enough to be Efram's gran. As her fingers grasped a clump of weeds by the roots, she peeked around the corner. "Queen's Crown, that's the assassin who killed Jakob Kornish," hissed Mara. "And he's definitely heading our way!"

"Why is he an assassin and not simply a thug and murderer?"

"He uses darts with poisoned tips." Mara tugged Efram around the back of the crypt, out of sight. "Quick, let's cast a veil of drabness!"

Efram nodded and they both murmured, "Drape us in a veil of gauze, hide us from inquiring eyes."

A gauzy film draped itself over them. Mara heard the man's footsteps, and she brought a finger to her lips. They stayed in a crouched position, leaning against the back of the vault, waiting for the man to make a move. She reached into her right boot and withdrew a dagger. The assassin shuffled one foot, then another, and Mara heard a thump above her head. She glanced up. The man's head was peering over the roof of the crypt, the rest of his body stretched out behind him. In his hand was a dart, which he started to bring up to his mouth. He couldn't actually *see* them through the veil of drabness, but perhaps he heard them breathing.

Mara wasn't taking any chances. She threw her knife, which lodged in the hand holding the dart. The man made no sound. He merely stared at the knife and continued to wrap his lips around his dart. Efram leapt up at the man, jamming his sword into the man's mouth and driving the poisoned dart down his throat. The assassin gagged and flailed his arms, tumbling off the top of the crypt to the ground.

Mara reached the man first. He worked his jaw a few times, managing to utter, "Clock man." His eyes glazed over.

Efram knelt down next to the man. "What did he say?"

Mara told him, adding, "It makes no sense."

Efram retrieved her knife, wiped it off on the grass, and handed it to her. He cast a hasty veil of drabness over the dead man. "There's something really strange about that man. I registered zero emotions emanating from him, as if he were a block of wood or a piece of metal."

"Arnesto said the same thing about him."

"He's not what he seems." Efram rolled the man over and pointed to a thin red line along the base of his neck. Using the tip of his short knife, Efram cut a small incision along the red line. He fished inside the opening and withdrew a round metal disc the size of a coat button. He held it up for Mara to see. "Some sort of a mechanical device."

Mara thought about what the man had said after Efram's sword struck him. She stared at the disc in Efram's hand. "I think he was trying to tell us he was under the control of this mechanical device—he was a *clockwork man*. I don't think he could stop himself from killing. Something was compelling him."

"And you say he killed someone else?"

"Aye, a baker by the name of Jakob Kornish who'd recently moved to the area to work for Chef Desna. The constables have no idea why Jakob Kornish was a target." She thought of the grihms at the preserve. "I suspect a similar device was inserted into the grihms at the preserve, who started rampaging a few days ago. I don't know if they received a command, or if the device inside their heads malfunctioned."

"Perhaps the same might be true of this man."

Mara glanced around the cemetery. "Why did you bring us here in the first place?"

Efram snorted. "I figured we could arrive without drawing anyone's notice, but that clearly wasn't the case."

"But the clockwork man wouldn't have known we were coming." Mara re-sheathed her knife inside her boot. "So why did he attack us?"

"Let's discuss this in private." Efram's mists curled around their legs and waists. He whisked them away in a puff of vapor and deposited them inside the largest mausoleum in the cemetery, the final resting home for a dozen members of the same family. The interior smelled of rat droppings and mildew. Efram conjured an egg-shaped light like Yelenarra's, although his was lime green. Mara gritted her teeth at the spider webs crisscrossing the interior. Mara felt a spider climbing up her leg and gave a little screech.

"What was that all about?" she whispered.

"I wanted to move us somewhere less exposed."

"And this was the best you could do?" grumbled Mara.

Efram ignored her grumbling. "I've been thinking about the fires, which seemed to target fays or their close allies. Then there's the 'accident' that injured Arnesto, the seemingly random killing of Baker Kornish in the pub, and this senseless attack on us, by a clockwork man who didn't know we'd be here. See any patterns?"

Mara flicked the spider off her leg. "Whatever your theory is, let's have it so we can get out of here, find Vas and a few others I'm sure will help us, and go rescue Arnesto and Remy."

"You make it sound so easy."

Mara sighed. "Think about what we've been through this past year. This won't be easy, but we've had practice standing up to Fallow sorcerers and necromancers before, and we've won."

"Not without losses," Efram reminded her. "Heart-breaking losses."

"I know," said Mara softly. "Tell me what pattern you're seeing. Why do you think the assassin targeted us?"

"My guess is that he'd been programmed with a set of targets. You were on that list. So was Jakob Kornish. So was Arnesto, although in his case, the driver of the locomobile ran him down. What do you, Arnesto, and Baker Kornish have in common?"

"Other than the fact Baker Kornish worked briefly for Chef Desna, and Arnesto and I worked for the chef for a day, there's no connection that I can think of. Oh, and Remy is a baker apprentice, also working for Chef Desna."

Efram rubbed the stubble on his chin. "That's an awful lot of coincidences involving one chef."

"Yes and no. Vas sent Arnesto and me to the bakery to find work and snoop around. We wouldn't have been there otherwise."

"Even so, Jakob Kornish is dead, Remy has been taken, Arnesto was injured on purpose by a locomobile driver, and you were just targeted by the clockwork man."

"How do we know I was the target? He could just as easily have been targeting you. We were right next to each other."

"Fine, I'll concede I might have been the target." Efram

waved his hand holding the light, which flickered and almost went out.

Mara yelped. "Don't let that light go out. This place is almost as creepy as the realms of the dead."

Efram ignored her outburst, but he kept his light steady as he spoke. "Maybe we were both 'general' targets, and it didn't matter who he might have killed?"

Mara shrugged. "And maybe Jakob Kornish was just in the wrong place at the wrong time. He could have been simply a test case to see how well the clockwork man followed orders."

"Alright. I don't think it matters much at the moment. We've got some people to recruit to face Bazra and rescue my brother. Where to first?"

Mara ran down her short list of names and places, beginning with Vas's well-fortified brick house. She figured Vas was running the provisional government out of his front parlor, since the old savings and loan building had been reduced to rubble. Mara had no compunction about relying on Efram's mists, along with a veil of drabness for concealment, to translocate from the cemetery to Vas's gravel driveway. They had a lot of territory to cover, and very little time to plan their operation.

CHAPTER 24

Mara rapped the brass knocker on the dark green door and waited, while Efram constantly scanned their surroundings for any signs of dark fays or undead monsters. She thought Efram was more paranoid than usual, but then again, his brother had been captured practically under his nose.

Qwidd opened the door, his bushy eyebrows raised in surprise at her black tunic and leggings with sparkly gold stars. Mara hastily brushed some cobwebs from the shoulder of her cape. "Miss Pensk, we'd been given to understand you were detained caring for Mr. Luca. Who is your companion?"

Mara made the introductions, Efram bowing elegantly. He was almost as much of a showman as his younger brother. Qwidd invited them inside and led them down the hall to a small library. "Vas is in a conference right now, but he'll want to see you. How is young Mr. Luca doing?"

Mara's voice dropped low. "He's been kidnapped by the dark fays. That's why we're here, actually. A battle is brewing over the future of Valerra and Havynweal. We need all the help we can get to defeat the dark fays and rescue Arnesto, as well as Remy, who was also taken."

Qwidd's demeanor changed, from a polite but slightly bored fencing coach and part-time butler, to Vas's chief of staff and military advisor. He drew his shoulders back. "I'll inform the colonel immediately. This act of aggression must not stand."

Mara noticed he reverted to using Vas's former military rank. When the Glenbarrans overran Bellaryss, demolishing both military and magical defenses in the city, Colonel Martel Revas became simply Vas, a resistance leader. Later, Vas became the provisional president. However, to his former marines, Vas would always be the colonel.

She heard murmuring in the parlor and then quick footsteps. Vas burst into the room, his exhaustion evident in the dark circles beneath his eyes. "What's this about dark fays kidnapping Arnesto and Remy? And a battle for Valerra?"

Mara gave Vas an overview of all that had occurred since she'd last seen him, including the locomobile incident that injured Arnesto, her battle with the grotesque creature in Havynweal, and the threat from Bazra. Efram described the circumstances surrounding Arnesto's capture, and the significance of Remy's red sword falling into Bazeerka hands.

The lines on Vas's forehead deepened, and he ran a hand through his hair. "And you're saying we have about twelve hours to assemble a fighting force and enter the barrens—"

Efram interjected, "Technically it's the outer demesnes, located between the barrens and the realms of the dead."

"Alright then, we need to enter the outer demesnes, rescue our people, and take down this Bazra fellow?"

"Bazra is the dark fay king. His power in the outer demesnes is nearly absolute," Efram pointed out.

"I think he might have struck a deal with King Roi," said Mara, before Efram tried to offer up any more explanations about dark fays and their king. She knew Vas, and his focus would be on protecting Valerra and finding King Roi, who'd slipped through his fingers once before.

"Why do you say that?" barked Vas, who Mara knew from previous missions became increasingly prickly and irritable as their likelihood of success diminished.

Mara explained her theory about the Glenbarran king using necromancers to raise an undead army for Bazra, in exchange for something—that something likely being Bellaryss itself.

Vas stared up at the wood-paneled ceiling and then leveled his gaze on Mara. "An excellent though chilling theory, one that had not occurred to me. It does line up with what we know about King Roi and explains why he would be operating along our southern border, which is far from his home base and has nothing to offer other than proximity to the barrens. I think we need to operate under the assumption that Roi and this other fay fellow—"

"Bazra, the dark fay king," supplied Efram.

"That Roi and this Bazra fellow are in cahoots. A Fallow sorcerer king and a dark fay king teaming up against Valerra—"

"And Havynweal," added Efram.

Vas sighed, clearly annoyed at Efram's constant inter-ruptions. "Aye. They are teaming up against Valerra and Havynweal, but to what purpose? What is their end game?"

"To crush Serving magic so no one can oppose the rest of their plan."

Mara jumped. She hadn't noticed Chief Inspector Talias's arrival on a cloud of mists.

Vas walked over to Talias and grasped her hands in both of his. "Do you really believe that, Penray?"

Talias nodded. "Without a doubt. We must do what we can to stop them, although I fear it may be too late."

Vas's expression darkened. "Don't say that. We've faced daunting odds before, and we've found a way to beat them."

"We didn't face the Bazeerka before. I'm afraid we are woefully unprepared for a fight with Bazeerkalim's descendants. But you're right. There may yet be a way to disrupt their plans." Vas draped an arm around the chief inspector's waist, and she leaned her head on his shoulder. In another time and place, Mara would have said something, teased them in a lighthearted way, but there was nothing blithe about their current situation. Bazra would be breathing down their necks soon enough, and Arnesto and Remy were his prisoners.

Qwidd asked, "What is their plan, beyond destroying Serving magic?"

Talias said, "It's clear the dark fays intend to vacate the outer demesnes. They've been biding their time for centuries, waiting for the means to leave, and now they've got it."

"I'm not sure I'm following you," Qwidd's eyebrows drew together, two bushy caterpillars in a face-off.

"They needed a human king stupid enough to invite them onto human lands."

Vas stared at Talias. "Are you suggesting King Roi has invited Bazra to inhabit Valerra?"

Talias nodded. "Aye. I believe that's the likeliest explanation."

Mara waved her hand. "But Roi has no authority here. Valerra is run by Vas and the provisional government."

"That's not entirely true," Talias sighed. "At least not according to fay customs."

"Huh?" Vas thrust out his bottom lip. "What's this about fays not recognizing my authority?"

Talias explained, "Bazra adheres to the old ways. A king, even a crazy king with a rag-tag following, is an authority figure."

"But we defeated King Roi." Vas scowled.

"But did we really? Has he conceded defeat yet? Are all his thugs and sorcerers rounded up and in jail? Are we able to rebuild without fear of insurrection, stirred up by Roi and his Glenbarrans?"

Vas dropped his head, suddenly deflated. "Point well taken."

Talias punched him lightly on the arm. "Stop that right now."

"Stop what?"

"Stop looking at this situation as a personal failure. This is not about you or me or any one person. Although I suspect there is more to Arnesto's kidnapping than meets the eye." Efram and Mara glanced at each other but didn't say anything. Some secrets had to remain just that. "You have no standing army, very little political capital outside of Bellaryss, and far too many ignorant anti-magickers who believe Serving mages and fays should be 'de-fanged' as they call it."

"It's ironic," said Efram. "The anti-magickers are playing right into the hands of the dark fay king and Roi's necromancers."

"Aye, true enough," agreed Talias. "And the most ignorant of them all is Harlan Lewyn, who is a Serving mage, although he's disavowed all magic. I believe he sees this as a way to gain enough political clout to challenge Martel for the presidency."

Vas shook his head. "But Lewyn has been so supportive up until now. He's providing the government with low-interest loans and free boarding for our horses in his stables."

"He's also been running the grihm preserve, and we know how that turned out," said Mara.

Vas stared at the opposite wall, filled with leather-bound books and a few very old scrolls, as if searching for inspiration. He narrowed his eyes and turned to Mara. "I certainly hope you're wrong about Harlan Lewyn having a direct hand in what happened to the grihms, but I don't like coincidences. His anti-magic movement might have taken a dangerous turn."

Mara nodded at Efram. He reached inside his cape, where he'd placed the metal disc from the clockwork man, after first carefully wrapping the thing in a linen handker-chief. Mara told them about their encounter with the assassin in the cemetery and his attack on them. Efram unwrapped the disc and handed it to Vas, who picked it up between his thumb and forefinger and carried it to an open window for a better view.

"Penray, what do you make of this?"

The chief inspector joined Vas, standing together in the patch of sunlight from the window. "It appears to be of the same design as the metal discs removed from the grihms who'd rampaged at the preserve."

Vas rubbed his beard. Mara heard the clock on the mantel ticking the seconds. Everyone waited as the provisional president considered the evidence and his options, which were few and unlikely to succeed without more loss of life. Vas turned the metal disc over in his palm and then handed it to Penray. "Please keep that as evidence, once we figure out who inserted it into the murderer's skull, when the surgery occurred, and to what purpose. In the meantime, we have a dark fay king to defeat, a crazy Glenbarran king to arrest for his war crimes, and friends to rescue." He glanced at the clock above the fireplace. "And we now have little more than ten hours to come up with a plan. But first, tell me who else you're planning to recruit from Bellaryss."

Mara ran down her very short list. He nodded his agreement. "I'm surprised by that last one, but I can see your point. Alright then, Penray is able to transport my team and me to Havynweal. You and Efram will round up the rest, and we will see you soon enough on the grounds of Dame Yelenarra's manor. But first, we are going to take a moment to gather up our weapons down below."

Mara felt a grim sort of relief that Vas would be helping. She needed him and the others to help rescue Arnesto and Remy. She only wished she could guarantee their safety—and survival—in the outer demesnes.

CHAPTER 25

By the time Mara returned to Havynweal with Efram, pops of brilliant color filled the wide lawn surrounding Yelenarra's massive home. The fays who responded to the aidirasa had set up campsites, their yurts turning the hilltop into splashes of blue, red, green, and yellow. Mara was pleased to see Zornamayne and her clan had come. She had no doubt they would need the feline hybrid's remarkable healing skills.

Gloria arrived by Mara's side in a flutter of wings, rapidly clicking her beak. "I was worried, milady. You were gone over long in the human realm."

"Any news about Arnesto?" Mara reached down to rub Gloria's mane.

The griffin dipped her head to the side and purred from her throat. "Nay, milady. However, over two hundred fays have responded to the aidirasa—not a small showing by any means."

"Aye." Mara continued stroking Gloria's mane, wondering how badly outnumbered they would be in the outer demesnes. Perhaps it was best not to know.

"Pretty colors," grunted Farleigh, waving one paw at the yurts dotting the hill.

"Blue nicest," yipped Jerdahn. The enthusiastic young grihm had practically bowled Mara over when she and Efram arrived at the farm on the outskirts of Bellaryss to pick up Farleigh. Mara was thrilled to discover Jerdahn had been one of the grihms who'd escaped from the preserve, along with a whiney older grihm named Yeller. The two escaped grihms had managed to find their way to Farleigh, using their superior sense of smell and Farleigh's evening howls to track down his whereabouts.

Vas's farmer friend had called in an animal healer to deal with the grihms' injuries, mostly scrapes and cuts on their paws and a gash on Yeller's hind leg. At Vas's request, the healer searched for any recent incisions on the back of their necks. Sure enough, the healer had discovered and removed a metal disc from each of the grihms.

Efram led Mara, Gloria, and the grihms to a huge gazebo on Yelenarra's side lawn, near the large blue yurt that Penray had conjured for herself and Vas. Two other blue yurts stood nearby, one for Nahn and Gemala, and the other for Qwidd and Sami. A third yurt, red and yellow striped, sat on the other side of the gazebo. Mara gaped when Inspector Foxx and Chef Desna emerged from the tent. Neither of the men had been on her shortlist for this battle. While she could understand why Talias would have recruited her trustworthy constable for this mission, why was the most famous baker in Bellaryss standing next to Yelenarra's gazebo, completely at ease in Havynweal?

Desna's ice-blue eyes twinkled at Mara. "It seems you're surprised to see me standing here on Yelenarra's hilltop, Miss Pensk. However, this is not my first visit to Havynweal. My grandmother was fay. She used to bring my brother and me to Havynweal when we were boys, to pet the unicorns and visit the festivals. The first time I tasted a full puff pastry was at a little tearoom in harvest fall. I promised myself then and there that I would master baking—without magic, since I inherited very little of my gran's abilities—but that's a story for another day." He nodded at Inspector Foxx. "When Vincens stopped by the bakery to say goodbye and explain about the threat from the Bazeerka, I closed the bakery early and came along with him and Penray."

Inspector Foxx supplied the missing information. "Not many people realize Chef Desna Foxx and I are brothers."

Mara glanced at the brothers' baldheads; any trace of their blue-streaked hair would have long since fallen out or been shaved off. She realized poor Bea could have stopped dying her hair to hide the blue, without incurring Chef Desna's displeasure. If anything, he would have protected her right to become a baker's apprentice. Mara smiled. "I'm grateful you've come to help us."

She didn't feel it was her place to ask the Foxx brothers about their fighting skills. While she assumed Vincens's training as a constable involved a variety of weapons, she couldn't fathom Chef Desna's skills. His eyes crinkled at the corners. "You may be wondering what a pastry chef can do on the battlefield. Rest assured I am quite adept with my blades." His hands moved almost as quickly as Arnesto's when he was using his fast-math skills. In a blink, Desna held twin short swords in his beefy hands, their silver blades gleaming in the afternoon sun. He twirled the swords, sheathing them again at his sides. "Anyone employed in a kitchen ought to know how to use a knife, lass."

"Thank you all for responding to my aidirasa." Yelenarra used her commanding voice to project across the hill-side. She stood in the open turret of her manor home. Once used as a lookout tower during the fay clan wars, it over-looked the yurt-dotted grounds. Yelenarra's earlier indecision was gone, and she spoke with heart and conviction about the dangers before them, as well as the consequences of allowing the Bazeerka to escape from the outer demesnes.

When she finished speaking, Yelenarra stepped back from the turret wall. Katrine took her place, dressed for battle with the undead in her silver cape and tunic, a coil of golden rope slung over each shoulder, and a longsword at her waist. Katrine used her commanding voice, which was even more powerful than Yelenarra's. She reinforced Yelenarra's main points, and then explained the strategy. "Yelenarra will call us into the great hall after we have ensured everyone has eaten, since we do not know when we'll enjoy our next meal. Once in the hall, we shall divide ourselves into groups by clan and then by weapon mastery. In the meantime, please run your own practice drills."

Yelenarra and Katrine conjured platters of sausages, cheeses, toast points, and fresh fruit, which they sent round to each of the yurts. If Mara weren't so anxious about rescuing Arnesto and Remy, she would have laughed out loud at the sight of large platters of food moving across the hillside without any visible means of support, as if carried along by invisible servants. Next, Yelenarra and Katrine sent out a round of ginger beer, as well as jugs of fresh water from the stream that ran behind Yelenarra's labyrinthine garden.

After the platters had been emptied and everyone had their fill, Yelenarra rang a bell from the top of her lookout turret. The various clans began collecting their weapons and entering Yelenarra's home through the rune-covered archway, the runes lighting up as each clan passed beneath them. As each clan entered the enormous great hall, they gathered in small groups on the wooden floor, organizing themselves by weapon mastery as Katrine requested.

Mara and Efram entered with Yelenarra, Katrine, and Vas and his team, which now also included Penray Talias, Chef Desna, and Vincens Foxx. They sat in the center of the great hall, where Yelenarra and Katrine would be able to call out instructions when the time came. Once everyone had assembled inside the massive hall, Yelenarra nodded at Katrine, who clapped her hands. Mara sensed the ground begin to shake beneath her. At first, she thought it might be an earthquake, and then she feared it was the Bazeerka thundering into the room. Instead, the great hall itself was moving. Efram leaned over to explain they would pass through harvest fall and frosty fall, before arriving in dead of winter, which was the only season in which fays were permitted to speak of war.

Mara was slightly nauseous by the time the hall stopped shuddering. Her teeth began chattering as frost spread across the ceiling, walls, and floor, and snowdrifts gathered in the corners of the room. Katrine clapped her hands again, and Mara's black cape gained a fleece lining. She reached into the pockets and withdrew a pair of thick leather gloves. An ensorcelled lasso appeared over each of her shoulders, crisscrossing her chest. Mara glanced around and noticed everyone else wore suitable winterized clothing, either magicked by Katrine or self-conjured.

Katrine clapped once more and shouted, "Let the aidirasa begin!" The great hall erupted into forty different conversations, as fays debated the best means of accessing the outer demesnes without alerting the Bazeerka. The debate continued for two hours at least, perhaps more, but since fays didn't bother with clocks or timepieces, Mara couldn't be certain. She wondered when someone would actually make a decision. Meanwhile, Talias, Vas, and the rest of their "clan" discussed the best means of rescuing Arnesto and Remy. Mara stewed and worried and chewed her knuckles. She hated indecision and inaction and was anxious to do something.

A thunderous crash reverberated across the great hall, followed by a cracking sound, like a whip across a horse's back, and then screams. The hall shook and rattled, as icicles fell from the windows and doorframes. One huge boom and then a series of smaller booms echoed the length of the cavernous room, which began breaking apart. Everyone was knocked off their feet, tumbling to the floor in a jumble of arms and legs. Although Mara attempted to jump back up, the ground shook so much she couldn't find any purchase. She scrambled to her hands and knees, swaying with the motion inside the hall.

Mara heard what sounded like fabric tearing, as if a healer were ripping a length of cotton to use for bandages, although there was no healing in this noise. The ripping and tearing felt as if the world around her were being shredded from its foundations. The floorboards continued vibrating beneath her and pieces of plaster fell from the ceiling, showering her head and shoulders. Mara didn't know whether to pull out her lasso or her blades, deciding to wait for the shaking to subside before attempting to handle anything sharp.

Another explosion rocked the hall, which resembled a battlefield rather than Yelenarra's gathering place, with people sprawled all about, some bleeding from head injuries, others knocked unconscious. Mara gagged as the stench of death filled her nostrils, her stomach curdling with fear at what came next—monsters.

Hulking, screeching, undead creatures clambered up through the floorboards and flooded in through the shattered windows. Some looked like the tearoom beast, a cross between a panther and a lizard; others slithered along like snakes, but they had eight legs like spiders and mouths filled with pointy teeth. Whatever forms they took, thick, sharp bristles covered their hides, and their eyes glowed red.

Mara felt darkness pressing in on her from all sides. She entered a black void inside her head that chased away every happy thought, crushed her will to resist, and forced her spirit into submission. Although a small part of her brain knew this overwhelming sadness came from beyond the grave and had a life outside of her physical body, she found it impossible to withstand. Mara crumbled onto the uneven floorboards, realizing Yelenarra had been right. She lacked the fortitude to face this onslaught.

Gloria lay on her side nearby with a nasty gash across her abdomen. One of her wings drooped at an odd angle. Mara watched as one of the snake creatures turned its fiery eyes toward her griffin. The beast scuttled on its eight spidery legs toward Gloria, who moaned but was unable to move.

"No!" Mara was unable to utter more than a pitiful whimper. "No!" she repeated, this time a bit louder. She discovered if she repeated "No!" inside her head, her sadness slowly unwound itself, and she could begin to think for herself again.

Mara scrambled to her feet, but stayed in a low, crouching position. She reached inside her boot shanks and withdrew her twin blades. The snake monster was almost on top of Gloria. It opened its jaw wide, moving in for the kill. Mara, gripping a blade in each hand, leapt up and jammed the daggers into the creature's eye sockets. The snake monster roared, rearing back to strike at Mara, as yellow liquid streamed from both eyes. The creature wavered and fell to its side, where it withered into a mound of bristles and ash.

Mara picked her blades out of the sooty ash and crawled over to Gloria, who clicked her beak weakly. "Thank you, milady. Now go rescue Arnestarious and the others."

"Not until I'm sure another one of these monsters isn't going to eat you!"

Zornamayne, bleeding from a cut above her eye and panting heavily, laid a paw on Gloria's abdomen. "Gloria is right. I shall look after your griffin and the others here in need of healing. You must go now." Zornamayne pointed to the largest crack in the floor. For some reason the undead monsters were retreating into the crack and dropping into the abyss below. "Bazra could only give them a few minutes of half-life outside of the realms of the dead—even he cannot control that many creatures for any longer among the living. Follow the undead down to the lowest realms. They will lead you to the dark fay king. You must stop Bazra and rescue Arnestarious."

"How can I possibly go alone?"

"You won't be alone. Others will follow. But you were the first to break through Bazra's bonds, so you must lead the rest. Now go!"

Mara looked in the direction Zornamayne was pointing. The panther-lizard creatures had already dropped out of sight. Mara's heart thundered in her chest as she chased after the last of the slithering snake monsters and leapt into the fissure that ran the length of the great hall. She glanced upward as she fell and saw that Zornamayne was right. Others were following her lead, most of them bleeding from scratches and cuts, their clothing shredded from wrestling with the bristly beasts. Talias, Vas, and his team tumbled after her, as well as Katrine, Yelenarra, and Efram. Desna and Vincens Foxx followed them, along with Farleigh, Jerdahn, and Yeller, screaming all the way down. About a dozen fays leapt in after them, blades and arrows at the ready. Mara suspected more would have followed, but many fays had been injured during the explosions that rocked the great hall.

Her stomach in knots, she swallowed hard as she peered into the gray gloom below. Why was it so much louder and hotter than the first time she'd leapt through a portal to the lower realms? The creatures who'd retreated ahead of her screeched and screamed from somewhere below; a few of them reached upward to swipe at her legs and boots. She kicked away one razor-sharp claw and heard a yowl of pain. Beads of perspiration collected on her forehead and dripped into her eyes, the heat inside the realm nearly suffocating. She'd have to lose her fleece-lined cape as soon as she landed.

Why was she still falling? The last time, she'd tumbled for maybe ten or twelve seconds and landed on soft, spongy ground in the lowest realm. But she'd been dropping for at least half a minute, maybe longer. She hoped wherever she landed, she would have a few moments to regroup with her friends before having to face the undead again. After all, she was now entering their territory—they held the upper hand.

The soles of her boots scraped against loose sand, and she toppled onto her hands and knees, grinding her teeth to keep from yelping in pain. She pushed herself off the ground, grabbing her daggers from the sandy soil as she stood, legs flexed and all her senses alert. She pivoted on the ball of one foot, ready for an attack that didn't come. Mara was alone, surrounded by shadowy forms that rocked to and fro but thankfully didn't advance. She spun around again, her spine tingling. Something landed onto her head and she screamed, bending over and shaking her ponytail until a hairy brown spider fell onto the ground.

Mara *hated* spiders. She'd rather face Bazra's undead monsters than pull spiders out of her hair. She lifted her boot and smashed the spider, yellowish-brown liquid oozing out beneath her heel. Three more spiders fell onto her head and shoulders, and then four more. Mara ran around in a strange circular dance, shaking herself and hollering, not caring who heard her. She managed to pull up the hood of her cape, only to yelp when a large gray spider crawled out. Screaming, she flung the cape away. Was this what Yelenarra meant when she said Bazra would test her to her very limits?

"Mara! Where are you?" hissed Efram somewhere off to Mara's right.

She glanced around, her eyes adjusting somewhat to the constant gray gloom. The shadows that shifted from side to side weren't monsters at all, but spindly, leafless trees, their limbs swaying in the hot air currents that swirled around the realm. "I'm standing inside a ring of trees, and there are spiders everywhere!"

"Huh? I don't see any trees or spiders, but there are giant rats peering out of holes in the ground. One of them bit me in the leg."

"Keep talking. I'm going to make my way over to you."

Mara heard a clattering sound, as if Efram had tossed a

knife at something and missed. "Hurry up, one of them ran off with my dagger!" Efram howled as if bitten, and Mara ran through the trees, flailing her arms at the spiders that continued dropping down from the limbs. She ran past the last of the trees and found Efram cowering on the ground, stabbing empty air in front of him with his longsword. She saw no holes and no rats.

"What do you hate more than needles?" she shouted above Efram's yelping at the imaginary rodents.

"Rats. I abhor them," whimpered Efram. "And they keep coming at me."

Mara bent down to pick up Efram's dagger. "Run right through them. Trust me, they're not there. Neither were the spiders I hate, though I would have sworn they were dropping on me from the trees that weren't there either."

Efram glanced at Mara. "Ugh, you're holding a rat by the tail."

"I'm holding your dagger, silly. Now get a grip. We're here to rescue your brother, and we're going to need to find the others first."

Efram straightened and ran toward Mara, kicking at the imaginary rats along the way. He stopped a few feet from her. "That was awful. This place is awful."

"Do you think we're in the lowest of the realms? It sure doesn't look like it did the last time I was here. And it's a lot hotter too."

Efram shrugged. "I have no idea, and if there's anything worse than giant rats, I don't want to know."

"Big hairy poisonous spiders."

"Not nearly as bad."

Mara rolled her eyes. "Let's find the others." She handed Efram his dagger, which he took cautiously. They paused to listen.

Mara thought she heard faint screaming. She pointed at a sand dune, which she started to climb, her boots sinking into the sandy soil with each step. "Come on. Someone's hollering on the other side."

Mara reached the top of the sand dune first, her leg muscles aching from the steep climb. She used the sleeve of her tunic to wipe the sweat from her brow. "I think that's your aunt and Katrine over there waving at us."

Efram came alongside her and squinted into the gloom. He waved back. "Aye, it's them. But I don't see anyone else down below—just a wide stretch of damp sand. The tide must be low, because I can just make out a body of water in the distance." Mara and Efram jogged down the dune and were greeted with hugs by Yelenarra and even Katrine, who was not the hugging type.

Yelenarra leaned on her tall staff, which Mara learned was the elder fay's weapon of choice. Her long blue hair was in disarray, having tumbled out of her normally neat bun. "Oh my stars, at least you've not been taken!"

"Who's been taken?"

"Everyone else," said Katrine. Her tunic was ripped, her mouth bleeding, and her eyes looked slightly unfocused.

"You mean Vas and Talias?" asked Mara.

Katrine sighed. "Aye, plus the rest of Vas's team, and all the fays who jumped into the portal with us. They were surrounded by Bazra's guards and loaded onto his ship. They must be at his compound by now."

Mara had trouble visualizing Bazra possessing a ship and a compound, but she supposed if the dark fays had been banished here for a millennia, they would have done some construction during that time. "How did you two escape?"

Yelenarra shuddered. "Goblins."

Katrine grunted. "Bats."

"Excuse me?" Mara tilted her head to one side. "Oh, I think I understand. Yelenarra, you battled goblins, and Katrine, you fought off bats, until you realized they were illusions."

"They felt real enough to me," grumbled Yelenarra.

Katrine agreed. "I was bitten several times. But you're right, lass, they were not real, at least not in the sense we would think of them as real."

"But why wasn't everyone else affected the way we were?" Efram scratched his chin.

"Oh, but they were. In their case, it was group hysteria. Everyone screamed they were under attack from an army of undead riders. There was no army—just a dozen or so armed Bazeerka, who forced them onto a Bazra's ship."

Mara frowned. "What about the grihms and the hybrids? Were they also taken prisoner?"

Katrine and Yelenarra glanced at each other and then shook their heads. Yelenarra said, "I didn't notice any grihms or hybrids on that vessel. I don't know where they could be."

"Then we need to find them. They have to be around here somewhere." Mara scanned the wide beach and saw nothing but wet sand, clumps of gray grass, and the dunes behind her.

"Aye, and we shall. But first, we must find a way to rescue Arnestarious and Remy." Yelenarra used her staff to pound the sand for emphasis.

Efram pointed to a small black dot in the distance. "Is that Bazra's compound?"

Katrine nodded. "Aye. We need to find a means of crossing the river to reach it though. Bazra's compound is on an island in the second lowest of the realms of the dead.

If we could fly upward through the levels, we would find ourselves standing in the barrens. If we descended, we would be standing at the junction of the falls, where the river meets the lake of fire in the lowest of the realms of the dead."

Mara had been in the lowest realm once before and had no desire to repeat the experience. She tucked a loose chunk of hair behind her ears. "What sort of magic works down here? Can we use your mists to translocate us?"

Katrine shook her head. "Only elemental magic works in the realms of the dead, and the only one of us with any real elemental power is Arnesto."

Efram grumbled, "It should have been me who was taken; at least then Arnesto could have done something about it. I feel useless."

"Stop that negative talk this instant, Eframallium. It is not helpful," scolded Yelenarra.

Efram pressed his lips together in a straight line and glanced away, toward the small dot of an island.

"If fay mists won't work down here, then I suggest we start walking." Mara sheathed her daggers inside her boots and withdrew her longsword, which lit up blue along its blade. "At least this magic is still active."

Yelenarra gripped Mara's shoulder. "Of course! The Swords of Five were forged by a giant and then sprinkled with magic dust from the ancient forests by a powerful fay girl. Your sword is a perfect melding of magical elements and works as well in the lowest of the realms as in Havyn-weal or Valerra. Your sword will be able to help us do more than fight Bazeerka."

Katrine slapped her hand to her forehead. "That's brilliant! Why didn't I think of that sooner?"

"I'm not following either one of you." Efram spread his

hands wide, palms outward. "But if you have a plan, let's hear it."

"Mara is going to use her sword to get us onto that island." Yelenarra pointed her staff in the general direction of Bazra's compound.

"How am I going to do that?" Mara held her sword aloft and rotated it, examining the blade from all angles. The hieroglyphs glowed vivid blue, the only bright spot of color in the otherwise dull gray gloom of the second lowest realm of the dead.

Yelenarra closed her eyes and murmured in her buzzing fay way. Mara had seen Chief Pryl do the same thing when he was recalling a scrap of prophecy or an old incantation. Yelenarra opened her eyes. "You will need to Focus, Funnel, Find, Flow. Which in this case means focus your sword's magic, funnel your mental energy, and find us a conveyance in the flow of elements."

Mara lowered her sword. She'd learned a slightly different version of the Serving mage's mantra in school. "You want me to use my sword to conjure something that will transport us to the island?"

"Aye. That's right. Conjure us a means of crossing land and sea."

"Like what?"

Efram suggested riding on top of a giant whale, but that wouldn't help them cross the wide sandy beach. Yelenarra thought horses might work, if they could traverse the river, but Katrine said the river's current would be too swift for the horses to safely cross.

Mara tapped her boots on the sand while they debated. "Fine, I'll conjure us something that will work on both land and sea. But don't complain if you don't like what I come up with."

Yelenarra nodded. "Go right ahead, lass. Get us onto that island. You won't hear any complaining from me."

Mara drew her brows together and focused on the image she had in mind; while she'd never ridden on one, she'd certainly seen the artwork and read the old fay tales. She struck the sand with her sword three times and was nearly knocked over by the magic's power as she shouted:

> *"Come hither, great one, without delay—*
> *Take us to the lair of the dark fay.*
> *Our quest is honorable and worthy:*
> *Bazra to stop, his captives to free.*
> *Come hither, great one, we are ready."*

Mara heard an indignant bleat and felt a blast of hot air on the back of her legs, followed by the smell of singed leather. Mara glanced down and noticed that her boots were smoking and her calves felt warm. For a brief, horrible moment she feared she'd conjured an undead beast.

"Oh lass, what have you done?" squealed Yelenarra. Katrine and Efram stared at the creature standing behind Mara, their mouths open in shock.

Mara turned around slowly, her stomach a mass of anxious knots.

An enormous dark green dragon, with golden flecks on its scales and wings, shifted impatiently on its hind legs, waving its forearms about as if directing traffic on High Street. The creature stood two stories tall, with a spiked tail the length of Yelenarra's side lawn. The dragon's teal eyelashes were as long as Mara's fingers and curled upward delicately, leading Mara to believe the dragon was a female. The dragon lowered her head to ground level and stared at Mara through intelligent emerald eyes.

Flaring her nostrils somewhat, the dragon opened her mouth to speak. Efram yanked Mara backward, out of range of any stray fire bolts the dragon might accidentally emit when she spoke. "I am called Xenestra, of the Suporra-Draca clan. Who are you and why have you brought me to this dreadful place?"

"I am called Maragold. I have brought you here to help us rescue a group of citizens from Havynweal and Valerra, who are being held against their will by Bazra."

Xenestra snorted, sending a burst of fire out of each nostril. Mara had to remember to thank Efram for pulling her out of range. "I have no quarrel with the dark fay king. He has not taken any dragons."

This is all I need, thought Mara, *a self-centered dragon with her own political agenda.* "Today, fays and humans are being held prisoner by the dark fay king. Tomorrow, it could well be dragons. We need your help to rescue our prisoners and prevent Bazra from taking anyone else."

"I am sorry to disappoint you, but I have no intention of doing anything that could jeopardize the Suporra-Draca clan. Now send me home."

Mara didn't think Xenestra was sorry at all—proud and uncooperative, more like. "No!" Mara clenched her jaw to keep her teeth from chattering.

Xenestra drew herself up to her full height. "No?"

Mara folded her arms, hoping the dragon didn't notice how badly her knees were shaking. "You heard me, Xenestra of the Suporra-Draca clan. I will not send you home until you have helped us accomplish our mission. You will fly us to Bazra's island compound, deposit us in a safe place, and wait for us to free the prisoners. And then you will fly all of us, including the freed captives, up to the top of this abyss." Mara pointed upward, and the dragon lifted her face to peer through the gloom.

"And these are the conditions of our arrangement?"

Mara was about to agree, but Katrine cleared her throat. She stepped into line beside Mara and introduced herself to the dragon, using her official title of "Interim Chief of the Fay Nation." This was the first time Mara heard Katrine publicly lay claim to her leadership role and perhaps also acknowledge that her half-brother, Chief Pryl, might not be returning to Havynweal anytime soon.

Xenestra greeted Katrine respectfully and then repeated her request to be sent back home. Katrine echoed Mara's demands, adding, "We will send you home once every one of our prisoners is rescued and delivered to Havynweal in safe, stable, and intact condition. If you need to make more than one trip to accomplish this, or engage in defensive maneuvers, then you shall do so." The dragon started to open her mouth to roar her objection, but Katrine hastily added, "In exchange for such outstanding service to the Fay Nation and the Valerran kingdom, I shall grant the Suporra-Draca clan access to the disputed Toomsenbarra Parkway, next to the Unicorn Sanctuary within harvest fall."

"Unlimited access?"

"Aye, unlimited access. Do we have an accord?"

Xenestra used a talon to write something in the damp sand. She dusted the sand from her talon and waited for Katrine to sign their agreement. Mara found the dragon script unintelligible, but Katrine didn't hesitate to sign the agreement. When Katrine finished, she rose and wiped the sand from her fingers. Xenestra said, "May I borrow a small dagger?"

Mara handed the dragon one of her blades. The dragon gripped the knife in her talon and pricked the flesh of her forearm. She dribbled five drops of her blood over the message inscribed in the sand. "Our accord is sealed in dragon blood. If any party forfeits, the other has first rights." Mara had no idea what "first rights" meant and she had no intention of finding out.

Katrine bowed and waved her hand to indicate everyone else should bow as well. "Aye, we concur. Now let us be on our way. Maragold will lead us, as it was her magic that brought you here."

Xenestra dipped her large head in acknowledgment. "I await Maragold's directions." The dragon handed Mara's dagger back to her hilt first.

Mara sheathed her blade. "First, can you please tell us how to mount you? It would help if we can see the island from your vantage point."

Xenestra lowered her belly to the sandy soil. "Climb onto my tail, but take care to avoid the spikes. Ascend my back until you reach my shoulders. Use the raised plates on my spine as hand grips whilst you climb and again when we are airborne."

Mara scaled the dragon's tail and back, careful not to slip off as she made the steep climb up the bony ridge of the dragon's spine. She cut her hand a few times on the sharp, raised plates along Xenestra's back. She quickly learned to grip the plates from behind, where they were not so sharp.

Mara reached the spot between Xenestra's shoulders and stood up for a better view. Her heart sank at her first real glimpse of Bazra's compound: a squat gray building that looked as if it had been constructed with matchsticks and glue. At the rear of the building stood a crooked black tower. Sadness and despair hung like low clouds about the island compound. She closed her eyes and thought of Arnesto. *I'm coming for you. I won't leave you in that horrid place.* She felt a stab in her chest, and a momentary ache ran through her shoulder and thigh. *Is Arnesto in pain? Or is he trying to warn me of the dangers?*

Mara compressed her lips. She decided that either way, she would not back down. Arnesto needed rescuing, and so did her ex-boyfriend, the provisional president of Valerra, the chief inspector of Bellaryss, and everyone else who'd responded to Yelenarra's aidirasa.

No one was going to be left behind on Mara's watch.

CHAPTER 26

MARA WAITED UNTIL EVERYONE ELSE WAS IN POSITION BEHIND HER, gripping Xenestra's bony plates for support, and then she gave the order. "Xenestra, let's be off. Please circle the island so we can determine the safest spot for landing."

Xenestra snorted a puff of smoke from each nostril. "We shall not find a *safe* spot for landing. If we are very lucky, we shall find a *suitable* spot where we might not draw Bazra's immediate attention. This is a foolhardy mission, but I have agreed on behalf of the Suporra-Draca clan, and I shall not forfeit."

Xenestra ran forward on her powerful hind legs and spread her wings, which glimmered gold, teal, and green— an achingly beautiful sight amidst the dull gray gloom of the second lowest realm. If Mara weren't so filled with dread at facing the Bazeerka, she would have enjoyed the short flight. Xenestra circled high above Bazra's island, giving them a dragon's-eye view.

The only possible landing area for the giant dragon was a broad expanse of sandy beach surrounded by black dune grasses. The rest of the island was either enclosed by tall, spike-topped fences or covered in sharp rocks. A large, black, hulking ship, its charcoal sails hanging motionless in the dead air of the Bazeerka's enclave, sat in a small cove beside the beach. Mara figured Bazra used elemental magic to propel his ship since there was no wind whatsoever.

Yelenarra called out over the flapping of Xenestra's wings. "Cast a veil of drabness, lass, but channel it through your sword."

"Will that work?" hollered Mara.

"Theoretically, it should."

Mara told Xenestra to wait to descend until she could cast, or try to cast, a veil of drabness. Mara shouted, "Drape us in a veil of gauze, hide us from inquiring eyes," while holding her sword aloft. A bright blue light sparked at the tip of her sword. She sensed the veil of drabness draping over them, obscuring the dragon and their landing party in the same gray, gauzy gloom that permeated the second lowest realm.

Xenestra touched down with surprising grace on all four legs. They landed in the shadow of the hulking ship, which offered additional cover, if anyone from the creepy castle were peering down at the beach. The dragon turned her enormous head around to address Mara, gazing at her through one emerald eye. "I shall be flying overhead, Maragold. Use your sword to call me down, and I shall come for you and the others. Good luck, if such a thing is possible against the dark king."

Xenestra waited for their small group to descend from her back and then she took a running start, soaring into the sky. The veil of drabness hid her until she was well away. Mara just hoped their arrival went equally unremarked by Bazra and his guards.

Efram hissed, "Now what? We have no floor plans of

this monstrous building and no idea where the captives are being held."

Mara sighed. Sometimes Efram's pessimism really got on her nerves, especially when his brother had been kidnapped right under his nose. Not that she blamed Efram, but still, why couldn't he have stuck around and waited for Arnesto? The two of them together might have been able to fight off the undead creatures sent by Bazra. Now Arnesto was stuck somewhere in the bowels of that rotten building, perhaps even now having his blood drained for its unique properties. Something about Arnesto's bloodline, as well as Efram's and Yelenarra's, stirred an idea at the back of her mind, but she couldn't quite grasp it. She knew not to force such things. Odd bits of inspiration generally arrived just in time.

Yelenarra poked Efram in the ribs. "Use your noggin, lad, not your mouth. Where would you place a large group of prisoners?"

Efram winced at the sharp poke. "Either very high up, like in that tower up there, or very low down, in a basement dungeon. Both places would be well fortified and difficult to reach."

Katrine said, "Good thinking. Now one more question —on an island with a high water table, where would you secure your prisoners?"

Efram pointed at the tower. "Up there."

Yelenarra and Katrine glanced at Mara. "What do you think?"

Mara nodded. "I agree that's the most logical place. Now we just have to find a way in, dispense with any dark fays we meet along the way, and rescue everyone."

"Bazra will not let Arnestarious go without a fight," said Yelenarra.

"You said earlier we would need the red sword to stop him. Then we'll need to free Arnesto and the red sword—hopefully at the same time."

"Aye," Yelenarra nodded. "But that will be only half the battle."

"What do you mean?"

Katrine answered Mara's question. "Yelenarra is referring to the undead called forth by Bazra for this battle. And let's not forget your theory about King Roi joining forces with Bazra. Given the position of this compound, Bazra and Roi would be able to tap into a steady supply of undead creatures from the lowest realm. With the threat of eternal death in the lake of fire, the undead will be quite pliable. In order to defeat Bazra, we'll need to return the undead to the lowest realm."

Efram squinted up at the foreboding tower above them. "I'll stick close to Arnesto and help him guard the red sword."

"I believe our best hope is for all of us to stick together." What Mara didn't say was that she wasn't about to let Arnesto out of her sight again, and she wasn't leaving his safety up to Efram again. She still trusted Efram, but she didn't think he'd proven himself as reliable as she would have expected, given his field experience and his skills as a fay. Perhaps losing Wreyn had dislodged something within him, making Efram less of the whole person he'd been before.

Mara squared her shoulders. "Alright, here's the plan. We'll watch the guards for a bit and find a way to enter the compound without raising an alarm. We'll confirm the location of the prisoners and then go release them. Once they're freed, I'll call Xenestra and have her begin ferrying our people back to Havynweal. And then we'll take on Bazra and the undead."

"Let's just hope it happens in that order," grumbled Efram. "And that we survive long enough to tell of our exploits afterward."

Mara strengthened the veil of drabness, using her sword to channel the magic. The four of them crept from the beach to a wooden guardhouse, which looked like it had been constructed from driftwood and held together with thick ropes and wooden stakes. The Bazeerka guards looked more like skinny wraiths than fays, probably due to the constant gloom of the second lowest level. They were dressed like street urchins in moth-eaten morning coats, patched up trousers, and a variety of headgear ranging from peaked caps to turbans and top hats. Their weapons consisted of battered swords, spears, and bows and arrows, all of them looking as if they'd been lifted from an army of the undead. Perhaps they had.

Mara noticed every one of the dozen guards wore odd-looking spectacles made from glass bottles shaved off at the bottom and attached to their heads with bits of leather, like goggles. She wondered whether living for centuries in the realms of the dead without access to sunlight had rendered them nearsighted. She didn't have time to figure out how to test the theory since a fresh unit of guards arrived, equally rag-tag, to relieve the first group.

Mara hoped they would pick up some gossip from the guards before they crept inside the compound. So far, their presence had gone unnoticed.

One of the new guards, wearing a red velvet smoking jacket and yellow trousers, pointed behind him. "His Highness is already celebratin' his victory over the sunlight fays."

"Is he now? Don't 'e think they'll be comin' fer their folks?" asked one of the guards getting ready to go off duty.

"Oh he's expectin' 'em to come, but he don't seem too worried. Says he's got sumptin' special waitin' for 'em."

The guards going off duty grunted their goodbyes and trooped through the massive wooden door of the compound, which also appeared to be constructed of driftwood, old stakes, and thick ropes. Mara suspected Bazra used elemental magic to hold his massive compound together. There was too much rotten wood for the building to be stable otherwise.

Mara waved her team forward. They crept alongside the off-duty guards, still hidden by the veil of drabness, which Mara prayed would remain in place until they could find somewhere to hide. They passed half a dozen guards, as poorly dressed as the rest, accompanying what appeared to be four kitchen maids. The serving women wore shifts made from old gunnysacks, gathered at the waist with pieces of rope. One woman carried a basket of hard bread crusts, another woman held a platter filled with bits of smelly cheese, and the last two women carried pitchers of water. Although the women didn't wear goggles, they squinted when a guard addressed them, and peered about as if in need of direction. "Come on, lasses, up the stairs ye go. Them captives ain't feedin' theirselves."

Mara couldn't believe her luck. These serving women were going to lead them right to Arnesto and the others. Mara started up the stairs toward what she assumed was the tower, but someone gave her a hard pinch on her upper arm. She nearly yelped but bit her tongue.

She turned around with a scowl to see Katrine with a finger to her lips, pointing to a small cloakroom. As soon as the four of them scuttled inside, Mara whispered, "Why did you pull back?"

"Our veil of drabness was fading fast. We had less than a minute of coverage left. We're not going to be able to sneak around like this, not without using your sword's magic, which is going to draw the wrong kind of attention."

"Aye, your sword isn't exactly subtle," griped Efram.

Mara ignored Efram's last remark and hissed. "Alright, any ideas on how to find the prisoners?"

Yelenarra shrugged. "Those women look pretty miserable. Maybe we can barter with them."

"What would we have that they could possibly want?" asked Efram.

"Freedom," replied Mara.

Efram gaped at her. "Freedom? You want to help those dark fays leave this place? They've been banished, in case you've forgotten."

"I haven't forgotten, but that was over a millennia ago. These dark fays look like a pretty downtrodden, pathetic bunch. A few of them might be willing to help us, or at least look the other way, in exchange for their freedom. The guards didn't sound all that impressed with their king."

Katrine looked uncomfortable, as if the entire experience had left a bad taste in her mouth. "Unfortunately, I'm not able to offer these fays their freedom. Banishment is final."

"Even to the tenth generation?" asked Mara.

"Even so, according to fay laws and customs."

Mara found herself feeling saddened by the fate of the serving women and their ridiculous guards. "Then we'll need to find another way to creep around this compound unseen. Any ideas?"

"Aye," Yelenarra whispered. "We're in a cloakroom, but

instead of cloaks, all I can see are stacks of raggedy cast-offs. Let's layer ourselves in these rags and sneak about like those guards."

"Auntie, I hate to be the pessimist here, but how are we going to do that without getting caught?"

Yelenarra folded her arms. "Do you have a better idea, Eframallium? Because if you do, let us hear it."

Efram shook his head. "I just don't think four of us can all pretend to be guards. I think one or two of us needs to pretend to be something else."

"We can't pretend to be prisoners. They've already been taken somewhere, and we'll raise immediate suspicion," said Katrine.

Mara snapped her fingers and then immediately regretted making any noise at all. Everyone else looked at her as if she'd lost her mind. "Sorry. What if two of us pretend to be healers? I suspect that some of the prisoners are in need of potions and salves."

Yelenarra and Katrine agreed, volunteering to play the part of fay healers, which meant that Mara and Efram would serve as their guards. They scrounged about in the stacks until they found suitable disguises for each of them. Yelenarra and Katrine wore long black robes with pointy sleeves and runes along the hems and cuffs.

"I think you look more like necromancers than healers," whispered Mara.

Katrine shrugged. "We'll make sure we can play either part, in that case."

Efram found a pink smoking jacket, brown pants, and a ratty purple top hat. He also managed to find an actual pair of goggles, which he donned. Mara slipped into a long green duster with one sleeve shorter than the other, a blue turban that hid her blonde hair, and an eye patch. She rolled up the sleeves of her tunic, so they wouldn't peek out from the duster. Mara made sure the hallway was clear before waving the group out of the cloakroom and toward the stairs.

They took ten steps before someone shouted, "Hold it right there. Necromancers that-a-way. There's a meetin' in the boardroom startin' soonish." A bored-looking guard in a brocade jacket missing all its buttons waved them down a different hallway. Efram grunted an acknowledgement, and they did an about-face.

A boardroom inside Bazra's creepy castle? How much weirder could this place get? Mara peered in each doorway, hoping to locate a second stairwell. They heard the murmur of voices toward the end of the dim corridor. "That must be the meeting of necromancers."

"Keep on going," whispered Efram. "This whole operation is taking way too long."

Mara skirted around a long, low-ceilinged room filled with two rows of black-robed men and women sitting on hard benches and murmuring an incantation. She didn't stop to listen but kept walking until she found the second stairwell. Mara slipped inside, confirmed it was quiet, and held the door open for the others.

"Did you hear that incantation?" asked Yelenarra. "Where did all those necromancers come from?"

Katrine's voice was grim. "My guess is they are Fallow sorcerers sent here by King Roi as part of his deal to secure Bellaryss for himself. Bazra is probably in there somewhere leading the ceremony. While they're distracted raising the undead, we need to find Arnesto and the others."

Mara started jogging up the twisty, wobbly wooden stairs, hoping their gamble would pay off and they'd find Arnesto in the tower. She didn't think they'd be able to run around the compound for very long without drawing notice, especially once the necromancers finished their business. A chill ran down her spine at the thought of having to confront so many necromancers inside the realms of the dead. After all, this was their turf.

Mara's calves and thighs burned by the time she reached the top landing. She paused while the others finished their climb. She half-expected Yelenarra to not be able to keep up, but the eldest member of their team was barely winded. Mara put her hand on the door handle and started to turn it, but Efram put his hand over hers and put a finger to his lips. She glanced around, not seeing anything but wooden beams and mud walls. Then she heard it—a faint knocking that was coming from the other side of the wall. Mara withdrew a dagger and tapped the wall four times, one for each member of the rescue team. There was silence and then she heard twelve taps in return. It wasn't everyone who'd been taken, but it was a start.

"Oh thank the stars!" whispered Yelenarra. "We've found Arnestarious after all."

Efram said, "Steady on, Auntie, we still have to rescue him and the others."

Mara took a deep breath, her pulse racing at the thought of seeing Arnesto on the other side of that wall. "Let's do this." She pushed open the door, took one step into empty air, and yelped, grabbing for the door handle.

The tower had no floorboards.

Katrine yanked the collar of her green duster and pulled her back to the landing. Mara leaned against the tower door, grateful for solid wood at her back. Her stomach churned as she fought against the nausea rising in her throat.

"This is going to be even harder than we thought," she whispered, her voice quivering. "There's no floor out there."

"What next?" muttered Efram, scrubbing his face with his palm.

"Undead creatures by the dozens," sighed Katrine wearily. "We need to figure something out, and fast. I'm liking our odds less and less."

Yelenarra asked Mara to move aside and then took a peek through the door. She pulled her head back in. "There are no floorboards, but there is scaffolding. Mara and I can skirt around the edge of the tower. We shall be able peer through the bars at the top of each door and identify the prisoners, both fay and human. Katrinareus and Eframallium, could you guard the door and warn us if anyone is coming?"

Efram withdrew his sword and stood near the stairwell. "If anyone is coming, I'm going to knock them out first and then warn you." Efram nodded, more to himself than to the rest of them, and his voice shook. "I'll not let anyone harm you, Auntie, nor anyone else. We will see this through."

Yelenarra gripped Efram's shoulder. "You are a good lad." Efram bit his bottom lip and turned away, but not before Mara noticed him swipe his eyes.

"What about the other entrance to the tower?" asked Mara, thinking of the serving women and guards they'd passed by earlier. They were delivering dinner to the prisoners using the stairs on the opposite side of the tower. How did they manage without floorboards?

Katrine peered out at the opposite side of the tower and shook her head. "That door is even less accessible to the prison cells than this side. The guards must lay down some boards to make it across to all the cells. Let's move quickly, determine who's in the tower, and hope no one comes up that side until we're finished."

"Alright, I'm ready." Mara straightened up, unwilling to reveal how scared she'd just been. She didn't relish the idea of falling thirty feet to her death in the second lowest realm, with a bunch of dark fays and necromancers nearby.

Mara pushed the door open again. She placed one boot on the scaffolding to her right, and then her second boot, and leaned against the curved mud wall of the tower, her legs shaking. She slowly scooted along, transferring her grip from the handle on the door leading to the landing, to the cell door on her right. Holding firmly to the handle on the cell door, Mara swung her left boot around so she faced the door and not the long drop below, and then she stood on her tiptoes to peek through the bars at the top of the door. She spotted floor mats and bodies curled up on their sides, but it was too dark to see who was in the room. *Please, let Arnesto be inside...and unharmed.*

Mara leaned forward and hissed through the bars, "Psst! Over here!"

"Mara, is that you?" whispered Nahn, who hobbled over to the door, her hands and feet bound together with the same thick rope Mara had seen elsewhere in the compound. "My stars, I didn't think I'd ever see you again."

Gemala's head popped up. "You were crazy to come, and I love you for it."

"Who else is here with you?" *Please say Arnesto.*

"All the women are here," said Talias softly. "There are twelve of us."

"Where are the men?" *Where is Arnesto?*

Talias pointed, her hands and feet bound up as well. "They've split them up into two rooms, on the other side of the tower."

Mara nodded. *It's alright. He's just across the scaffolding. Not much longer now.* "How often do the guards make their rounds?"

"Only at mealtime, and they just fed us what passes for dinner around here," grumbled Gemala, the pub owner.

"We're going to break you out of here all at once. Things are going to get noisy here pretty quickly. In the meantime, here's a dagger. Start working on those ropes."

Mara swung her right boot back around, so that she faced the scaffolding again. She waved to Yelenarra, who'd made it around to the first door on the other side. Yelenarra shrugged; that cell was empty. Mara pointed at the last two cell doors. Yelenarra nodded to indicate she understood. Mara leaned against the mud wall and crept along the scaffolding until her right hand reached the next cell door handle. She repeated her maneuver, swinging her left leg over so she faced the door.

Mara peered through the bars, longing to see Arnesto on the other side. "Quick—I'm here to help."

"Queen's Crown, Mara, what are you doing here?" Remy's voice was strained.

"Excellent job at tracking, lass. You are my favorite spy, bar none." Vas's teeth flashed in the semi-gloom, and she knew he was attempting to break the tension. Vas tried to stand, but his hands and feet were trussed together like the women in the other cell. "Am I correct in assuming you have a plan for our escape?" he whispered, hope evident in his voice.

"We haven't much time. How many are in there with you?" *And why hasn't Arnesto spoken up yet?*

"Nine in here, and roughly the same in the other cell. But Mara, they've put Arnesto somewhere else. He's not up here with the rest of us." Mara's mouth went dry and her chest tightened, making it hard to breathe. *Arnesto isn't here? But then where is he? No matter what, I'm not leaving without him.*

"Sit tight, sir, we're getting everyone out of the tower together." Mara handed over her other dagger. She would help these prisoners escape and then she'd look for Arnesto. She prayed Bazra wouldn't harm him in the meantime.

She rotated around and faced Yelenarra, who held up eight fingers. Mara held up nine fingers, and then shook her head to indicate Arnesto wasn't with them. Yelenarra's head fell to her chest, and Mara feared the old woman would fall. Mara felt as bereft as Arnesto's aunt. But before they could search for Arnesto elsewhere inside the gloomy compound, they had prisoners to rescue. Arnesto would have to wait a bit longer.

Yelenarra slowly raised her head and stared at the roof overhead. Mara looked up, surprised to see the center portion of the roof was gone. Or perhaps, like the missing floorboards, this part had never been completed. Mara narrowed her eyes, concentrating. *Aye, it just might work.* She waved to Yelenarra and pointed to the landing. They both scuttled back along the scaffolding and slipped inside the stairwell. Mara told Yelenarra and the others what Vas had said, about Arnesto being taken somewhere else. She explained her idea for rescuing the tower prisoners, which Efram thought was crazy, but Katrine and Yelenarra thought was wild but doable.

Mara took a deep breath. "I'll be calling Xenestra in a moment, but I'll not be returning to Havynweal—not without Arnesto."

Katrine and Yelenarra exchanged a look. Katrine sighed. "I'd rather stay here and help you fight Bazra, but someone has to keep Xenestra honest. I'll make sure we complete this rescue, and then I'll be waiting to see you and Yelenarra on the other side."

Efram squared his shoulders. "I'm staying as well. I'm not about to let the two of you have all the fun."

Mara punched him in the shoulder. "It wouldn't be the same without you."

Arnesto's brother rolled his eyes. "I think there's a compliment in there somewhere."

Mara smiled and then stepped over to the landing door and pushed it open. "Ready?" she asked Katrine.

Her fay boss nodded. "Aye."

Mara withdrew her blue sword, her fears evaporating as she focused on the mission at hand. "Hold on tight."

Katrine grasped the door handle, while Yelenarra and Efram gripped the stairwell railing. Mara raised her sword and concentrated on the green and gold dragon that would become the stuff of legend this day. She could almost imagine her father reading aloud to her the tale of Xenestra, the giant dragon who rescued twenty-nine innocent prisoners from evil King Bazra.

Mara used the same incantation she'd used earlier, this time substituting Xenestra's name. She struck the mud wall with her sword three times. Mara was tossed against the door as the entire tower started to shake. Xenestra arrived with a trumpet blast and a burst of flame, scorching the remainder of the tower roof. Chunks of roof tile fell to the ground below.

Mara opened the door leading out to the prison cells and cupped her hand over her mouth. She had to shout up to the dragon to make herself heard above the yells and screams from the captives.

"Xenestra! We need to move quickly. There are prisoners in three cells. Starting with the women, please lower your tail into their cell and tell them to climb up. I'll coax them from this side."

Xenestra bleated, "This is a most irregular evacuation, but I shall do my best." She used her talons to grip the edge of the tower's mud walls and swung her tail around to clear debris from the roof before lowering her tail into the first prison cell.

Mara maneuvered herself around to the women's cell and hollered to be heard above the screaming. "Listen up! This is your only means of escape, and you have just a few minutes. Climb up Xenestra's tail and hold on tight. We will have one chance to get this right. Move!"

Talias, Nahn, and Gemala helped the other women climb up the dragon's spiky tail and then jumped up themselves. Gemala called out, "You've just earned dinner for life at the Cracked Cauldron. Now go rescue our men."

Mara ducked as Xenestra swung her tail wide and dropped it down into the next cell. She watched as Remy climbed up Xenestra's bony ridge, and then gave a hand up to Chef Desna and his brother Vincens. Vas hopped on last and shouted down to Mara, "Make sure I see you on the other side."

Remy yelled, "He's right, Mara. Please be careful."

Mara waved as Xenestra swung her tail around, smashing the last cell door as she lowered it for the prisoners. The third group was better prepared, having watched through the bars of their door as their fellow prisoners escaped. They made quick work of scrambling up the dragon's very crowded back, grabbing onto any available bony plate. Mara scuttled around as Katrine arrived at the last cell from the other side of the scaffolding. Yelenarra had crept around to the opposite side of the tower, which she now guarded, her staff in hand. Efram stood in front of the door they'd entered through, his sword drawn.

Katrine gave Mara a quick head nod. "Well done, lass. Don't be long now, or I'll have to come back for you." Katrine leapt onto the tip of Xenestra's tail just as the far door, where Yelenarra was standing, blew off its rickety hinges, sending Yelenarra tumbling into thin air.

Efram yelled, "Auntie, No! No!"

Mara shouted up to Xenestra, "Go now!" She stifled a sob for the indomitable Yelenarra, the most amazing octogenarian she'd ever met.

Katrine pounded her hand to her chest and called down, "Save Arnesto!"

The giant dragon flapped her wings, creating a downdraft that nearly knocked Mara off her feet. She grasped what remained of the cell door to keep from falling off, when she felt a knife whizzing past her left ear, followed by a second knife, which struck her in the shoulder. Mara cried out at the searing pain. She heard swords swishing off to the side, where she knew Efram had been standing guard. A third knife sliced into her upper thigh, and she sank to the threshold of the damaged prison cell with a moan. They were trapped, pinned down without backup.

Mara felt as if she'd poured everything she had into this rescue, and she still hadn't found Arnesto. She'd never even told him she'd forgiven him or how she really felt about him. Now she'd never get the chance. She was out of time and ideas for how to find him.

And then she heard a most welcome sound: wolves howling in the second lowest realm, followed by the roar of very large cats. Farleigh was here with his friends, as well as the hybrids from Zornamayne's clan. Perhaps the Bazeerka had kept them somewhere else, in a different part of the compound. No matter—they'd escaped their confines and were on the move, as Mara could hear screams and shouts following the howls and roars. A loud bell clanged frantically somewhere below, and the guards retreated from either doorway to answer the call.

Mara spotted Efram lying at an awkward angle, half inside the stairwell, half across the scaffolding. He didn't move when she called his name.

CHAPTER 27

Mara hollered again, "Efram! Can you hear me?"

Efram groaned, "Aye, stop yelling. I'm injured, not deaf."

Mara expelled a puff of air. At least she still had one grouchy fay to look after. "Stay put. I'm coming over to you."

"I'm not going anywhere."

Mara dragged herself across the scaffolding, picking up several large splinters in her uninjured thigh. She grimaced as she hauled herself beside Efram. "Oh no, oh Efram!"

Efram was on his side, clutching his abdomen, which bloomed red between his fingers, his blood dripping through the wooden beams to the ground below. His right arm had been slashed open and was also bleeding heavily.

"Let me take a look."

"No, don't. I'm beyond your help. You need to find my brother and get out."

"I'm not leaving you."

Efram tried to chuckle, but it turned into a wheeze.

"That's true, as I'll be leaving you. At least my spirit doesn't have far to travel, just one realm down and across the river."

Mara wiped a tear from her face. While Efram could be incredibly annoying at times, he'd also been there for her and her Valerran friends, when very few fays had been willing to help them fight the Glenbarrans. She didn't want to lose him too. She told him how much his loyalty and Wreyn's had meant to her, and how much she'd learned from him.

Efram thanked her, his voice growing weaker. "Now listen. The hourglass of my life is nearly spent." He coughed. "My blood—it will help you control the undead. Take some and smear it on your sword."

Mara was horrified. "Absolutely not. We're getting you out of here."

"Mara," groaned Efram. "Do this one, final favor for me. It's the only chance you'll have of saving Arnesto. It's my fault he was taken. You know it's true. I should never have left him behind in that apartment."

"Why did you?"

"I was jealous of my own kid brother getting the red sword. After all, Arnesto is already the youngest twelfth-level fay wizard in history. Did he have to possess one of the Swords of Five too? And I was sick and tired of looking after him all the time. So when Arnesto suggested I return to Havynweal with your sword, I figured why not?" Efram choked on his last words. "Please don't tell Arnesto...just look after him for me." His breath came in short gasps, and then his chest stopped heaving.

Mara didn't wipe her tears this time but let them flow freely down her face. She and Efram had been more alike than she'd ever realized. Mara had been a jealous girl not so very long ago, envious of her friend Linden's superior magic and popularity, and even jealous of the time her father spent with her younger sisters—time that he no longer spent with her. She couldn't change the past, but she could do better, be a better person in the future. She'd already apologized to Linden, and if she ever saw her sisters again, she'd make sure they knew how much she loved them.

Mara wiped her face on the sleeve of the green duster, which she removed and draped over Efram. She said a silent prayer for the safe passage of his spirit through the lowest of the realms. Then she reached beneath the duster and ran her fingers across his abdomen. Gritting her teeth against the bile rising in her throat, she smeared her sword with Efram's lifeblood. This was his departing gift to her and Arnesto, and the only reason she could bring herself to touch it.

Mara wiped her hands on the duster and used her sword to push herself to a standing position, whimpering at the pain in her thigh and shoulder. She listened for any sounds of fighting on the stairs but heard nothing; the guards had defeated her and her team and moved on. Or had something prompted them to leave, like that clanging bell? She centered herself and brought up an image of Arnesto. *Where are you?*

A shot of pain passed through her chest again. And then the image of Arnesto in the midst of a windstorm, his arms raised to the gray sky, came to her once more. This time, she saw where he was standing—on the bow of an ugly black ship. Mara sent Arnesto a mental reply: *I'm coming!*

Mara whispered goodbye to Efram before dragging herself to the wooden steps leading down from the tower. She peered over the top landing, half-expecting one of

Bazra's wraith-like guards to throw another knife at her, but the winding staircase was empty. Mara crept down from the tower, holding her sword aloft and using the curved mud wall as support. Each step sent a jolt of pain through her leg. She didn't think she would last long in a swordfight, but perhaps that's not what Efram had in mind when it came to facing the undead.

When she reached the bottom of the tower, Mara tried standing on both legs and sucked in her breath. She debated pulling out the knives, still protruding from her shoulder and thigh, but she worried about the additional blood loss. If she made it back to Havynweal, Zornamayne would see to it for her. In the meantime, Mara didn't think she could walk without support.

She glanced around the stairwell, looking for anything —a stick, cane, staff, even a block of wood—to serve as well as the mud wall for support. She settled on a broken chunk of scaffolding that had fallen from the top of the tower stairs. Leaning heavily on the beam of wood, she gripped her sword in her right hand and listened.

She heard screams and shouts, as well as running footsteps, and the raspy grunts made by Bazra's undead creatures. The necromancers had stopped incanting by now; perhaps they were doing some of the screaming. Off near the beach she heard the grihms howling. Farleigh would help her rescue Arnesto, if she could reach him without being stopped by guards, necromancers, and an undead army.

Mara was in no condition to face guards or beasts on her own. She waited until most of the screaming subsided before opening the door. The corridor had transformed into a battlefield. Guards, servants, and a few robed necromancers lay where they'd fallen. Mara felt sorriest for the malnourished serving women in their limp gunnysack gowns; they had zero chance against the undead creatures. She gasped in recognition at one of the dead necromancers —Harlan Lewyn, slain by his own hypocrisy. He'd led the anti-magic movement in Valerra and was almost certainly behind the uprising at the grihm preserve and the creation of the clockwork man. All this time, he'd been secretly allied to King Roi.

Mara dragged herself down the dim corridor to the nearest exit, careful not to disturb any of the bodies. She pulled open a side door and stepped into a dreary gravel courtyard. Mara heard the raspy screeches of the undead coming from the direction of the beach, as well as the shouts of the remaining necromancers, who were beginning to sound desperate. Grihm howls and feline-hybrid roars followed, and then came the screams of the dark fays, terrified by whatever was happening. Mara hobbled around a corner, past the fencing surrounding the compound, and got her first glimpse of the pandemonium on the beach.

Mara thought perhaps in all the commotion she could slip away quietly with Arnesto. She should have known better, at least where Arnesto was concerned. He was never one to go quietly. The twelfth-level fay wizard stood on the bow of the ship, surrounded by hybrids from Zornamayne's clan and Farleigh, Jerdahn, and a third grihm she assumed was Yeller. His arms raised to the gray sky, Arnesto shouted an incantation. Mara felt a slight breeze on her cheeks, a faint movement of air in the second lowest realm. The breeze gathered speed and power, becoming wind gusts that stirred the clumps of gray grasses and dead trees along the shore.

Mara's first reaction to seeing Arnesto was overwhelming relief he was alive and relatively unharmed, at least as far as she could tell from this distance. She wanted to race across the sandy beach, climb aboard the ugly ship, and draw him into her arms. In reality, she could barely walk, and there were scores of undead creatures roving about between her and the ship.

Her second reaction was awe, mingled with a small amount of panic that Arnesto's magic could command the elements and raise up a wind inside the realms of the dead. Why would the most powerful and best-looking fay wizard in Havynweal want to pledge himself to a human girl like her? Although he'd confessed his feelings in his letter, Mara still couldn't understand why.

She didn't have time to reflect further, since a lightning bolt lit up the gray sky, causing all the prickly lizard-panthers and snaky monsters to caterwaul and surge toward the ship. The robed necromancers had lost all control over the undead; several were trampled, and the rest began running down the beach. A few of the monsters made it to the water's edge but couldn't go farther. Something about the water kept them contained to the sandy shore. *Good to know*, thought Mara, *but then we're at an impasse, and sooner or later, Bazra is going to show up.*

Mara could have kicked herself for even thinking it because the tallest of the necromancers, his black robe covered in gold and silver runes, climbed a leafless tree and called down commands at his undead army, which the beasts ignored. He followed up with threats to send them to the eternal lake of fire. That angered them, and the creatures surged around his tree. He wisely shut up and scuttled up to the highest branch. Bazra's plans at overtaking Valerra and Havynweal would not succeed that day, since he couldn't get his undead creatures to obey him.

That still left Mara stranded on a gravelly beach in the

second lowest realm of the dead, and Arnesto standing in the bow of a ghost ship with an army of undead monsters between them. Mara glanced at her blue sword with the dried smears on it. She recalled Efram's last words to her. She had no idea what she was doing, but that had never stopped her before. Mara looked about for a perch of some sort. Climbing a tree was out of the question with her injuries, but she wanted to be visible to all the undead when she used her sword.

Mara hobbled back to the deserted guardhouse, which had been constructed on a raised platform that stood about ten feet above sea level. Groaning with each step, she pulled herself up the stairs to the platform and shuffled over to the rickety railing. Meanwhile, Arnesto's wind whipped up the waves on the sea, causing the ship to rock and sending sprays of water onto the beach. The creatures backed farther away from the water's edge.

Mara took a deep breath and called forth all her anger at Bazra and the undead, and all her pain at losing Efram and Yelenarra, and all her weariness at the machinations of men like King Roi and Harlan Lewyn. She formulated an incantation in her head, and raising her blue sword, she shouted:

> *"Undead creatures, your rest disturbed,*
> *Stop and listen to my command—*
> *Return at once to the lowest realm*
> *Return from whence you were called."*

Very, very slowly, the bristly lizard-panther monsters and spiky snake creatures turned away from Bazra in the tree and Arnesto on the ship and shuffled around to face Mara. They lifted their misshapen faces and fiery orbs up to hers, and rocked to and fro in an odd symmetry. Mara had their attention. Now came the most important part, and the most dangerous.

She took her sword and swept it over all their heads, from one side of the beach to the other. "You shall return to the lowest realm and rise up no more! If you ignore the necromancer's commands and listen to me, I will not dispatch you to the lake of fire. This is your sole chance, the only offer of mercy you will ever receive. Think on it and act now."

At first nothing happened, and Mara figured she was done for. But then a crack opened in the sandy soil in front of the guardhouse, and several of the undead dropped out of sight, followed by several more. Soon, all the creatures save one had jumped or slithered to the lowest level. The last creature, a huge lizard-panther not unlike the others she'd battled, stared at her, his mouth open wide. He uttered one word, turning it into a question, "Mercy?" before he dropped into the fissure. The portal closed over his head.

It's finished, thought Mara. *I can call back Xenestra with my blue sword and take Arnesto home.* Then she thought of the empty manor, without Yelenarra and Efram, and her eyes welled up again.

A nasty, raspy cackling sent fresh shivers through her. Bazra had descended from his tree and waved his arms about wildly. His eyes looked almost as fiery as the undead he called forth, and his complexion as gray as the gloom of his homeland. Around his waist he'd strapped the stolen red sword, which Mara hoped would remain a dull gray for as long as he owned it, the blade's hieroglyphs dormant until claimed by its rightful owner.

Bazra shouted his necromantic incantations again. The

ground shook as another portal started to open along the beach. Mara's anger at Bazra resurfaced, along with uncertainty. How was she supposed to fight him? Didn't she and Arnesto need the red sword? Or had the seers gotten it wrong? Perhaps what they'd seen as they peered into the future was her blue sword with its reddish brown smears. Prophecies were notoriously imprecise, often conflicting, and sometimes dead wrong.

Mara raised her sword, thinking about how to subdue the dark fay king inside his own realm. Yelenarra had claimed his power was nearly absolute, although even that had been overstated, more legend than reality. His compound was a rickety, rotting mess, his subjects miserable, and his undead disobedient. While she considered how to handle Bazra, Arnesto solved the problem for her. His windstorm dislodged the black tree behind the dark fay king, tearing it out of the ground roots and all, and smashed it over Bazra's head.

The dark fay king and his tree toppled into the wide crack he'd just opened. Mara waited for the portal to close again, but nothing happened. She frowned, worried that undead creatures would begin pouring out through the new portal. Mara waved her sword over the fissure and shouted, "Close up, and do not reopen!" The crack in the beach narrowed until nothing more than a thin line in the sand remained, and then that disappeared too.

Mara glanced up and down the length of the beach. The remaining few guards and serving men and woman bowed low to her and called out a single word: "Mercy!" She'd find a way to show them mercy somehow, although that would be for another day. She made her way down from the platform, one painful step at a time. She hobbled halfway across the beach and couldn't go any farther. She'd lost too much blood and was bone weary.

"I want to go home," she murmured, gripping her sword in her hand. "Xenestra, take us home."

Mara wavered and felt herself tumbling backward. Before her head hit the gravelly sand, a pair of strong arms caught her.

CHAPTER 28

Mara slept for two days and dreamt of horrid, bristly creatures and murderous clockwork men pursuing her down gloomy alleys or across sandy beaches. She never seemed able to run fast enough or far enough to escape them. She moaned when a healer—was it Zornamayne?—removed the blades from her leg and shoulder and repaired the internal damage.

People whispered around her, but she lacked the strength to open her eyes. Gloria clicked her beak softly and often nestled at the foot of her bed. Arnesto took her hand at some point and brought it to his lips for a kiss. He leaned over and whispered, "Maragold Gracelyn Raeburn Pensk, you must wake up soon. I cannot bear the waiting...or the loneliness."

Mara smelled bone broth mixed with angelica root, aniseed, and turmeric. She opened her eyes and blinked several times, certain she was still dreaming. She was lying on the soft feather mattress of the large bed in the Amber Room, which she'd begun to think of has her room. The kind, careworn face of Yelenarra stared down at her. "Oh my stars, dear lass, you have finally woken! Arnestarious has been beside himself with worry. I was going to call for Zornamayne soon if you had anymore nightmares, you poor dear."

"Yelenarra," croaked Mara, her voice hoarse. "I saw you fall—I thought you were gone." A crazy thought ran through her befuddled head. "Did Efram survive, too?"

Yelenarra's eyes moistened. She withdrew an embroidered handkerchief from her pocket to dab them. "Nay, our dear Eframallium was not so lucky. As I fell, my staff became lodged in the scaffolding, breaking my fall and my arm."

Mara noticed the sling supporting Yelenarra's right arm. "I'm so sorry I couldn't do more for Efram."

Yelenarra shook her head. "There was nothing more to be done. We brought him home with us on Xenestra's back and held his funeral rites yesterday in the wildflower meadow at the base of our mountain. It was his favorite spot as a boy, a place where he would dream of becoming one of the fay heroes of legend."

"He was very brave." Mara's voice was tight, her tears threatening to spill over.

Yelenarra nodded. "Aye. He was a courageous lad, though always a bit in the shadow of his younger brother, which is never easy. Arnestarious misses him terribly."

Mara thought back to the last few minutes in the second lowest realm, before she collapsed on the beach. "Is Bazra...?"

"You sealed him into the lowest realm. A fitting place for a most unfit king."

"But he has the red sword."

"Aye. And one day, we shall retrieve it. But we have more pressing concerns at the moment. I must build housing for the Bazeerka I brought back with us. The fay council, of course, is furious with me—and not for the first time, I might add. But what could I do? I simply had to rescue those pathetic, broken fays from Bazra's crumbling compound. Katrine agreed with me, but she's unable to convince the council of the rightness of my decision. I have offered them sanctuary on my mountain, in exchange for an honest day's work."

Mara smiled, patting Yelenarra's good arm. "Thank you for showing the Bazeerka mercy. It's what I would have wanted, had I been conscious at the time."

"I heard how you commanded an entire army of undead monsters, telling them they had one opportunity to accept your mercy. Well done, lass. This is the true path, and what separates Serving mages from Fallow sorcerers."

Mara remembered Farleigh, Jerdahn, and Yeller. "What about the grihms? They will need sanctuary somewhere, since their preserve has been destroyed back in Valerra."

Yelenarra held a spoonful of bone broth up to Mara's mouth. She swallowed the bitter medicine, trying hard not to grimace. Yelenarra arched an eyebrow, and Mara meekly accepted another spoonful. She hoped the medicine improved with repeat exposure, but she didn't think it likely. "You need not worry about the grihms. Zornamayne has offered them sanctuary, and further, she said your debt is paid in full."

Between mouthfuls of broth, Mara asked, "How come?"

"Her clan's population has been dwindling, and the trolls have been encroaching. With three sturdy wolf-man crossbreeds to protect their boundaries, the trolls have retreated back to their own lands."

"Have Vas and the other Valerrans returned home?" Mara wanted to ask about Remy, but she feared it might be awkward, since she was pledged to her nephew. But she needn't have worried.

"Aye, all the Valerrans have been returned home. President Vas assured me King Roi and his necromancers shall be hunted down in the barrens and brought back to Bellaryss for a trial. Chef Desna said you may have a job with him whenever you like, but he believes your talents lie elsewhere." Yelenarra tilted her head to the side. "By the way, young Remy seemed particularly confused. I trust that the unremembered spell cast by Arnestarious shall smooth out over time. As it was, he seemed to think you and he were, ah, a special couple. I assured him he was mistaken."

"You're quite right. Remy was very much mistaken." Mara asked Yelenarra why Arnesto had been on Bazra's ship in the first place, and not in the tower with the rest of the prisoners.

"Bazra chose to imprison Arnestarious on the ship because he wanted to isolate him from the others. He wanted to ensure Arnestarious was better fed and better rested, so he could extract my nephew's blood for a long, long time and use it to control the undead."

"How did Arnesto break free?"

"We have the grihms and hybrids to thank for my nephew's escape. They had been imprisoned together in a shed behind the main building. The wooden slats were so rotted they burst through them and frightened the guards, who fled. The grihms and hybrids made it to the ship and tossed Arnestarious's guards overboard."

Yelenarra placed the empty bowl of broth on the nightstand. "Arnestarious shall demand to see you the instant I tell him you are awake. Would you like me to brush your hair before I alert him?"

Mara nodded. "Aye, thank you. And perhaps I could have a mirror and a damp towel?"

Yelenarra produced the towel, hairbrush, and mirror. Together, they made Mara as presentable as she was going to be, until she was fully healed. Her wheat-colored hair fell in loose waves around her shoulders. Yelenarra freshened her pale blue nightgown with a bit of her fay magic, and nodding, rose from the chair. She left in a puff of mists, taking the empty bowl and damp towel with her.

Mara wished she had a tenth of Yelenarra's magical abilities. But then she stopped to consider her own sword magic, which she'd used to call a mighty dragon from the fay lands to the second lowest realm of the dead, and to send the undead back to their own realm. Perhaps she ought to be grateful for what she did have and stop comparing herself to others or wishing for their gifts.

There was an impatient knock at her door. She barely managed to call out, "Come in!" when the door burst open.

Arnesto dashed into the room and then abruptly stopped. He folded his hands and furrowed his brow, but he did not approach the bed.

"Why are you standing there?"

"I am awaiting your response to my note. I do not wish to cause you any further pain or embarrassment, not after you were injured rescuing me and banishing Bazra to the lowest realm."

Mara shook her head. He was so thickskulled he didn't even comprehend *she* could have feelings for *him*. But Arnesto mistook her meaning. He dropped his eyes and said, "I see. I shall bother you no further."

The mists rose around his ankles and legs, though Mara noticed the vaporous tendrils were slow to rise up his torso. He was delaying his departure. Her mouth twitched slightly. "Arnestarious Aziel Windstorm Lucato the Four-teenth!" Mara's heart hammered inside her chest as she pronounced each syllable.

Arnesto's mists evaporated. "This is the first time you have called me by my full name. Is there something that you need from me?"

"Could you please come closer? I can hardly see you standing over there by the door."

"Of course." Arnesto walked up to the foot of her bed and stopped. "Can you see me better now?"

Mara sighed. "Not really. Could you please come sit here by me?" She patted the side of her feather mattress.

Arnesto swallowed and complied, sitting gingerly on the edge of her bed. She inhaled his rich scent of loamy earth mixed with tangy citrus, so unusual and so like him. Arnesto looked everywhere but at her face.

He cleared his throat. "I am sorry about—"

"Oh Arnesto, please don't say anything more about it."

He finally peered at her, his frown lines deepening. "But I do not understand."

"Of course you don't." Mara reached out her hand and touched his ridiculously handsome face. "Come a bit closer."

Arnesto arched one eyebrow upward, and the other downward. "You mean..."

Mara drew him down for a kiss, and then another, and another after that. She ensured the youngest-ever twelfth-level fay wizard understood he'd been forgiven, and that this particular human girl was perfectly content to be his special friend, with all the strings attached.

BOOKS BY TONI CABELL

A fast-paced adventure full of magic, romance, humor, sword fighting, dangerous creatures, and the power of light versus darkness, **Serving Magic** is a YA Epic Fantasy series with Steampunk and Regency vibes. Winner of The Wishing Shelf Book Awards and recognized by Indies Today as a Top 5 YA Fantasy series by an indie author:

- *Lady Apprentice, Book 1*
- *Lady Mage, Book 2*
- *Lady Liege, Book 3*
- *Lady Spy, Book 4*
- *Lady Reaper, Book 5*

In the arid hills of Toresz, there's one thing more dangerous than divining for water... falling in love with the enemy. **Water Witch** is YA Romantasy duology packed with action, danger, intrigue, royal politics, and romance. Winner of The Wishing Shelf Book Awards:

- *The Lightness of Water, Book 1*
- *The Way of Water, Book 2*

If you're looking for sweet, slow-burn romance with swoony kisses, second chances, and funny, heartwarming characters, don't miss the complete **Faeries of Door County** series. Winner of Best Paranormal Romance, each novel is a standalone story set in the same cozy small town:

- *Rhyme, Riddle, and Romance*
- *Half a Faerie*
- *Return to Mooncrest Inn*

Find all Toni's available books and upcoming new releases on tonicabell.com and Amazon. All her novels are also available in audiobook format on Audible and Apple Books.

About the Author

When Toni told her fifth-grade teacher that she wanted to be a writer, neither of them expected Toni's journey to include stints as a nurse's aid, personal banker, instructional designer, real estate broker, systems analyst, and youth director. Toni is thrilled to be an indie author and does at least half her writing in the middle of the night, which may explain her wild plot twists and unforgettable characters.

Today, Toni writes award-winning fantasy stories filled with spunky gals, protective guys, imaginative magic, and romance that sizzles without the spice. Whether you're a fan of fast-paced, YA fantasy adventures with a dash of swoon or cozy paranormal romance packed with heart-stealing kisses and small town charm, you're sure to find something to love.

Toni's novels have earned Silver and Bronze Medals in The Wishing Shelf Book Awards, two Gold Medals in the Global Book Awards, and Best Paranormal Romance from Indies Today.

She makes her home in a small village along the shores of Lake Michigan with her handsome husband, where she enjoys generous supplies of strong coffee, too many pastries, and more books than she can ever read.

Want a free novella and to stay current on Toni's upcoming releases, sales, and giveaways? Then visit tonicabell.com and sign up for her newsletter.

Toni posts regularly about her indie author journey, life lessons, what inspires her, and her books on Instagram and Facebook. Also consider joining her Reader Group on Facebook, @onceuponaswoon, where she hangs out with some of her closed-door author friends and readers like you.

Soli Deo Gloria. ✝

www.ingramcontent.com/pod-product-compliance
Lightning Source LLC
Chambersburg PA
CBHW061556190726
48288CB00007B/2055